'You told  whispered, between his

'I am living. This is what I want. Lo— *Love me!*' she continued.

Her own body was so aroused that she wondered how it could still obey her. But then she was operating on instinct. And love.

Cassian tore his mouth away, his face strained. 'But afterwards—'

'Forget afterwards. This is now,' she said fiercely.

The ecstasy in her body was nothing to the joy in her head, her heart and her soul. Cassian would possess her.

Childhood in Portsmouth meant grubby knees, flying pigtails and happiness for **Sara Wood**. Poverty drove her from typist and seaside landlady to teaching, till writing finally gave her the freedom her Romany blood craved. Happily married, she has two handsome sons: Richard is married, calm, dependable, drives tankers. Simon is a roamer—silversmith, roofer, welder, always with beautiful girls. Sara lives in the Cornish countryside. Her glamorous writing life alternates with her passion for gardening, which allows her to be carefree and grubby again!

Recent titles by the same author:

MORGAN'S SECRET SON
THE KYRIAKIS BABY

THE UNEXPECTED MISTRESS

BY

SARA WOOD

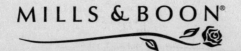

All the characters in this book have no existence outside the imagination of the author, and have no relation whatsoever to anyone bearing the same name or names. They are not even distantly inspired by any individual known or unknown to the author, and all the incidents are pure invention.

*First published in Great Britain 2001
Harlequin Mills & Boon Limited,
Eton House, 18-24 Paradise Road, Richmond, Surrey TW9 1SR*

© Sara Wood 2001

ISBN 0 263 82573 6

*Set in Times Roman 10½ on 11¼ pt.
01-0202-51323*

*Printed and bound in Spain
by Litografia Rosés, S.A., Barcelona*

CHAPTER ONE

CASSIAN lounged contentedly on the roof of the large rented house which he shared in typically cosmopolitan style with two English strippers, a Buddhist from Florida, and a Moroccan herbalist. It was late, the sky a dense black scattered with stars, the air warm and still.

He and his literary agent were watching the snake charmers and acrobats performing in the *Djemaa el Fna*, Marrakesh's extraordinary market square. His agent's mouth had been almost permanently open since they'd emerged onto the roof ten minutes ago and Cassian's dark eyes hadn't stopped twinkling in gentle amusement.

'A tad different from central London,' his agent marvelled with great understatement, goggling at a group of Saharan nomads who were sweeping majestically through the square.

Men in rags, walking like kings, Cassian thought, reflecting on his belief that outer trappings often concealed the real person beneath.

'Same world. Different values and desire. Life stripped to its bare necessities. The need to eat, to find shelter and love,' he observed lazily.

Stirred but not staggered by the scene below, Cassian poured coffee from the silver beaked pot and offered his agent a sweet pastry. After living here for a year, it had all become gloriously familiar to him; the huge lanterns illuminating the storytellers, the contortionists, the clowns and boy dancers, and the crowd of Berbers mingling with an incongruous sprinkling of awestruck tourists.

By now his ears were attuned to the din. Drums, cymbals and western music drowned the hubbub of voices—and also, mercifully, the groans coming from the stall of the dentist who was enthusiastically wielding his pliers.

A willing slave to intense feelings and sensuality, Cassian delightedly inhaled the powerful aroma of humanity mingling with spices and the smell of cooking from the blazing braziers dotted around the square. And he wondered curiously where his passion for living life to the hilt would take him next.

'So,' said his agent in bright cocktail-speak, clearly uncomfortable with the culture shock he was experiencing. 'Now you've finished the book, I suppose you and your son are both going home for a while?'

Cassian sipped his Turkish coffee, appreciating its richness. 'Jai and I have no home,' he said gravely.

And yet... As if to contradict that statement, an image had come unexpectedly into his mind. Instead of the black night and the ochre buildings, the blazing torches and the patchwork of bright colours below, he saw emerald-green hills laced with grey stone walls, ancient woodlands and small stone villages by a cool, rushing river. The Yorkshire Dales. And, specifically, Thrushton.

Astonished, he inhaled deeply as if he could feel the freshness of the champagne air in his lungs. For the first time in his life he felt a pang of longing for a place he'd once known and loved.

That startled him: he who'd spent his adult life passionately embracing a setting, teasing out its darker side to create one of his popular thrillers...and then leaving without regret for new sensations, new horizons.

'Still, you must have a great sense of relief,' his agent persisted. 'You've got your freedom back, for a start. No more sitting hunched over a PC for hour after hour,' he added jovially, attempting to penetrate the mysterious psyche of the man he knew only as Alan Black.

'I never lose my freedom. If I ever felt it was threatened,' Cassian replied quietly, 'I'd stop writing at once.'

'Hell, don't do that! We've got another film producer offering us an option on your next book!' panicked his agent, seeing twelve per cent of a fortune vanishing overnight.

But Cassian had stopped listening. His sharp ears had heard an unusual noise in the narrow alley beside the house. Moving to the low parapet, he could see a man there, curled up in a foetal position and moaning with pain. Someone was running into the darkness of the souk beyond. Without making a fuss, he politely excused himself and went to investigate.

It was a few minutes before he realised that the bruised and battered man he'd hauled into the house was Tony Morris, his old enemy from that very part of England which had sprung to mind so surprisingly at the mention of the word 'home'.

As Tony blubbered and whimpered, and he silently washed the blood from the flabby face, Cassian found his longing for Yorkshire increasing quite alarmingly, the memories coming hot and fast and extraordinarily insistent.

Ruled by his instincts, he acknowledged that perhaps it was time to go back. Time to immerse himself in the landscape which had reached like loving arms into his unhappy soul and given him solace and peace of mind. Time also to face the devils that haunted his dreams.

And then Tony offered him the opportunity on a plate to do just that.

Laura slammed two mugs on the table and doled out the last of the coffee granules with a preoccupied expression. Coffee wasn't the only thing she'd have to eliminate from her shopping list. Poverty was staring her in the face.

'Sue,' she said urgently to her life-long friend, 'I've got to get a new job sharpish.'

Sue looked sympathetic. 'Nothing yet, then?'

'No. *And* I've been searching in Harrogate all this week!'

'Wow!' Sue exclaimed, suitably impressed.

Her friend was the only person who knew what a huge step that had been. It was a month now since she'd lost her job. Night after night, Laura had lain awake worrying about her child's future, his poor health, his fragile state of mind. For Adam's sake she *must* find work! She must! she'd thought with increasing panic.

No work was available in Thrushton where she lived, nor in the small community of Grassington nearby. None, either in nearby Skipton.

Up to now her entire existence had been confined to the rolling dales and picturesque stone villages surrounding the River Wharfe. Of the rest of Yorkshire, she knew nothing— let alone England—and the thought of travelling further to work had made her blanch with apprehension.

It was a stupid reaction, she knew, but not one of her making. If she had ever been born with self-assurance and confidence, then it had been crushed by her restrictive upbringing. If she'd ever had ambition then that too had withered and died, thanks to the critical tongue of her adoptive father's sister, Aunt Enid, and the scorn and cruelty of her father's son Tony.

She knew she was submissive and reticent to a fault. But the needs of her own child meant a radical rethink of her life. It didn't matter to *her* that she wore jumble sale clothes, but she had to earn good money and buy some decent gear for Adam—or he'd continue to be bullied unmercifully.

'I'd do anything,' she said fervently, 'to ensure we can stay here. This house is my…my…'

'Comfort blanket,' supplied Sue with a grin. 'Be honest. It is.'

Laura glared at her horribly perceptive friend and then let her tense mouth soften in recognition.

'You're right. But I need stability and familiarity in my life. Adam too. We'd both go to pieces anywhere else.'

'I know, duck. I think you've got real grit to pluck up the courage to hunt for work in Harrogate.' Raising a plump arm, Sue patted Laura's long and elegant hand in admiration. 'But…it'd be a bit of a nightmare journey without a car, wouldn't it?'

Laura grimaced. 'Two buses and a train and a long walk. What choice do I have, though? Nine-year-old boys can eat for England. Mind you, employers weren't exactly falling over themselves to take me on. I'm fed up! I've exhausted every avenue,' she complained crossly.

'Must be *some*thing out there,' Sue encouraged.

Laura rolled her eyes. 'You bet there is. Lap dancing.'

Tension made her join in with Sue's giggles but it was frustrated resentment that made her jump up and perform a few poses around an imaginary pole. She adopted an 'I am available' face and moved her body with sinuous grace. It seemed an easy way to earn money.

'Crikey. I'd give you five quid!' Sue said admiringly. 'Madly erotic. But then you've got the most fab legs and body. That monumentally baggy shirt would have to go, though,' she advised. 'Wrong colour!'

Hastily smoothing her tousled hair, Laura subsided breathily into the chair and wriggled down her slim skirt—which she'd acquired like most of her clothes from the local jumble sale and which was almost a size too small.

She felt quite shaken by her erotic performance. She was a natural. Perhaps these things could be passed on genetically, she thought gloomily. After all, she was a bastard. That had been rammed into her enough times.

If only she knew what her real mother had been like! Then she wouldn't have to wonder if her mother *had* been a tart, as Aunt Enid had claimed.

'She was a slut!' Enid—her father's sister—had claimed. 'Your mother slept with anyone and everyone. And married to your father, a respectable solicitor! Diana brought the name of Morris into disrepute.'

Laura would never know the truth. Would never know why her mother had been unfaithful. Would never know the identity of her real father. Nobody else knew that she *wasn't* George Morris's child.

As soon as Laura was born, her mother had run away and George had had no choice but to bring Laura up as his daughter. Which he'd resented. That explained his indifference and total lack of affection.

Misty-eyed, she looked around the comfortable, stone-flagged kitchen with its huge Aga and deep inglenook fireplace, wincing as she imagined the uproar when her mother's infidelity had been discovered. And she understood how hard it must have been for her 'father' to accept his wife's bastard.

Together with Aunt Enid, he had created a regime so narrow and unbending in an effort to keep her on the straight and narrow, that she had turned into a timid mouse. Albeit, she thought wryly, with unrivalled domestic skills and a posture a ramrod would be proud of. Pity she didn't have other qualifications. She might be more employable.

'You know, Sue,' she confided, 'sometimes I've felt as though I'm *prostituting* myself at interviews with all that smiling, all that looking eager and charming and willing...oh, I hate it all!'

Close to losing control, she thumped the table, and Sue jumped in surprise at Laura's unusual vehemence.

'Something'll turn up,' her friend soothed, not very convincingly. 'I've got my dental appointment later, in Harrogate. I'll get the local paper for you to look through the Jobs Vacant column.'

'I'll do anything decent and legal. I'm willing to learn, conscientious and hard-working...but the downside is that I'm plain and shy and my clothes are out of the Ark,' Laura muttered. 'I see all the other applicants glowing with confidence in their make-up and attractive outfits and I know they're laughing at me behind their smooth, lily-white hands!' Glaring, she held up her own. 'Look at mine! They're rough enough to snag concrete. I tell you, Sue, I'd be just as good as them, given a lick of lippy, a decent haircut and a ten-gallon drum of hand cream!'

'I've never known you so forceful,' Sue marvelled.

'Well. It's because I'm angry.' Laura's blue eyes flashed with rare inner fire. 'When will the world recognise that appearances aren't everything? That it's what's here—' she banged her chest vigorously '—and here—' her head had the same treatment '—that's important! And what's that removal van doing outside?' she wondered, breaking off with a frown.

'Getting lost,' suggested Sue without interest. 'Nobody round here's moving that I know about.'

Built from local rock in the Middle Ages and enlarged in the Georgian period, Thrushton Hall stood at the far end of the twenty other stone houses that comprised the tiny village, a cheerful cottage garden separating the handsome manor house from the narrow lane outside—which led only to the river.

Laura leaned across the deep window embrasure and peered through the stone mullioned window. Clearly the van driver had missed a turning. And yet the name plaque on the low drystone wall seemed to satisfy the removal men who'd jumped from the cab, because they brought out a flask and sandwiches and proceeded to settle themselves on the wall to eat.

'Well, unknown to us, we've become a designated picnic spot!' Laura declared wryly. A battered four-wheel drive cruised up and drew to a halt behind the small van. 'Here's another picnicker!' she called back to her friend. 'Huh! We'll have a coachload of tourists here in a minute and I'll have to give them sun umbrellas, waste bins and loo facilities! Sue, come and…!'

But her words died in her throat. From the Range Rover

emerged a tall, slim figure in black jeans and T-shirt. The breath left her lungs as if they'd been surgically deflated.

'What's the matter?' Sue hurried up, then grabbed Laura's arm with a gasp. 'Blow me! Isn't that...?'

Laura's eyes had grown huge, her lashes dark against the unnatural pallor of her face.

'Yes!' she choked. 'It's Cassian!'

His appearance was so unexpected, so utterly bizarre, that she stood rooted to the ground in numb disbelief while he chatted to the men. And then he began to turn to the house. Like children caught doing something naughty, she and Sue hastily dodged back out of sight.

'What a hunk he's become!' Sue declared. 'He's absolutely scrummy. But...why's he here—of all places?!'

Laura couldn't speak at all. Her mind was whirling, confused by the sight of the dark and sinister figure, whose sudden arrival seventeen years ago—and equally sudden disappearance five years later—had split her family apart.

She'd been ten at the time. Her father had begun to talk of nothing but a female client who'd come to his legal practice. One day he had announced that he was to marry the artist he'd been defending—and that his bride and her twelve-year-old son would be moving in. It was only then that Laura had realised George must have divorced her mother.

Tony, up till then the adored and spoilt only son, had been scarlet with fury at the news. For her, the arrival of Bathsheba and Cassian had been a revelation. Suddenly the house had burst into life with colour and laughter and music and Laura had quickly become familiar with the smell of turpentine mingling with that of the herbs and spices of exotic dishes.

But almost immediately there had been titanic rows over Cassian's behaviour. Laura could see him now; a silent and glowering boy who couldn't behave conventionally and who'd refused to fit into the community.

Vividly she recalled his defiance in the face of Aunt Enid's rigid rules and the way he'd disappeared for days, seemingly existing without food or comfort.

And while she'd envied his independence and stubborn refusal to be anyone other than himself, she'd feared that very freedom he exemplified. He had been untameable, with an adventurous, bohemian past and he came from a greater world than she or her friends could ever know or understand.

And so they were strangers to one another. She had admired and watched him from afar, wishing she had his nerve, envying his daring.

As he had grown into a young man, the depth of his inner assurance had attracted the girls like bees to a honeypot. He was the local Bad Boy, and women longed to be noticed by him. One or two were. The chosen dazed and dazzled girls had huddled in Grassington square, discussing with awe the passion they'd unwittingly unleashed, while she'd listened in horror.

And, she was ashamed to say, with a secret excitement. Not that she'd want to be part of his life at all. He scared her though she didn't know why, and she couldn't fathom what made her heart race whenever she set eyes on him.

It was quickening now, bringing a flush to her cheeks. Squirming with dismay, she took a cautious peek out of the window. Cassian had resumed talking to the removal men, one foot on the low wall, an expressive hand gesticulating as he described something.

A strange exhilaration caught hold of her, something that coiled warm and throbbing in her veins. She stared, mesmerised. Cassian had charisma. He had always been different, magnetic, special.

Laura shot a glance at Sue. Even her sensible, down-to-earth friend was gazing open-mouthed at him, her expression nakedly admiring. And Sue was in a state of tension, her fingers gripping the curtain tightly.

Just as she was, Laura thought in surprise, releasing the creased curtain in embarrassment. She didn't like being disturbed like this and she felt uncomfortable that her nerves were jiggling about all over the place.

Why should he make her pulses leap about so erratically? It didn't make sense. Oh, he was good-looking enough in a foreign kind of way. Handsome, she supposed. But so were many other men who'd walked into the hotel where she'd worked: young, affluent and personable, and she'd been indifferent to them. And they to her, of course!

Bemused, she scrutinised him carefully in an effort to solve the mystery. And felt her fascination go up a notch or two. His hair was still dark—black and gleaming with the richness of a raven's wing—but it was shorter now, the rebellious curls sleekly hugging the beautiful shape of his head.

His face... Well, those high cheekbones and carved jaw would make any woman's heart beat faster coupled with the dark, intense eyes and sexily mobile mouth. She suppressed a small quiver in her breast.

'What's he doing?' hissed Sue.

'Don't know.'

Her voice had been hoarse because his liquid and relaxed gestures had caused the muscles to ripple beneath his black T-shirt in a way that left her breathless.

'He's beautifully toned,' Sue whispered, eyes agog. 'Not over-developed—just perfect. Wow! And he used to be so skinny.'

No, Laura wanted to say. He was always strong and wiry. But she didn't want to betray her ridiculously chaotic hormones by speaking. His shoulders and chest had certainly expanded. Cassian's torso was now a devastatingly attractive triangle of powered muscle and sinew.

She watched him, her eyes wide and puzzled. He was more than just a perfect body. He...

She stiffened, suddenly realising what drew her to him.

Cassian possessed what she—and many others—might search for all their lives. Something that money couldn't buy. Total self-assurance.

She let out her tightly held breath. Cassian was sublimely at home in his own skin, whereas she had lived in the shadow of someone else's rules and had moulded her behaviour to the will of others. She was someone else's creation. He was his own.

And she longed to be like him.

Suddenly he laughed, and she felt a sharpness like a vice in her chest as she was almost bowled over by the sheer force of life which imbued his whole body—his brilliant white teeth flashing wickedly in the darkness of his face, the tilt of his chin, the warmth in those hot, dark eyes.

'Now that's what I call sex appeal!' Sue whispered in awe. 'Isn't he like his mother? What was her name?'

Laura swallowed and found a husky voice emerging. 'Bathsheba.'

'Unusual. Suited her.'

'Exotic,' Laura agreed.

His mother had been the most beautiful and vibrant woman she'd ever known. Bathsheba had dark, wavy hair, eyes that flashed like scimitars when she was happy, and a face with the same classically chiselled bones as Cassian's.

For the five years that Bathsheba had been her stepmother, neither she nor Cassian had taken much notice of her. But then Enid had kept them apart as much as possible.

And tragically, during the time that Bathsheba and her father were together, Laura had witnessed how two people could love one another but be incapable of living with one another. They were torn asunder by their differing views— particularly where the disciplining of Cassian was concerned.

'Bathsheba and Cassian vanished overnight, I remember,' Sue mused.

Laura nodded. 'They *walked* out into the night, taking

nothing with them! I was appalled. I wondered where they'd live, how they'd cope. George never recovered, you know.'

Her eyes softened. It seemed incredible that one person could have such an effect on another. Her stern, unbending father had died of a broken heart. She shivered, shrinking from the destructiveness of passion. In her experience, it had never done anyone any good.

'Well, Cassian's got over his feelings about Thrushton. He's coming up the path!' Sue marvelled. 'Oh, why does something riveting like this have to happen, when I'm going on holiday tomorrow?!'

Laura couldn't believe her eyes. 'He's hardly likely to stay long. He hated this house!' she said, feeling an irrational sense of panic. 'This can't be a social call. He never noticed me, hardly knew I existed. And he just loathed Tony—'

She gasped. A key was rattling in the lock. There was a pause. Cassian must have realised that the kitchen door wasn't locked at all. The latch was lifted. Laura couldn't breathe. *Why did he have a key?*

The door creaked open a fraction. And then it was flung back with considerable force.

In an instant, the room seemed to be filled with him, with the blistering force of his anger. She cringed back instinctively by the half-concealing fall of the curtain, afraid of his potency and bewildered by the physical impact he had on her.

Cassian simmered with a volcanic rage as he scanned the kitchen with narrowed and glittering eyes. And all too soon, the full force of his incandescent fury became focussed directly at her.

CHAPTER TWO

THE smell of freshly baked bread had hit him immediately as he'd opened the door—even before it had swung fully open. Although his senses had enjoyed the aroma, he'd tensed every muscle in his body.

It meant one thing. A sitting tenant. And a legal mine-field ahead.

Unsettled, he'd paused to collect himself. He had wanted to be alone here when he first arrived. To chase away the past. That was why he'd left Jai in Marrakesh, exploring the High Atlas mountains with one of their Berber friends.

Instead, it looked as if he'd have to chase a tenant out first! Furious with Tony for not mentioning that he'd rented the place out, he'd thrust at the door with an impatient hand and stepped into the room.

His heart had beat loud and hard as he'd entered the house where he'd cut his teeth on conflict, toughened his character and learnt to deal with Hell. He'd steeled himself.

And then he'd seen Laura.

The shock rocked him. It was a moment before he could collect his wits, a fearsome scowl marring his features and his eyes narrowing in disbelief as he realised the situation.

'*You!*' he growled, his voice deep with disappointment.

Of all people! She ought to have gone years ago, left this house and made a new start in life!

When she flinched, obviously struck dumb by his greeting, he scowled harder still, silently heaping vicious curses on Tony's fat head. Her huge eyes were already wary and reproachful. Instinctively he knew that she'd weep pathetically when he turned her out and he'd feel a heel.

'Hi, Cassian!'

He started, and glanced sideways in response to the cheery greeting from a strawberry blonde.

'Sue,' he recalled shortly and she looked pleased.

In a second or two he had assessed her. A ring. Biting into her finger. Married for a while, then. Weight increase from children or comfortable living—perhaps both. Her clothes were good, her hair professionally tinted.

She didn't interest him. He turned his gaze back to Laura, drawn by her mute dismay and her total stillness. And those incredible black-fringed eyes.

'W-what…are you doing here?' she stumbled breathily.

Cassian's mouth tightened, his brows knitted heavily with impatience. She didn't know! Tony had taken the coward's way out, it seemed, and not told his adopted sister what he'd done with the house he'd inherited on his father's death. Little rat! Selfish to the last!

'I gather Tony didn't warn you I was coming,' he grated.

Her lips parted in dismay and began to tremble. For the first time he realised they weren't thin and tight at all, but full and soft like the bruised petals of a rose.

'No!' She looked at him in consternation. 'I—I haven't heard from him for nearly two years!'

'I see,' he clipped.

The frightened Laura flicked a nervous glance at the removal van. Her brow furrowed in confusion and she bit that plush lower lip with neat white teeth as the truth apparently dawned.

'You're not…oh, no! No!' she whispered in futile denial, her hands restlessly twisting together.

And he wanted to shake her. It annoyed him intensely that she hadn't changed. This was the old Laura, self-effacing, timid, frightened. He did the maths. She'd been fifteen when he'd left. That made her twenty-seven now. Old enough to realise that she was missing out on life.

His scowl deepened and she shrank back as if he'd hit her, then with a muttered exclamation she whirled and frantically grabbed a tea towel, beginning to polish the hell out of some cutlery that was drying on the drainer. It was a totally illogical thing to do, but typical.

Cassian felt the anger remorselessly expanding his chest. His eyes darkened to black coals beneath his heavy brows.

She'd always been desperately cleaning things in an attempt to be Enid's little angel, not realising that she would never achieve her aim and she might as well cut loose and fling her dinner at the vicious old woman.

It appalled him that she hadn't come out of her shell. Well, she'd have to do just that, from this moment on.

'Just stop doing that for a moment.'

Grim-faced, he took a step nearer and she looked up warily, all moist-eyed and trembling.

'I—I need to!' she blurted out.

'Displacement therapy?' he suggested irritably.

Close up, he was surprised by the sweetness of her face. It was small and heart-shaped with sharply defined cheekbones and a delicate nose. Her rich brown hair looked nondescript and badly cut—though clean and shiny in the morning light which streamed through the window. His sharp senses picked up the scent of lavender emanating from her.

And signs of fear. Although her body was rigid, there was a tiny twitch at the corner of her mouth where she was trying to control a quivering lip. Perhaps she knew his arrival presented some sort of threat to her beloved security, he mused.

'I—I don't know what you mean!' she protested.

Her whole body had adopted a defensive pose. Arms across breasts. Shoulders hunched, eyes wary. He sighed. This wouldn't be easy.

'I realise this is a shock, me barging in, but I didn't expect to see anyone here,' he said gruffly, softening his voice a little without intending to.

'Tony gave you a key!' she cried, bewildered.

'That's right.'

'Why?'

He frowned. She'd sussed out the situation, hadn't she? 'To get in,' he said drily.

'But...'

He saw her swallow, the sweet curve of her throat pale against the faded blue of her threadbare shirt. Noticing his gaze, she blushed and put down the tea towel, her hand immediately lifting again to conceal the tatty collar.

His body-reading skills came automatically into use. Obviously she was poor. And she was proud, he noted. Slender hands, roughened from physical work. Pale face... Indoor work, then. She must be on night shifts—or out of a job, since she was home on a weekday.

Not married or engaged, no sign of a ring. But several pictures of a child in the room. Baby shots, a toddler, a school snap of a kid a bit younger than his own son. He felt intrigued. Wanted to learn more.

'I'm confused. That removal van...' She cleared her throat, her voice shaking with nerves. 'It can't...it doesn't mean that...that Tony has let you stay here with me?!' she asked in a horrified croak.

So that was what she'd thought. 'No. It doesn't. But—'

'Oh!' she cried, interrupting him. 'That's a relief!'

He was diverted before he could correct the conclusion she'd drawn. Laura's slender body had relaxed as if she'd let out a tense breath, the action drawing his eyes down to where her breasts might be hiding beneath the shirt which was at least two sizes too big.

Fascinated by her, he kept his investigation going and finished his scrutiny, observing the poor quality of her skirt and scuffed sneakers. Long legs, though. Slightly tanned, slender and shapely.

He felt a kick of interest in his loins and strangled it at birth. Laura wasn't his kind of woman. He adored women of all kinds, but he preferred them with fire coming out of their ears.

'Laura,' he began, unusually hesitant.

Sue jumped in. 'Hang on. If you haven't come to stay, why bring a removal van?' she asked in a suspicious tone.

'I'm about to explain,' he snapped.

He frowned at her because he didn't want her to be there. This was between him and Laura. Like it or not, Laura would have to go and he didn't want anyone else complicating matters when he told her the truth.

He'd tell her straight, no messing. Disguising the news with soft words wouldn't make a scrap of difference to the situation.

He sought Laura's wondering gaze again, strangely irritated by her quietly desperate passivity. She ought to be yelling at him, demanding to know what he was doing, persuading him to go and never return. But she meekly waited for the world to fall in on her.

He wanted to jerk her into life. To make her lose her temper and to see some passion fly. At the same time, he felt an overwhelming urge to protect her as he might protect a defenceless animal or a tiny baby. She was too vulnerable for her own good. Too easy to wound. Hell, what was he going to do?

In two strides he'd breached the distance between them. With the wall behind her, she had nowhere to go though he had the impression that she would have vanished through it if she could.

Grimly he took her arm, felt her quiver when he did so. Looking deeply into her extraordinary eyes, he saw that she recognised he was going to tell her something unpleasant.

'Sit down,' he ordered, hating the way she made him feel. Firmly he pushed her rigid body into the kitchen chair.

And inexplicably he kept a hand on her shoulder, intensely aware of its fragility, of the fineness of the bone structure of her face as she stared up at him in fear and apprehension, drowning him, making him flounder with those great big eyes.

'What is it?' she whispered.

Feeling distinctly unsettled by her, he dragged up a chair and sat close to her. Immediately she shrank away from him, covering her knees with her hands primly. His mouth tightened.

He loathed seeing her like this, a slave to her past, to the constant belittling by Enid which had relentlessly ground away her confidence. It had been just like the elements, the wind and the rain out there on the moors, grinding down solid rock over the years. She needed to leave. To find life. Her true self.

Confused by his own passionate views of Laura's future, he plunged in, eager to send her out into the world.

'When I said that I'm not staying here with you, Laura,' he said firmly, 'I meant that *you* won't be living here at all. I've bought Thrushton Hall from Tony. I'm moving in.'

'Moving…in?'

She was blinking, her eyes glazed over as if she didn't understand. He tried again so that there would be no mistake.

'Correct. You, Laura, will have to move out. Pronto.'

Laura let out a strangled gasp. Her stomach went into free fall, making her feel faint.

'No!' she whispered in pure horror. 'This is my home! All I've ever known! Tony wouldn't do that to me!'

'Yes, he would,' Sue muttered. 'He's a loathsome little creep.'

'That's true,' Cassian said in heartfelt agreement.

Laura stared at the implacable Cassian, her brain in a fog. 'This is ridiculous! I live here!'

'Not any more.'

She gave a little cry. 'I've been paying the bills and maintaining the house ever since Tony disappeared! You— you can't turn us out of here!' she said weakly.

'Us.'

Suddenly alert, he turned to scan the photographs around the room, his eyebrows asking an unspoken question.

'My son,' she mumbled, still dazed by Cassian's announcement. 'Adam,' she added blankly as tears of despair welled up in her eyes. 'He's nine.' She saw Cassian's eyes narrow, as he began to make a calculation and she jumped in before he could say anything. 'Yes, if you're wondering, I was eighteen when he was born!' she defied hysterically, bracing herself for some sign of disapproval.

Cassian, however, seemed unfazed. 'You and your son,' he said quietly. 'No one else living with you?'

Suddenly she wanted to startle him as he'd startled her. Panic and fear were making her unstable. A spurt of anger flashed through her and with uncharacteristic impetuosity she answered;

'I'm totally alone. I never *had* a husband—or even a partner!'

Everyone here knew how the travelling salesman from Leeds had flattered her by pretending she was beautiful. He must have seen a gauche, nervous and drab female in ill-fitting clothes and decided it would be easy for his silver tongue to dazzle her. Laura realised now that her transparent innocence, coupled with her teenage desperation to be loved, had been her downfall.

She flinched. There had been one fateful evening of bewilderment and repugnance—on her part—and then the arrival of Adam, nine months later. The shame of what she'd done would live with her for ever. And yet she had Adam, who'd brought joy to her dreary life.

Annoyingly, Cassian took her confession in his stride. 'I see,' he said non-committally.

Laura stiffened. 'No you don't!' she wailed. 'You stroll in here, claiming you've bought Thrushton Hall—'

'Want to see the deeds?' he enquired, foraging in the back pocket of his jeans.

The colour drained from her face when she saw the document he was holding out to her. Snatching it from him, she frantically unfolded it and read the first few lines, her heart contracting more and more as the truth sank in.

This was Cassian's house. She would have to leave. Her legs trembled.

'No! I don't believe it!' she whispered, aghast.

Despite the harshness of her childhood, this house held special memories. It was where her mother had lived. Deprived of any tangible memories of her mother, it comforted her that she walked in her mother's footsteps every day of her life. And Cassian intended to drive her away.

'You have no choice.'

Her head snapped up, sending her hair whirling about her set face. A frightening wildness was possessing her. Hot on its heels came an urge to lash out and pummel Cassian till his composure vanished and he began to notice her as a person instead of an irritating obstacle he needed to kick out of his way.

Her emotions terrified and appalled her. They seemed to fill her body, surging up uncontrollably with an evil, unstoppable violence. She fought them, groping for some kind of discipline over them because she didn't know what would happen if she ever allowed those clamouring passions to surface.

'You don't want this house! You can't possibly want to live here!' she whispered, hoarse with horror.

His calm, oddly warm eyes melted into hers.

'I do. I can.'

She took a deep, shuddering breath but she was losing a battle with her temper. Her child's security was threatened. She wouldn't allow that.

'This is my *home*!' she insisted tightly, clinging for dear life to the last vestiges of restraint. 'Adam's home!'

He shrugged as if homes were unimportant. 'I had the

impression that it was Tony's. Now it's mine. Do you pay rent?'

'N-no—'

'Then you have no legal rights to stay.'

Laura gasped, her hand flying to her mouth in consternation. 'Surely I do! I must have some kind of protection—'

'There could be an expensive legal case,' he conceded. 'But you'd have to go eventually. You'd save time and hassle if you did so straight away.' He smiled in a friendly way, as if that would console her. 'You'll find somewhere else. You might discover that moving from Thrushton turns out to be a good idea in the long run.'

She glared and was incensed when his eyes flickered with satisfaction. It was as if he welcomed her anger!

'What do you know?' she yelled. Dear heaven! she thought. She was losing control, acting like a banshee— and couldn't stop herself! 'It's a stupid idea! For a start, I don't have any money!' she choked, scarlet from the shameful admission. But he had to know her circumstances. 'There's nowhere I can go!' she cried in agitation. 'Nowhere I can afford!'

He continued to gaze at her with a steely eye, his heart clearly unmoved by her plight. And she knew that her hours in her beloved house—*his* house, she thought furiously— were probably numbered.

'It's true. She's dead broke. Lost her job,' confirmed Sue, suddenly butting in. Cassian jerked his head around in surprise as if he, like Laura, had forgotten Sue was there. 'I reckon she can stay put if she chooses—'

'I don't deny that.' Cassian flung an arm across the back of the chair, his eyes relentlessly fixed to Laura's. She flinched as his expression darkened, becoming unnervingly menacing. 'But you ought to know that living with me wouldn't be pleasant,' he drawled.

'Meaning?' Sue demanded.

He shrugged. 'I'd be…difficult.' His eyes seemed to be issuing a direct challenge. 'I'd eat her food, play music late at night, change the locks…' There was a provocative curve to his mouth, something…unnerving in his expression as his gaze swept her up and down. 'Laura, I'm not changing my way of living for anybody, and I have the distinct impression that you'd be shocked by the way I wander about half-naked after my morning shower, with just a small towel covering me and my—'

'Please!' she croaked.

'I'm just warning you,' he murmured with a shrug.

She felt hot. The rawness of his huge energy field reached out to enfold her in its greedy clasp and she instinctively flattened herself against the back of the chair.

She blushed, ashamed to be assailed by the unwanted rivulets of molten liquid which were coursing through her veins. His sexuality was too blatant, too unavoidable. This was something alien to her and she couldn't cope with it. Didn't want it at all. Living with him would be a nightmare.

'It's no use! I can't stay if he's living here!' she declared to Sue shakily. 'Sharing would be impossible!'

'Don't you give up!' Sue snapped. She glared at Cassian. 'Laura's been far too sheltered all her life to manage anywhere else—so you leave her alone, you ruthless, selfish brute. Push off back where you came from!'

Cassian rose, his eyes dark and glittering. 'I'm not going anywhere, whatever insults you choose to hurl at me. I'm moving in, once the removal men have finished their early lunch.'

'*Lunch?*' With a start, Sue glanced at the kitchen clock and let out a groan. 'Oh, crikey! My dental appointment! Never mind. I'll cancel it,' she offered urgently. 'You need backup, Laura—'

'No,' she said quickly, sick with nerves, hating the wobble in her voice.

This was her battle. Sue was making things worse.

Cassian had visibly tensed when Sue had shouted at him.
He'd listen to logic, she was sure, but he wouldn't be bullied.

Proud and erect, she stood up with great dignity, conscious, however, that her five-seven didn't impinge on
Cassian's six foot.

And they were now only inches apart, waves of heat
thickening the space between them, pouring into her, the
heavy, lifeless air clogging up her throat. Laura gulped,
feeling that all the power was draining from her legs till
they trembled from weakness.

'Well! Are you fighting me, Laura?' he taunted.

Rebellion drained away too when she met his challeng-
ing eyes. His confidence was daunting. How could she fight
him when he held all the cards?

'I—I...'

'Still the mouse,' he mocked, but with a hint of regret
in his dark regard. 'Still meekly huddling in the corner,
afraid of being trodden on.'

'You rat!' Sue gasped.

'It's true!' he cried, his voice shaking in an inexplicable
passion. 'She can't even stand up for her own flesh and
blood!'

'Leave her alone!' Sue raged.

'I can't! She has to go! I have no intention of having a
lodger around!' Cassian snapped.

With a whimper, Laura jerked her head away and found
herself staring straight at the photo she'd taken of her son
on his ninth birthday. Her heart lurched miserably.

Adam looked ecstatic. They'd spent the day at Skipton,
where they'd explored the castle, picnicked by the river,
and splashed out on a special treat of tea and cakes in a
cosy café. Cheap and simple as day trips went, but a joy
for both of them.

The recriminations surrounding his conception had been
hard to bear. Yet, even in the depths of her shame, Laura

had felt a growing joy. This child was hers. And when he was born, her emotions had overwhelmed her, unnerving her with their unexpected intensity.

Love had poured from her and it had felt as if her heart would burst with happiness. She'd never known she had such feelings. Her child had reached into her very core and found a well of passion hidden there.

For hours she had cuddled her baby, his warm, living flesh snuggling up to her. And it had been more than compensation for the hard, unremitting drudgery which Enid had imposed on her as a punishment for her 'lewd behaviour'.

She'd hardly cared because she had had her son to love. Someone to love her back.

Laura squared her shoulders. She would never let him down. Adam was horribly vulnerable and deeply sensitive. Cassian couldn't be allowed to uproot them both. Did he honestly imagine that they'd pack their bags without a murmur, and tramp the streets like vagabonds till someone took them in?

She flung up her head and spoke before she changed her mind. 'You're wrong about me! I *will* fight you for my home! Tooth and nail—'

'To defend your lion cub,' he murmured, his voice low and vibrating.

Her eyes hardened at his mockery. 'For the sake of my son,' she corrected in scathing tones, infuriated by his condescension. 'Sue, get going. I can deal with this better on my own. Besides, I'd rather you didn't witness the blood he sheds,' she muttered through her teeth.

'Sounds promising,' Cassian remarked lazily.

Laura ignored him because she thought she might choke with anger if she said anything. The situation clearly amused him. For her, it was deadly serious.

'Come on, Sue. Off you go and get those molars drilled,' she ordered tightly.

Secretly astonished by her own curt and decisive manner, she pushed her protesting friend towards the door.

Naturally, Sue resisted. 'I can't believe this! The worm turns! This I've gotta see!'

'I'll get the camera out,' Laura muttered. 'Please, please, go!'

'I want close-ups!' Sue hissed. 'A blow by blow account, when I get back!'

'Whatever! Go!'

It took her a minute or two before Sue could be budged but eventually she went, flinging dark and lurid warnings in Cassian's direction and promising Laura a stick of rock from Hong Kong to brain Cassian with if he was still around.

Quivering like a leaf, Laura shut the door, braced herself, and turned to face him. With Sue gone, it felt as if she was very alone. And she would be—till the following afternoon. Adam was going to his best friend's house after school and sleeping over. It was just her and Cassian, then.

Her heart thudded loudly in her chest at the strange pall of silence which seemed to have fallen on the house, intensifying the strained atmosphere.

Cassian was looking at her speculatively, his eyes half-closed in contemplation, a half-smile on his lips.

'It's a problem, isn't it?' he said mildly.

'The camera or the blood?' she flung back with rare sarcasm.

The black eyes twinkled disconcertingly. 'You and me. In this house together.'

The huskiness of his voice took her by surprise. It contrasted oddly with the intensity of his manner. There was a determined set to his jaw and the arch of his sensual mouth had flattened into a firm line.

'You can live anywhere. I can't—' she began.

'You must have friends who'd take you in,' he purred.

'I couldn't impose!'

'You don't have a choice.'

She felt close to tears of anger and frustration.

'You don't understand! I have to stay!' she insisted frantically.

'Why?'

'Because...' She went scarlet.

'Yes?' he prompted.

She stared at him, unwilling to expose her fear. But she saw no other way out.

Her eyes blazed with loathing. 'If you really want to know, I'm scared of going anywhere else!' she cried shakily.

He raised a sardonic eyebrow. 'Then it's time you did.'

She gasped. So much for compassion. But Cassian would never know what it was to be uncertain and shy, or to be uncomfortable in unfamiliar surroundings. Her pulses pounded as her heart rate accelerated.

'There's more,' she said, her lips dry with fear.

'Yes?'

She swallowed. This was deeply personal. Normally, wild horses wouldn't have dragged this out of her, but Cassian had to realise what this house meant to her.

'My...' She felt a fool. He was looking at her with cold hard eyes and she was having to expose her innermost secrets. For Adam, she told herself. And found the strength. Her eyes blazed blue and bright into his. 'My mother lived here,' she began tightly.

'So?'

She drew in a sharp breath of irritation. This wasn't going to get her anywhere. But...he'd adored his own mother. Wouldn't he understand?

'Cassian,' she grated. 'Is your mother still alive?'

He looked puzzled. 'Yes. Why?'

Thank heaven. Maybe she had a chance. 'You still see her, speak to her?'

'She's remarried. She lives in France, but yes, I see her.

And I speak to her each week. What are you getting at?'
he asked curiously.

She offered up a small prayer to the Fates. 'Imagine not
knowing anything about her. Not even how she looked.
Think what it would have been like, not to know that she's
beautiful, a gifted artist, and full of life and fire!' Her eyes
glowed feverishly with desperate passion.

'I don't see the—'

'Well, that's how it is for me!' she cried shakily. 'No
one will speak of my mother and all trace of her was removed the day she left.' Her voice broke and she took a
moment to steady herself. 'I wouldn't know anything at all
about her if it wasn't for Mr Walker—'

'Who?' he exclaimed sharply.

'He's someone in the village. A lonely old man with a
vile temper but he can't walk far so I do his weekly shopping. He gives me a list and money for what he needs. I
lug his shopping back, he complains about half of it and
we both feel better.'

Her eyes went dreamy for a moment. Out of the blue,
Mr Walker had once said that her mother was lovely. In
his opinion, he'd said, Diana had been wasted on boring
George Morris.

'What did he say about her?' Cassian asked warily.

She was surprised he was interested, but she smiled, remembering. 'That she was passionate about life.'

'Anything else?'

'Yes. He said she was kind and very beautiful.' Laura
sighed. 'Since I'm nothing like that, I think he was probably winding me up. When I asked him for more information he refused to say anything else.'

'I see,' he clipped, dark brows meeting hard together.

'The point is that this house means more to me than just
bricks and mortar and general sentimentality.' Desperate
now, she felt herself leaning forwards, punching out her

words. 'Thrushton Hall is all I have of my mother!' she jerked out miserably.

'Surely you must know about your mother—!'

'No! I don't!' Wouldn't he listen to her? Hadn't he heard? 'I don't know what she looked like, how or why she left me, *nothing*!'

She was aware of Cassian's stunned expression and took heart. He would see her plight and take pity on her.

'Cassian, other than the house, I have nothing else to remember her by, not one single item she ever possessed. Everything has vanished. The only actual trace of her is *me*!'

She steadied her voice, aware that it had been shaking so strongly with emotion that she'd been almost incoherent.

'I don't believe this!' he muttered.

'It's true!' she cried desperately. 'I've had to rely on my imagination! I've visualised her in this house, doing everyday things. That is where she must have stood to wash up, to cook,' she cried, pointing with a fierce jab of her finger. 'She must have sat at that very table to eat, to drink cups of tea. She would have stood at that window and gazed at the view of the soaring fells, just as I do. I can imagine her here and think of her going about her daily life. If—if I leave Thrushton,' she stumbled, 'I would have to leave behind those fragile half-memories of my mother. I'd have nothing at all left of her—and the little that I have is infinitely precious to me!' she sobbed.

She saw Cassian's jaw tighten and waited seemingly for an eternity before he answered.

'You must make enquiries about her,' he muttered, his tone flat and toneless.

Laura stared at him helplessly. How could she do that?

'I can't,' she retorted miserably.

'Afraid?' he probed, his eyes unusually watchful.

'Yes, if you must know!' she retorted with a baleful glare.

'Laura, you need to know—'

'I *can't*,' she cried helplessly. 'She's probably started a new life somewhere and I could ruin it by turning up on her doorstep. I couldn't do that to her. If it was all right for us to meet, she would have come to see me. I can't take the initiative, can I?'

He was silent, his face stony. But she knew what he was thinking. That perhaps her mother hadn't wanted to be reminded of her 'mistake'.

Closing her mind to such a horrible idea, she lifted her chin in an attempt to appear tough. Though even a fool would have noticed her stupid, feeble trembling.

'You must learn the truth—' he began huskily.

'No!'

She wrung her hands, frustrated that he couldn't see how scared she was of confronting her mother. Maybe she was flighty. Maybe she'd had a string of lovers. Maybe…

'Cassian,' she croaked, voicing her worst fear, 'I can't pursue this. I—I just couldn't face being rejected by her.'

'I don't think—'

'How the devil do you know!' she yelled. 'She left me, didn't she? Though…I suppose she knew that George would have won custody, whatever she did. She'd run away. He'd been looking after me and was a lawyer, after all. Mother must have known she didn't have a chance. To be honest, I don't even know if there was a court hearing about me. There might have been—and she might have tried to take me with her. I'll never know. Nobody would ever talk about her.' Slowly her head lifted till her troubled eyes met Cassian's. 'Mr Walker said she was full of life. Knowing how *your* mother felt, I understand why anyone with fire and energy would have found it difficult to live here,' she said with dignity.

Cassian looked uncomfortable. 'Laura,' he said in a gravelly voice, 'this is nothing to do with me. Not one of your arguments is sufficient reason for you to stay. Excuse me.'

He strode into the hall. She heard the sound of men moving about, presumably bringing in his possessions. She buried her head in her hands. She'd failed.

Cassian saw her emerging from the kitchen a few moments later, her eyes pink from crying, silver tear-track streaks glistening on her face. He gritted his teeth and continued to organise the stacking of his few belongings in the spacious hall.

Behind his bent back, he could hear the fast rasp of her breathing and sensed she was close to hysteria. And he felt as if he'd whipped a puppy.

'All done, guv,' announced one of the men.

Grateful for the diversion, he gave Len and Charlie his undivided attention. 'Thanks. Great meeting you,' he said warmly, shaking the men's hands in turn.

He slid his wallet from his back pocket and handed over the fee plus a tip, brushing away their astonished refusals of such a large sum of money. What was cash to him? It came easily and went the same way.

Charlie had told him about his new baby and Len was nearing retirement. They could both do with a little extra and he believed passionately in circulating money while he had the earning power.

'I had a windfall. Might as well share it, eh?' he explained. Like an obscene advance from a film company.

'Yeah? You're a gent,' said Len in awe.

'Thanks,' added Charlie, looking stunned.

'Have a pint on me.'

Len grinned. 'Treat the wife to a slap-up meal and a holiday, more like!'

'Buy a baby buggy!' enthused Charlie.

He saw them out, found them shaking his hand again and accepted an invitation to visit Charlie's baby and to have tea and cakes with Len and his wife. After much scribbling of addresses, he returned to the tense and angry Laura.

'What are you trying to do by gossiping out there—drive me to screaming pitch?!' she demanded furiously, her hands on shapely hips.

He stole a moment to admire them. 'Being friendly. Would you prefer I dismissed them with a curt nod and a growl?' he enquired.

She flushed. 'No…oh, you're *impossible*!'

He felt pleased. Her eyes were sparkling, a hot flush brightening her cheeks. If only he could release her emotions…

He bit back an impulse to invite her to stay so he could do just that, and followed up her remark instead.

'I just live by a different code from you. Now…will I push you into suicide mode if I just check I've got all my possessions here?'

She blinked her huge eyes, dark lashes fluttering as she eyed the stack of boxes, his luggage, and three bags of shopping.

'Do you mean…that this is all you own in the whole world?'

'It's all I need. Books, computer stuff and a few mementoes. Plus a few changes of clothes and some food stores.'

'I don't understand you,' she muttered.

'Not many people do. Now, this is what I've decided,' he said brusquely, suddenly needing to get away from the censure of her accusing eyes. 'I'd booked a room in a hotel in Grassington because I didn't know what state the house would be in. I'll go there now and leave you to start looking for temporary accommodation. Someone will take you in for a few days till you can find somewhere permanent. I'll be back in the morning. To take possession.'

He turned on his heel. Flinched at her horrified intake of breath as it rasped through emotion-choked airways.

'Cassian!' she pleaded in desperation.

But he'd opened the door, was striding up the path and

ignoring the sound of her weeping. It would be good for her, he kept telling himself, wrenching at the door handle of his car.

She needed to find out the truth about her mother. But first she'd have to stand up for herself, to gain some strength of will—and being forced to move would make her take her life in her hands at last.

He crunched the gears. And accelerated away, angry with her for making him feel such a swine.

CHAPTER THREE

WHEN he turned up the next morning she was beating the hell out of a lump of dough and he couldn't help smiling because her small fists were clearly using it as a substitute for his head.

Her glare would have put off a seasoned terrorist but, knowing how normally reclusive she was, he could only be pleased. This was precisely the reaction he'd hoped for.

'Any progress?' he asked, coming straight to the point.

'No.' She jammed her teeth together and kneaded the bread with a fascinating ferocity. 'If you must know, I didn't try! And if you're looking for coffee,' she said, as he opened and shut cupboards at random, 'you're out of luck. There isn't any.'

He went to find some in the supplies he'd brought, came back and put on the kettle. The bread dough looked so elastic she could have used it for bungy jumping.

'You did discuss leaving with your son, didn't you?' he enquired.

Laura slammed the dough into a bowl and covered it with a cloth. 'You didn't give me a chance to tell you,' she said grimly, pushing the bowl into the warming oven to prove and slamming the heavy iron door with some force. 'Adam's been with a friend. I won't see him till this afternoon after school. Besides…' Her face crumpled and he realised that she looked very tired and pale as if she'd been up most of the night. 'I can't tell him!' she confessed helplessly.

'You can. You're stronger than you think—' he began.

'But *he's* not!'

Quite frantic now, she began to fling fresh ingredients

37

into a mixing bowl and he began to think that the resulting cake would weigh a ton.

'In what way isn't he strong?' he asked quietly.

'Every way,' she muttered, measuring out flour carelessly. 'Cassian, *you* know what it's like to be uprooted from somewhere familiar. You loved the narrow boat where you lived with your mother before you came here after her marriage, and you loathed Thrushton—'

'Not the house itself, or the countryside,' he corrected, wondering what she'd say if he brushed away the dusting of flour on her nose and cheeks. It made her look cute and appealing and he didn't want that. It was very distracting. 'Just the atmosphere. The stifling rules,' he said, miraculously keeping track of the conversation.

'Well, moving is traumatic, especially when you're a child. Can't you put yourself in Adam's place and see how awful it would be for him to leave the place of his birth?' she implored, pushing away her hair with the back of her hand. 'Making friends is hard for him. He'd find it a nightmare settling into another school.'

'Life's tough. Children need to be challenged,' he said softly. He passed her a coffee.

'Challenged?!' She flung in the flour haphazardly and began to fold it into the cake mixture as if declaring war on it. 'He's sensitive. It would destroy him!' she cried, her face aflame with desperation.

'Here. That'll turn into a rugby ball if you're not careful. Let me.'

He took the bowl from her shaking hands, combined the flour and the abused mixture with a metal spoon then scooped it all into a cake tin. Gently he slid the tin into the baking oven and checked the clock.

She stood in helpless misery, her hands constantly twisting together.

'Thanks,' she mumbled.

'You say your son is sensitive,' he mused. 'Is he happy where he is at school now?'

She frowned. 'N-no—'

'Well, then!'

'But another one could be worse—!'

'Or better.'

'I doubt it. He'd be such a bag of nerves that he'd turn up on his first day with "victim" written all over his face,' she wailed. Her eyes were haunted. 'You can't do this to my child! I love him! He's everything I have!'

His guts twisted and he had to wait before he could speak.

'And you? How will you feel, living elsewhere?'

His voice had suddenly softened, caressing her gently. She drew in a sharp breath and shuddered with horror.

'I can't bear to think of going,' she mumbled pitifully. 'I love every inch of this house. I know it, and the garden, the village, the hills and the dales, as well as I know the back of my hand. There's no lovelier place on God's earth. My heart is here. Tear me away,' she said, her voice shaking with passion, 'and you rip out a part of me!'

'I'm sorry that you will both find it hard,' he said curtly. 'But…there it is. That's life. One door closes, another one opens.'

Laura gasped at his callousness. It was as she feared. He was determined on his course of action. She turned away as tears rushed up, choking her. Her hands gripped the back of a chair for support as she imagined Adam facing a new playground, new teachers, new, more intimidating bullies…

'All right, Cassian!' She whirled back in a fury. 'You open and close all the doors you want—I'm staying put!'

He smiled faintly and his slow and thorough gaze swept her from head to toe.

'Flour on your face,' he murmured.

Before she knew it, his fingers were lightly travelling over her skin while she gazed into his lazily smiling eyes,

eyes so dark and liquid that she felt she was melting into a warm Mediterranean sea.

By accident, his caressing fingers touched her mouth. And instantly something seared through her like a heated lance, tightening every nerve she possessed and sending an electric charge into her system.

She struggled to focus, to forget the terrible effect he was having on her. He was throwing her out. Going gooey-eyed wouldn't help her at *all*. Rot him—was he doing this deliberately? Her eyes blazed with anger.

'If you want me to go, you'll have to get the removal men to carry me out!' she flung wildly.

'No need. I'd carry you out myself. I don't think it would be beyond my capabilities,' he mused.

In a split second she saw herself in his arms, helpless, at his mercy…'Touch me and you'll regret it!' she spat, thoroughly uncomfortable with her treacherous feelings.

'Yes,' he agreed slowly, apparently fascinated by her parted lips and her accelerated breathing. 'I think I might.' Equally slowly, a dazzling grin spread across his face. It was at once wicked and beguiling and made Laura's stomach contract. 'But,' he drawled, 'that wouldn't stop me from doing so.'

She blinked in confusion. There were undercurrents here she didn't understand. Somehow she broke the spell that had kept her eyes locked to his and she looked around desperately for a diversion.

'I'd fight you!' she muttered.

'Mmm. Then I'd have to hold you very, very tightly, wouldn't I?' he purred.

Her throat dried. Almost without realising, she began to tidy the dresser, despite the fact she was so agitated that she kept knocking things over.

Cassian came up behind her. Although there had been no sound, she knew he was near because the hairs on the back of her neck stood on end and her spine tingled. Sure

enough, his hand reached out, covering hers where it rested
on a figurine she'd toppled.

'You'll break something,' he chided, his breath whispering warm and soft over her ear, like a summer breeze in
the valley.

'I don't give a toss!' she jerked out stupidly, snatching
her hand away.

He caught the flying figure deftly and set it on the
dresser. His arm was whipcord strong, his hands big but
with surprisingly long, delicate fingers.

'Laura, surrender. You can't fight the inevitable.'

She blinked, her huge eyes fixed on his neatly manicured
nails. Her body was in turmoil and she didn't know why.
It was her head that ought to be in frantic disarray.

She should be panicking about her eviction. Instead, she
was finding herself totally transfixed by his breathing, the
cottony smell of his T-shirt, the accompanying warm maleness...

Oh, help me, someone! she groaned inwardly, trying to
gather her wits.

'It can't be inevitable! Have pity on us!' she whispered.

'I am. That's why I'm chucking you out. And when I
do, would you like a fireman's lift, or something more conventional?' he murmured in amusement, turning her to face
him.

Laura's knees weren't functioning properly. She wobbled
and he steadied her. He was incredibly close, his smooth,
tanned face sympathetic and kind. It didn't make sense. But
his gentle smile broke her resistance. For a terrible, sham-
ing instant, she was horribly tempted to reach up and kiss
that inviting mouth so that the tingling of her own lips
could be assuaged.

Her eyes widened at her temerity. This was madness!
Where were her inhibitions when she needed them? She'd
never felt like this. Never had such an overwhelming urge

to abandon what was decent and proper and to submit to physical temptations!

It was a relief that he couldn't know how she felt. The unguarded, unwanted and definitely unhinged response of her own body shocked her. It felt as if she was glowing. Erotic sensations were centred in places where he shouldn't have reached. It was awful. Like finding she enjoyed sin.

Shame brought high colour to her cheeks. A terrible thought flashed through her mind. Perhaps she was a slut. Perhaps her mother had been... *No!* Her hand flew to her mouth in horror, dismayed where his casual behaviour had taken her.

'Laura,' he murmured, drawing her imperceptibly closer.

'Let me go! I told you!' she moaned, wriggling away from the pressure of his hands and emerging hot and flustered because of the skin-tingling way they had slid down her arms. She moved back warily. 'I don't want you to touch me!' she stormed. 'Let's get this straight! If you do force me out, I'll come straight back in!'

His eyes danced with bright amusement. 'I'd lock the door.'

'I'd break a window!' she retorted heatedly.

'Do you intend your son to use the same point of entry?'

Laura ground her teeth in frustration. Her argument was futile and they both knew it. That didn't help her temper much.

'So you turn out a woman and a child, both of whom were born in this house! How do you think you'll be treated by people in this village?' she flared.

'Like a leper. However, it's not something that would disturb my sleep,' he replied gravely.

No. It wouldn't. Cassian never worried about the opinions of others. In her desperation she tried another tack. A last-ditch attempt to find a scrap of compassion in Cassian's granite heart.

'Adam is asthmatic. Emotional upsets can bring on an

attack. Do you want his health on your conscience?' she demanded.

'That would be unpleasant for all of us,' he admitted. 'What do you suggest we do?'

Her mouth fell open. 'What?'

Quite calmly, Cassian perched on the kitchen table, one long leg swinging freely and his steady gaze pinning Laura to the spot.

'I've bought the house. I want to live in it. So do you. That suggests a conflict of interests. How do you propose we deal with the situation?'

She was astonished. She hadn't expected negotiating tactics.

'Tell Tony you've made a mistake! Get him to buy it back!' she pleaded.

Cassian shook his head. 'No use. He'll have paid off his debtors to save himself from being beaten up again.'

'Again?! What do you mean?' She felt the colour drain from her face. 'Where is he? What's happened to him?' she asked in agitation.

'You're surprisingly concerned, considering Tony's indifference to you,' he observed. 'If I recall, he was the favoured child. He went from public school to university, whereas you were destined to leave school early. It never bothered him that your lives were unequal. You didn't figure in his life at all.'

'There was a crucial difference between Tony and me,' she pointed out sharply.

'Sure,' Cassian scathed. 'He was a selfish jerk. You were a doormat—'

'I—I was…!' OK. She was a doormat. He didn't have to say so! 'I was hardly in a position to demand my rights,' she said stiltedly. 'I had no blood ties with anyone in this house and you know that. It's hardly surprising he had all the advantages. I was lucky—'

'Lucky?' he barked, leaping to his feet angrily.

'Yes! They brought me up. I was fed and clothed—'

'You were crushed,' he snapped. His eyes blazed down at her, sapping her strength with their ferocity. 'And you're *grateful* because they offered you the basic human needs! Laura, they systematically browbeat you. They punished you for what your mother did to the oh-so-important George Morris, solicitor of this parish. They turned you into an obedient, colourless, cowering mouse, afraid of opening your mouth in case you said the wrong thing—!'

'Don't you criticise my family!' she cried hotly. 'It's none of your business how we lived! I don't care what you think of me…!'

She gulped. Because she did care. It upset her that he saw her as such a wimp. An obedient, colourless, cowering mouse! That was an awful description. Was she that pathetic?

Muddled, she stood there, her chest heaving, wondering why he was so angry and why she kept losing the composure which had always been such an integral part of her.

That was because he'd flung her into her worst nightmare. He was knocking away all her props. Leaving her with nothing. Perhaps she could plead with Tony herself…

'Tony,' she reminded him, her voice thin with panic. She sat down, shaking. 'Just tell me what's happened to him!'

Cassian felt like shaking her. She still saw justification in the way she'd been treated as a child. And yet cracks were beginning to appear in her armour. Rebellion simmered inside that tense body. She might have been taught to abhor passion but it was there, nevertheless and the thought excited him more than it should.

Inexplicably he'd wanted to press his lips on her pink, pouting mouth and her unavailability had only made the urge stronger. He couldn't understand his reaction. He'd been celibate for a long time and many women had tried to steer him from his chosen path, using all the tricks in the book and then some.

Tricks he could deflect. This was something else. Whether he liked it or not, Laura was reaching something deeper in him without even knowing what she was doing.

Curbing his rampaging instincts, he set about hurrying her departure before her temptations proved his undoing. Women could be dynamite at the best of times. He dare not get tangled up with someone like Laura. That would be dangerous in the extreme for both of them.

Pity, he found himself musing recklessly. It was such a luscious, kissable mouth... And he hungered for it more than was wise.

Grimly Cassian subdued his lurching passions. He could be hard on himself when necessary. And this was essential.

'I met Tony in Marrakesh—' he began at a gallop.

'*Marrakesh!*' she exclaimed, as if it were the planet Mars.

He gave a faint smile. To her, it probably was.

'Stupidly he'd swindled some thugs and they'd beaten him up. I got out the sticking plasters, let him stay for a while—'

'You have a house in Marrakesh?' she asked, wide-eyed.

Cassian perched on the table again. 'No, I rented rooms. Tony hotbedded with Fee, a stripper, who I—'

'*What?*' Her eyes were even wider, her mouth now joining in the amazement. She was wonderfully transparent. 'You...lived with a...stripper?!'

'Two, actually.' Before her jaw dropped any further and she did herself an injury, he added, 'We weren't cohabiting, I hasten to add. Same house, different rooms. Loads of space, no obligations to one another, come and go as you like...a perfect arrangement. No commitment, company when you want it, solitude when you don't.'

'But...strippers?'

Disapproval came from every line of her body. He decided she needed to have her judgement shaken up.

'Don't let the job fool you. Fee's a sweetie, with a very

strict moral code. Comes from Islington. You'd like her. Runs a shelter for sick animals in her spare time.'

'You're kidding me!' she scoffed.

'No, word of honour. It's partly why she let Tony stay. She has a warm heart.'

'I bet. So…what does…"hot-bedded" mean, then?!' she asked warily.

He couldn't help but smile again, seeing that he was stretching her knowledge of the world a little too fast, a little too far.

'It's not as interesting as it sounds. The strippers worked at night so Tony had the use of Fee's bed in their room. During the day they slept, and he mooched about on the roof. It's flat. A kind of garden,' he explained.

'Warm-hearted or not, I don't see why they'd let a stranger invade their privacy.'

'It was a favour to me.'

'Oh?'

It was a very meaningful and glacial Aunt Enid kind of 'oh', but he wasn't going to explain how he'd got the girls out of trouble with the police, who'd been harassing them in the hope of some 'action'.

'Anyway,' he said, 'I suggested an answer to his cash flow problem. He was relieved to sell up. I got the impression he felt nothing for the Dales.'

'No, he didn't,' Laura admitted.

'Last I heard, he was planning his escape to Gibraltar with what was left of the cash.' He glanced at her sharply. 'How soon can you go?'

She bit her lip. 'You're heartless!' she flung.

He grunted. 'Practical. I'm not good at living cheek-by-jowl with other people.'

'I remember,' she said caustically and he gave a lop-sided grin. 'Cassian…' She paused, then seemed to pluck up courage. 'Let me explain the difficulty of my situation.'

He frowned. 'You've done that already, at extraordinary length.'

'Please! Give me a chance!'

Her huge blue eyes transfixed him. He saw that she was close to tears and felt a pang of sympathy. Even though her plight had shaken him more than he would have liked, he could cope with this. He'd handled any number of awkward situations in his life.

'All right. I'll listen—briefly. But, I warn you, I won't change my mind.'

'Do you blame me for trying?' she asked, her face wan.

'Go on, then. Make your pitch if you think it's worth fighting for. Tooth and nail, I think you said. And Sue will expect to see blood on the floor when she next calls in,' he mocked, deliberately goading her.

Rebellion flared in her eyes and brought a new strength to her trembling mouth.

'She's going to Hong Kong for two weeks. It'll have dried by then,' she said tartly.

Cassian laughed. 'Well give it a go,' he encouraged, eyes crinkling in amusement.

She took a moment to compose herself, knowing that she must be calm. Adam's future depended on what she said and how she said it. This time, she must let Cassian know her son's needs.

'I want to tell you about Adam in a little more detail,' she said gently. 'The kind of person he is. Why I'm so anxious about him.'

Cassian marvelled at the change that came over her. The expression on her face had became suffused with tenderness and he felt his heart soften. She could love, he thought, his pulses quickening.

'Yes?' he snapped.

His curtness had no impact on her at all. She was totally absorbed in thinking of her beloved son. That's pure love, he mused. And marvelled at the luminous quality of her eyes.

'He was born prematurely. I think now,' she said softly, 'that when I was pregnant I did too much physical work around the house for too long.'

'Sounds like Enid. Perhaps she wanted you to lose your baby,' he muttered.

She winced. 'Perhaps. I can't deny that's a possibility. She made it clear that my pregnancy was all the more reason for me to pull my weight. Anyway, he was a sickly baby and cried a lot. I found myself protecting him, watching out for the slightest indication that he might be starting another chest infection. And then, one day, he—oh, Cassian, it was so awful!' she whispered.

'Tell me,' he said softly.

His heart went out to her. She'd been treated very badly. Someone ought to give her a good time, make her happy...

'He had his first asthma attack. I thought he was dying! He was rushed into hospital and put in an oxygen tent. I knew then that he was more important to me than life itself. From that moment on, I've had to watch his health very carefully,' she said, her voice low and so tender that he almost envied the child. 'It's important that he's not stressed. If he's badly upset then he gets an asthma attack. I've had to work around them, of course. It's what mothers do.'

He grunted. 'Work at what?'

'I did a computer course,' she replied. 'I did well, had a natural aptitude, but I had to abandon it. Adam was ill so often that I couldn't take on anything full-time or permanent because I had to look after him.'

'Tough,' he conceded, his eyes narrowed as he studied her.

She showed no signs of resentment that her son's health had imprisoned her in a financial straitjacket. Pure love shone from her eyes. He wondered idly what it would be like to win the heart of a woman with such deep, hidden passions.

Frightening, he decided. She'd expect total togetherness. His idea of hell.

'It's not tough,' she said, her expression tender. 'He's so uncomplaining and I...like being with him,' she added more briskly, as if reluctant to express affection for her son.

'How did you survive? Social Services?' he hazarded.

'No!' She looked shocked. 'I worked for ages as a waitress in a Grassington hotel but the new owner has daughters who can do my job.' She put on a bright smile. 'They're gorgeous blondes with big bosoms,' she explained with a laugh of self-deprecation.

He tried to stop himself, but he found his glance flicking down and the way she was hugging herself revealed more than she knew, the shirt pulling tightly over firm, high breasts, lusher than he could have imagined.

He felt heat suffuse him and frowned with annoyance. He'd seen breasts before. He wasn't a curious teenager any more.

'Pulls in the trade, you must admit,' he said shortly.

'Oh, I can't blame him for employing his family, or anyone who's really attractive,' she said without rancour. 'I have no illusions about myself.'

You should look in the damn mirror! he thought sourly in the pause that followed. How could she miss what he could see? And yet he dared not tell her. For a start, she'd never believe him—and he didn't have time to convince her. Nor would it be in his interests.

'And, as you have already said, you're out of work again,' he said flatly.

'With a sickly child,' she emphasised.

She crossed and neatly arranged her eye-catching legs. Her face lifted to his earnestly. Cassian hardened his heart. The welfare state would provide.

'So?'

'I can't just walk out and rent somewhere. I have no savings. But I am actively searching for a job and when I get it, I'll pay *you* rent. You don't want this house. You can't want it. You bought it out of the goodness of your heart, to get Tony out of a hole—'

'Huh! If he were in a hole, I'd hire an excavator to make it deeper,' he drawled, moved by her situation despite himself. Yet common sense argued that it was still in her best interests to leave. 'I'm not charitable where he's concerned. I'm here because I want to be.'

'But—!'

'No buts. This has gone on long enough. I'll make it easy for you, Laura. A compromise. Pack your stuff. When your son comes home I'll drive you both to a hotel of your choice and I'll pay for you to stay there till you find a job. Can't say fairer than that.'

He leaned back, pleased with his generous solution. Laura looked defeated. For some reason that didn't give him the satisfaction he'd expected.

The muscles in her heart-wrenchingly sweet face tightened as she struggled not to cry and he had a wild moment when he almost moved forwards to take her in his arms and soothe her panic with promises he couldn't keep.

The tears defied her, trickling from the corners of her eyes. Cassian gritted his teeth to stop himself from backtracking.

'I couldn't let you pay our hotel bill!' she croaked shakily.

'I couldn't do otherwise,' he found himself saying.

'I have my pride.'

'So has the entire population of Yorkshire.'

'It's your revenge, isn't it?' she mumbled.

Cassian frowned. 'What for?'

She hung her head. 'For what Enid and my f-father did to you,' she sniffed.

He was appalled. 'No! I—'

'Then *why?*' she wailed.

'That's my business. I want you to go. Don't you see that—'

She wasn't listening. Her head was angled in an attitude of listening. He heard the sound of feet: someone running—stumbling—up the path.

'It's Adam! Something's wrong!' she jerked out, with a mother's inexplicable certainty.

Hastily she rubbed her tear-stained face with her fists then jumped up and flung open the door. Past her rigidly held body, he saw a mud-splattered boy with dishevelled blond hair and a panic-stricken expression come skidding to a halt outside.

'Adam!' she whispered.

Cassian frowned and rose to his feet. The child was obviously in distress, and by the looks of him he'd been in a fight, but neither he nor his mother were making any move towards one another.

They both stood as if frozen to the ground, staring in consternation, some kind of signal going between them that prevented them from physical contact.

A chill went down his spine. Enid's tongue had removed something more crucial than defiance from Laura. It had killed Laura's ability to show love.

'I—I fell over!' Adam claimed, trying to be brave. But his mouth was all over the place.

'Oh, Adam…!' Laura was evidently distressed. Her hands hovered in front of her as if she was desperate to cuddle her son but had been forbidden to do so. 'I—you…! You—you should be at school—'

Cassian could bear no more. He pushed Laura aside and placed a firm arm around the quivering child's shoulders.

'Cup of tea, I think,' he declared cheerfully, easing him through the door. 'Then a scrub down with the yard brush and a bit of TLC for those bruises. Falling over's quite a shock, isn't it?' he chattered, getting the shaken child into a comfortable armchair in the kitchen and crouching down beside him. 'I did it a lot as a child.' He grinned. 'I seemed to get in the way of other boys' feet.'

He tensed when Laura's hand came past his ear and brushed the hair back from her son's forehead to reveal the bruise which Cassian had already spotted. He was an expert on bruises. And bullying. Particularly from adults.

'Poor Adam!' Laura leaned forwards and hesitantly kissed the purple bruise and then briefly touched her son's hot face. 'I'll put the kettle on,' she said huskily, as if overcome.

'Thanks, Mum.'

Adam bent to untie his shoe laces and Cassian knew he was trying to hide his tears. To be strong. To cultivate a stiff upper lip. Anything to stop real emotion from emerging. Emotion was a bad word at Thrushton Hall.

He could hear George Morris's voice now, echoing down the years.

'Stop crying!' Morris would beg the temperamental Bathsheba in horror. Or…'Don't laugh so loud!…' 'Don't dance like that—it's…unseemly, you're a married woman!…' Or maybe 'Calm yourself!…Don't yell…'

Ridiculous. The man had married his mother because he'd adored her exuberance. And then had set about curbing it so that she fitted in with the silent and repressed household over which he'd presided.

It wasn't surprising that the deeply repressed Laura was afraid of expressing her real feelings.

Cassian found the situation interesting. There seemed to be a kind of agreement between Laura and her child. A tacit acceptance, perhaps, that there should be the minimum of affection displayed, one or two small gestures sufficing for deep concern.

Intriguingly, she had put her hand on the arm of the chair where Adam was sitting. Cassian had noticed that Adam had imperceptibly leaned in that direction so that his body was inches from his mother's restless fingers.

He couldn't believe what was happening. This was a kind of distant comfort, practised by two people who didn't dare to let go in case they betrayed their emotions.

The situation struck deep at his heart and he was moved more than he would have liked. Wordlessly, hampered by no inhibitions, he reached out to hug the shaking child and to let him know what human warmth could be like. He rubbed the thin, bony back in sympathy.

'Let's get your muddy shoes and jumper off, shall we?' he suggested gently.

As the child complied with a worrying submissiveness, Cassian reflected that the relationship between Laura and Adam couldn't be more different than the closeness between him and Jai. Laura would be shocked if she ever saw their mutual expressions of love. He and his son had no problems about expressing their emotions.

A surge of longing careered unhindered through him. He wanted his child near him. Missed him like hell. In a reflex action, he clutched Adam more tightly.

'Who...are you?' Adam asked timidly.

He smiled down mistily. 'Cassian.'

The trembling stopped. Tears were knuckled away in a gesture that mimicked Laura's.

'Gosh! I've heard of you!'

He grimaced. 'Don't tell me!' he said, pretending to groan. 'I was surly and rude and ignored your mother while I was here!'

Adam shook his head, his blue Laura-eyes bright with eagerness.

'I dunno about that. But Mum said you knew every plant and insect and bird and you could find your way around the countryside blindfold!'

Cassian glanced at Laura in amusement. 'Your mother is very kind to concentrate on my few good points.'

'Cassian's come to stay,' Laura said, putting a mug of tea by Adam's elbow. Her eyes challenged Cassian to say anything further.

'Oh, gosh, cool!' enthused Adam.

Cassian frowned at Laura. He'd deal with her later. He fixed Adam with a sober but friendly gaze.

'So. Spill the beans,' he said quietly. 'What happened?'

'I—' Adam faltered, clearly unable to look into Cassian's steady eyes and tell a lie. There was a long pause. It was the silence before a confession and Cassian waited patiently for the child to begin. 'Well…at break-time they said my Mum was a stupid feeble wimp, like me, and—and that we're silly drips with marshmallow instead of guts!' he said with a huge, indignant sniff.

There was another pause. Cassian prayed that Laura wouldn't react or speak. The boy needed a silence to fill with words. Any interruption might make the kiddie clam up. To his utter relief, Laura didn't even move and after fiddling with his fingers for a while, Adam began again.

'I t-tried to ignore them, like Mum said, but they pushed me into the nettles then jumped on m-me and pinched my packed lunch!'

Tears rolled down his cheeks again and Cassian felt his heart aching for the distressed child.

'Here,' he said huskily, grasping Adam's hands strongly in his.

'Oh, my darling!' Laura sobbed.

And to Cassian's surprise, she pushed him aside and drew her son into an awkward embrace. She was crying too, utter misery on her face.

Cassian rose, made two more mugs of tea and took the cake out of the oven. It pained him to see Laura rocking her child and trying to control her weeping.

They needed love and support. Someone to give them confidence. Bullying made him feel sick. Even the thought of it disrupted his laid-back approach to life and made him irrational, his emotions churning chaotically as anger, resentment, pity and past terrors filled his head.

He'd been secretly bullied by George Morris. Taunted, spat upon, and beaten by older kids at senior school. The sheer helplessness had made him seethe with rage and frustration.

And he was seething now, hurting for Adam's sake, loathing those who attacked anyone who didn't conform to some imaginary 'norm'.

He couldn't bear it. He wanted to crack heads together, yell, terrify…anything so that Laura and her child would never weep like this again. He wanted to hug them both, tell them he'd deal with the problem, see their tears dry up and their faces turn to him trustingly. To see them smile.

He found himself shaking—whether from passion or fear at where his thoughts were leading, he wasn't sure.

At that moment, he knew that he couldn't turn them out—not yet, anyway. And the cold certainty iced his spine with apprehension.

He was walking into dangerous quicksand. He loathed living with other people. Found their pettiness and knee-jerk rules irritating. Yet the urge to offer a temporary respite for Laura and Adam was so overwhelming that it couldn't be denied. It seemed he cared about them.

He drew in a sharp breath. For a man who needed to be free that was extremely worrying.

CHAPTER FOUR

Laura crossly banged pans about as she prepared a scrap lunch. How Cassian had persuaded Adam to go up for a bath without protest—and got him giggling as well in the process—she'd never know.

But before she could think straight, Adam had come hurrying back downstairs in a holey old jumper and faded jeans, his face pink and shiny with eagerness as if something exciting awaited.

She supposed it did. Cassian.

Now Adam sat in smiling assent while Cassian gently and expertly smoothed the cuts and bruises with some cream he'd dug from his First Aid kit.

Adam had spurned her usual stuff, beguiled by the promise that Cassian's remedy was herbal and 'brilliant, I use it all the time when I fall off mountains and things'.

Huh! What was she suddenly? Redundant? The mince suffered a fierce pounding with the spoon. Cassian had made her look both callous and, now, hopelessly inadequate.

When she'd seen Adam struggling desperately to be brave, she hadn't known what to do. Should she respect his attempt or give in to her maternal instinct and comfort him?

It had always been an unwritten rule between them that Adam should try to overcome the bullying on his own. He'd made that clear the first time she'd indignantly tried to interfere on his behalf.

But now Cassian had changed the rule. And, even more infuriating, his tactics of firmness, humour and sympathy had worked, defusing Adam's shock and making him feel better about himself.

With vicious strokes, she grated some cheese and put it aside then flung carrots, onions and turnips into the mince to make it go further.

Adam ought to be sitting with his shoulders hunched, chest heaving, clinging for dear life to his asthma inhaler. That's what invariably happened after something like this.

Instead, he was laughing at some improbable tale Cassian was relating about walking in the foothills of the Himalayas—Him*ar*leeas he pretentiously called them— when he'd slid over fifty feet down a slope and ended up in a particularly magnificent heap of yak manure. Huh! As if!

'We ought to let the school know you're here, Adam,' she said shortly, interrupting Cassian's fairy stories.

'Phone them after lunch,' Cassian suggested with a languid stretch.

'We don't have a phone.' Crossly she met his astonished eyes. 'Too expensive. I'll have to go to the school—'

'That's ridiculous!' he protested. 'It's a four-mile round trip. Take off that hair shirt. You can use my mobile or take my car.'

'I'll phone. Thank you,' she muttered.

'Mum can't drive,' explained Adam.

'Perhaps I should teach her,' Cassian growled.

There was a sudden silence. She looked at Cassian, startled and flustered by his remark. Though he looked more than a little startled too. Her heart thudded. Surely this meant she had a reprieve! Long enough for her to learn to drive!

Adam looked impressed. She knew he dearly wanted her to join the human race and acquire a driving licence. But what was the point if she couldn't afford to own a car? Yet that didn't matter. The reprieve did.

'You won't tell them what happened, will you, Mum?' Adam asked anxiously.

'I can't have you being hurt like this—' she began fretfully.

'Please!' he begged, looking petrified. 'You'll make it worse!'

She looked at him helplessly. What did you do? What was right, in the long run? Did she make her son a total outcast by complaining, or was he to be battered on a regular basis?

Extraordinarily, she found herself searching out Cassian, wondering if he had an answer to the problem. She quivered. There was a melting tenderness in his eyes and it confused her.

'*You* were bullied,' she said to him in a low tone, remembering the torn clothes, and the cuts and bruises he'd often be sporting. He'd always told Aunt Enid that he'd been in a fight, but had never asked for help. And suddenly the bullying had stopped. 'What do *you* think?'

'I didn't want adult interference,' he said quietly. 'But that's because I wanted to find my own way of dealing with the bullying. There isn't one solution. Each person has a different need. Some don't have the resources to cope alone. Adam, if you think you can change from being a victim to a winner, then go for it.'

He was wise, she thought, seeing her son straighten as if he was growing in stature. Suddenly she saw that Cassian could help Adam so much. A tremor took her unawares, making her lips part at the thought of Cassian here, taking a part in their daily lives.

'How long are you staying?' Adam asked him.

She winced at the wistful note. Her son was revelling in male company. Suddenly she felt isolated.

'A while. Moving in tonight,' came the easy reply. It was coupled with a dazzling smile.

'Cool!'

She shot a glance at Cassian and found that he was regarding her wryly. The odd sensations crept into her loins again. They were like small spasms, tugging and relaxing.

Quite unnervingly enjoyable. She bit her lip and clenched all her muscles hard.

'...yes, I was twelve when I first came to Thrushton,' Cassian was saying.

'Did you like it here?' Adam asked eagerly.

'Hated Aunt Enid, loved Thrushton,' Cassian replied with blistering honesty.

Adam giggled. 'Why?'

'I regret to say that Enid was a cow. A strict and humourless woman who thought children should be neither seen nor heard. I think she would have preferred them to have sprung from the womb as fully trained adults with a degree in silence and obedience.'

'Cassian!' Laura reproved, while Adam gazed in delighted shock.

'I can hear her voice now,' he said, looking pointedly at her and Laura blushed in bitter recognition because she'd caught herself reproving Adam's small and rare misdemeanours with Enid's sharp little voice. Cassian had the bit between his teeth and was galloping on. 'Her favourite word was "don't",' he said blithely. 'And her tongue had been dipped in snake venom. She had a way of gnashing her teeth that makes me think now that she could have crushed Terminator I, II and III in her jaws.'

Adam laughed, awe-struck by Cassian's frankness. 'But you liked Thrushton,' he said, pleased.

'Oh, yes. Out there...' He paused. Laura gulped, her senses beguiled. His face had become soft, quite beautiful in its dreaminess. 'It's wild and free and open. Magnificent scenery. Takes you at once from your small, inward world and places your life in a greater context. Don't you think?'

Laura was stunned to learn how he'd felt. That was why he'd spent days at a time on the fells. It had been more than an escape from the confines of the house. He'd seen more than beauty in the Dales. Like her, he'd found something special, spiritual, uplifting.

Thoughtfully she listened while Cassian continued to answer the hail of questions coming from Adam, speaking to her son as if he were an adult. It disturbed her that Adam was chattering—*chattering!* when he was usually so monosyllabic!—and it disturbed her that Cassian's lazy, deep voice seemed to be soothing her own agitated mind and slowing her movements till she was wafting languidly about the kitchen and catching herself hanging on every improbable word.

But her son was undeniably happy in Cassian's company. And although she might resent Cassian for being the one who'd taken Adam's mind off the bullying, she was grudgingly grateful.

'Sometimes you must have got soaked to the skin, when you wandered off for days on end!' Adam was saying. 'Wasn't that awful?'

'Not often!' laughed Cassian. 'I checked the chickweed. Failing that, the spiders.'

Adam grinned. 'Chickweed?' he scoffed.

'Sure. It closes up if it's going to rain. And spiders are only active in fine weather. If they remake a web around 6—7 p.m., you can be almost sure it'll stay dry. If it's raining and they're altering their web, it'll clear up. You have to read the signs. For instance, a red sunset tells you that dry air is coming. A yellow one indicates it'll be damp. You can read clouds too. I'll show you sometime.'

Sometime, she thought. Another indication that they wouldn't be leaving soon. Her hopes rose.

'Cool! But...what did you eat?' asked Adam, wide-eyed with admiration.

'Trout, usually. You start downstream, place a light close to the water, and the fish come to look. With care, you can flick one out. I'll show you. There's plenty of food if you know where to look. I can lend you a book about finding food in the wild. But make no mistake,' he warned, 'walking the Dales over a period of days is not something anyone can do—not even an adult. I took no risks, Adam. I learnt the lie of the land first, practised and learnt the art of survival till I could light a fire in a howling gale and tell by sound and smell and feel alone where I was.'

'You mean...' Laura eyed him in amazement. 'You were so determined to escape Aunt Enid that you spent weeks preparing yourself?'

'I think it took two years of concentrated effort before I was sure I knew what I was doing,' he said quietly. Then he smiled. 'I wanted to escape, not die! It was wonderful out there on a starlit night,' he mused softly, his face radiating pleasure. 'The silence was awesome.'

Adam moved a little closer to his new hero. Laura watched, her gratitude towards Cassian a little eclipsed by a wary concern. Adam wasn't tough. She didn't want him trying to emulate Cassian.

'Weren't you horribly afraid?' he asked timidly.

Cassian's eyes liquefied with warmth. 'Sometimes. Especially when the night was black and I hadn't reached the shelter I'd chosen. But I always knew where I was heading, and never left anything to chance. I started with small trips, graduated to longer ones. And each success made me stronger, more confident.'

'And...er...' Adam persisted, 'you weren't popular at school.'

Laura held her breath. He'd slipped the question in as if it were casual. Would Cassian see that her son wanted some reassurance about popularity—and help with the bullying?

'No. Because I was different,' Cassian answered gently, and she felt the air slowly sift from her lungs. He'd be kind to Adam, she felt sure. 'Kids don't like people who stand apart. I was categorised along with the boys with National Health glasses and too much weight. We were bullied as a matter of course. It's a very primitive thing, Adam, a caveman attitude. Part of what they call the biological imperative. That means that it's part of our survival instincts. Oddities are rejected to allow survival of the fittest. The world has moved on since Neolithic times, but unfortunately civilisation hasn't always impacted on some primeval brains!' he finished with a grin.

Adam laughed too. 'What did *you* do when you were bullied? Actually *do*?' he asked with an exaggeratedly nonchalant tone which fooled nobody.

Laura stiffened, turning to face the two of them where they were sitting with cosy familiarity on the old sofa. He'd never talked so openly before. He trusted Cassian, she thought in shock. More than *she'd* ever been trusted. Or were mothers naturally ruled out as confidantes?

'I learnt about pain,' Cassian replied ruefully. He smiled down at Adam, his manner relaxed and inviting.

'Nothing else?' her son asked in disappointment.

'Plenty!'

'What?!'

Eagerly, Adam tucked his legs up on the sofa, his body curled against Cassian's. Laura felt her heart lurch. Her son was looking at Cassian as if he held the Holy Grail in the palm of his hands.

'Well, obviously you know that my solutions won't necessarily be yours,' Cassian flattered, and Adam nodded in sage agreement. 'You'll know that you have to decide how to deal with *your* problem and work out what *you* want—'

'To be tough!' Adam blurted out.

Cassian's arm came about Adam's shoulders and he was nodding as if they both had much in common. To Laura's astonishment, Adam reached up a puny arm and boldly felt Cassian's biceps. She couldn't believe what her reserved and shy son was doing. For the life of her, she couldn't recall him ever touching anyone.

But Cassian was incredibly seductive and...touchable. She went pink, thinking how close she had come to breaking her own rules about personal space.

'My decision exactly.'

'Did you, uh…have the same plan as me?' asked Adam tentatively.

Laura could have wept. Her son desperately needed help and she hadn't seen that. All his stubborn insistence that he was fine had been a cover-up. She couldn't bear it.

'You tell me! I chopped wood,' Cassian confided, perhaps deliberately emphasising the muscle definition of his chest by leaning back, his arms behind his head. Shocked to be distracted, Laura found herself mesmerised by his physique, her throat drying in an instant recognition of his visceral appeal. 'I walked miles too,' he reminisced. 'Climbed hills. At first, I puffed like an old steam train, then I graduated to running up them. I heaved rocks about, making dams on the fells where no one could see me fall or fail or yell in frustration. I suppose that's the kind of thing you've decided to do.'

'Yes!' Adam cried with shining eyes.

Laura felt a shaft of pain that her son had seen a glimmer of hope on the horizon. And she hadn't been the one who'd put it there. She felt a tug of admiration for Cassian's technique.

'Thought so.' Cassian yawned. 'Lucky that everything you need is on the doorstep, isn't it? Logs, hills, rocks. Makes getting fit a piece of cake.' He looked up, saw Laura stupidly holding the saucepan as if she'd been welded to the floor, and smiled. 'No time like the present, Adam,' he said briskly, leaping from the sofa. 'You can start flexing those muscles by mashing the potatoes while I fetch something for pudding.'

'Me?' her son's mouth dropped open and Laura was just about to say that she did all the cooking and housework while Adam studied or rested, when he scrambled up and rushed to her side. 'Right. Er…what do I do, Mum?'

'Bash.''

Tight-lipped, she handed him the masher, wordlessly dropped a knob of marge into the pan and added seasoning.

Out of the corner of her eye, while Adam pounded the potatoes with messianic concentration, she saw Cassian tipping fresh raspberries into a dish which he'd hauled from the cupboard.

'Make yourself at home,' she said tartly.

'I am, aren't I?' he murmured.

She gave him a scathing look and inspected the potatoes. Her brows knitted in a frown at the lumps but before she could say anything to Adam, Cassian squeezed himself between them.

'You're doing great,' he enthused, praising her son where she would have criticised. 'Nearly got all the lumps smashed, I see.'

Adam's eyes rounded in dismay. Hastily he pulled the pan towards him and set about reducing the potato to a creamy consistency.

Laura stood transfixed. Cassian had achieved the required result with consummate skill, craftily ensuring that it was Adam himself who'd decided the mash wasn't up to standard.

'Penny?' Cassian murmured, his palm touching the small of her back.

She felt she'd been set on fire. It had been a mere enquiring touch and yet her body had reacted so violently that it seemed her heart might leap from her breast.

And all the while her mind was teeming with new thoughts, excitement mounting as she examined the idea of praise and suggestion as a replacement for criticism— which up to now had been the only method of shaping a child's behaviour that she'd ever known.

It was as if she'd stumbled on treasure. In a way, she had.

Half-turning, her face now inches from Cassian's, she smiled delightedly into his dark, pooling eyes and instantly became light-headed. Joy was unsettling, she thought warily. Then decided to succumb. What the hell.

'My thoughts are worth more than that,' she said happily. She could have danced. Almost did. Her toes wriggled. She grinned. 'Thank you.'

He raised a heavy eyebrow. 'For what?'

Close up, his mouth looked devastatingly sensual. Again she felt the light pressure of his hand on her spine and she had to struggle to remember what they'd been talking about.

With solemn delight, she met his bone-melting stare. It was the revelation that was making her so delirious. And she wanted to keep her new-found knowledge to herself.

'For showing Adam how to make the perfect mash,' she breathed.

'My pleasure.'

There was a brief pressure on her tingling back and then Cassian had moved away, leaving a cold gap she wanted immediately to fill. With him. To have him close, touching her, gazing into her eyes…

'Inspection!' ordered Adam excitedly, banging the pan in front of her.

She was jerked back to reality. 'Wow!' she marvelled. 'Totally smashed mash! Eat your heart out, celebrity cooks of the world!'

'Bread smells fabulous. Fancy some wine?' Cassian enquired, waving a bottle of red at her.

She beamed, feeling suddenly hedonistic. Wine was a luxury. And a wicked indulgence at lunchtime! 'Yes, please!' she said recklessly, knowing she was being silly, but unable to stop herself. After lifting out the golden brown bread, she picked up a serving spoon—and then on an impulse she handed it to the glowing Adam. 'There you go. Pile the potato on top of the mince, add the cheese, grab the oven gloves and push the dish into the oven. It's ready when the cheese is brown and sizzling. I'm going to put my feet up and luxuriate in the high life.'

Flushed and happy, she sat neatly in the armchair while

Cassian opened the bottle. The sunlight danced on the planes of his face. He looked relaxed and at ease and she felt her entire body responding to his mood, softening and slowing down as if she too were laid back and uninhibited.

Her fortunes had changed. Cassian had now met Adam and seen his needs. Instinctively she knew they'd be staying for a while—and perhaps she could even come up with some means of sharing the house till he grew tired of such a narrow world and drifted off to pastures new.

A little fragment of doubt interrupted her plan, a small voice telling her that Cassian wasn't an ordinary man, that she was already disturbed by his deep sensuality. But she could surely curb her mad thoughts if it meant she and Adam could stay at Thrushton.

Perhaps she could cook and clean and do Cassian's washing in addition to holding down a new job. No man would refuse free housekeeping services!

Dreamily planning, she surveyed him from beneath her lashes. With the enjoyment of a true sensualist, he was passing the opened bottle beneath his nose, his face rapt as he inhaled the aroma. Her senses quickened.

Slowly he filled two glasses and carried one over to her. 'Enjoy,' he murmured.

Their fingers touched as she took the glass. A flash of heat melted in the core of her body and she felt Cassian's sharp exhalation of breath warming her lips before he re-treated to the sofa again. She was afraid he was annoyed by her gaucheness, but he said nothing. Fortunately, he was totally indifferent to her.

Instead, he concentrated on his wine, quietly studying its colour, sniffing it again and then taking an absorbed sip.

'What do you think of it?' he asked, as if her opinion mattered. He shot her a look and his dark eyes suddenly glowed.

She pressed her parted lips together hurriedly and picked up the glass. 'I don't know anything about wine.'

'You have taste buds!' he growled.

She took a cautious sip. And then another.

'Describe what you feel,' Cassian coaxed.

'I feel warm. From cooking,' she said, ducking the issue and omitting to say that he had added to that warmth.

When he remained silent, she concentrated harder, tasting the rich, dark red wine and trying to find words to explain the glorious sensation in her mouth and the wickedly pleasurable feeling as the alcohol pooled seductively in her stomach.

'I love the smell,' she decided, playing safe. 'It makes me feel rich.'

'Let me sniff, Mum!'

Laughing, she held her glass up to Adam who rolled his eyes and declared he was a millionaire.

'Not far off the truth,' Cassian acknowledged. 'Nothing better than good food and wine, to love and to be loved.'

Laura felt a tightening in her chest. He had someone, she thought, quite irrationally disappointed. It had never occurred to her that the wolf that walked alone would have found a soul mate, but there was no mistaking the depth of emotion in his words. He wore no ring, but then Cassian wouldn't allow any woman to curtail his freedom.

'I've got Mum,' Adam said, treading where angels and she feared to tread. 'Who've you got?'

'My son,' Cassian said softly.

Laura almost spilled her wine. She put it down on the table, her mind whirling. 'Your son?' she repeated stupidly.

'Jai. He's ten.'

'I'm nine!' Adam cried in delight.

Cassian grinned. 'I know. Small world.'

Adam began rattling off questions. Quickly she realised that this was why he'd had such a sure and empathetic touch with her son. Cassian had practical experience of his own.

And what, she thought in quite extraordinary agitation,

about his partner? The woman who'd won his heart, who'd slowly, seductively stripped the clothes from that lithe and lean body…

Laura gulped, appalled at herself. Without any reason whatsoever, she was horribly, stupidly, jealous. She wanted to be close to Cassian…perhaps because it would be wonderful to have the power to conquer someone so quietly strong and independent that his very kiss would be an acknowledgement that she was unique among women. She wanted to sit with him, to be enclosed in his arms and to be soothed by his steady calmness…and to be fired by the passions that lay beneath.

Dear heaven, she thought in horror. What was happening to her?

'*Marrakesh?*' Adam's exclamation made Laura jump.

Cassian hastily got up and opened the oven door, taking out the pie then prepared a pan for the frozen peas he'd produced. Now *he* was entering into displacement activities. Anything, he thought, to avoid Laura's captivating face as she dreamed of…what?

All he knew was that his willpower was being sorely tested and every nerve in his body was begging him to go over and relieve his desire to kiss her soft mouth till his senses reeled. Suicidal!

'Yes,' he said, waiting for the water to boil and glad of an excuse to keep his back to her. 'Jai's hiking in the High Atlas mountains with friends. They'll put him on a plane to Heathrow and he'll make his way here in a couple of days or so, I'm not sure when.'

There was a deafening silence. Glancing round, he saw that Laura's eyes were nearly falling out of their sockets.

'A ten-year-old, finding his way on his own?' she said in horror. 'Don't you think that's stretching independence too far? Anything might happen to him! There are bad people out there, Cassian—'

'Allow me to know how to manage my own son,' he

said irritably. 'Maybe I've arranged for someone to watch over him. Maybe he's thrilled at the thought of planning his own journey. Maybe he has travelled alone before and has developed strategies to stay safe.' His jaw tightened. How dare she assume he hadn't thought of Jai's safety? 'Maybe,' he said sarcastically, 'I don't care if he's robbed or attacked or abducted by—'

'OK, OK, I'm sorry!' she muttered awkwardly.

He grunted and tipped half the frozen peas into the pan, securing the remainder in the bag with a twist tie. He knew he'd overreacted but no one, just no one, interfered between him and Jai, whose life he'd guard with his own.

'Here,' he growled lobbing the bag at Adam. Who fumbled and dropped them. An easy catch. Poor kid had much to catch up on, he mused and softened his expression. 'Freezer?' he suggested, when Adam looked at him with a puzzled frown.

'Oh, yeah.' The lad disappeared into the scullery and the door banged shut behind him.

He remembered that scullery. He'd stood peeling potatoes for hours there, till his hands were raw. And Laura's father had been furious, Cassian thought darkly, because he'd been unable to break Cassian's will.

Of small victories like that, Cassian knew his character had been forged. And consequently he had his own ideas on how to bring up children. Not by making them peel sacks of potatoes, of course! Gradual responsibility. The acquisition of life skills. Knowledge is power.

Hearing Adam fumbling around in the freezer, he took the opportunity to confront Laura. 'It looks as if we're going to be together for a short while. The shorter the better, I think. But while we are under the same roof, you can keep your thoughts to yourself where Jai is concerned. We have our own way of living and we're happy with it. Any problems, bring them to me. You won't nag Jai and tell him to put his coat on because it's cold. You won't tell him to be careful if he decides to cook. He does what he's capable of. Understand?' he snapped.

'So long as Jai's behaviour doesn't affect Adam,' she said, her eyes wide and anxious.

'Maybe that would be an improvement.'

She bristled, as he knew she would. 'How d—?' Adam walked in again and she broke off, biting her lip. 'How long do you think, before you take those peas off?' she amended, filling in the awkward silence. But her eyes told him how angry she was. And he felt a small leap of triumph.

'Now.'

Cassian spun on his heel and took the pan off the heat for straining. But he was thinking all the while that if he strode over and kissed her passionately on that soft, quivering pink mouth then she might unwind a little. And she and her son might begin to live.

She came to his side, fussing with the plates and he let her take over because otherwise he'd grab her arms and pull her against him so he could rain kisses on her long, slender neck and tousle that perfectly tidy hair.

He wanted to muss her up. To murmur wicked, seductive words in her ear, to rouse her beyond her prim and restrictive responses till she cried out his name and begged for him in husky, unrecognisable tones.

Crazy. The lure of the unattainable. Or perhaps he needed the release of sex. If so, he needed a woman who wanted fun and no strings, not the uptight, emotionally repressed Laura who'd probably expect a ring on her finger if he went so far as to hold her hand.

Grimly he sat at the table. Adam chattered and he answered as best he could. The kiddie had a sweet temperament but was as vulnerable as hell. He itched to set him on the right road. Hated to see a child crushed by life, condemned to feeling inferior to others.

Like Laura. He tore off a piece of crusty new bread and

chewed irritably. She'd annoyed him from the first moment he'd set eyes on her, with her mimsy little voice and breathy uncertainty, scuttling to do the evil Enid's bidding. If his mother hadn't told him to leave Laura strictly alone, he'd have dragged the kiddie off on his attempts to toughen himself up. Though everyone would have imagined they'd been up to no good.

Angrily he replenished Laura's glass and his own. He wasn't used to walking on tiptoe around people and the next few days were going to be foul. It was his habit not to pussyfoot around but to be straight with people. If he did that, he and Laura would be in the sack and Adam would be doing press-ups in the garden each morning.

'Is the pie all right?' Laura's anxious voice impinged on his thoughts.

He looked at his plate and realised he hadn't been eating. 'It's great,' he said honestly, tucking in. 'And the bread is wonderful.'

At least she could cook. That suggested *one* sensual delight in her repertoire.

'I'm glad you like it!'

He looked up and was shaken by her pleased smile. His jaw clenched. She was terrifyingly vulnerable too. One wrong word from him and she could be seriously wounded. It was a hell of a burden to carry.

'I'm going out,' he said when he'd finished. 'Excuse me—'

'But…your pudding!' she cried.

Impatiently he sighed. 'It's not compulsory.'

She flushed and he was back into whipping puppies again. 'But…you haven't even unpacked yet,' she pointed out hesitantly as if he might have forgotten.

'I know,' he bit irritably and she had the grace to look contrite. 'But that can wait and I want to walk.'

Before she could come up with some other conventional chain to wrap around his neck, he strode out.

It wouldn't work, he thought darkly, changing into walking boots and slinging a small rucksack on his back. Laura and he would never live in the same world. Somehow he had to force her out. Before he did something he'd regret for the rest of his life.

Or he could sell up. Perhaps coming here had been a mistake after all.

He set off at a blistering pace, walking off his frustrations.

By the time three hours had passed by, the magic of the fells had made his heart sing again. His route had taken him way beyond the ruined buildings of the medieval lead mines above Thrushton, and past the narrow fourteenth-century hump-backed packhorse bridge with its ankle-high parapets, designed so that a train of forty mules could pass with their laden panniers unimpeded.

Taking delight in treading in the footsteps of history, he walked along the corpse way. He could almost feel the weight of the past, hear the mourners as they carried a loved one to the church, along the narrow path and over the treacherous stepping stones from some remote settlement.

From the track he had climbed high above the beautiful valley where the River Wharfe glinted and sparkled far below and as he climbed he felt a soaring joy at being alive.

The air was sharp and clear and filled with swooping swallows creating a ballet in the air. Overcome by powerful emotions which shook him to the core, he sat on the edge of a limestone pavement, watching an adder drawing the last vestiges of warmth from the late afternoon sun.

He closed his eyes, almost pained by the beauty of his surroundings. And he knew then that he had to spend time here. Wanted… His breath knifed in, snapping his eyes open again. Shock ran through his body. For a brief moment it had crossed his mind that this would be a suitable place to settle. To put down roots.

In a dazed blur, he saw himself creating a herb garden and feeding hens. And then, totally unbalanced by such uncharacteristic dreams, he leapt up and headed at a half-run for Grassington, determined to drink or wench away any potential curbs on his personal freedom.

'I can live here,' he muttered to himself like a mantra, his loping stride swiftly devouring the ground. 'But there's no way I'm going into pipe and slippers mode!'

The beer was good. The women less so. He smiled ruefully on his way back to Thrushton Hall. Women had recognised him. Fluttered their lashes in the hope that he'd remember their totally unsatisfactory teenage embraces. He'd raised his glass in acknowledgement and remained aloof. The loner.

And despite the attentions of what he assumed to be the landlord's 'bosomy' daughters, he felt nothing; no desire, no stirring, no interest whatsoever.

Worse, he found himself comparing them with Laura. Her quiet beauty. Solemn eyes of cerulean-blue, the colour of a Mediterranean sky. Untouched lips he wanted to explore. The body of a siren and the innocence of an angel.

A woman alone. Unique. Unaware that she was close to spilling out her long-hidden passions and needing someone who wouldn't hurt her, who wouldn't damage her fragile self-esteem but who would build it up till she realised her full potential.

And he wanted to be that man. Even though he knew he couldn't give her what she would want. Marriage. Security. Two point four children and a mortgage and the ritual of cleaning the car every Saturday morning after doing the weekly shop.

So he had to keep his hands and his eyes to himself. And save them both from disaster.

Trying to settle his thoughts, he walked down to the

river, knowing the narrow path so well that the occasional light from the thin crescent moon was enough when the clouds lifted, and so he did not need to use his torch.

He let the soft rush of water soothe his mind. Listened to the scops owl, the sounds of badgers snuffling up roots somewhere in the mid distance. Simple pleasures which money could never buy.

It wasn't until after midnight that he returned, letting himself into the house silently. He took a deep breath to steel himself. Now he would face the house, at its darkest and most sinister and chase away the memories till only stone and mortar remained.

CHAPTER FIVE

LAURA had been unable to sleep. It bothered her that Cassian hadn't stopped to sort out which bedroom he'd use or even unpacked his night things. Did he think he could come back in the early hours and wake her up, demanding sheets and pillows? she thought crossly.

So here she was, having to stay awake to tell him that she'd made up a bed in the back room. It was typically selfish of him that he did his own thing and never mind anyone else!

Her mouth pruned in. That was him now. Grudgingly she admitted that he had been extraordinarily quiet, but she had been waiting for that slight creak of the door, her ears tuned like interstellar radar to an invading Martian.

Flinging her cosy blue dressing gown over her short cotton nightie, she angrily tied the cord around her waist as if girding herself up for battle.

Her head cocked on one side. Instead of coming up the stairs, he was moving around in the dark downstairs. That was the study door opening. Her eyes narrowed. What was he doing?

She listened but there was no sound from below. Then the boards creaked in the hall and there came the unmistakable sound of the latch being lifted on the dining room door.

Well, she thought grimly, if he was looking for money, he'd be disappointed! Curiosity got the better of her and she tiptoed onto the landing, intending to catch him red-handed at whatever he was doing.

At the top of the stairs she froze as Cassian's dark figure crossed the hall beneath her and glided stealthily into the sitting room. With the utmost care she crept down and by the time she peered into the room her nerves were strung along wires.

He stood with his back to her, his bulk just visible in the pale light which filtered through the thin curtains. He seemed to be listening, his very muscles and sinews straining from powerful emotion as he remained rooted to the spot with that deep inner stillness which was peculiar to him.

Laura frowned. Something about him kept her from calling out. He wasn't searching for anything. More like… making a reaquaintance with the house.

She stiffened, her hand going to her mouth as she realised why he was creeping about like a burglar. Earlier on, he hadn't ventured into the rest of the house but had remained in the kitchen, and briefly, the hall.

Intuitively she knew that he must be reliving bad memories. A chill iced her spine.

'Cassian!' she breathed, aching to see what this was doing to him.

But he ignored her because no sound had emerged from her dry throat.

Unaware that he was being watched from the darkness of the hall, he scanned the sitting room with painstaking slowness. Half-turning, his eyes focused on the inglenook and she felt her heart lurch. In the gloom she could see that his face was bleak, his jaw rigid with tension.

'Cassian!' she pleaded in soft concern.

His body jerked. When he swung around she saw with shock that his eyes were silvered and as hard as bullets.

'This is private!' he said fiercely.

She felt like an intruder in her own house. His house. 'But—'

'Don't crowd me! Leave me alone!' he snapped.

Taking a deep breath, his face set, he strode to the fireplace. Picking up a log from the stack, he weighed it in his hand then sniffed its resiny smell. Slowly he returned it to the neatly-stacked pile. Placing his palm on the massive granite lintel across the fireplace, he stared moodily at the hearth.

Laura swallowed, knowing what must be going through his mind. He'd chopped logs in all weathers and had never complained or run to his blissfully unaware mother. Bathsheba was usually engrossed in painting her wonderful landscapes but, even so, Laura had found it hard to understand why Cassian had suffered in silence.

'I chopped those,' she said, desperate to lighten the oppressive atmosphere. 'My axe technique's improved over the years.'

His head lifted but he didn't look at her. 'I'm not in the mood to chat. Please go. I can lock up,' he said icily, his profile taut and uncompromising.

She bristled. 'I thought I'd better wait up because—'

His eyes blazed at her, black and glittering. 'I'm not a child!'

'But I made up a bed for you!' she protested tremulously. 'You wouldn't have known where to sleep…' She stopped, cut short by his irritable sigh.

'It didn't matter. I would have curled up on the sofa,' he said dismissively.

'But you would have been uncomfortable—'

'Laura! That's my problem, not yours!' He paused, gazing at her in consternation. 'I thought you knew me better,' he reproached.

She was shocked by her reaction to his disappointment. She wanted to understand him, to please him. And she had no idea what she'd done wrong.

'Don't live my life,' he went on, his face tight with restraint. 'Don't fit me into your ordered, conventional routine!'

'I was being thoughtful,' she said unhappily.

He looked at her helplessly. 'I know. You were. Hell.

Where do I begin? We both lived in this house for five years and you have no idea about me, do you?'

'We weren't close,' she sulked.

But, she realised to her astonishment, she'd always longed to be.

'OK. It was a misunderstanding. You were being kind—but I had no idea you'd take it on yourself to look after me. I thought—wrongly—that you knew me better and you'd leave me to my own devices. It never occurred to me that you'd prepare a bed for me—so you can't be annoyed with me for keeping you up.'

'No. Suppose not,' she muttered grudgingly.

He sighed. 'I don't know where to begin. Look, I can see it's hard for you to understand how I live—but please don't think you need to run around after me. I've slept on mud floors and bare mountains. I can take care of myself. To be honest, I'm not comfortable with being fussed over. It's…stifling. It's up to me if I eat pudding or not and it's my fault if I'm hungry as a consequence. I'm an adult. If I choose, I can stay out till morning, sleep downstairs or even outside in a field if I want.'

She was beginning to see his point of view. And she had known how independent he was. Unfortunately habit died hard, and the arrival of guests meant looking after them. She'd forgotten that Cassian wasn't an ordinary man.

'I understand,' she said, subdued.

Did he ever need anyone? Flashing into her mind came the unexpected thought that she wanted to care for him, to make him comfortable, happy. But he'd loathe that! She bit her lip and vowed not to push the lone-wolf Cassian into a domestic straitjacket.

'I know I'm difficult, Laura,' he said ruefully. 'I did warn you. I've inherited from my mother an abhorrence of being organised.'

She smiled and lifted bright eyes to his. 'Oh, yes! I remember her yelling at Father about that! I won't do it again.

You can organise yourself in future. But…if you happen to be passing the back room any time, you'll see I've made up a bed for you there. You won't have to cosy up to a sheep tonight,' she said lightly.

'Thank you. I appreciate your trouble. Goodnight.'

He hadn't smiled back at her attempt at levity. His tone was tight and strained and she knew he wanted to be alone.

'Goodnight,' she said, unwilling to go.

She almost told him what time breakfast would be, but realised he'd expect to sort himself out. He didn't need anyone. Especially her.

Upset at that thought, she left the room, her bare feet silent on the cold stone. Back in the sitting room Cassian gave a harsh exhalation of breath and she hesitated, her pulses racing.

'Hell!' he muttered in the silence. His voice had broken up as if emotion was choking him. 'Give me strength,' he growled shakily.

Laura was appalled. Was he pleading for strength to cope with her? She listened, her ears straining in the stillness of the night.

'You nerd. It's a cupboard,' she heard him mutter.

And her heart seemed to leap to her throat. The cupboard. He'd been banished there more times than she could remember. It had been unlit then, with a freezing stone floor and huge spiders.

Cassian was testing himself. That's the kind of man he was. Before he felt able to stay here, he needed to come to terms with the harshness of his treatment at Thrushton.

Her eyes darkened as her tender heart went out to him. And yet…if he did conquer the past then she would definitely find herself without a home. From her point of view it might be better if Cassian never overcame the bad memories which filled the silent corners of the house.

She could leave him to it. Hope that he discovered he hated the atmosphere still, and that the reminders of her adoptive father and her aunt were too powerful even for him to be comfortable with.

But even as that thought raced through her head, she knew she had to help him. His distress cut into her very heart and nothing would stop her from offering solace, not even his scorn or his anger.

Soundlessly, she tiptoed back to the doorway, initially keeping well hidden in the shadows.

As she'd expected, he stood in front of the cupboard, his fists tightly clenched, his shoulders high. A rush of emotion hurtled through her. This had been his hell. And she couldn't just walk upstairs when her soul was reaching out to him in sympathy.

Quietly she crossed the soft carpet and stood so close to him that their arms touched. For a moment it seemed that he leaned nearer, though she might have been the one to do so. The fact that he hadn't yelled at her was encouraging and she even believed that his tense muscles had relaxed a little.

'Don't do this, not now,' she whispered into the thick, cloying silence.

'I must.'

Stricken by his choked reply, she astonished herself by putting an understanding hand on his increasingly rigid back. Looking up at him, she saw that his jaw was set and his eyes seemed distant as if he remembered every incident, each indignity, the slaps and the punishments which had made up his days.

With a suddenness that took her by surprise, he lurched forwards and wrenched open the cupboard door. The breath became strangled in her throat. His face was white and he was sweating, beads of perspiration standing out on his forehead.

Her fist went to her mouth. 'Oh, Cassian!' she whispered.

He didn't speak. For a long, agonising time he stared into the black recesses of the deep cupboard and she relived her own terror of all those years ago when he'd nonchalantly walked in there, his head held high in defiance as if he were entering a paradise.

The hackles rose on the back of Laura's neck. For the freedom-loving Cassian this must have been a terrible ordeal.

Seconds ticked past and his facial muscles tightened till she couldn't bear it. 'Cassian—'

'Shut me in.'

She jerked in a shocked breath. *'What?'*

'Do it.'

He stepped in and turned, his eyes commanding her.

'No!' she breathed in horror.

He glowered, his jaw clenched. 'Do it!' he commanded.

She gulped. And knew she must. Mesmerised, she clasped the latch in a shaking hand and slowly closed the door. Aghast, she stared at the oak panels with wide, anxious eyes. For several long minutes she waited, cold and shivering, her pulse thundering in her ears as she imagined what must be going through his mind.

There was a light knock on the door. With relief she stumbled forwards to open it again and Cassian emerged: shaking, breathing heavily, but with the light of triumph in his eyes. Laura gave a little cry and ran to him, briefly hugging him before moving back in confusion.

'You're freezing!' he said with a frown. He reached out and rubbed her arms.

'I'm all right,' she croaked, still reeling from the feel of his strong body against hers. 'Are you?'

'Fine.'

His hands were slowing and warmth was flowing into her—though it was nothing to do with any external temperature. She picked off spider threads from his shirt and suddenly felt overcome with the intimacy of such an action.

'I was just worried about you,' she babbled.

'I was OK. I'll put a key on the inside so no one can ever be locked in. It's all in the past, now.'

'I really didn't want to shut that door. It wasn't your favourite place of all time. Was it really awful, being locked in there when you were a kid?' she asked, and could have kicked herself for such stupidity. Of course it had been awful.

'It was a lesson.'

Puzzled, her small face lifted to his. And she saw the strength there, the fierce willpower which she had always admired and envied.

'In what?' she asked in awe.

'Detachment. Mind over matter.'

'But you must have dreaded going in there each time,' she persisted, for some reason wanting him to acknowledge the horror of sitting in a small, dark cupboard on a solid stone floor for hours on end.

'Sometimes, Laura,' he said huskily, 'you have to face your fears to become stronger.'

'But…' Her face grew perplexed. 'Everywhere you look in this house you must see things you'd rather forget.'

'If you can live here,' he said softly, 'so can I.'

'I'm different—'

'You can say that again,' he murmured wryly.

She flushed, wishing they weren't light years away from one another. But persisted with her point. 'We are total opposites. You and your mother were like…like wild birds!' she exclaimed. 'You both craved freedom! I, however, have always been tractable—'

'Laura. Don't be mistaken; we are all passionate about the things we love.' His hot, dark eyes burned into hers till the breath came short and fast in her throat and she could feel the increased pressure of his hands around her arms. 'Even you. You are passionate about your son—'

'Am I?' she breathed in amazement.

'Fiercely. Your love for him overrides everything else.'

His smile dazzled her, sending her nerves into a tailspin. 'As for me, I don't know why I have to be here, only that I felt an irresistible pull the moment Tony mentioned the house. And,' he went on huskily, 'when I saw the sun on the fells, glinting on the drystone walls and Thrushton nestling on the slopes, my heart leapt in my body. I need to be here and I will come to terms with my past. That is just a cupboard and it holds no terrors for me any more. I must live here to make this house ordinary in my mind again. I think it's part of my rites of passage.'

She grasped that, but would never fully understand him, she thought, stunned by how sad that made her feel. She would never know what drove him, pleased him, made him tick. Would never reach the impenetrable depths which made him so fascinating and desirable.

The past and the present collided. Tension had torn at her nerves making them raw. Cassian always unsettled her, turned her life upside down, upset her. She began to cry silently but didn't know why, and turned away blindly so that he didn't suspect.

But he knew. His hands were on her shoulders, strong, firm, comforting. Gently he coaxed her around and then suddenly she seemed to be crushed against him, weeping quietly into his shoulder.

'I—I'm sorry!' she mumbled in dismay, trying to pull back. He resisted her efforts and she was secretly glad. 'I shouldn't—'

His finger lifted her chin and she did her best to stop her stupid sobbing. 'If you need to cry, then cry,' he said softly. 'There's no point in bottling it up.'

There was. Miserably she blinked in a heroic effort to stem the flood, her tongue desperately mopping up any tears which headed near her mouth. Something told her that if she really let go, then all her carefully constructed world would start falling apart.

'I have to stay in control!' she mumbled.

'Why?'

'Of course I must! Everyone should! Where'd we be otherwise?' she said wildly.

'Laura!' he husked.

His hand slid around to cradle her jaw. Through the veil of tears she could see that his eyes were bright, his lips parted in consternation.

There was a tenderness in his expression which made her heart lurch. Suddenly she felt giddy, as if she were being lifted off her feet by a whirling wind and carried into the sky. Her eyes seemed to be closing of their own accord. The sensation persisted, even intensified and she had the impression that there was no solid ground beneath her feet any more.

She could smell him. A wonderful, alien, male smell that tantalised her nostrils and increased the beat of her heart. Beneath her palms his chest was firm, the pressure of his body a delight.

A soft sigh escaped her as she revelled in the contrast between his masculine strength and her own soft yielding.

'Cassian,' she found herself murmuring.

His embrace enfolded her more securely and she felt an extraordinary elation. Although she was intensely aware of her nakedness beneath the robe and thin cotton nightdress it didn't bother her.

Drowsily her eyes opened. A sudden rush of warm breath raced over her face and she tensed expectantly, straining upwards for the wonderful moment when their mouths would meet.

'Would you…?'

Laura smiled invitingly, delighted by his huskiness. 'Mmm?' she prompted gently.

He cleared his throat. 'Would you like my handkerchief or are you all right now?' he shot out.

They both stepped back from one another; Cassian's expression unreadable, hers transparent with disappointment till she managed to haul the shreds of her tattered dignity about her again.

'I'm OK,' she lied jerkily, avoiding his horribly perceptive eyes.

OK? Her whole body was screaming for him, like a child having a tantrum because it has been deprived of a favourite toy.

'I don't know why I cried—' she mumbled.

'You don't need a reason. Or to give me one,' he said softly.

'I'm not a wimp—' she began.

'I know. I think you're brave.'

She met his eyes then, and found herself caught by them. 'Brave?' she squeaked, feeling her body reaching melting point again.

'Strong, too, and determined. It can't have been easy, bringing up Adam on your own with Enid presumably breathing fire and brimstone and calling all kinds of damnation on your head.'

She gave a wry smile. 'It was a bit like that.'

'You could have given him up for adoption,' he suggested.

'Never!' she declared in horror. 'He was my baby! I loved him from the start. I'd have sooner cut out my heart than give him away!'

'I thought so,' he said gently. 'Laura, I want you to listen to me very carefully. This is important.'

He was smiling at her. She responded with one of her own and was thrilled when she saw a glow light up his eyes.

Kiss me, she told him, with every ounce of her being.

'I'm listening,' she said, deceptively demure. And intensely hopeful.

Cassian touched his lips with the tip of his tongue and Laura swallowed, her eyes huge with longing.

'I believe in Kismet. Fate,' he said thickly.

It had brought him here. 'Me too,' she breathed, her face radiant.

Tight-jawed, he folded his arms, a gesture which immediately put a barrier between them. Laura's hopes and dreams began to fade.

'My arrival releases you,' Cassian said, still hoarse, but perhaps with embarrassment and not desire.

Laura stared in dismay, her mouth suddenly unruly and refusing to obey when she tried to stop it quivering.

'From…what?' she mumbled with difficulty.

'Everything that's kept you here. For you,' Cassian continued more curtly, 'the next journey in life is to shake off the shackles of this house and this village and to take your son and yourself somewhere new.'

'No!' she cried in horror.

He frowned down at her, no longer someone she could trust, but a cold and determined stranger.

'You are strong and you are brave, and your devotion to Adam will ensure that you both survive. I know you can do it,' he rasped. 'I'll give you a week to tell Adam and to get used to the idea. After that, you're out on your ear.'

CHAPTER SIX

THE sound of music woke her, seeping through the house with a soft insistence. Glancing in outrage at the bedside clock she saw it was only six-thirty.

Wretched Cassian! She needed that extra half-hour after tossing and turning all night, seething with anger at how badly she'd misread Cassian's intentions! Far from being close to kissing her, he'd been searching for a way to tell her she wasn't welcome in his house.

And now she was horribly, thoroughly awake.

Muttering under her breath, she dived into the bathroom and showered, dressed and made her bed all in record time. And apart from the few moments when she wielded her toothbrush with unusual vigour, her teeth were angrily clamped together for the whole fifteen minutes.

As she passed Adam's room, she saw that the bed was already made. That meant Cassian had woken him too!

Determined to lay down a few ground rules before putting over her housekeeping plan, she stomped down the stairs, astonished to be met by the delicious smell of bacon.

And then she was confronted by the shocking sight of Adam, scarlet in the face—a fever, perhaps—and yet he was checking the six rashers sizzling gently on the grill which he was holding at a very careful arm's length.

She gasped. He was ill. Alone. Cooking without super-vision! Of all the reckless, thoughtless…

'Adam!' she exclaimed. 'What the—?'

'Hi, Mum! Shall I do you some?'

She didn't know where to begin her tirade. She identified the source of the music. It came from a small, state of the art personal stereo. The wonderful swelling sound was washing gently through her brain, doing its best to soothe her temper.

But she wouldn't be placated. First she'd deal with Adam's fever. Then she'd find Cassian and flay him alive.

'Sweetheart, your face is terribly flushed,' she said bossily. 'I ought to take your temperature—'

'Morning, Laura. He's fine, it's only a healthy glow. We've been out for a run,' came Cassian's voice from the scullery beyond. 'Found some mushrooms on the way,' he added, coming into the kitchen.

Laura's eyes popped. True to his earlier threat, he was wearing nothing but a bath towel! Acres of tanned, muscular chest speedily impressed themselves on her retinas so indelibly that she wondered if she'd ever find room for any other vision again.

'M-morning!' she gasped.

'Chanterelles, parasols, ceps. Not bad. I've brushed them clean,' he said to Adam, casually adding the mushrooms to the grill and drizzling on a few drops of oil.

She blinked, all the better to clear her fogged eyes and brain and to see the interesting movements of muscle beneath the flawless back, which was so smooth and glowing that she could hardly hold back from reaching out to caress it.

Briefly she let her gaze wander to the narrow hips and the small, tight rear beneath the thin, clinging towel. It was an awful mistake. Terrible things were beginning to happen to her. Delicious sensations. Wicked yearnings.

But sex-god or not, her boring, Aunt-Enid generated conscience told her sternly, this man was ruthless and heartless and she'd better not forget that.

'Now Cassian—!' she began angrily, all set for a showdown.

'Just a sec—' He wasn't paying her any attention, his alert and watchful eyes constantly on Adam. 'Looks great, steady as she goes,' he said in his deep, calming voice, leaning nonchalantly against the Aga rail.

'Will the sausages pop?' Adam asked nervously.

'Not on the simmer plate. You've got a splatter guard, anyway. Just show them you're the boss. The pan will be safe and steady if you hold the handle firmly.'

'Like that?' Adam assumed a more commanding position.

'Perfect,' beamed Cassian. 'It's like everything; success is a matter of application and keeping focussed on the task.'

'The sausies look a bit brown on their bottoms,' Adam said uncertainly.

'You're right.' Cassian handed him the tongs.

Laura sullenly admired his technique. He hadn't said the sausages needed turning, but had waited till Adam had noticed that fact for himself. The edges were rubbed off her anger. She couldn't help but be impressed by Cassian, callous brute though he may be.

She sat down, non-plussed, her gaze sliding surreptitiously back to him as he raised a hand and slicked back his hair which was still wet and shiny from his shower. Absently he rubbed his damp palm on his rear. No noticeable wobble. Taut muscles. Small and neat...

Laura tried to breathe normally. She couldn't cope with so much nakedness, so much male beauty. It was too early. And to make matters worse, she had the distinct feeling that she was being superseded.

A sausage sizzled menacingly as Adam wielded the tongs. And she jumped up again.

'Cassian! The fat—!' she cried in alarm.

'Sound effects, nothing more,' Cassian said airily. 'There's virtually no fat at all, the way we're cooking. He's safe, I promise you.'

She glared. If her son was burned, she'd...

'Great grub, isn't it?!' enthused Adam, failing dismally to turn any of the sausages.

She took a step to help but felt a heavy hand descend on her shoulder pushing her back into the chair. Cassian's carefully draped towel brushed her leg. His hip was an inch from her eyes and she almost craned her neck to follow the delicious aroma of fresh soap that had accompanied his sudden movement.

'Little beggars, sausies, aren't they?' sympathised Cassian, releasing his hold on Laura. 'Oh, well done. They give in eventually. One down, three to go.'

Her mouth opened and closed. The burning imprint of his hand remained on her shoulder.

'What was this about a run?' she queried icily.

She peered hard at Adam for signs of exhaustion. There were none. That should have pleased her but it made her crosser than ever and she felt horribly guilty because of that.

'Cassian asked if I'd like to go with him. We were up before six,' Adam said proudly. 'We walked and jogged and ran then walked and jogged and ran,' he explained. 'It's a good way to start exercise. I could have gone on,' he boasted, 'but Cassian said he was starving so I agreed to come back.'

'Oh, yes?'

Laura's cynical glance made Cassian grin and shrug his shoulders in amusement behind Adam's absorbed back. Cassian was so fit he could have run to London and back without breaking into a sweat. But at least, she thought, Cassian had been careful not to drive her son to the limit of his endurance.

'This is a first. You never eat breakfast,' she pointed out to her son, having tried for years to interest him in more than a meagre slice of toast and a glass of orange.

It annoyed her that Adam didn't answer. He was occupied in looking blankly at the egg which Cassian had handed to him as if he'd never seen one.

'I'll do the first, you do the next,' Cassian murmured,

sotto voce. 'Watch. Small tap with a knife, fingers in carefully, open it up very slowly…break it into this cup and tip it into the poacher.'

He was behaving like a conspirator, Laura thought huffily. For the first time in her life, she was playing second fiddle to someone else in Adam's life. And she couldn't bear it.

To her amazement, Adam managed the tricky operation and grinned up at Cassian in delight, receiving a slap on the back.

'Eggsellent!' Cassian said with a grin.

Laura looked at her giggling son as if he'd betrayed her. 'So now you're a fan of cooked breakfasts,' she said lightly, trying to keep the scouring jealousy out of her tone.

'I didn't have the benefit of fresh air and exercise before,' he said absently.

He pushed back a blond hank of hair with a busy hand and cracked another egg with great success. It was as if he'd scored a goal for Manchester United.

'Hey! How about that?' he cried in delight, taking a bow.

'Brilliant,' conceded Laura, squirming at his pleasure. This wasn't her son. It just wasn't.

Cassian put an arm around Adam's shoulder. They looked very much at home with one another. Her eyes clouded.

'There's plenty for you, Laura,' murmured Cassian, 'if you want some. I bought loads.'

She could be proud and stick to toast and marmalade, or give in to her hysterical taste buds.

'Thanks,' she said stiffly, managing a compromise. 'I'll do myself some in a moment.'

She stalked over to the fridge for the juice and stood in amazement at the sight that met her eyes.

'Is this…yours?' she asked Cassian, overwhelmed by the amount of food crammed into the small space.

'And yours. I just grabbed a few things on my way here.'

'Few?' Steaks. A joint of lamb, chocolate eclairs...
'We...we can't—'

'Oh, Mum!' complained Adam. 'We can! It can be his
rent for staying here, can't it?'

Her teeth ground together. 'You answer that,' she said
sweetly to the amused Cassian.

'The food is for us. My contribution to the well-being of
our stomachs,' he fudged, his eyes mocking.

'Sending us off into the blue, well-fed?' she queried
waspishly, prompting him to come clean about his presence
in the house.

He smiled and didn't rise to her bait. 'With all the exercise Adam's intending to take, he'll need plenty of sustenance,' he said easily.

'It's brilliant having you here, Cassian. And isn't this
music triff, Mum?' Adam declared, going off at a tangent
and totally oblivious to Laura's fury. 'Andean pipes.
S'posed to sound like condors, soaring over mountain
peaks. Condors are big birds of prey, Mum.'

'Are they?' she replied drily.

But she lifted her head and listened to the music, hearing
the sound of wind on feather, the chillingly beautiful echo
of the pipes—as if they were rebounding from one mountain top to another.

She was aware of Cassian watching her intently and lowered her gaze, annoyed to be caught out enjoying the music
and disturbed that her senses had been so deeply stirred.

'I've made Turkish coffee for myself. Want to try some?'
he murmured.

Even now, though she knew his intentions towards her—
eviction—her body trembled at the sound of his low, me-
lodious voice. Even, she thought, wryly, at the crack of
dawn.

If he could have this kind of effect on her, in a kitchen,
with the smell of sausages pervading the air, what could he

achieve over a candlelit dinner for two and a splash of aftershave?

'All right,' she said with a shrug.

Cassian poured some treacly liquid into a small cup from an exotic-looking silver jug with a beaked nose.

'Do you think everything's done now?' he asked Adam innocently.

'Um…yes, I reckon so,' he replied, flushing with pleasure at being given the responsibility to decide.

Laura shrank into herself even further. The two of them dished up and carried their heaped plates to the table. All very cosy, very intimate and chummy. Laura sat sipping the rich, sweet coffee, feeling utterly miserable and gooseberryish.

They chattered, she was quiet. Adam didn't slump as usual, or eat at a snail's pace. And he looked Cassian directly in the eye, instead of that hesitant, sideways glance he normally gave to people.

It was astonishing. In a few hours, her son had changed. A few culinary skills, a jog across the fields, and he'd gained in confidence.

A sharp pain sliced through her and she hastily got up to cook herself some breakfast. She was a failure. Adam had needed a father—or at the very least, a different mother, she thought, racked with guilt. But she'd done everything she could to protect him. Cared for him, sacrificed much. Why then, should she feel deeply inadequate?

Miserably she looked up, hearing Cassian offer her son a lift to school. She almost told Adam to do his teeth but daren't, not with Cassian's dark eyes upon her in warning.

'I'll go and do the gnashers,' Adam declared. 'Um… what do I need today?' She opened her mouth to reply, but closed it again around a piece of sausage, waiting for her son to work that one out for himself. Perhaps because he wasn't used to doing that, there was a long pause. 'I'd better check what lessons I've got and get my stuff together,' he said eventually. 'Then I can do some extra work on my project till it's time to go.'

'Mmm,' she enthused, and gave him a beaming smile of encouragement. 'You do that, darling.'

Adam dashed out and Cassian raised his coffee cup to her in admiring salute. Laura only just managed to stop herself from blushing coyly and joining the Cassian United Fan Club. But she knew how Adam felt, she mused. Heady, happy, pleased.

She glared at the seductive triangle of Cassian's back. He was already clearing dishes and running water for washing up, his feet planted firmly apart on the stone flags as he tested the temperature of the water and squirted in some of the ecologically friendly washing up liquid he'd bought.

Nice feet, she couldn't help but noticing. Well-shaped, with no ugly lumps or bumps. And muscular calves...

Furious with herself for finding him so attractive, she leapt up and stacked plates on the counter, then grabbed a tea towel. All madly domesticated, she thought grimly.

'Now, look,' she snapped. 'We need to talk.'

'Shall we save it till Adam's at school?' he suggested amiably, working away at an eggy plate.

'No! I can't wait! Now!' she hissed.

'You could shout at me more easily if he's not around,' Cassian pointed out, infuriatingly right.

Laura hauled in a huge breath, ready to explode, but she heard Adam thundering down the stairs and shot Cassian a vicious scowl instead.

'All right. Later,' she grated.

'Look forward to it,' Cassian murmured.

'Hey! I just had a thought,' Adam said excitedly, gazing at Cassian with a hopeful expression. 'Do you know anything about Ancient Egypt?'

'Lived in Cairo and Aswan for a couple of years,' Cassian replied and smiled at Laura when she let out a quiet snort. 'What do you need to know?' he asked Adam.

And soon they were both huddled over Adam's project, with fascinating stories being faithfully recorded—stories so well-told and interesting that Laura found herself moving quietly so that she didn't miss a word.

There were tales of Pharaohs, of greed and ambition, murder and achievement—all woven into a tapestry of facts and figures which made them seem all the more believable.

He was amazing. A walking encyclopaedia, she thought, deciding that everything he said was probably true. A devastatingly charismatic man—and already Adam had fallen under his spell.

She couldn't blame him. If she didn't know Cassian's intentions, she'd be sitting goggle-eyed at his feet, too.

Seeing her child's awe-struck face and shining eyes, she knew that he'd be terribly hurt when Cassian revealed that he owned Thrushton Hall. And she couldn't bear to see Cassian leading Adam on. If they did have to leave, then Adam would find it hard to deal with Cassian's two-faced betrayal.

'Time you went, darling,' she said, sounding choked. 'Got everything?'

'Oh, Mum—!'

'Come on,' Cassian said cheerfully. 'Plenty of time tonight to do a bit more after we've had our run.'

'Another?' Adam looked shocked. 'I usually watch TV—'

Cassian shrugged. 'Whatever you prefer—'

'Oh, a run!'

Laura glared. This was hero worship on a grand scale and it had to stop. '*After* your normal homework,' she put in quickly.

'I knew that!' protested Adam.

And Laura felt a shock go right through her. He was annoyed with her, for the first time in his life.

'I suppose I'd better get dressed,' Cassian said loudly. 'I

imagine towels aren't usually worn on the school run. Be down in a moment.'

'Sorry, Adam,' she said quietly, when Cassian had bounded up the stairs two at a time. 'I shouldn't have nagged.'

'It's OK, Mum. I usually need reminding.' They smiled at one another, friends again, both confused by the small crack in their relationship. 'Isn't he fab, Mum?' Adam enthused.

'Fab,' she managed with a smile.

And suddenly the future seemed even more uncertain than ever. If they left, they'd have problems adjusting to a new and hostile world. If they stayed...

She bit her lip. She'd have to watch her own child worshiping the ground Cassian walked on. She wouldn't be needed any more. The truth was, that Cassian had the advantage of maleness. They'd do men's things together.

And Cassian's extraordinary magic would act as a magnet to the impressionable Adam. She had no fascinating experiences, no exotic background or a storyteller's gift.

She just loved her child. And, she thought forlornly, it seemed that wasn't enough any more.

It was a long time before Cassian returned. She kept looking at the clock, wondering when he'd come back and rehearsing what she'd say.

Everything had been dusted twice, all surfaces wiped down, cobwebs whisked away. The house gleamed and smelt deliciously of lavender but it felt empty and silent after the chatter of the early morning.

Prompted by the deathly quiet, she fiddled with Cassian's stereo and managed to make it eject the condor music and accept something called 'Flames of Fire'.

The house throbbed to a deep and intensely sensual music that sent shivers down her spine and made her think unwisely of Cassian's warm eyes and erotic mouth.

Catching herself breathing more heavily than her recent bout of dusting should have produced, she decided to swap the flames of fire for something that didn't make her erogenous zones tingle. Like a party political broadcast. But she never made the switch.

'You there, Laura? I'm home!'

She stiffened at Cassian's voice, coming from the hall. 'Oh, no, you're not!' she muttered under her breath. This was her home. He merely owned it.

'What do you think of the music?' he asked cheerfully, immediately seeming to fill the sitting room with energy.

'I was just going to turn it off,' she grumped.

'Do that. And get smartened up. I'm taking you off to look for a job.'

Her mouth tightened stubbornly. 'I want to talk to you first—'

'Do it on the way.' He waited expectantly.

She tossed her head in defiance. 'Don't boss me around! I don't like being organised any more than you do—'

'But you need a job.'

'I can go on the bus,' she said, cutting off her nose to spite her face. A lift would have been marvellous. But not with *him*.

'Seems silly. I'm going anyway. So if you don't come with me, your heart to heart talk will have to wait till tonight.' He smiled at her sulky face. 'Come on. You might as well use me, mightn't you? And think of the yelling you can do, while I'm driving.'

He was utterly impossible! She glared. 'Put like that...'

With a show of reluctance, she stalked over to the door, expecting him to move aside. He didn't, and clearly wasn't intending to. The stereo whispered out a deeply passionate refrain that made her entire body contract.

Summoning up all her willpower, she slid past Cassian, totally, intensely aware of the feel of his moleskin trousers, the softness of his brushed cotton shirt, the flurry of warm breath that disturbed her hair…and her senses.

Hot and flustered, she scurried up the stairs. Her heart pounded as she scrabbled out of her clothes and dug out her interview suit. Bottle-green, second-hand and badly fitting. Crisp shirt, well-polished court shoes, well-worn. Ditto handbag.

Smooth the mussed-up hair. How had that happened? Cold water on face. Done.

He was waiting outside. Took one look at her—clearly disapproving, from the quick frown—and opened the passenger door without a word.

Composed now, she climbed onto the high step, hampered by her skirt. Cassian gave a brief push on her bottom and she slid into the comfortable seat pink with embarrassment but determined to use her time usefully.

'I have a proposition,' she announced briskly as they pulled away.

'Uh-huh.'

'You know all the reasons I want to stay.'

'Yup.'

Her hands fidgeted nervously in her lap. Cassian reached over to her side and she flattened herself against the back of the seat. With a curious look at her, he turned on the radio and pushed in a cassette.

Laura groaned. Loin-stirring flamenco music.

'Well,' she said stiffly, 'I've thought of a way to solve the problem.'

Cassian didn't look too pleased about that. 'Oh?' he grunted.

'You can live at Thrushton Hall.'

'Thanks. I'm with you so far,' he drawled.

She took a deep breath. The next bit was tricky.

'I get a job, stay at Thrushton too—and pay rent, and I do all the housework and cooking and washing for you!'

She looked at him anxiously. The signs weren't good. Beetled brows, furrowed brow, tight mouth.

'One teeny flaw. I don't need a housekeeper or a cook or someone to do my washing,' he declared.

Her heart sank. She felt stupid for not realising. Cassian would bring over his woman to Thrushton. It was too painful to contemplate.

'I'd forgotten. You've got your wife. Partner. Whatever,' she floundered miserably.

'No wife, partner or whatever. My wife died when Jai was born,' he snapped.

Now she'd hurt him. 'I'm sorry,' she mumbled.

'Laura, please try to tune in to the kind of man I am. I've always looked after myself. I need no woman for that.' His glance seared into her. 'I've never needed a woman for anything other than love.'

Love. He had sounded very sad as if he was remembering the woman he'd adored so much that he'd risked his love of freedom and gone willingly into marriage. And his wife had died tragically. How awful.

There was a long silence. Then timidly she ventured again.

'You and Jai would be alone?'

'It's how we like it.'

'But I could save you from doing domestic things. They're boring. You'd have more freedom,' she enlarged, 'if you didn't have to do chores—'

'You're very persistent.'

'It's very important!' she replied. 'Well?'

'No.'

Her stomach lurched at the finality of his tone. 'Why not? You hate restrictions! Shopping and cooking—'

'I don't shirk responsibility,' he corrected. 'I just don't do things that are unnecessary.'

'Please, think about it—' she begged, horrified that her great plan had been so casually rejected.

'No.'

She pressed her fist to her mouth and tried to stop the tears of disappointment. She'd really failed this time. For a moment she contemplated the abyss that was her future.

It would be terrible. She felt sick. Adam would be devastated. Her head jerked up. Adam!

'In that case...' She choked, swallowed, and tried to find her voice again. 'In that case,' she cried hotly, 'if we're out on our ears at the end of the week, then leave Adam alone! Don't get close to him!' The flamenco rose to a crescendo and she found herself shouting angrily over the fiery beat. 'You'll destroy him, Cassian! You're not blind. You can see he thinks you're Mr Wonderful. You sit there, telling him stories, behaving like—like a *father* to him, the father he's always wanted, and yet in a few days' time you'll be rejecting him! You can't do that!' she stormed, beating her fists on her knees. 'You can't hurt him, I won't let you...' She broke off. He was pulling over, driving onto the verge. 'What are you doing?' she flared.

'Out.' He jerked his head at her.

Her mouth dropped open. 'You don't mean—?'

'No, I'm not abandoning you,' he said wearily. 'But this is important and I can discuss this more easily when I don't have to concentrate on the road.'

'Discuss?' she raged, half-falling out of the car in her eagerness to get out before he helped her. 'There's no point in talking! You won't listen to me. You don't care what happens to Adam and me. You have no heart! It doesn't matter that he'll be distraught because his god has turned out to have feet of clay and that—'

'Laura!' Cassian was shaking her, his grip firm on her arms. 'Laura, *I do care*!'

CHAPTER SEVEN

HE COULDN'T believe he'd admitted that. He felt her freeze, every muscle, every breath in her body halted by his claim.

'What?' she whispered, searching his face.

'I care about Adam,' he said shortly, and released her. 'Come and sit in the sun.'

'I'm all right here!' she yelled.

'As you wish.'

Touched by her wonderful stubbornness, he settled himself on the low stone wall and stared out at the valley, hoping his inflamed senses would simmer down.

Laura had been more passionate than he could have believed possible. Yesterday he'd watched her responding to the music and enjoying the wine, an excitement surging within him as he saw her long overdue awakening to the pleasures in life.

His body had known little rest since. It demanded that he should introduce her to the greatest pleasure of all.

His eyes closed to the warmth of the sun, feeling his very bones melt at the thought of making love to Laura. Despite the terrible green suit.

'Cassian.'

There was a lurch in his loins. She had come to sit near him.

'Mmm?' he grunted.

'If you care—'

'It's because I care, because I see a child longing to be part of the hurly-burly of the world,' he said grimly, determined to deny himself the pleasure he wanted, 'that I'm determined to extract you both from your shell. He must

101

take his life in his own hands. He's desperate to be liked at school. I've never seen a kiddie so anxious to please—'

'What do you mean?' she demanded, suddenly alert. 'Something happened, didn't it? Tell me!' she cried, grabbing his arm with both hands.

He glanced quickly at her fiery eyes and only just managed to drag his gaze away and fix it on a distant peak.

'Oh, some kids making fun—'

'Of Adam?' she cried, aghast.

He sighed, and decided he'd better explain. 'They were actually pointing at—and mocking—what they imagined to be my rucksack. It's orange, you see. Day-Glo. So I got out and told them it was my paraglider and offered to show it to them.'

She frowned. 'You mean those parachutes with a sort of strap seat thing beneath it? You fling yourself off mountains for fun?'

'Something like that.' He was amused by her description of one of the most exhilarating sports in the world. To fly. To soar into the sky, to stay airborne by reading the contours of the ground and assessing the thermals... Breathtaking. 'It's a little more complicated, but that's the general idea,' he acknowledged.

'Then what happened?' she asked curiously.

Bedlam. He grinned and played the whole thing down. 'We got quite a crowd around us. I answered questions about it and then a woman with a letterbox mouth came over and told us all off for not hearing the bell.'

'Miss Handley,' Laura said, her mouth curving into a reluctant smile.

'Yes. The Head. I apologised, said it was all my fault and why and before I knew what was happening, she had me in there giving a talk during her assembly.'

Cassian watched a sparrowhawk spill out the air from its wings, mastering thermals without knowing how.

'I can imagine.' To his relief, Laura sounded drily

amused. Then she frowned. 'I suppose Adam is madly impressed.'

And he sighed. Even now he felt upset by Adam's pitiful delight to be associated with someone 'cool'.

'Adam helped me with my talk,' he said in a low tone. 'Unwrapping my wing. The parachute,' he explained. 'He sat in the seat while I held it.'

He didn't want to say any more. He could see the child's face, bright with joy to be regarded with such envy by the entire school while he talked of flying with black vultures over Spain and with the condors in South America. It hurt him to remember.

Laura was silent. He was glad, needing time to push some steel into his backbone because somewhere a little voice was becoming more insistent, saying that Laura's solution was workable, that he could help them both.

Then common sense reasserted itself. He wasn't God. Shouldn't meddle. She had to find her own way. All he should do was to put her on the road.

Dippers bobbed about on the rocks in the turbulent river below. A heron flapped lazily across the meadow. Far in the distance he could see that a deer had become trapped in a field, enclosed by the high stone walls.

It ran up and down in panic, unsure how it had got there, incapable of finding its way back to safety. He realised that this was what he was doing to Laura and Adam: flinging them into an alien space where there were no recognisable landmarks. Yet, like the deer, they wanted to hide in safety—

'There's a deer trapped!' she cried with concern. And she pointed.

'I know.'

'I forgot. You don't miss a thing, do you?' she said ruefully. 'It's scared, Cassian. Can't we go down the valley and help it somehow?'

'No.'

'Surely we must—'

'Laura, I hate to see it so frightened but we'd scare it even more if we started waving our arms and trying to get it back to the wood. It could hurt itself on the wall—break a leg, perhaps in its panic. Or get caught up in the barbed wire at the top end of the field.'

'It looks so frightened,' she said in a small voice.

He laid his hand on hers. 'It must find its own way,' he said gently.

And, extraordinarily, he wanted to keep Laura safe with him, and not send her out into the wide world. His jaw clenched. He was just missing Jai. Needed company. Someone to hold.

'What is it?' Laura asked softly.

'Jai.' His voice was choked with emotion.

He knew she nodded, though he kept staring straight ahead.

'You're a very caring man. Jai is very lucky to have you as a father.'

He sought her eyes then, almost faltering at the beauty of her misted blue gaze.

'A callous brute like me?' he joked.

She smiled wistfully. 'I know you think you're doing the right thing—that you believe it's ''good'' for us,' she breathed.

Her face lifted to his, the wind ruffling her hair. And he felt his heart lurch. She was entering his very bones. Shaking the cells in his body. It was purely a yearning for the softness of a woman, nothing to do with her personally.

Do it, a satanic voice urged. Wake her up. Kiss her.

'I think we'd better go job-hunting,' he said in strangled tones, his eyes hopelessly enmeshed with hers.

'OK. But…about us staying on. Reconsider. A trial period. Please.'

Passion suffused her face. She looked radiant. And he could resist no longer. His mouth closed on hers and he groaned with hunger as she responded eagerly, inexpertly...but oh, so sweetly, the taste of her more succulent than the most exotic fruit, the pressure of her hand on his arm more welcome than he could ever have imagined.

Her hand slid to his neck. He drew her close, absorbing her into him, the needs of his mouth becoming more and more desperate as he sought to kiss life into every part of her.

To his astonishment, his neck was encircled in crushing arms, his head forced down till his mouth and thus his kisses became bruising. Laura had erupted. She was clamouring for him, moaning, crying, urging with a vehemence that startled and thrilled him to the core.

He lifted her onto him, her skirt riding up and her legs sliding around his waist. They clung in total abandon, not caring that anyone might drive by—although it was a rarely used road—oblivious to everything but the sensational release of long-held desires.

Her skin felt like velvet. Her hair tumbled over her forehead, silky and faintly perfumed of rosemary and he explored every inch of her face with impassioned delight.

He was weakening, kiss by kiss. Each wickedly innocent caress of her work-roughened hands aroused him more than any artful, silken finger. Laura was without artifice, her passion real and untaught.

That dazzled him, made his head spin with wonder. If he could have this glorious woman in his bed, he'd...

'Cassian!'

She had tensed. But he hadn't sated himself with her yet. So he continued to kiss her, to coax her now stubbornly closed mouth, sliding his tongue over it, enticing it open.

Except that it stayed resolutely closed, despite the sexual shudders which racked her body.

'Laura,' he murmured pleadingly.

'*No!*'

Oh, God, he thought, seeing her stricken face. She regrets what she's done. His arms fell away.

She looked down at her skirt, at the long lengths of slender tanned thigh which were making his loins liquid with their promise, and she gasped in horror then scrambled awkwardly away. With his reluctant help.

She turned her back, her face scarlet, eyes huge and glistening. Her skirt found its correct position. Her jacket was buttoned up, her hair hastily pressed smooth. And he saw with a wrench to his heart that her shoulders were shaking.

'Laura,' he ventured gently.

'No! Don't touch me! Don't come near me!' she squeaked.

'We just kissed,' he tried, playing it down.

Just! He'd seen stars. Been in heaven for a while. Dreamed impossible dreams.

Her head lifted and he dearly wanted to kiss the sweet nape of her neck.

'*You* might be used to grabbing women and—and—'

'Kissing them,' he supplied, seeing that she was struggling.

'Well,' she demanded, whirling around, all fire and passion again. 'Are you?'

How he wanted to take her in his arms again! That energy of hers needed an outlet—his, too.

'Not with such spectacular results,' he admitted, thinking how easily she'd aroused him.

She swallowed, as if horrified by his answer. And ran to the car. He didn't help her to get in. He didn't think she wanted to be touched.

He put his hands on the wall to steady himself because his legs seemed like water. His hands were shaking too.

Several deep breaths later, he'd come to the conclusion that he'd made things worse. Laura's hidden depths had come to the surface but he'd been almost drowned in the process. Of course he'd known from the start that Laura wasn't a run-of-the-mill woman. Whatever she felt, she felt fiercely.

So long as he realised that her uninhibited response hadn't been to him, *for* him, but was a reaction to her stifled emotions, he'd be all right. She would never want sex without strings. Whereas that was all he'd allow himself.

He gave her a moment to compose herself. Below, he saw that the deer had gone. It had found sanctuary. Perhaps, he mused, some people thrived better in their own small worlds.

The thought hit him like a sledgehammer. He could be wrong about extending Laura's field of vision, enlarging her horizons.

Yet now he'd kissed her, she could never remain at Thrushton—not if she wanted to stay out of his bed.

He muttered a low curse, went back to the car and settled himself in the driver's seat without comment.

'It never happened!' she whispered hoarsely.

He shot her a cynical look. If she thought he could ever forget that moment, she had another think coming.

The gears ground beneath his jerky grip. 'Let's concentrate on finding you employment, shall we?' he suggested, grinding the words out through his teeth as harshly as he'd ground the gears.

The beautiful scenery was lost on him. He kept blaming himself, trying to understand why he'd acted so precipitously. The desire for pleasure, he supposed. And, for a short time, what pleasure!

Once in Harrogate, he marched her off to a boutique. And, ignoring all her bad-tempered protests, coldly persuaded her that she'd get a job a hell of a lot faster if she wasn't wearing one of Aunt Enid's 'costumes'. If that's what it was.

Sulkily she saw the sense of what he was saying and insisted on paying him back out of her future wages. The assistant whisked Laura off and he lounged in an armchair, being plied with coffee and biscuits by a pretty redhead. Her legs weren't as good as Laura's. Nor her cheekbones.

'What do you think?' trilled the assistant smugly.

He turned his head and gulped like a teenage boy faced with a nude woman for the first time. Only this one was far better than nude. Dressed, she was absolutely breath-taking.

Finding his mouth was open, he closed it and summoned up as near-normal a voice as he could.

'Perfect.'

Laura's eyes had deepened to a startling sky-blue, en-hanced by the soft navy dress. It skimmed her body but any connoisseur of women could see that she had a fabu-lous figure and the unbroken length of the sleeveless dress, grazing her collarbone and falling smoothly to just below the knee, made her look taller and more imposing than before. Helped by the elegant high heels and…surely new, sheer stockings.

As she moved in response to the assistant's instructions, he realised that Laura had incredible poise, her carriage as graceful as a model's.

'And there's a jacket to go with it that matches Modom's eyes,' the assistant crowed, bustling to put it on the increas-ingly astonished 'Modom'.

'Do you like it, Laura?' he asked dead-pan, entranced by her rapturous face.

She eyed him uncertainly. 'I do. I think it's gorgeous! But I don't think I'd be able to afford it—'

'Your…leaving present, then,' he suggested in clipped tones, finding the words ridiculously hard to say.

Her eyes widened in consternation. 'Leaving! Oh, yes. Leaving.' She gulped. The idea was obviously terrifying to her. He thought of the frightened deer. 'I—I don't know—'

'I do.' Feigning a frown, he stood up and handed over his credit card. 'I'm not hanging around any longer,' he said, with a good attempt at irritation. 'People to see. I've got an office to set up.'

'An office?' she repeated in amazement. '*You?*'

'For a colleague,' he growled. And realised he'd have to be careful if he was to keep his business a secret. 'Come on. That outfit is fine.'

And so with a little judicious bullying and much tutting at his watch, he rail-roaded her into accepting an expensive designer outfit, the shoes too, and a handbag which the assistant hastily found.

By the time they drove back later that day he'd leased a large Georgian building overlooking the green and had ordered the necessary office furniture and computer equipment. Sheila was due any time and he didn't want his charitable foundation to suffer any delays.

He wasn't the only one who'd had a successful day. Laura had four good job offers to consider. Success had wiped away her earlier distress and made her glow with pride. She looked utterly ravishing and he found it hard to keep his mind on the road.

This was a turning point for her, he thought. And wondered if she'd change, and become hard, efficient and slick.

Hopefully not. Since the incident in the restaurant when the waitress had flung banoffi pie over his arm, she'd mellowed towards him. That meant she had a soft heart. May it never harden. Wherever she went.

His stomach sucked in. There it was again. A pain. He didn't want her to go. Suddenly it was difficult to pump breath through his lungs. He felt as if he was panicking and set his mind to conquering his weak and wayward body.

'I'm in a total whirl!' she confessed as they bumped through Grassington's cobbled square. 'Which job do *you* think I ought to accept, Cassian?'

'It's your decision.'

His tone was abrupt enough to make her sink back into her seat and work out the pros and cons of each offer in silence.

Cassian couldn't understand why her success should bug him. What was he afraid of? He wanted her to extend her horizons and to become self-assured. Wanted her to have a better standard of living. Yet her imminent departure filled him with unease. No—be honest—misery. How could that be?

Appalled, his thoughts winged back to Jai again. It must be that he felt lonely. He and his son had never been apart for so long. That was it!

With a screech, he brought the car to a halt overlooking Thrushton village, the relief surging through him in waves.

'Got to ring Jai,' he explained, before leaping out.

Even in her bewildered state and with several job offers to consider, Laura noticed his urgency, the way he fumbled with the mobile attached to his belt and punched numbers with an almost frantic haste. He dearly loves his son, she thought soberly.

And the happiness that lit up his face when he spoke to Jai made her heart somersault. He didn't trouble to disguise how he felt. He looked thrilled, amazed, tender and amused, all in the space of a few moments.

He couldn't keep still, but strode about, gesticulating excitedly with his free arm, occasionally pushing a hand through his hair till it tumbled about in gypsy curls and made him look boyishly appealing.

If only she could be that free, that much at ease with Adam!

'Good news?' she queried, unable to hold back a smile. Cassian looked elated, his eyes sparkling like black diamonds.

'He's heading back!' Cassian leapt energetically into the car, beside himself with delight. 'Arriving later this week, depending on when he can get a flight. Isn't that fantastic?!'

His happiness was infectious and she found herself beaming. 'Wonderful,' she said huskily, wishing she could bring such a light to his eyes. 'We've both got something to celebrate.'

The light died a little. 'Yes. We have,' he said slowly.

And he suddenly jerked around, setting the car in motion again, his profile a confusing mix of pleasure and regret and anger.

Laura was puzzled. In fact he'd been odd ever since they'd met up after going their separate ways and she'd announced with pride how well she'd done in her interviews. His praise had been less generous than she'd expected and it seemed as if he was almost…sorry, yes, sorry, that she would soon be out in the world of commerce.

Had he hoped she'd fail? It didn't seem like Cassian. He was too big-hearted, too adamant that she should stop hiding herself away.

She glanced at him surreptitiously. He was frowning, his mouth grim. The tension in his hands would have been obvious to anyone. Perhaps his day hadn't been to his liking.

'What's wrong?' she asked softly.

His body contracted. He continued to glare at the road. 'Thinking.'

From the harshness of his tone, he didn't want to be disturbed. He shifted in his seat, drawing her attention to the flatness of his stomach, the stretch of soft moleskin over his thigh.

She drew in an involuntary breath before she knew what she was doing. He flicked her a sharp glance and the air seemed to thicken. She could feel her blood racing around her body, scalding her from within and she looked away, quickly.

Already she'd made a fool of herself. Perhaps that was what he was worrying about—wondering if she'd embarrass him in front of his son. She groaned inwardly. He must have been shaken by the way she'd responded to his kiss. Or had she made the first move? It had all been so sudden, so inevitable.

Whatever had happened to her? Had she unwittingly encouraged him? Had he—being acutely perceptive—read the signals she'd tried to hide…and acted on what he knew had been surging within her body?

She cringed, remembering with shame how abandoned she'd been, taking that kiss several stages too far. Cassian must have been appalled.

But… She bit her lip, frowning. Something had snapped inside her and she hadn't been able to stop herself. Her lack of control scared her. She needed to keep a tighter rein on herself.

So what about Cassian? Why had he taken up her unintentional invitation? Racking her brains, she remembered that they'd been talking about Jai. Heaven help her, she thought. She was a love-substitute. Cassian had wanted to be with his son—and he'd kissed her in an expression of his own loneliness.

Idiot! Stupid, arrogant dummy that she was! She stared into the window, seeing her own blurred reflection. A dull mouse; now dressed up in fabulous clothes, but clad in ghastly bottle-green yuk when they'd kissed.

She couldn't believe that she'd imagined he'd been interested in her. Would a man like Cassian ever be attracted to a homebody? Her eyes darkened. No. He'd go for the Bathsheba type: hot, passionate, simmering and unpredictable.

Her fingers touched her lips, every nerve in her body reliving the pressure of his mouth. It seemed that she had become hopelessly addicted to Cassian. Ever since he'd arrived there'd been a current of electricity linking them, setting her on fire.

Adam might hero-worship Cassian, she thought soberly, but so did she, after his behaviour today. His actions had proved him to be the kind of man she'd always admired. Thoughtful to others, courteous, easy company.

Lunch had been such fun. And he'd been so nice to the waitress, when the rather shaky-handed older woman had dropped the pudding onto his sleeve then burst into floods of tears.

To her amazement, he'd jumped up, put an arm around the woman's shoulders and drawn her aside, talking to her for a while and calming her down—totally ignoring the tight-lipped head waiter.

'Her husband's up for shoplifting,' he'd explained, when he finally returned to the table with profuse apologies for his absence. 'She thinks he might have Alzheimer's.'

'That's awful!' Laura had said, her eyes rounding. 'The head waiter was awfully mad—'

'Not any more, he's not.' Cassian accepted a substitute banoffi pie from a smiling waitress.

'Got you a big helping,' the young girl whispered. 'And thanks. That's my Mum you saved from the sack.'

'She'll be OK,' Cassian assured her quietly. 'I've arranged with the management that she can have time off to organise a decent defence—and a medical check for your father.'

For Laura, the rest of the meal had been spent in a haze of admiration. Now watching the houses of Thrushton loom nearer, Laura leaned back in her seat, her head filled with thoughts of Cassian and his kindness to people.

She knew that it hadn't been a show for her benefit. Kindness was ingrained in him. When she'd arrived early at their arranged meeting-point, she'd wandered through a department store and had seen Cassian unfolding a baby buggy while a young woman juggled child and shopping. Carefully he had tucked the toddler in, making it giggle while the mother had stowed away her laden bags. And they'd parted in smiles.

More important to Laura, a few moments later he'd

checked to see if she was in sight—not knowing she was following behind him—and made a point of going around the square to slip money into the hands of the young men who were begging there.

That had really touched her heart and melted any doubts she had about his values. It always upset her to see people reduced to such terrible indignities. Maybe some of them were 'fake'. But plenty were not. How did you ever know?

'Cassian…'

'Uh,' he grunted.

She searched for a diplomatic way to bring up the subject. 'Did you notice the beggars today?'

'Hmm.'

She waited for him to announce his generosity, but gradually realised that he wasn't the kind of person to boast about his good deeds.

'I never know what to do,' she confessed. 'Whether I'm condoning a drink or drug habit by giving them money, or if I'm actually helping them to buy a meal… What do you think?' she asked anxiously.

His mouth softened. She saw his shoulders drop and realised he'd been holding them in tension.

'There's no easy answer, no right or wrong. It's a question of conscience and judgement, isn't it?' he said gently. 'I like to make contact with them. I look into their eyes and talk to them and see if they're still on this planet and then decide. The method works whether you're in Yorkshire or Egypt, Russia or Columbia. However, I do give to the support groups—the hostels and so on. One day I hope that no one will be without a home. It's a basic human right.'

Laura considered this, remembering how he'd stopped to chat to each one, touching them, treating them like human beings instead of parasites or objects of loathing. He is compassionate, she thought shakily. And the knowledge brought her a quiet joy.

'It breaks my heart to think they have nowhere to be warm and safe,' she said in a small voice. 'I can't bear it. So I always give them money even though I don't know how to tell if they're on drugs or not.'

'But you're on the breadline yourself,' he said huskily.

Her eyes were big and dark with distress. 'And I have a home and a child who loves me! They have nothing, nobody! Imagine what that's like, Cassian!'

'I do,' he muttered bleakly. 'Often.'

She felt intensely disturbed by the depth of his caring. He was very special. Even as a child she'd known that. On several occasions she'd come upon him, secretly nursing an injured animal back to health. He had a way with animals; strong, gentle hands and a softly reassuring voice that encouraged trust. Dogs, cats, horses...they all fell under his spell.

Whenever he'd been with animals, there had always been a softening of the surly, angry expression he'd habitually shown to the world. And she remembered thinking how lovely it must be, to be tended with such devotion.

Laura hung her head. What must he think of her? That she was cheap and easy? She shuddered, wishing that she hadn't kissed him with such desperation. More than anything in the world, she wanted him to like and admire her. It baffled her why that should be.

Trying to unravel to mystery, she stole little glances at him, compelled to look, driven to gaze on him so often that he might have been her lover.

She stopped breathing for a moment. Lovers couldn't tear their eyes away from one another. *Love*... Could that explain the huge swelling sensation in her chest? The feeling that her mind had been electrified by a thousand volt charge? That she wanted to bury herself in him, to hold him and never let go?

Her muscles tensed. The extent of her passion was terrifying. Hot and trembling, she slid off her jacket after a

complicated manoeuvre with the seat belt. And her senses
screamed when Cassian's helping hand brushed her bare
arm.

'I can manage!' she croaked.

'I'm sure you can,' he replied in a low and husky voice.
'But it would have been bad manners not to have come to
your aid.'

'Sorry,' she muttered, feeling awful for snapping at him.

'It's OK. I imagine you're a bit preoccupied thinking
about the jobs you've been offered,' he said generously.
'I'll leave you in peace.'

Peace! If only!

There was a brief touch of his hand on hers. She almost
clasped it and gave it a fierce squeeze. Instead, she merely
trembled.

Horrified, she realised that she was utterly infatuated
with a man she hardly knew. A ridiculous situation.

Except…she felt as if she did know him. Perhaps she'd
had these feelings before—when they were younger. She
frowned. When he and Bathsheba had left Thrushton, had
her sense of loss been so heart-wrenching because she'd
believed herself to be in *love* with Cassian? Even at the
age of fifteen?

And…had she unwittingly carried a torch for him all
these years, perhaps even flinging herself at the salesman
from Leeds because he too was dark and travelled about
the country and had an air of independence like Cassian's?

Restless with the significance of her half-formed
thoughts, she crossed her legs. And noticed his eyes lingering on the curve of her thigh. Her heart beat faster. Then
she told herself that all men looked at legs. What she
wanted, was a man who was interested in her. And that was
highly unlikely where Cassian was concerned.

Anger set her eyes flashing and a fierce shaft of longing
tightened her entire body. She wanted him with a ferocity
of purpose that she'd never known before. Yet sheer com-

mon sense told her that at the best she'd be a woman to
kiss and fondle. Nothing more. Nothing deep and lasting.

And in only a few days they would part, perhaps never
to see one another again. She felt frantic at the thought, her
heart cramping now that they were drawing up to the school
to wait for Adam. It was all too late. Cassian would for
ever remain a man she adored, his heart untouched.

Overcome with misery, she flung open the door and
jumped out, her pulses thumping chaotically. It felt as if
her life was disintegrating into tiny pieces. She knew at
that moment that she had fallen headlong in love with
Cassian.

It was a certain and instant knowledge. She'd always
dreamed of being in love. But in her dreams her love had
been returned and her lover had proposed marriage. She
had imagined a Happy Ever After scenario but life wasn't
like that. It was cruel and kicked you down whenever you
got to your feet. One step forwards, two steps back.

Cassian had released her emotions; making her angry,
afraid and defiant. With the opening of the flood gates, her
passion for love had been also released from its prison of
restraint, and she had joyfully emptied her heart to him.

But if you stuck your head above the parapet, there was
a chance that you might get wounded. And wounded she
was.

Choking back the sobs, she stood in forlorn silence, steel-
ing herself to the fact that for the rest of her days she'd
never find another man to match Cassian.

She loved him. Wanted him. But knew, with a sense of
utter desolation, how hopeless her desires were.

CHAPTER EIGHT

LATER, she changed out of her finery and after a monosyllabic evening she sat pretending to read in the sitting room, while a silent and thoughtful Cassian sat opposite working on his laptop computer.

After school, he'd touched her heart still further by taking Adam for a walk then helping him with his homework and cooking supper. Steak and chips. Treacle sponge. Which Adam helped to make. Then treating Adam to a thrilling bed-time story, all off the top of his head.

Why did he have to be so flaming perfect?! she thought crossly. She was useless. OK, she conceded, maybe she'd landed those jobs and everyone had seemed more than anxious to have her on their staff... That was quite an achievement...

'You've been deep in thought for hours. I suppose you must have decided by now,' Cassian said quietly.

His eyes bored into her and she dropped her startled gaze in case he saw her naked adoration.

'Not yet. Toss up between the legal secretary and admissions clerk in the clinic,' she fudged, having hardly given them a thought at all.

'You must have been a brilliant interviewee.' His gaze held hers and she tried not to sink into a jellied heap but his voice was soft and dark as chocolate and persisted in rippling through her in silky rivers. 'Now do you believe me when I say you can do anything you want, if you want it badly enough?'

She smiled sadly. If only he knew what she really wanted! 'I hope that's true! But my references helped. People said some kind things about me.'

'They told the truth. Anyone can see how genuine you are; that you're honest and sincere and totally trustworthy,' he said quietly. 'It's plain that you'd be a conscientious and dedicated worker, and wouldn't contemplate giving anything less than one hundred per cent to your work.' He laughed at her open-mouthed amazement. 'I'm not kidding! Workers like you are few and far between. You have rare qualities, Laura.'

'Well, they only became apparent when I wore decent clothes,' she pointed out wryly, intoxicated by his words. Rare! She felt delirious from his praise.

'They got you noticed, I go along with that. Unfortunately people pay attention to appearances. But you won those job offers on your own merit so don't put yourself down. It's quite an achievement.'

She felt her breathing rate increase as hope spilled into her dulled brain. What had Cassian said? Something about applying yourself? If she wanted him to notice her, to respect her—and she did, oh, how she did!—then she needed time. Which she didn't have. Unless she very quickly made herself indispensable.

He wouldn't love her, she had to accept that. But could she settle for mutual friendship? Adam would benefit so much from Cassian's strength.

Living with the man she loved—and keeping her adoration a secret—would be agony. But it was better than never seeing him again, and for Adam's sake she must do everything she could to ensure that they remained in the house.

Looking at him from under her brows, seeing his long limbs draped easily over the armchair, she felt every inch of her body becoming fluid with adoration.

Quite subtly, so he wouldn't realise, she'd have to produce such gorgeous meals and make life here so incredibly comfortable, that he wouldn't want her to leave—whatever he'd said about being able to manage for himself.

He'd love being looked after—providing, she warned herself, she didn't ever curtail his freedom.

'You look sad,' she said gently. 'Are you thinking of Jai?'

His eyes flicked to hers and then darted away, his expression bleaker than ever.

'Something else.'

She had to bite her tongue to stop herself from asking 'what'. He'd tell her if he wanted to—and it seemed he didn't. It felt as if he'd slapped her around the face. It was all very fine, being Rare, but that didn't stop her from being excluded from Cassian's inner life.

She wanted to call out *Look at me, I'm here! Talk to me, confide in me!* But she couldn't bear the prospect of rejection. He didn't need her, he'd made that plain.

Her idea wouldn't work, she thought, her fragile confidence wavering. She'd never be able to hold back because she loved him so much. The sensible thing would be to close down. To shut out her feelings and become detached.

Her mouth shaped into a stubborn line. But she didn't want to! She wanted it all—the house, the job, Cassian. *Impossible.* Her eyes filled with tears.

Dimly she heard the trilling of a mobile phone and hid her wet face with her hand in case he noticed that she was being a wimp again.

'Cassian here,' he murmured into the phone and she flinched at his warm, rich tones. 'Hi, Sheila!' he said enthusiastically and she flinched again, this time because she wanted to be greeted with delight like that. 'How's things?'

There was a long pause during which Cassian's brows drew close together and his expression became concerned. Tactfully, Laura rose and slipped into the kitchen, wondering who Sheila might be that she could elicit such affection from him at first, and then reach into his heart to cause that look of deep consternation.

What a cloth-head she was! she thought grumpily, stoically drying her eyes and beginning to set out the breakfast things. Sheila was probably gorgeous. With ninety-four-inch legs, a degree in astro-physics and a background of extensive world travel. Oh, how could she ever have imagined that Cassian would give a damn about her—friend or otherwise?

And supposing he did, what then? They were too different for any relationship to blossom. She'd witnessed a similar disaster between her father and Bathsheba—and they'd been madly in love.

Little Miss Mouse, terrified of her own shadow, living on another planet to Cassian... The tears seeped inexorably upwards, clogging her throat.

'I'm going to bed.'

He'd spoken from the hall, his voice tight with strain. Scowling, she shot a quick look at him, surprised to see how defeated he looked.

Whatever Sheila had said, it had shattered him. Laura swallowed and furiously tried to stem the newly threatening tears. She wanted to affect him like that!

'Night,' she muttered, hoping he'd stay and tell her what troubled him.

He didn't move. It seemed as if all the stuffing had gone out of him. Her body ached with the yearning to run over and enclose him in a hug. But that wasn't her way.

'I'm going into Harrogate tomorrow,' he said flatly. 'Do you want a lift?'

So she wasn't to be his confidante. Bereft, Laura slammed the marmalade on the table.

'No. I'm shopping for Mr Walker.'

'What?'

Conscious that he was barely listening to her, she dealt out cutlery with unusual carelessness. Her life was one long round of fun, she didn't think.

'I told you about him. He's the one I shop for.'' Seeing he was still staring blankly into space, she felt compelled to let off steam. 'He's smelly and bad-tempered and he does nothing but moan and complain. I walk the two miles to Grassington, get everything he wants, walk the two miles back laden with bags, unload his shopping while he pretends I've got the wrong variety and have spent too much, and then I make him a cup of tea, settle him in his chair with a rug around him and we watch TV for an hour together. That's my excitement for the week. That's what I am,' she said with a sob. 'Miss Exciting. I really know how to live life, don't I? No doubt you're *riveted*!'

'Laura!' he cried, his brow furrowed in bewilderment. 'You're upset! Why—?'

'It doesn't matter!' she snapped, turning her back on him.

He pushed her around to face him again but she jerked her head to one side. Unfortunately her tears betrayed her and he gave a sigh then held her in his embrace.

'It does matter.'

'Only to me! And d-don't ask me if it's that time of the month,' she snuffled, 'because I'll scream!'

Cassian merely held her tighter. 'It's been an emotional few days for you,' he murmured in her ear. 'I would be surprised if you *weren't* on a roller-coaster.'

His hand lightly stroked her hair. It was a lovely sensation and she relaxed into him. But, to her dismay, he gently moved back.

'I didn't mean what I said about Mr Walker,' she mumbled. 'I do care. It's an awful life for him being confined to his house.'

'How long have you been doing all this for him?' Cassian asked quietly.

'I don't know. Ever since his wife died. I used to help her do her hair. She had arthritis in her fingers.'

Cassian drew in a long and hard breath. He seemed to be thinking about something and while he did, his finger lazily toyed with her fringe. She froze, afraid that any movement she made might make him stop.

'How badly do you want one of those jobs, Laura?' he asked hesitantly.

Blue eyes met brown. 'Desperately. I need a job to survive, you know that! How else can I afford champagne?' she jerked.

He smiled at her brave joke, took out his handkerchief and handed it to her. 'There's another job you might be interested in.'

'Sounds like an embarrassment of riches,' she commented, handing back the handkerchief.

Cassian pulled out a chair for her and sat nearby. Absently he rearranged the higgledy-piggledy cutlery in front of him and she waited, realising that he was searching for a way to tell her something.

'I…have a friend. A very good friend—'

'Sheila,' she hazarded.

How good, how friendly? her mind was demanding. Very? Bed friendly? Snuggle up together and exchange personal secrets kind of friendly?

He nodded. 'She runs a charitable organisation. Handing out money to deserving causes.'

Cassian's friend *and* with a wonderful job! Lucky Sheila. 'I envy her,' she said with a sigh.

Cassian felt his pulses race. She'd be perfect. Honest, reliable, conscientious and warm-hearted, with a love of humanity and a desire to help people in need. There was no one else he could turn to at such short notice. And yet common sense was telling him this would increase her involvement with him…

'She's had to give it up,' he said, pushing the words out before he got cold feet. The charity had to come first, whatever his doubts. 'She's flying to the States to look after her three nieces. Her sister and brother-in-law were killed in a car crash yesterday.'

'Cassian!' Laura cried in horror. 'That's terrible! The

poor little kiddies. Poor woman! Is someone with her? Do you need to go with her?'

She was holding his hand, giving him comfort. He could feel the firmness of her grip, the roughness of her work-worn fingers and somehow her concern was making his heart tighten as if it were in a vice.

'No. Her partner has gone with her. But…Laura, she's frantic about leaving the charity in a lurch. It's a small operation but it needs someone at its helm, someone who can be trusted not to misappropriate funds. People like that are hard to get—particularly at short notice.'

'I imagine so,' she said in concern.

Amazing, he thought. She had no idea of her qualities. Even now she had no idea that he was alluding to her. He took a deep breath, his passion for the charity overruling any personal wariness.

'Laura, I told her she could go immediately because I knew someone who could do the job.'

She smiled sadly. 'That's great. Sheila must have been relieved—'

'You,' he said. 'I thought of you at once.'

Her eyes widened, the spiky wet lashes blinking furiously. He wanted to kiss her. To take her to bed. He snatched away his hands and she looked upset at his rejection, her lush mouth trembling.

'You can't mean me! You can't be suggesting I take her place!'

He tried to keep his head—even if his body had decided to betray him and go off the rails. He cleared his throat and wondered if he had a cold coming.

'Who better? I've just set up an office for the charity in Harrogate—'

'Well, there you are. That lets me out. How do I get there? It's impossible, Cassian!'

His heartbeat quickened. She'd sounded deeply disappointed. 'You would commute, and get in whatever time you can. There aren't any rules attached to this job. Or I could drive you in sometimes. Then *you* will learn to drive. The charity will supply you with a car.'

Wistfully she said, 'And when Adam's ill?'

'No problem,' he said firmly. 'Much of the time—when he's ill, or if you have something special you need to do at home, you can operate from the house—'

'Sure. With no phone, no computer—'

'You're determined to find obstacles,' he said, amused. 'A phone line can be installed. This isn't the Sahara Desert. In the meantime you can use a mobile. The charity will set you up with everything you need, including a computer at home, plus anything else you need.'

'But…the cost—!'

'—would be a drop in the ocean. Particularly if the position goes to someone reliable and honest. There are a lot of sharks about. Money is a huge temptation and whoever runs this charity has carte blanche to sign cheques for massive amounts of cash. Appointing the right person is a real headache.'

'But…wouldn't you like the job?' she asked, puzzled.

'Me?' He hesitated. 'I'm…already employed.'

'Oh. I thought you must be looking for something. You've only just come from Morocco and you haven't exactly joined the 9—5 brigade,' she explained, looking excited at the prospect of landing the job.

'I…took time off.'

'What do you do?' she asked eagerly.

'Computer work. Laura, never mind me. What do you think?'

She chewed her lip. 'I don't know. It's a huge responsibility. I'm not sure I could do it—'

'You could! Listen. There's a fund. The income from its investments can be spent every year. Applications come in and the fund director—you—'

'Me? A fund director?' she asked, pink and beaming.

He laughed. 'That's what you'd be. And you'd sort through the applications, interview people from the charities applying, and write a cheque to those you think worthy, honest and with sound business plans. Simple. A matter of judgement. The salary would be at least double that of the jobs you've been offered—'

'Good grief! I couldn't take that much!' she protested. 'Not from a charity—'

'For heaven's sake, Laura!' he said impatiently. 'Value yourself! You'd earn it, I can assure you!'

'Well,' she said with a huge smile. 'I can always give the extra away, can't I?'

Typical. The people with least money were the most generous. He desperately wanted her to be financially secure.

'You'll do the job?' he asked, hardly daring to breathe.

'Don't I have to be interviewed? See a board of directors or something?' she asked with a frown.

'I told you. Sheila runs it. The directors are…kind of sleeping. She's left the matter of her replacement in my hands.'

'Why? What's your connection with the charity?'

'I contribute to it on a regular basis,' he said, omitting to tell her he was the only contributor.

She sighed. 'You are so generous. And, judging by the state of your four-wheel drive, you're not rolling in money.'

This wasn't the time to say he wasn't bothered about material goods and if a car moved, then he was happy with it.

'I get by,' he said blithely. 'Forget me. Say you'll do the job. It'll be a load off my mind and I know you'll be cracking at it.'

'I can't believe this! Yes, yes, I'd *love* to. Absolutely adore it!' she replied, her eyes shining brilliantly.

'Fantastic! Thank you!'

In sheer relief he caught her hands and grinned at her, completely bowled over by the delight on her face. Somehow they had moved closer and her lips were recklessly within reach. There was nothing in his lungs, not one breath. The very air seemed suspended as slowly he leaned towards her, a centimetre at a time so that she didn't take fright.

Her eyelids closed, her face lifted and he felt his heart soar as if he were being lifted on a thermal. Gently he placed a hand behind her head and let his lips touch hers. She quivered throughout the length of her body.

'Thanks,' he muttered.

The sweetness of her smile, the tenderness of her gaze, created mayhem in his head. This wasn't happening to him. Mustn't happen.

'I want to kiss you again,' he said with reckless disregard for sanity.

Solemn and painfully beautiful, she seemed to sink more deeply into his arms.

'It would be very unwise,' she said, encouragingly unsteady.

'Why?' he asked, his voice as thick and slow as a treacle.

'Because I'm going at the end of the week.'

His teeth clamped together. He had the impression that she was angling for an alteration to their arrangement. But if she stayed much longer than the next few days, he'd seduce her. And he must not do that. She was too precious, too vulnerable to handle a brief relationship. But a kiss or two would be all right.

'All the more reason to kiss you before you leave,' he murmured, pushing back the knowledge that he was deliberately deceiving himself.

She looked confused. 'Why do you want to kiss me?'

Cassian bit back an exclamation. He'd never been interrogated like this before! Trust Laura. He smiled at her, his finger running down the side of her soft cheek. She gave a little gasp and he knew she longed to let go. It would be good for her, he rationalised. A release of passion. Hell—it would be good for him too!

'Your mouth,' he husked recklessly, 'is soft and warm and far too near for me to ignore it. I like its taste. I like holding you in my arms…like your scent, the way your body yields, responds, matches mine for passion…'

She surrendered. With a series of little sighs, she let her lashes flutter down and allowed her lips to part. Gently he pulled her close. Felt her heart beating hard against his chest. The exquisite softness of her high, fast-heaving breasts and the tight hardness of her nipples, apparent even beneath the material of her shirt.

His head began to whirl. She wore no bra. It would take just a movement of his hand and…

He swallowed, checking himself ruthlessly. A kiss. Nothing more.

'You're so beautiful,' he breathed.

Her eyes snapped open, startlingly blue so close to his. 'What?'

The lightest of kisses. 'Beautiful.' Another one, delicate, whispering, tantalising every inch of his body with the effort of denial. 'Beautiful.'

'Oh!' she sighed in bliss.

He had no reason to be doing this except for sheer sensual pleasure. And pleasure it was. The smell of her, the feel of her hair beneath his fingers, the way she fitted him…

And he was using her. It wasn't fair. Wasn't right. Somehow he must extract himself from this situation without hurting her. Hell. Oh, hell, hell, hell.

Just a little more, a voice was telling him. A few kisses, a little more passion, the pressure of her mouth infinitely irresistible, the winding of her arms around his neck all that he could have wished for.

Against his chest her nipples were rock-hard now and

her mouth had become more daring, exploring his with a thoroughness that thrilled and unnerved him.

He had to get out of this, he thought hazily, crushing her closer. Willpower, that's all it took. All! When his entire body throbbed, his blood pounded so loudly in his ears that he couldn't have heard if she'd yelled, when his heart was in danger of going into cardiac arrest and his hunger had never, never been so desperate...

Somehow—who knew how?—he gentled their kisses, moving a fraction of an inch back each time. And wondered how he could do this when she was as hungry as he, willing, dizzy with desire...

'You,' he croaked, like a rusty hinge, 'are gorgeous.'

Her smile was intoxicating, lighting up her whole face. He couldn't leave it like this. She'd imagine this was the beginning of a courtship.

Cassian cursed himself for succumbing. It had been a mistake. Cruel.

He could hardly breathe. Certainly couldn't walk yet. He'd ache for hours.

'I know I shouldn't have done that,' he admitted hoarsely. 'But I can't say I'm sorry. I hope I haven't offended you...' A slight movement told him that she was moving away, both mentally and physically. 'I just had to kiss you,' he confessed with all honesty. 'An impulse. I was grateful—delighted that you'll take on the charity. And...you looked so lovely. Hope you understand. Forgive me?'

His eyes pleaded with her, begging her not to be hurt. Like an angel, she accepted his reasons, saw nothing evil in what he'd done. Perhaps because there had been no evil intended.

Her slow and seraphic smile mesmerised him. 'I understand.' Her eyes lowered, her mouth mischievous. 'It was a thrilling moment and it bowled me over,' she murmured. He tensed, every nerve in his body straining. And then he was stunned by his intense disappointment when she added demurely, 'To be offered such a wonderful, worthwhile job.'

'My gosh! You look terrible!' Laura said in amusement, when he staggered in from his run with Adam the next morning. 'Unshaven, bleary-eyed…what *have* you been doing?!'

'Bad night.'

'Why's that? Bed uncomfortable?' she asked innocently.

He was rescued by Adam. 'Race you to the shower!' Adam crowed, already leaping upstairs in his socks.

But Cassian didn't take up the challenge. He unpicked his laces, put his boots beside Adam's and slumped in a chair.

Now, mused Laura, usefully pouring him a black coffee, is this a man who's sexually frustrated and has spent the whole night trying to stop his hormones holding him to ransom?

She smiled a little smile of triumph. She did hope so! And she hugged her glee to herself that—for a brief time— he had found her mouth quite irresistible.

'I'm doing scrambled eggs. Shall I add some for you?' she asked serenely.

'Uh. Please.'

Grumpy and haggard and bemused. Looking at her legs again, slowly surveying her rear, her breasts… Her eyes gleamed. He was interested. He did like her. Respected her enough to offer her a high value job. That had meant a lot to her. And to top it all, she was both rare *and* gorgeous.

Her mirror that morning had agreed. After a deep, utterly contented sleep, she had woken to find someone else looking back at her—a confident, sparkling-eyed woman who oozed vitality.

She sang happily to herself, adding a few home-grown chives and tiny tomatoes from the garden to a buttered dish and slipping them in the oven to grill. For the first time, she really believed that she could achieve her life-long dream. Her voice strengthened, bursting with joy, the notes clear and true, every inch of her body surrendering to happiness.

Cassian slowly stumbled out of the kitchen, his tread heavy and laboured on the stairs. Her singing grew louder, more ecstatic.

It took Mr Walker only a short time, however, to bring her down to earth again. Morose and uncommunicative, Cassian had acted as chauffeur so that she could do Mr Walker's shopping and then be free to investigate the office in Harrogate.

'I hope you don't mind,' she said hesitantly, when the old man opened the door, 'but I've brought—'

'Cassian!' Mr Walker cried in delight. 'Cassian!' he added with soft affection.

Laura was open-mouthed when Cassian strode forwards and gave Mr Walker a gentle bear hug.

'Tom,' he said fondly. 'You old reprobate! Sitting around like Lord Muck, and letting a tame dolly bird do all your shopping…you ought to be ashamed of yourself!' he teased.

'Man's gotta get what pleasures he can at my age,' chuckled the old man. 'Sight of those legs of Laura's sets me up for the whole day!'

Blushing, the astonished Laura went into the tiny kitchen and began to unpack the groceries, oddly pleased that there was some kind of bond between the two men.

'You know each other, then,' she commented when they both appeared, Cassian with his arm around Mr Walker's frail, shawl-wrapped shoulders.

'Go a long way back.' The old man eased himself painfully into the rocking chair by the iron stove. 'Cassian used to come here when he was a lad. We went fishing together. My Doris lent him books. Great reader, my Doris.

Devoured encyclopaedias, Cassian did… Hang on a minute, lass!' he protested. 'That's not proper ham!'

'It's what you always have,' she said calmly, conscious of Cassian, dark-eyed and silent in the corner.

Mr Walker muttered under his breath, picking over his supplies for the week. 'I've told you I don't like big oranges. And those sprouts look manky. Useless woman,' he goaded, picking up the bill and glaring at it. 'You bring me rubbish and there's twopence more on the bill?' he snapped.

'I know,' she said with a sigh. 'I'm awfully sorry—'

'You're on the wrong track,' Cassian said to Tom Walker, suddenly alert. 'Try attacking something she cares about.'

Mr Walker's watery eyes narrowed. She thought there was the suspicion of a smile on his sour face before he said in contempt,

'Her? She's a waste of space. And her kid's as dopey—'

'Don't you dare talk about my son like that!' she flared, her eyes scorching with anger. 'I can take your bad temper and your ingratitude because I feel sorry for you but Adam's off limits! *Do you understand?*' she yelled, banging the table so hard that the vegetables jumped in shock and rolled to the floor.

To her astonishment, Mr Walker grinned so hard that his toothless gums showed. Cassian was laughing.

'Now *that's* your mother talking!' cackled Mr Walker.

She froze. *'What?'* she ground out furiously.

'I've bin trying for years to get you angry, lass!' he wheezed, tears of laughter running down his face. 'Wanted to see if you'd got your ma's fire in your belly. Almost gave up. All you did was apologise like you was made of milk and water. But you're like her all right,' he said more gently. 'More life in her than most. Lovely woman. Miss her, something chronic, I do.'

She sat down, her legs weak. 'You…you devious, mean

old man!' she said shakily but she couldn't hide her pleasure. 'Am I…am I really like her?'

'Spitting image. Beautiful, she was. Had a temper on her,
though.'

'Tell me!' she begged. 'I know nothing about her, nothing! Please! Tell me the circumstances surrounding my
birth. Everything.'

'Well, I'm blowed. I thought you knew *that*. Well, let's
see. I know George Morris didn't treat her right. Bullied
her. Any fool could see how unhappy she was and that she
longed to be loved proper, like. Anyroad, she fell headlong
in love with the American who took over Killington Manor,
down the dale just beyond Little Sturton, where I worked
as a groom. Found she was pregnant—and George hadn't
touched her for over a year. But, proud devil that he was,
he wouldn't agree to a divorce so she tried her level best
to settle back into her marriage. Doomed, it was, though.'

'My…father was…American?' she said faintly.

'S'right. Nice chap,' said Mr Walker. 'Jolly sort—'

'More!' she begged. 'I want to know more!'

'More, eh? He was tall, dark, smiling eyes, if you know
what I mean. Easy-going hospitable type. Publisher. Crazy
about your mother, but then few could resist her lovely
nature.'

'All this time I've known you…why…*why* didn't you
tell me all this?' she wailed.

'Thought you knew bits and pieces, lass. When I realised
you didn't have much of a clue, I thought I'd better keep
my trap shut. Not my business to interfere. Wasn't sure you
were tough enough to hear the truth.'

'They didn't speak about her mother,' Cassian explained.
'It was a taboo subject.'

'But…*you* knew!' she stormed at him.

'Yes,' he admitted. 'But until you told me a few days
ago that Thrushton Hall was the only link you had with
your mother, it had never occurred to me that they hadn't

told you the basic facts, or that you had no tangible memories of her—photos, possessions…I still can't believe they'd do that to you! Poor Laura. This is outrageous…'

Clearly upset, he put his arm around her shoulders. Gratefully she leaned into him, touched by his anger on her behalf. She felt nothing but contempt for George and Enid's refusal to explain her background.

'But why did my…' She checked herself. Never again would she call George Morris 'father'. 'Why did George get custody?'

'Because everyone thought you were his child,' Cassian said gently.

Laura felt a sickening sensation clutch at her stomach.

'Didn't my *real* father claim me? She must have gone to him, surely? Didn't they run away together? Didn't they want me?' she asked miserably.

The old man looked uncertainly at Cassian, who brought her close to him as if protecting her.

'She can deal with it,' he said in low, quiet tones.

Laura's hopes collapsed. 'Oh, no!' she groaned. 'You're not telling me they're…*dead*?'

Mr Walker's eyes were gentle, his expression loving and full of regret.

'Both of them, lass. Her and the American. It was filthy weather. Tractor came out of a field and into the Harrogate road and killed them outright two weeks after you were born. He was bringing you and your mother back to Killington Manor to live with him. George Morris brought you up as his daughter and only a few of us knew the truth.'

A sob escaped her. She had been so close to having a truly loving home. And her mother had been denied the happiness she'd hoped for.

It was unbelievably sad. Laura gave a moan and flung her arms around Cassian's waist for solace.

'They never said!' she mumbled. 'All these years I privately feared that she'd rejected me, *abandoned* me—led on by heavy hints from George and Enid. Oh, that was cruel, Cassian, cruel!'

She burst into floods of tears. There were years of weeping inside her but the two men just held her and patted her and waited while she mourned the parents she'd never known.

Dimly she became aware that the men had been talking for a while.

'...say goodbye properly. Got a map, Tom?' she heard Cassian ask quietly.

A map! She felt indignant but kept her head buried in his middle hearing the rustle of paper. Cassian wanted to look at a route to somewhere, when she...

'Just there,' said Tom Walker. 'That little lane...'

'And the gate?' Cassian asked softly.

Her heart turned over. Guilt swept through her as she realised what Cassian was doing. Bless him, she thought. Bless him.

'Take me there!' She pleaded, choking and hoarse, the words disappearing into his soft shirt.

His hand was infinitely gentle on the silk of her hair. 'Come,' he muttered, his voice cracking. 'We'll pick some flowers from the garden. We can make a lovely bunch for your mother from the roses, agastache, helenium, salvia...'

'And if you come round one day, both of you,' said Mr Walker kindly, 'we can have tea and talk about your parents, if you'd like. I'm very fond of you, pet,' he added. 'You're like a dear daughter to me.'

'I'd like,' she said in a small voice. And kissed him. Suddenly she felt overcome with emotion and her arms tightened about the skeletal frame and she held him tight. 'See you soon,' she whispered.

He nodded, his eyes filled with tears. 'Say hello to her from me,' he rasped. 'Good friend. Warm heart. Like you. I promised her, at her funeral, that I'd keep an eye on you. She'd be proud of you, Laura.'

She couldn't speak for emotion. In a blur she saw Cassian clasp Tom Walker's hand, an unspoken message of affection exchanging between them.

'Old times,' Cassian said softly. 'We have a lot of catching up to do, Tom. Till then.'

Gently he ushered Laura out of the door. His arm was around her as they walked along the street to the manor house, guiding her feet, holding her firmly when she stumbled because the tears were obliterating her vision.

But he stood back while she picked the flowers, knowing that this was something she needed to do on her own. These were her gift to her mother.

And even though he waited a yard or so away, his tenderness enfolded her, protecting her like a supporting blanket. Without him she would have broken down. With him, she felt she could cope.

'How did you know that Mr Walker was goading me?' she asked in a pitifully little voice.

'Partly because he's a kind man and I could see from his eyes that his heart wasn't in what he was doing, and partly because I'd been trying to do the same.'

Her eyes widened and accused him. 'Provoke me, you mean?'

'Sort of,' he confessed. 'When you talked about Adam, I could see that underneath you were a woman of deep passions and fierce beliefs. For your sake, Laura,' he said gently, 'I wanted you to find your guts before you were thrust into the world. It's a wonderful and exciting place. I wanted you to enjoy it.'

She heaved a sigh. The end of the week was a long way away at the moment.

'I'm finding my emotions all too easily,' she said jerkily. 'You're stripping away all my barriers and I'm left raw and open and hurt!'

His eyes softened. 'But you're in touch with your heart.'

'It's a painful process,' she muttered.

'There's joy too,' he promised.

'Really?' she mumbled, her face wan.

Because she wasn't sure she believed him. A chill went through her. Passion, she thought, gripped in an icy fear. Was it truly worth the anguish that came with it?

CHAPTER NINE

IT WAS a fifteen minute drive to the accident spot. For the rest of her life she would remember the powerful musky perfume of the roses in the confines of the car, and the comfort of Cassian's reassuring hand on hers when they finally reached the place Mr Walker had described.

'Wait. I'll help you out,' Cassian offered.

So kind and tender. He seemed to know instinctively what to do, what to say, when to be silent.

Her pulses drummed. Her face was almost as white as the mallow flowers in her hands. Shakily she clambered down and lifted her head up high.

Alone, she walked to the farm gate, thinking only of her mother's tragic death and of the American man who had been her mother's lover. Her father. A man she would have loved if she'd known him. What had he been like? She didn't know. She couldn't visualise him.

Her eyes filled with tears again. It was awful, not knowing either of her parents. She bit her lip. For most of her life she'd unwittingly lived a lie created by George and Enid Morris.

Fervently she asked for her mother's forgiveness for doubting her. Laura had been swayed by the endless falsehoods and half-truths. Cheated of her past, deceived, and twisted so that she fitted into a mould of George Morris's choosing.

She could have been lively and passionate and beautiful, given the chance. She might have been the kind of woman who flung her arms around people, like Sue, and breezed through life without hang-ups.

138

Her heritage had been taken away from her. And now she didn't know what kind of person she was.

And yet despite her sadness, Laura felt the inexorable beauty of her surroundings seeping into her. The lane ran along a valley, eroded long ago by the meltwater from an ice sheet. Close by were the remains of a medieval village, abandoned in the plague. Buttercups made the valley golden in the September sun. In early summer, she mused, the meadows would be a riot of colour, red clover, pignut and cranesbill vying with the buttercups and marguerites.

The high drystone walls were thick with lichen and moss and she reached out to touch the soft green mat covering the massive limestone rocks. Here in this lovely valley she could imagine her mother's spirit. Here she could find solace and comfort.

'I love you, Mum,' she husked, an overwhelmingly powerful emotion deepening her voice and making it shake. She didn't find it odd to be standing in a country lane and talking aloud. It seemed right and natural and it unburdened her heart. She took a deep breath and continued passionately. 'I wish I'd known you and Father! Wish I'd lived with you! Oh, I wanted that so badly. We could have been happy, the three of us.'

Again she thought how different she might have been. More open, less guarded, more ready to laugh and cry. Less afraid to show her love. To be loved.

Her heart aching, a hard, painful lump in her throat, she strewed the flowers about the lane and bowed her head while goldfinches chattered sweetly nearby.

'I'll make you really proud of me,' she promised. 'I won't let myself become like Aunt Enid: mean and caustic, critical and unfulfilled. I will go for happiness…follow my heart. I will hug people if I feel the urge. I won't let my life go to waste, I won't!' she sobbed. 'And I'll help Adam to be strong, now I know how. You'd love him, Mum, Dad…'

She couldn't speak for crying. It felt as if her heart was full of love and sorrow at the same time. It seemed to be expanding from where it had been lying cramped and afraid in her chest. Now it beat with her mother's blood, her father's passion. And she felt whole at last.

She shivered and a moment later she started when she felt a jacket being gently draped about her shoulders.

'You're cold. You've been here a long time,' Cassian said huskily.

Her forlorn, tear-washed face lifted to his, instinctively seeking something from him.

'Hold me,' she pleaded.

With a mutter of concern, he took her in his arms and let her squeeze him as hard as she could. After a moment the violent tensions in her muscles eased and she sagged against him.

'They…sound as if…they were lovely people,' she sniffed jaggedly.

'And you are their child. Remember that. You are like them,' he answered, stroking her back.

'That's a n-nice thing to s-say.'

'Just the truth,' he breathed into her hair. 'Perhaps now you can be yourself. Be free.'

The thought comforted her. She could start again. Despite her anguish, she felt an uplifting feeling. 'Can we walk?' she mumbled.

'Whatever you like, whatever you need. Hold my hand, you're shaking,' he said softly.

With infinite care, he helped her over a ladder stile and into the field beyond. For a long time they strolled quietly with just the plaintive cry of the lapwings eerily breaking the silence.

They found a sheltered spot to sit. They gazed at the view from high above the strip lynchets, the terraced fields which had been hacked out of the hillside centuries ago, even long before the Black Death in the fourteenth century which must have parted so many loved ones.

The wind ruffled her hair and brought sharp colour to her cheeks. This was her beloved Yorkshire. The place where her mother and father had fallen in love and where they had died. And she would do anything to stay here for the rest of her days on earth.

His hand gripped hers tightly. His eyes were like liquid velvet and she felt more cherished than she had in the whole of her life.

And for no reason at all, her tears suddenly cascaded down her face in torrents.

'Laura, Laura!' he whispered, turning her to him.

His lips touched her cheekbone then travelled around her face stopping each tear that fell. She felt a desperate need to be comforted by him, to lose herself in his kisses.

Lifting her mouth, she caught his face between her hands and let her eyes do the asking.

'Kiss me properly,' she moaned.

Cassian stared helplessly. 'Don't mistake what you're feeling,' he rasped. 'You're—'

'I want to be kissed!' she insisted.

'Because you want to be comforted.' He sounded bitter and his teeth were clenched together hard. 'I'll hold you, but I won't do more—'

'Why?' she demanded, shuddering with intense fervour.

'You'd regret it later, when you're not so distraught—'

'I won't!' she whispered, adoring his mouth, the smoothness of his face beneath her fingers.

Desperate to lose herself in his lovemaking, she explored his mouth with a thoroughness that shook her. She laced her fingers through his hair, subtly trapping him, her body pressing hard against his.

It was wonderful when he responded, a groan preceding his impassioned surrender to her wiles. They couldn't get enough of each other, their hands clutching, roaming, invading...

She was caught up in the intensity of her feelings, her mind closed to all but the sensations surging through her frantic body, everything centred on the need to touch Cassian, to be touched...loved, not to miss a moment of life and happiness.

If she loved him, and she did, she wasn't going to waste time being coy. She'd take what she wanted, be what she wanted, obey the call for love that was overriding everything else in her mind and body.

She was crying and gasping, moaning and panting just like him. His hands wove magic spells in her body, every part of her seemingly set alight by his caress.

Each breast quivered, bloomed, tightened unbearably from the gently erotic movement of his questing fingers. The heat of his loins burned into her till she thought she must have reached melting point.

At some time they must have sunk back to the ground. Here, her arms demanded, legs slithered urgently, pelvis arched in throbbing hunger. She was dimly aware that her mouth knew now every inch of his face and throat, the hard satin of his chest, the hollows of his stomach.

Her clothes had largely disappeared, like his, though when he—or she—had removed them she couldn't have said. Her desperation matched his. Her desire to kiss and touch every inch of him was echoed by his unstoppable ravishment.

The surface of her skin felt hot and tingling as if it had been electrified. Each of Cassian's fierce, impetuous kisses stirred her very blood and pushed her to a more intense state of excitement.

'I can't bear it!' she whispered, seeking without success to undo his belt.

She felt him kick away her skirt, and, unhampered, she wound her legs about him so that she could drive her pelvis harder into his body and ease some of the terrible need within her.

His mouth swooped on hers, enclosing, warm and almost frantic in its kisses. The pressure of his hand cupped around the cleft between her legs and even through her small cotton briefs she could feel the heat, the glorious movement of the heel of his hand. And then, with a wriggle, she had ensured he touched her flesh.

'Ohhhhh…'

'Laura!' he croaked.

Her loving hand stroked his face, her eyes anxiously encouraging him.

'Please,' she whispered.

'I—this is not right…I—'

'I need you, Cassian!' she rasped. And touched him.

His eyes closed as he did battle with himself. Gently she moved her hand, feeling the leap of power beneath her fingers.

'No, no, no…' he moaned.

'You told me to live!' she whispered, slipping her tongue between his lips. 'I am living. This is what I want. Love me. *Love me!*' she moaned into his mouth.

She mimicked the act of making love, her own body so aroused that she wondered how it could still obey her. But then she was operating on instinct. And love.

Cassian tore his mouth away, his face strained. 'But afterwards—'

'Forget afterwards. This is now,' she said fiercely.

She took his hand, let his fingers meet the throbbing bud between her legs and uttered a long, low moan of pleasure. This was what she'd longed for. Physical release with the man she loved.

The ecstasy in her body was nothing to the joy in her head, her heart and her soul. Cassian would possess her. She would know him and he would know her. If she died tomorrow, she would have been a part of him.

He could feel her mouth bruising his. Heard the little gasps and moans, the outrush of her sweet breath as he rhythmically caressed her. The beauty of her body had stunned him.

The soft mounds of her breasts met his mouth and her nipples rose obediently to his gentle suckling as she bucked and shuddered beneath his arousing fingers.

Too far…he'd gone too far to step back. It terrified him, this sensation of losing total control, of being unable to master his passion. What had she woken in him? he thought, slipping further from reality, mesmerised by the alluring Laura, by her sublime eyes, her hungry mouth and fabulous, irresistible body.

Quite helpless, driven by something he didn't understand, he clawed at his belt and managed by accident rather than luck to undo it. In a moment they were both naked. Flesh to flesh. He trembled, intoxicated by the sensation.

'Are…' He tried again, swallowing back the choking emotion. Pausing only briefly to wonder what was happening to him. 'Are…you…sure?'

There was a beauty about her face, as it swam beneath him, that made his heart turn over. Her dreamy smile dazzled him, leaving him blind.

'Sure,' she breathed. 'More sure than I've ever been.'

A volcano was threatening to burst inside him but he caressed her gently, taking his time till her pleas were so loud and insistent that he knew she was more than ready.

A sense of wonder flooded his mind as he gently eased into her, their bodies sliding so naturally together that they had surely been made for one another.

And then his world exploded. All he knew was that something unbelievable was occurring, a scattering of his senses and a fierce high voltage arousal of every cell in his body.

A storm erupted in his head. Sweet torment surrounded every nerve, tugging and caressing, thrilling and teasing until he didn't know where he was or what he was do-ing…only that this was lovemaking at its most awe-inspiring and this was love with Laura and he never wanted it to end…

The pounding in his ears blotted out her cries—or were they his?—and his body erupted in a wild release of joy and pleasure. Warmth flooded him. And a deep, intense peace.

Her hands moved lazily over his back. Still in a state of disbelief, she smiled to herself. This was why people be-came obsessed with one another, then! Her heart was soar-ing. As free as that bird she could see high up in the sky…a lark, surely?

Now she fully understood her mother. When you found true love and a passion that matched your own, it was hard to deny. She was so happy. Madly, hugely, ferociously!

'Cassian,' she whispered into his ear.

'Mmm.'

She wound her arms around his neck. He lifted his head which had been buried in her neck and looked at her as if he was drunk. Her eyes shone, her adoration plain for him to see.

'Is it…always like that!' she asked, not sure if she could physically bear such sweet torment too often.

He kissed her soft mouth. 'Hardly ever,' he said wryly. 'What did you do, Laura? Drug me?'

She laughed and kissed him back. No. She'd only loved him. Given him everything. 'Good, was I?' she asked smugly.

His eyes darkened till they were like glittering black onyx.

'Sensational,' he growled.

She was going under again; the desire flaring up from the igniting of his body moving over hers. Her eyes closed, all the better to enjoy the unbearably slow, rhythmical strokes inside her and the delicious sensations chasing on and in and through each part of her.

'Cassian,' she murmured and slithered sensually against him, provoking him with her body, biting him, enjoying the tension of his muscles under her sensitive hands.

'Sweet Laura,' he said hoarsely, kissing her throat.

The little stabs of energy began to thrust at her and she let them take her over, revelling that she could abandon herself without fear. She trusted Cassian. And so she could dare to behave freely.

''Swunnerful,' she slurred, clinging to him.

He flipped her over, hauled her up, cupped her heavy breasts in awe and flicked his tongue over each engorged nipple. Then his hands pressed on her hips till she felt the deepest, most incredible completion of herself.

And she began to move, watching his face, seeing the infinite pleasure she could give him, aroused beyond belief by the blissful expression on his beloved face.

The climax came hot and fast, rushing up to take her unawares. It shot her up to a pinacle of sensation and then slowly released her, till she found herself safe and warm in the welcome of Cassian's strong arms.

It was a while before he dressed her. Tired and bemused, she let him do so, offering a leg or an arm like a docile child. She was far to 'high' to do anything for herself.

This was emotion—and she loved it, she mused, as his handsome face contorted with a frown while he tried to manoeuvre her skirt over her hips. With a sigh, she lifted her pelvis. Their eyes locked. Hot passion spilled between them, Cassian kissed her, hard.

'I can't leave you alone!' he muttered.

'Good,' she crowed.

'No, it's not…'

'Why?' She lifted her arms over head, intentionally provocative.

'Please, Laura!' he groaned. 'We have to get back. Harrogate's off, but you'll need to be home for Adam.'

'Is it that late?' she said in stunned surprise.

'We seem to have missed lunch,' he said, amused.

'No, we didn't!' she laughed and he kissed her tenderly.

In a daze they stumbled back to the car. Laura paused for a moment in the lane, trying to visualise her mother as someone alive and vital and very much in love, very loved, chattering happily as her lover drove her and their baby to Killington Manor.

Her mother would have been happy. As happy as she, Laura, was now. A long sigh escaped her parted lips. Today she had found great sorrow and great joy. This, she vowed, would be a relationship that would survive.

'Do you want to be alone?' Cassian asked with typical tact.

They were holding hands and she gave his a quick squeeze of thanks.

'No.' She didn't ever want to be alone again. 'Thank you for bringing me here. Let's go home,' she said, deeply content.

'Tom has told me where your parents' graves are,' Cassian said quietly. 'I'll take you there. And I think Adam should come too.'

She was overcome with gratitude. 'Thank you,' she said again.

They met Adam from school and took him to the small churchyard in a small village beyond Killington Manor, close to the river. Gently Laura told him about his grandparents while Cassian checked the gravestones.

'Here,' he said, holding out his hands to them.

Laura's heart pounded. She swallowed and gripped Adam's small hand in hers. Cassian enfolded them both in his arms, shepherding them towards a small, nondescript stone above an untended grave.

'I can't read it!' she mumbled, her eyes awash.

'It says…"Here lie Jack Eden and Diana Morris",' Cassian said huskily. 'Then there are the dates…and below it is written; "tragically taken from this world but together in the next." Tom Walker had that stone put up,' he told Laura. 'There was a scandal because George and Enid wouldn't pay for the funeral but those who worked at Killington had a whip-round for it. The house was sold and incorporated into your father's estate. Since your father hadn't changed his will, everything went to some distant cousin in New York. Tom was upset that you had nothing. He has watched over you ever since.'

'People are so kind!' she said shakily. 'I don't mind about the money. I have so much, compared with others.'

'Don't cry, Mum!' begged Adam.

She hugged him hard. 'I'm sad and I'm happy. Do you understand, darling?'

His big blue eyes softened. 'Yes, I do, Mum. I'm sorry they're dead. I'd have liked grandparents. But I'm glad they didn't abandon you.' His skinny arms wrapped tightly around her. 'I love you, Mum,' he said fiercely. 'Everything'll be all right now.'

She smiled and met Cassian's infinitely tender eyes. 'Yes,' she breathed, kissing her son's fair head. 'I think it will.'

That evening, when supper and the run and homework were all dealt with, all three of them sat on the sofa together and talked. And when Adam had gone sleepily up to bed, she curled up in Cassian's arms watching a documentary on TV.

Occasionally he kissed her. But most of the time it was enough that they were close. He was wonderful, she thought happily. And he seemed compelled to touch her. Not sexually, but just small touches; a stroke of her hand, the brush of his fingers down the side of her cheek, the increased pressure of his arm around her waist for no particular reason.

In her book, that meant one thing. Whether he knew it or not, he was rapidly finding he couldn't do without her. She hoped that was true. All her hopes were pinned on that fact.

'I wish I could take you to bed,' he growled in her ear.

'Well, you can't,' she said, secretly delighted with his regret.

'I know. It's torture. I want to fall asleep with you in my arms, to wake and find you beside me.'

'Me, too!' she whispered, overjoyed that he wanted her presence as much as she wanted his.

'I'll take you to the office tomorrow,' he rasped. 'And I will make love to you as you've never known it before.' Abruptly he stood up. 'I must go now, Laura,' he said, desperately running his hands through his hair. 'See you in the morning.'

She couldn't believe it. He needed her very badly. And everything he said suggested that it wasn't just sex but something deeper. Hopefully more lasting.

Walking on air, she floated off to bed and fell into a contented sleep the moment her head touched the pillow.

CHAPTER TEN

'THE blue or the green?' she asked the next morning in the Harrogate office, waving silky scraps of froth, which were masquerading as panties.

'Breen. Glue…Laura!' groaned Cassian, when she gurgled in delight at his confusion. 'My brain doesn't work when you prance around like that.'

'Like what?' She pranced. Tried a little modified lap dancing.

Naked and menacing, Cassian growled alarmingly and came straight for her. She squealed and dashed around the buttonback sofa. But not too fast.

'Temptress,' he muttered, catching her and covering her with kisses.

He bent her backwards, Silent Picture Style, and she fluttered her lashes at him, making Silent Picture Faces at him.

'I think I'm going to like coming here,' she said smugly.

'You won't get sex every time, you know,' Cassian said with a grin.

'Shame! I suppose I'd better get dressed.' Her eyes sparkled, a deep and intense blue. 'Have another glass of celebratory champagne while I shower. Then I'm handing out money to people who deserve it,' she said happily.

'You think you have everything you need?' he enquired.

She paused, her eyes glazing over. He was gorgeous. Standing there absolutely naked, totally masculine and unbelievably thoughtful. His hair was tousled, eyes drugged whenever he looked at her, body…quite breathtakingly beautiful. What more could a woman want?

Yes. She had everything.

'It's all perfect,' she said with a sigh.

150

Glowing with love, she cast her eyes about her. The offices were gorgeous too. High ceilinged and with the lovely proportions of a typical Georgian mansion, they had been tastefully decorated and fitted out so that the overall effect was that of a comfortable high class home rather than a business empire.

They were in the interview room, having made the best use of the deep cream carpet she could ever have imagined. Their clothes were strewn everywhere. The results of their shopping—wicked and seductive lingerie and two more outfits for her, plus clothes for Adam and small decorative touches to make the office more friendly—were heaped on the comfortable sofas.

When she was ready, she was to employ someone to open mail and to deal with her correspondence. Until then, she could settle in at her own pace. It seemed too good to be true. But it was real enough. She'd seen the letters asking for help and was anxious to get started.

'Thank you for this chance,' she said, beaming with pleasure.

'Thank *you*. You'll be wonderful,' he answered huskily.

Blowing Cassian a shy kiss, she wandered into the huge marble bathroom and turned on the shower. She was to work for a while and Cassian would help her with the mail, then they were going out to lunch.

When they arrived back at Thrushton Hall, Cassian and Adam would go out for their run and then on their return the house would be filled with the sound of laughter and noise and fabulous music, just as it had been last night.

She smiled, thrilled with the change in Adam. He *was* more confident, more feisty. And she'd listened to the sound of Cassian's voice in the house upstairs as he'd read some exciting story to her son, and her heart had seemed fit to burst with happiness.

A fabulous meal was in order tonight, she thought, mentally going through the recipe she'd chosen. With a month's advance salary in the bank, she'd felt able to buy something special to strengthen her plan to be totally indispensable to Cassian.

Fillet of beef rolled in herbs and porcini, wrapped in prosciutto. Her mouth watered as she stepped out and dried herself. Chocolate pots and sharp lemon wedges. Her eyes lit up. He'd adore it, while she'd adore cooking for the men she loved. And tomorrow there'd be succulent chicken in wine sauce followed by bread and butter pudding laced with whisky. Heaven.

'Champagne.' Cassian handed her a glass and switched on the shower for himself.

'To the future. Happiness for all,' she said, lifting the elegant flute, confident now that he'd want her to stay.

He smiled fondly. 'The future. Happiness.'

In a daze of delight she eased on her elegantly fitting Jackie-O dress and then, with great pride she settled at her huge desk with its view across the leafy park.

Her mind was teeming with thoughts of the future— Cassian falling in love with her, the two of them and their sons living happily together, perhaps a child of their own...

The shower door banged in the background and she hastily put her dreams on hold and began to tackle the post.

'So many people needing help!' she marvelled, when Cassian came in.

He grabbed a stack of letters and began slitting them. 'I know. It can be heartbreaking. But we...I mean, the charity can make a difference to some. I suggest you make a rough selection of "Good grief no's" and "so-so's" and "yes, desperate's", and I'll keep them coming.'

Her 'yes, desperate' pile was unnervingly large when they'd finished opening all the letters.

'Supposing I give out all the money in two months and there's none left?' she said anxiously.

'Then you have ten months of twiddling your thumbs,' he said, grinning. 'Relax, Laura. Use your intuition, make some appointments and hear what your favourites have to say.'

Solemn-faced to have such awesome responsibility, she applied herself with a will and began to enjoy the task. Her decision to enter every single applicant on a database had been greeted with approval by Cassian and her fingers flew over the keys as she entered the names and addresses.

'Time for lunch,' he murmured in her ear, seemingly a few minutes later.

She checked her watch. 'It can't be that late!' she exclaimed.

'You've been working non-stop. Take a break.'

'I'd rather continue. Could we have sandwiches?' she asked hopefully.

'I can do better than that.'

Cassian disappeared and returned later with smoked salmon, pasta salad and two wicked cream cakes.

'Pastry on your mouth,' he drawled lazily, when they'd finished. 'No, let me!' The tip of his tongue slid around her lips, making her tremble. 'Tasty.'

'You're supposed to be the office boy today, so go and make me an espresso,' she said haughtily, pretending she wasn't feeling hot throughout her body.

'Mmm. Ever had a fantasy about an innocent young office boy being seduced by his glamorous, high-flying boss?' he murmured, slipping his fingers to her zip at the back of the honey-gold dress. 'Across her executive desk?'

Her eyes gleamed as her body capitulated. She walked over to her desk and without taking her eyes off him, hitched herself onto it, her skirt high on her thighs.

'Come and learn a little office practice, *boy*,' she purred silkily.

She saw him swallow, knew he was hopelessly drawn to her. Elated, she leaned back, unable to believe he found her so enticing.

His mobile rang. He ignored it. And played the game to the full.

'Lunch hours have never been such fun,' she gurgled later, when they were mutually soaping one another in a haze of satisfaction. 'Enough!' she protested, when Cassian came dangerously close to arousing her again. *'Work.'*

Escaping, she pulled on her clothes and shakily returned to her lists. Time passed quickly again and it seemed only an hour or so before they were driving home. Somewhere in the depths of Cassian's pocket, his mobile rang.

'Can you answer that?' he asked.

'Yes, of course.' She dug it out. 'Hello?' she said uncertainly.

'Oh. Where's Dad?'

'It's Jai!' she squealed.

Cassian's eyes lit up like beacons. 'Can't stop here, too dangerous. See what he wants,' he urged.

'He's driving. Can I give him a message?' she suggested excitedly.

'OK. Can you tell him I'm sitting on the wall outside his house?'

Laura's eyes rounded. 'What? You've arrived? This is fantastic. He'll be over the moon—wait, oh, it'll be a good half hour or so before he can get to you—'

'No sweat,' said the composed Jai. 'I can wait.'

'See you soon,' she said happily. There was a casual 'OK' and then Jai rang off. 'He's there!' she told Cassian. 'At the house!'

'That must have been him, ringing earlier. I totally forgot to check if any message had been left. I can't wait for you to meet him. And Adam,' he said enthusiastically. 'We'll pick him up from school first.'

She beamed, thinking of them all together. Just like a family.

'I can't wait,' she replied.

* * *

The noise was deafening but she loved it. Jai had brought his father a tape of a local band playing in some market square in Marrakesh. Adam and Jai were excitedly chattering together, heads close, as Jai described the Berber houses in the mountains, where hospitality was so generous that he'd been overwhelmed by the excess of food and love. Cassian sat listening to the tape and occasionally adding to the stream of information coming from his son. His hand gripped Jai's, his eyes resting on his child with naked adoration.

And she was trying to get the meal together, having shooed away all offers of help, while at the same time she was doing her best not to miss a word of Jai's extraordinary tales of mountain passes, verdant valleys and ruined fortresses.

But mainly he spoke of the people. Her mind teemed with images and ideas, astonished that a ten-year-old boy should have experienced so much.

The vividly colourful clothes of the women, who worked in the fields and grazed the cattle and goats. The closeness of the families and the affection between them all. The remarkable fact that wherever they went, even in a remote valley, someone would appear. And that someone either spoke English or knew a villager who did.

She smiled, caught up in the excitement of Jai's arrival, thrilled to see how happy he was to be with his father. He was a handsome child. Dark, rangy, like Cassian, and clearly tough and self-assured. But sunny-natured, laughing a good deal, and never arrogant, never conscious that his life must be so different from most other children's.

Her eyes softened. She would never forget his meeting with his father. Cassian had leapt from the car as if ejected by a rocket. The two had flown together and had remained in a hug for ages; weeping, exclaiming, squeezing.

Without realising, her arm had gone around Adam too.

And she'd felt weepy when her son had cuddled her hard, his small face lifted to hers in love and happiness.

'Isn't life great now, Mum?' he'd said, starry-eyed.

'Great,' she'd agreed. And promised to herself that she'd do everything to keep it that way.

She hadn't stopped smiling since. Lifting the broccoli off the hot plate, she grinned at the laughing men in her life and coughed loudly to attract their attention.

'Supper's ready,' she announced, flushed pink from cooking and deep contentment. 'Jai, it's your choice. Eat here or the dining room?'

'Here, please!' cried Jai. 'It's smashing. Cosy and homely. Can we have candles?'

'I'll get them!' offered Adam, jumping up.

'I'll come too—'

The boys disappeared. Cassian looked up at her and if she hadn't fallen love with him before she would have done so then. There was such pleasure in every cell of his body and such exhilaration in his gleaming dark eyes that her heart somersaulted chaotically.

'He's wonderful,' she said shakily.

'I think so. I'm glad you do,' he replied.

He reached out his hand and she grasped it, both of them grinning idiotically at one another.

'I'd better put the meal on the table,' she breathed, afraid that she'd tell him how much she loved him. And she pulled her hand away.

'Crikey!' gasped Jai rushing in. 'Just look at that beef! Smells stupendous. I can't wait. I'm starving!'

Pleased, she began to carve. 'When did you last eat?' she asked in amusement, watching Jai pile potatoes and vegetables onto his plate.

'Umm… In Skipton, just before my minder put me on the bus.'

Adam giggled. 'I can't imagine what Skipton made of a

Berber in full ceremonial robes standing at a bus stop with you!'

'Did draw the crowds a bit,' Jai acknowledged. 'But Karim's got a degree in Psychology so he handled it. I love England, Laura. People are so friendly and smiley.'

'Are you sure?' she asked, a little astonished.

'I grin at them and they grin back,' Jai said blithely.

'I can imagine,' she said with a smile. He'd charm the birds off the trees. 'But we don't all have a tame Berber to help the conversation along.'

Jai laughed and sampled a piece of beef. 'Wowee, this tastes fab, Laura!' he declared. 'The absolute best!'

'Thanks,' she said warmly, won over by Jai's enthusiasm. 'I wondered what you'd think of the food in this country, after all the exotic stuff you've eaten.'

'But it's exotic here!' Jai claimed.

'*Yorkshire?*' hooted Adam.

Jai nodded. 'It is, to me. It's foreign. Exciting. I've never been to England before. Dad's talked about it a lot. In fact, he hardly ever *stops* talking about the Yorkshire Dales—'

'Exaggeration!' Cassian protested.

'In the last month or so, all I hear,' said Jai with the kind of affectionate scorn reserved for a wayward parent, 'is how beautiful it is, how green, the charm of the hills and trees and little fields and tiny villages. And do you know something, Dad?'

'I'm a bore?' he suggested.

Jai grinned. 'Never in a million years! No, you're right! This place blew me away. I know why you drooled about it.' He ducked to avoid an accurately hurled lump of bread. 'Seriously, though…is this going to be our home, now, Dad?'

'Could you really *live* here?' Adam cried hopefully, before Cassian could answer. But she saw he was frowning and a slight feeling of unease spread over her. 'We'd have a great time together,' Adam enthused.

'Yeah! Could you show me the corpse way you told me about?' Jai asked eagerly. 'And…what was it…Li'l Emily's Bridge? And the suspension bridge that wobbles and—'

'All of it!' broke in Adam. 'It's Saturday tomorrow, so I don't have school. We'll go early. And there are the remains of Roman lead mines above the village, and ruins of Victorian mining offices and a forge. It's dead interesting—'

'Dad!' Jai cried, his eyes shining. 'We can stay, can't we? Adam and me'll have a great time—'

He and Adam vied to coax Cassian. Laura suddenly couldn't eat. Her future—Adam's future—had been suddenly pushed to the forefront.

It had been obvious that Jai thought Cassian must be renting the house, as was his custom. She knew that he'd spent two years renting rooms in Morocco, two years in an Egyptian apartment before that, and a holiday home in Madagascar before then…

It puzzled her why Cassian hadn't explained he'd bought Thrushton Hall. Her eyes grew troubled. And she held her breath while he tried to make himself heard over the eager boys.

'I thought we'd stay for a while—' he began.

The boys whooped, waving their forks triumphantly in the air.

'Brill, Dad! Gosh, Laura, you don't mind?' exclaimed Jai.

'I—don't mind.' How could she? She adored him. And loved his father. 'I'd love to have you here,' she said warmly, aware that Cassian was frowning. But it was his own fault. He should have told Jai what he'd done.

Jai leapt from his chair and ran over, giving her a hug which left her breathless.

'It'll be like having a Mum around,' he said, misty-eyed.

'I've always wanted one of those but Dad wouldn't play ball!'

'Jai—' growled Cassian.

'It'll be like living in a real home, with a real Mum,' Jai said, not in the least bit unnerved by his father's ferocious scowl. 'I wish I had one. A Mum, I mean.'

'Is she dead?' asked Adam, with the typical bluntness of a child.

'When I was born. Dad said she was the most beautiful woman he's ever seen. I've got pictures of her, I'll show you. She was terribly clever. A novelist. He's never really got over her—'

'Jai!' muttered Cassian.

'Well, it's true, Dad! You told me you'd never love another woman, remember?'

Laura tensed, her stomach plummeting. This was awful. Could she ever make him forget this perfect wife, who'd tragically died before boredom or familiarity could set in? Who he remembered with rose-coloured spectacles?

'Yes,' Cassian said in a hoarse whisper. His face was unnervingly bleak. 'I remember.'

She felt sick. Cassian looked dreadful. He was carrying a torch for his late wife. Her hopes came crashing about her ears.

'Wish I had a father,' Adam put in, gazing significantly at Cassian, raw hope in his eyes.

She didn't know where to look. Her fingers trembled. The boys were voicing her dreams. Cautiously she stole a quick glance at Cassian. He was frowning at his plate, cutting up a piece of beef into increasingly small pieces.

'What happened to your Dad?' Jai asked gently.

'He didn't stand by Mum,' Adam said, his voice indignant. 'He left her in the lurch. But she's the best Mum in the world. You can share her if you like.'

'Can I?' Jai asked, his face wistful.

Laura's heart jerked painfully. 'Of course, Jai,' she husked. If Cassian would only let her...

'I thought you liked wandering the world, Jai,' Cassian said gruffly, still intent on dissecting the beef out of all existence.

'I do! It's cool!' Jai declared with passion. 'I love new places and getting my education first hand from you and where we are, instead of—'

'Wow! Your Dad teaches you?' Adam asked in awe.

'Yeah. Our life's too nomadic for me to go to school. Dad sets me work—like...doing the shopping in the souk, working out exchange rates, comparing prices and currencies in other countries, that kind of thing. Or...I do a study on the effect of land form and climate on people's lifestyles—that was my last project. Or local art—that's great, I get to talk to some real odd bods. And when Dad's finished writing for the day, we talk over what I've done.'

Cassian had stiffened imperceptibly. He was staring fixedly at the oblivious Jai—who was happily eating—as if he wanted to convey a message. Laura's eyes narrowed.

'Course,' Jai went on, prompting Cassian to tense up even more, 'when Dad's *really* motoring on a book, I have to create my own education. That's quite fun. I brush up on the local language or do a bit of painting. Sometimes I just read and read.'

Laura's mind was racing. Cassian's late wife had been a novelist. And he spent long hours 'motoring on a book'.

'I write thrillers,' Cassian said quietly, plainly reading the expression on her face. 'Under a pseudonym. I tell no one, *no one*, who I am. I don't like my private life invaded. We travel so that I can research a particular setting for a novel.'

'Wow!' Adam's eyes were popping. 'Are you famous?'

'I'll say!' Jai answered, matter-of-fact.

'But anonymous,' Cassian warned, and his son at last took the hint.

'We won't tell anyone. Will we, Adam?' Laura promised.

A writer, she thought. And if Jai hadn't innocently spilled the beans, she wouldn't have known. Even now, Cassian wasn't intending to tell her the name he wrote under. That hurt. He didn't want to share a huge part of his life with her. She felt suddenly flat and depressed. Where did she stand with him?

'You work on a computer?' she asked, remembering how he'd deflected her questions about his job.

His eyes begged her forgiveness for that evasion. 'I do.'

'Anyway,' Jai went on, 'it's a great way to live. I'm not knocking it, Dad. But for a while I'd like to be here. It's a super house, isn't it? And Adam and I are already good mates. Laura's my kind of Mum-substitute. I'd have chosen her out of a million other women—'

'Only a million?' Cassian asked, eyebrow raised.

'Ten,' Jai amended.

'A billion,' Adam said.

She waited for Cassian to make his contribution. An advance on a billion would have been nice. But he didn't.

'Jai, it's OK,' he said instead, quite unusually stilted in his manner. 'We're staying put for at least a couple of years. After then…I'm not sure. You know how it is.'

'Two years!' the boys crowed. Cassian opened his mouth and shut it, his jaw tight.

Laura almost joined in the cheers. She began to feel a little better, knowing that she had two whole years with Cassian. They'd live in close proximity. Judging by the way that they had instantly melded into a happy, friendly unit, they would all get on well. And Cassian would surely not want to break that unit up at the end of that two years.

Maybe she wouldn't ever be as special or as beautiful as his late wife, but she would be an important part of his life. And that was enough for her.

Serene amid the noisy, excited chatter, she smiled indulgently at the boys as their friendship blossomed.

'I'm shattered,' Jai announced with a yawn when they were all sitting in the drawing room around a cheery log fire. 'Mind if I go to bed?'

'Me too,' said Adam.

'I'll make up a bed,' Laura said warmly.

'Will I be in the same room as Adam?' Jai asked, his eyes so appealingly like Cassian's that she laughed, unable to resist his plea.

'If you like!'

She covered her ears when the boys shouted their delight and found herself enveloped in wiry arms, one dark head and one fair buried against her middle.

'I think you're a hit, Laura,' Cassian said in a thoughtful tone.

She heaved a huge sigh of pleasure and put away her niggling doubts about Cassian's love for his late wife.

'Has there ever been a more perfect day?' she marvelled, her eyes desperately hoping that he'd agree.

'It's been eventful,' he replied, with masterly understatement. 'Come on, boys. A quick bath each and bed. I'll tell you about the ghost of the miner's daughter who haunts Bardale Peak if you're tucked up in fifteen minutes.'

'Ten!' cried Adam and led the charge up the stairs.

Cassian followed Laura, his mind in turmoil. He could barely answer her comments as they moved the spare bed into Adam's room and made it up for Jai. He'd get through the next half hour and then he'd have to do some thinking.

She was humming to herself. Her entire face seemed luminous and he couldn't bear the pain that gave him.

'Adam will do so well, with Jai here,' she said softly, her eyes shining with happy tears. 'You…you don't know what this means to me, Cassian,' she continued. 'To see my child transformed, because of you, because he has found a trustworthy friend in Jai, means more to me than if I'd won the lottery.'

He understood. And because he did, because he knew that his own happiness depended largely on Jai's well-being, he felt doubly torn. She and Adam had changed beyond all recognition. Jai wanted them all to live like one big family.

And he...he even wished he could tutor Adam so the two boys learnt together. It was a fatuous idea. Of course it was.

'I'll chivvy those boys up,' he said shortly and knew she was disappointed that he hadn't acknowledged her happiness. She looked at him uncertainly and then went down-stairs.

He stood in Adam's empty bedroom and gave a token yell at the boys, his breathing hard and fast. He couldn't allow this situation to develop. Nor did he want to feel this deeply. Didn't want to be possessed, obsessed.

His freedom was seeping away and soon he'd be back in the nightmare of his youth. Trapped. Cornered as surely as if he'd been shut in a cupboard.

The sex was fantastic. But love...that was something else. He didn't want this compulsion to stay close to Laura, to touch her every few moments, to ache with a sense of loss when she wasn't within his sight.

Love struck deep inside you. It took over your muscles, your veins, your lungs and every single brain cell. He would fight it. Stay detached.

'Story!' yelled Jai, hurling himself forwards like a pro-jectile.

Cassian caught him and flung him on the bed, laughing despite his worries. And he did the same to Adam, because the child desperately needed some rough and tumble too.

God. What was he going to do, break three hearts?

CHAPTER ELEVEN

AFTER the story he told Laura that he had work to do, and went into the study, her image—soft, sensuous, loving—imprinted indelibly on his brain.

Of course he couldn't work. He couldn't think, either, and sat in a leather chair morosely nursing a whisky, wishing that life consisted of him and Jai and no one else.

Except…he sighed. Laura filled his mind, intruding on logical thought. Perhaps tomorrow he'd be more able to decide what to do. If the weather was suitable, he'd take a flight and let his instincts dictate his future.

Feeling extraordinarily tired and subdued, he wandered slowly along the darkened hallway to where Laura sat reading recipes in the sitting room.

The firelight cast a glow over her absorbed face. Her dark lashes were thick arcs on her flawless cheeks and her lips were parted as she frowned at the recipe book, perhaps, he mused, working out quantities or deciding which day she'd surprise them with another superlative meal.

But she was a meal in herself. Her lissom body was curled on the sofa, every inch of her desirable from the top of her gleaming scalp to the delicate, beautifully arched feet which he had kissed so fervently that very day.

Something hard and painful cramped in his chest and he bit back an urge to invite her to stay for ever. With a tremendous effort, he forced his voice to sound casual.

'I'm going up. Fantastic supper,' he said, extending his goodnight even though he wanted to hurry away to the isolation of his room. 'See you tomorrow. Night.'

She had risen, her eyes on his. He could turn away with

a curt nod... No. He couldn't. She held him fast, his feet were rooted to the ground.

'Goodnight,' she said softly, coming to put her arms around his neck.

He found himself kissing her, the sweetness of her mouth taking his breath away.

'I'm pleased Jai likes me,' she sighed, snuggling into his embrace more securely.

Unseeing, he stared over her head. Jai's longing for a mother had shaken him—together with the fact that his son had clearly wanted stability, too, a home of some kind.

The wanderer wants a home, he thought wryly. The homebody wants to wander.

'I've never kissed a famous author before,' she murmured into his throat. 'I suppose you're a literary genius and that's why you aren't rich beyond the dreams of Averil.'

He smiled at her joke. And felt safe enough with her, sure of her discretion, to come clean. He didn't want secrets from her. He wanted to share.

'I am rich,' he said gently. 'I just don't keep much of my money. It comes in, I keep what I think I'll need, and the rest—'

'Goes to the charity?' she gasped.

'I trust you not to breathe a word to anyone.'

Her hand lifted to caress his cheek. 'You are the most amazing man I've ever known,' she said shakily.

A wonderful sensation—pride, joy, contentment—meandered silkily through every inch of his body. 'You must get out more,' he chuckled. Kissed her small nose, and beat a hasty retreat.

With a crescent of Day-Glo orange spread out behind him, he checked the wind and cloud formations again. His narrowed eyes scanned the ridge of hills, now lit by the warm morning sun.

Tightening the strap on his helmet, he began the short run to the edge of the hilltop and launched himself into the air.

Freedom.

A huge sigh released itself from his tense chest. It was a long time since he'd flown and he'd missed the sensation of becoming unshackled from the world.

His feelings for Laura were more intense than any he'd ever known, but he had to remember that a permanent relationship came with strings that eventually strangled him.

Yet Jai would love to have her around.

Cassian searched for more lift, found it, and shot up a few hundred feet. Now he could see Thrushton and the manor at the edge of the village. What was it about this place that gave him such a sense of calm and well-being? It was as if he had come home—despite his troubled teenage years there.

Jai and Adam would be exploring Hangman's Wood by now. They'd come back, dirty, dishevelled and talking nineteen to the dozen and Laura and he would listen to their exploits and smile at one another...

He frowned. Laura. Laura, Laura! She never left him alone. Slid into his thoughts and his vision, forcing him to acknowledge how powerfully she had entered his life. Too far, too fast. He had to cool things down. And separation was the only way.

He'd never intended that she should stay. Jai and Adam and Laura had misinterpreted his remark when he'd said they'd be living at Thrushton Hall for at least two years. He'd been referring to Jai and himself. Now he'd have to clarify the situation.

No problem. A straightforward statement of fact. And yet he was shying away from even voicing it to himself.

Slowly he worked his way along the ridge in the direction of Thrushton, as though he couldn't bear to be parted

from it for long. The wind began to buffet him and he had
to stop thinking and focus hard on keeping up in the air.

But he was losing height and the wind was throwing him
around too violently so he made a running landing and
packed up for the day, feeling vaguely unsatisfied.

The flight had been enjoyable but it hadn't thrilled him
as it used to. He found he was hurrying to fold up his
'wing', eager to return…to Laura.

He groaned. Maybe if he steeped himself in her the ob-
session would pall. He'd go back, make love to her… His
body jerked in anticipation and he ruefully stowed the wing
in its sack, recognising that there was only one thing on
his mind. To hold Laura in his arms. To smell her, feel her,
hear her, look at her.

The journey was short, he knew, but even then it took
too long. And when he arrived, shouting to her, struck
dumb by the answering silence, he knew a disappointment
so keen that it unnerved him totally.

He'd wanted to see her smile at him, the cute lift of each
corner of her lips, the whiteness of her even teeth. To listen
to the warmth in her voice with its husky cadences as she
spoke to him. Her scent was in his nostrils now, tantalising
him; the clean smell of the shampoo she used, the subtle
elusiveness of her favourite geranium and orange soap.

But without her presence, there was nothing but emptiness in the big house. It was as if it had died.

Quite at a loss as to what to do, he wandered into the
garden behind the manor and passed the time waiting for
Laura by planning a herb garden. It would be dual purpose—culinary and medicinal, and he'd draw on what he'd
learnt from the Morrocan herbalist.

Mint to keep flies at bay. Nettles for pesticide—and to
flavour the soft fruit he'd grow, chives for blackspot and
aphids on the roses… Meadowsweet, heartsease, chamo-
mile…

He couldn't wait to start planting. And what else? Perhaps at the far end of the garden he'd build a chicken run so they could have fresh, new-laid eggs. Extend the vegetable garden of course—

He blinked, and leaned against the sunwarmed wall of the house, suddenly sure—absolutely positive—that he wanted to put down roots here. Not just for two years. For the rest of his life. His mouth curved into a smile, his decision giving him a peace of mind he'd never known before.

'You look happy,' came Laura's soft voice.

It trembled a little, as if emotion bubbled within her and her eyes were luminous. He felt his knees weaken.

'I am.' But he didn't tell her why. And he had to fight his longing to include her in his plans.

'So am I. I've been talking to Tom about my mother. It's so wonderful, getting to know her, Cassian!'

'I'm very pleased for you,' he said, lightly touching her arm.

And suddenly she was nestled up to his chest and the house, the garden, his life, seemed complete again. His lips caressed her forehead while fear and excitement tussled with one another.

Maybe his idea of sating his desire wasn't a good one. It went without saying that Laura gave him the kind of sexual satisfaction he'd dreamed about. But she also made security and a cosy family life seem appealing. When, in fact, it wasn't.

Her fingers laced in his hair. Her laughing eyes were melting into his. Every part of his body was alight, energised, strangely empty. With increasingly drugged eyes, he gazed at her soft lips and let her warmth seep remorselessly into him. He paused, his heart thundering. There was nothing he could do to draw back—his desire was too overwhelming.

'I want you,' he said hoarsely.

Detaching herself, she gave a beguiling smile and walked

to the door, the glance over her shoulder telling him that he was to follow.

And follow he did, hopelessly tied to a woman's smile, soft blue eyes, a lushly mobile body. And hoping that was all. Pure physical lust.

Gently, with near-reverence, he made slow and adoring love to her. The poignancy of her whimpers and sighs caused a bitter-sweetness within him that led him to extend her pleasure until she was almost weeping with frustration.

His climax, and hers, both awed and unnerved him. Nothing could be this good. He was imagining it. No two bodies could move in such harmony, feel so good, offer such mutual rapture, or make him wonder if he'd been be-witched or transported to a heaven.

He didn't want to move, but held her in his arms, lost in a state of unbelievable bliss. And fear. This was getting beyond his control. No one should feel so attached to some-one.

It was as if he depended on Laura for his very existence. A lump of terror came up in his throat, his heart beating frantically. And he finally detached himself.

They were both quiet when they wandered hand in hand downstairs later, and he wondered if she too was contem-plating their relationship.

His throat dried again. He had to make his position clear. It was only fair.

'Laura,' he croaked, as she began her bread-making rit-ual. 'I must talk to you. Get things straight—'

'Things?' she asked, her eyes instantly wary.

He took the precaution of staring out of the window. Without her glorious, sexually glowing face in his vision, he'd focus more sharply.

'I think, over the past few days,' he muttered, 'I've known every emotion in the book.'

'Me, too.'

Hearing the smile in her soft voice, he steadied himself,

his hands flat on the work counter. Behind him he could hear the dough being thumped and he hurried on, anxious not to hurt her.

'It's…it's happened so fast, been such a roller-coaster that I hardly know where I am—'

'I know. It's lovely but it's scary, too,' she murmured in agreement.

'We need to slow down a bit.'

He almost smiled at himself. Was this really him talking—advising caution? Was he actually suggesting they lived with their heads for a while, instead of their instincts?

'If you like,' she said casually.

His head lifted in relief. She wasn't going to tie him down, to demand further commitment. A load lifted from his mind and he turned to watch her as she deftly kneaded the dough. Not too violently. Normal. Rational. Serene. And she smiled encouragingly at him, a dazzling smile that made his heart ache.

'I'm glad you feel that way,' he husked.

'I wonder,' she mused, glancing out of the window behind him, 'where Adam and Jai have got to now? They're as thick as thieves, aren't they?' She laughed, her pearly teeth glistening in her rosy mouth. 'I suppose I'll have a heap of washing to do when they come in!'

He knew what she was implying. That their sons were now a unit. But, he thought with a frown, that didn't mean they all had to live together.

'Laura, I don't want to lose what we have, you and me—'

'Nor do I,' she said, her eyes far too tender and mesmerising for him to stay unmoved.

'You know, I hope, that I'm not a man to make commitments,' he warned with quick urgency. 'I don't want to be trapped—'

'What commitments? And who's trapping you?' she asked in amiable surprise. 'You come and go as you like and I don't ask where you've been or where you're going—'

'It's not just that,' he said gently. 'Let me explain. You told me once that I wasn't to make Adam too fond of me because I wasn't going to be part of his life for long—no, wait, hear me out,' he said, when it seemed she'd interrupt.

The dough was left unheeded on the table. Dusted appealingly with flour as usual, she stared at him wide-eyed, her arms hanging by her sides.

'I'm listening.' Her voice shook.

'We're in danger here of giving the kids the wrong idea.'

'Are we?' she asked, her eyes piercing blue and startlingly luminous.

He could kiss her. Brush her hair from her forehead, chide her for coating herself in flour...

He swallowed. This had to be said. 'I'm worried that we're all getting too cosy. We're moving into Walton territory.'

'Nothing wrong with that, except all those interminable "goodnights",' she said with a wicked little grin.

No way could he smile. He was too worried. 'And what if it all goes wrong?' he shot. 'You saw how Jai was about you,' he croaked, longing to take her in his arms and say it would be all right, that she wouldn't be hurt. But he couldn't promise that. 'He wants a mother figure and has fixated on you. But the last thing I want is for him to be upset. We don't know what will happen between us, you and me. We might stay together for a while and part, we might separate tomorrow. Nothing is certain in this world. We can't let the boys think we're heading towards something permanent.'

He could feel the pain in her. And it was tearing him in two. But he had to be honest.

'You can't protect Jai from everything,' she breathed. 'You've taught me that. What happened to seizing the day? To living life? Learning to cope with disappointments?'

She wouldn't accept what he wanted, he thought with a slicing fear. Laura would want commitment. A husband, children—he'd always known that. She ought to be married to a loving man, not tied to someone who couldn't bear the finality of marriage. His spine chilled. Almost certainly he'd lose her.

And yet honesty and decency made him plough on, even though he knew he was heading towards a separation he'd find hard to bear.

'Jai is impulsive and passionate. He thinks you're wonderful. I'll be nagged to put our relationship on a firmer footing. I can't do that. I'm just suggesting that we can cool things and make this more of a friendly relationship, if we detach ourselves a little.'

'How do you suggest we do that?' she asked, widening her big blue eyes. She looked at him with a suspiciously provocative tilt of her head. 'I do find it hard not to touch you, Cassian. And we look at each other ten times a minute. The boys aren't stupid.'

He frowned. This wasn't going the way he'd planned. 'We'd be less…obsessed with one another if we didn't live together. I never wanted that,' he said with unintentional sharpness. And although he wasn't looking at her—but examining his shoes with intense interest—he knew she had stiffened. 'I said to Jai that we'd be here for two years but I think you all assumed that you and Adam would be part of that set up. Nothing was farther from my mind. You and Adam must live somewhere else. In the village, maybe— there are a couple of houses for sale, or Grassington—I'd buy a house for you both—'

'So I'd be your secret mistress,' she said, suddenly cold.

Alarmed that she was withdrawing from him mentally, he took a step forward. And she took one back. He felt panic welling up inside him.

'We'd have a relationship,' he corrected huskily. 'We'd

spend a good deal of time together, going out with the kids, reading them bedtime stories, that kind of thing—'

'And I'd pop over for sex. Or we'd use the back of your car. Or a convenient field.'

His breath rasped in. 'It's not like that—'

'Yes, it is.' She folded her arms and her eyes were as dark as a threatening storm. 'Just *you* get *this* straight. I won't be used as a substitute mother for your son and to satisfy your sexual demands!'

'Don't misinterpret what I'm saying! We both agree we're going too fast and need to find a way to put the brakes on. This would achieve that. Please don't think I'm using you. I want more than that—' he found himself saying desperately.

'What?' she shouted. 'To fall asleep beside me? To wake up and find me in your arms?' she cried, tormenting him with the passionate words he'd spoken earlier. 'So what do I do? Commute? Leap up at dawn and hurry home? Do I find a baby-sitter to stay in the house so Adam is safe? No, Cassian! I don't want to be at your convenience, at your beck and call. I deserve better. Either I live here with you, or we part. I mean *really* part. You choose. Now.'

He gazed at her in horror, his hand scraping distractedly through his hair. That wasn't what he'd wanted. Just something slower, less threatening to his freedom. He couldn't imagine what it would be like without her…

'I've not made myself clear,' he said, choked.

'Oh, yes, you have!' she raged. 'It's your late wife, isn't it? You think you can't love another woman because she was so perfect. Well I'm not filling her shoes. I have shoes of my own. I am not her. I am me. And if you don't want me as I am, warts and all, then have the grace to say so. But don't use me to assuage your guilt because Jai needs a motherly touch, and don't use me as a sex object for your voracious appetite! It's not fair on me! I want sex too. But I want a hell of a lot more than that from the man I give my body to! So decide whether you want me, flesh and blood and living and breathing—or your late, perfect, beautiful wife who's dead, Cassian, *dead*!'

'You've got it wrong!' he said harshly, grabbing her arms. She put her hands to his chest and pushed, but he resisted, ignoring the flour and dough that now marked his shirt and rushing straight into his explanation. 'My wife wasn't perfect! Not anywhere near!' he hissed, his face ferocious as he remembered, felt the wounds, the misery, again.

'You married her!' she shot.

'And don't I regret it! I fell for her because I was only eighteen and ruled by my hormones and thought sexual pleasure was love. She was four years older with a hell of a lot of lovers in her past and a whore's skill in arousing men. But she didn't have an ounce of tenderness in her entire body! She lured me into a hasty marriage because she was already four months pregnant by another man— *yes*! Pregnant!' he snarled, when Laura jerked in horror.

'Jai?!' she whispered, appalled.

'Exactly,' he muttered bitterly.

'But...he's so like you!' she gasped.

He nodded, sick with misery. 'His mother was dark-haired. Spanish. Hence the similarity. She was beautiful, yes, but only on the outside.' He raised a harrowed face as memories came thick and fast. 'I knew her to be cruel and vicious to animals and her behaviour towards them made me want to retch,' he muttered. 'She had no compassion for the elderly, or those who were less than beautiful, and she made fun of them, ridiculed them unmercifully. Maria was an absolute bitch. I *loathed* her for trapping me into marriage!'

'But she's dead, Cassian—!' Laura said, infinitely caring.

'No. She isn't.'

'*What?*' she gasped.

He felt drained, as if the lie had taken away something

precious to him. His integrity. His belief in honesty at all times.

'She didn't die. I lied to Jai,' he confessed hoarsely. 'I never wanted him to come into contact with her, to learn the kind of woman she was. She'd tried to abort him. Her own baby, Laura!' He thought of the world without his beloved Jai and his eyes pricked with hot tears. 'She didn't care about him. He was a burden, something vile to her, because he'd ruined her figure. When Maria gave birth she dumped the baby on me, then vanished. I never saw or heard of her again and it took years for me to get a divorce and to free myself from her. Jai is not my son but—'

Laura froze. There had been a sound behind her. Ice chilled her entire body. Cassian was staring in horrified disbelief at something...someone...over her shoulder. And she knew before she turned who it must be.

CHAPTER TWELVE

IT WAS Jai. Dirty and dishevelled from his adventures outside. Looking suddenly small and pathetic, his mouth open in an O of despair, his eyes, his deceptively Cassian-like eyes dark and glistening with utter horror.

And then Jai gave a terrible shuddering cry like that of a wounded animal and he'd turned, lurching away in a sobbing frenzy before either she or Cassian could move their paralysed limbs.

'Jai!' he jerked out, in a horrific, broken rasping sound.

Automatically she whirled around, her hands lifting to stop Cassian from following. He cannoned into her, carrying her along a pace or two before he'd grabbed her to prevent them both falling over.

'No,' she said urgently. 'Not you.'

Pain etched deep in his face, his pain hurting her, knifing her through and through as if she was being stabbed over and over again.

'He's my son!'

His eyes squeezed tight as if he recognised the irony of that cry. And she felt the tears welling up in her own eyes and fought them. For his sake, for Jai, she must stay strong.

'He ran *from* you, not *to* you,' she said, as gently as she could. 'Let me go. Give us a while together.'

Without waiting for his reply, she flew into the hall where a bewildered Adam stood, his face as grubby as Jai's.

'Where did he go?' she demanded fiercely.

'Sitting room,' Adam cried. 'But what…?'

She hurtled in there. Nothing.

She bit her lip, wondering if he'd clambered out of the open window. But when she ran to it, she could see no sign

176

of him. Panic made her shake. The child would be so hurt. His world had come crashing down, all the fantasies he'd woven about his mother, the images he'd had of her; lovely, loveable, kind…

And then she heard a stifled, muffled sob. She blanched. It had come from the cupboard.

'Where's he gone?' rasped Cassian from the doorway.

She couldn't answer. But he read her appalled gaze and flinched. Her hand stayed him. Quietly she stepped close to the door and laid her hand on it as if consoling the child within Cassian's long-ago prison.

'Jai,' she said tenderly. 'It's me. Laura.' Her fingers closed on the latch and gently eased it up. But the door was locked. Jai had locked himself in from the inside with the key Cassian had so carefully fitted in the lock. Her eyes closed at the pity of it all. 'Don't cry, sweetheart,' she crooned, love and compassion in every breath she uttered.

The dam burst; from behind the heavy panelled door, she heard a storm of weeping. Anxiously she glanced around. Adam was holding Cassian's hand, his young eyes aghast at the bleakness of Cassian's face.

She had to make things right. She loved Cassian so much that she'd do anything to stop him from hurting so badly. Her hand waved Adam and Cassian back, indicating they should retreat from the room.

'No one's here but me,' she said to Jai. She imagined him, sitting on the cold stone floor, sobbing his heart out. It was hard for her to keep her voice steady because she was so distressed. 'Don't stay in there alone, Jai,' she coaxed. 'Come and cuddle up with me on the sofa. Let me hold you. Just that. Nothing more. And we can talk if you want, or just sit together. Trust me. I know what it's like for you. I heard terrible things about my mother that broke my heart. Come to me. I understand. I've been there too.'

There had been a lessening of the wild crying whilst she spoke and she knew he'd been listening. She held her breath in the long silence that followed her plea. A stray sob lurched out from Jai and then there came the sound of scrabbling, as if he was standing up. Quietly she stepped back. The key rasped and the door opened a fraction.

'Cassian isn't here,' she said softly. 'Just me.'

Around the edge of the door, a wrecked face appeared, the small features screwed up in misery, the dark hair shooting in all directions as if he'd thrust violent fingers through it.

Heartbroken, she opened her arms and with a moan Jai stumbled into them.

'There,' she murmured, guiding him to the sofa. 'Come on. Snuggle up. I'll hold you tight. Cry if you want. I'm waterproof.'

She stroked the weeping child's turbulent curls, her arms securely around him. He clung to her like a limpet and she occasionally kissed his hot forehead, waiting patiently until his tears had subsided. It was a long wait.

'My m-mother was a cow!' Jai wailed. 'She...she didn't *want* me—'

'But Cassian did,' Laura gently reminded him.

'No! He was lumbered with me!' Jai sniffed.

'You know that's not true.' Laura kissed his wet temple and brushed soggy clumps of hair from the furrowed forehead. His tears seemed to have got everywhere, carried on frantic hands. Poor sweetheart. 'Cassian is crazy about you. He really believes you are his son in every way except by blood. He's prouder of you than perhaps he ought to be. The sun definitely originates from your person,' she said with a gentle smile.

'I have a vicious tramp for a mother and an unknown father!' Jai's appalled eyes gazed moistly into her own, seeking comfort.

'That is awful for you,' she acknowledged gravely. 'I thought I was in exactly the same situation as you, once, so I do know how painful it is when your parents turn out

to be less than perfect. I was lucky. I discovered that my
mother had been maligned and she wasn't horrible at all.
My father too. I can't pretend that your mother was really
a saint. But maybe she was scared because she was pregnant and unloved. People do terrible things when they're
frightened, Jai. They seek self-preservation—think of themselves. That's how the human race is programmed when
there's danger about.'

She shifted him more comfortably on her lap, gently wiping his tear-channelled face now that he'd stopped crying.

'Perhaps your father didn't know your mother was pregnant. Perhaps your mother has regretted leaving you, and
you are never far from her mind. We can't ever be sure.
But there is one thing we do know.'

'What's that?' Jai mumbled, sweetly grumpy.

Her lips touched his soft cheek. 'Cassian loves you,' she
said, her voice shaking with passion. 'You are the most
important thing in his life. Few people have such love. That
makes you very special, very fortunate.'

'He *lied* to me!' Jai railed, screwing up his fists in anger.

'I know,' she agreed, soothing him with her gently stroking hands. 'And that only shows how much he cares.
Cassian doesn't lie as a rule. It's a matter of principle to
him. He's always honest—sometimes uncomfortably so,'
she said, sadly rueful. 'But for you he made an exception.
He couldn't tell you the facts about your mother. Perhaps
he might have done, when you were older, but you wanted
her to be wonderful, didn't you? So he invented a mother
you'd adore. And we don't know how much it hurt him to
keep up that pretence, how hard it must have been to say
that his ex-wife was a paragon of virtue when she had hurt
him and deceived him so badly. Do you understand why
he felt compelled to lie to you, Jai?' she asked anxiously.

Cassian, listening in silent anguish from behind the door,
his hand crushed by Adam's bony grip of sympathy, held
his breath. He was nothing without his son. Without Laura.

'Yes,' he heard his son whisper.

Heard Laura murmur something, knew she was hugging Jai, rocking him. He threw back his head and closed his eyes, swamped by relief and gratitude. And admiration. By her tact and loving heart, she had given him the gift of his son. And for that, he could never thank her enough.

She was… He searched for a word to describe her but found nothing that expressed his feelings. More than wonderful. More than compassionate and caring. Selfless, tender, utterly sweet and loveable…

'You OK?' whispered Adam, stretching up on tiptoe to get close to Cassian's ear.

Dimly he saw the blond child's anxious face, saw the same concern and love that Laura displayed so openly. Unable to speak, he nodded, swallowing, and received a friendly squeeze of his mangled hand in response.

'Shall we see if we can call your father in?' he heard Laura say.

'Mmm,' snuffled Jai.

Adam beamed up at him. Laura's smile.

God, he loved her!

'Cassian!' she shouted. 'Are you around?'

He couldn't move. He was rooted to the ground in shock. He loved her so much that his lungs had lost their power and his heart seemed to have stopped beating.

Because he had messed up. He'd been so blind—had feared for his freedom so much—that he'd offered to keep her like some mistress, *like a caged bird*—to appear at his bidding, to make his life complete on his terms.

'Cassian!' she yelled, and Adam tugged at his hand urgently.

Laura wasn't like Maria. She would never trap him. She'd respect his need for space. And suddenly he didn't want that space so badly—he wanted her, to be with her, to be here in the manor and bathing in the warmth of her. Cooking breakfast, doing homework with the boys, exploring the moors, developing the garden…but all with Laura. With her in his heart. With her loving him.

Distraught, he obeyed Adam's desperate tugs and Laura's calls. Like an automaton he walked stiffly to the door, everything a blur because of the tears of despair in his eyes.

'Oh, *Dad!*' Jai wailed.

A body hurled itself at him. His son in all but blood, every inch, every bone as familiar to him as his own. Now Adam, too, was hugging him. And someone…the smell of Laura came to him. Laura. She was drawing them all forwards.

He felt the back of the sofa against his calves and found himself being pushed down. The misery was so intense that he couldn't respond to his son's desperate apologies but eventually he realised how upset Jai was and he managed to put on a show of normality.

'No, I'm fine. Just got a bit emotional,' he said huskily. 'I love you, Jai, Never want to hurt you. I'm sorry—'

'No sweat, Dad. I understand. Laura explained. I'm OK about it. Honest. I've got you, that's the important thing. And now we've got Laura. She's what I dreamed of when I imagined my Mum.'

His son's face swam before his eyes. He couldn't say that Laura was about to leave their lives. It wasn't the time. But his heart felt as heavy as lead despite his cranked-up smile. And he knew he had to be alone to grieve for his lost love.

'Yeah. Great. Now how about you two getting off me so I can breathe and flinging your grotty selves into a bath?' he growled. 'You're a disgusting colour, both of you. Have you been mud-wrestling or something?'

The boys giggled and leapt up. Jai hesitated, then bent down to kiss him.

'Love you, Dad,' he said shakily.

'Love you, Jai,' he croaked.

And then there was the sound of elephants stampeding up the stairs, the sound of yells, water running…

'Cassian.'

Laura's voice, soft and gentle. Her hand stealing into his. What a fool he'd been. Freedom wasn't in being alone, doing your own thing. It depended on many factors.

It was like flying. He could only stay aloft if the wind was right, if the thermals were there, if he manoeuvred his wing properly—and if the wing was undamaged.

To be free he needed a base from which to fly. Somewhere secure and familiar. And he needed to be nurtured by the right person if he was to truly soar up into the heights of joy.

He drew in an agonised breath. He needed to be loved.

'I'm sorry, Laura,' he rasped.

'For what?' she murmured.

'Coming here.'

He couldn't look at her. Not that he'd see her if he did. The tears which he'd not shed through all the bullying, all the terror and desperation, were betraying him now and falling freely down his face. What would she think of him?

He struggled to control himself, to find his iron will. He'd need it. God, he'd need it in the next days, weeks, months.

'How do you mean?' she asked, not moving a muscle beside him.

'If I hadn't come—'

'I would still be a mouse,' she said. 'I wouldn't have a wonderful job. Adam wouldn't know how much I love him.'

'OK. Some good has come out of it,' he granted.

She watched him struggling and longed to help him. But stayed quiet. Patience, she told herself. All would be well.

'I think it would be better for us all if—after a decent interval—I left. You and Adam can stay in the house.'

'Oh.' She thought for a moment. 'Can I take in lodgers?' she asked with apparent gravity.

'Lodge…?' He scowled. 'Suppose so. It'll be your house.'

'And…' Risking all, she said quietly, 'If I fall in love. Would you mind if my lover came here?'

His teeth drove hard into his lower lip. She could feel all his muscles tightening till they were rigid and quivering from tension.

'Your house. Your decision,' he clipped.

His distress, his pain, spurred her on.

'So,' she whispered, snuggling up close. 'When are you moving in?'

For a moment or two she thought he hadn't heard. Not a breath lifted his chest, not a flicker of his eyes betrayed the fact that he was a living man and not a frozen statue.

'What…did you say?' he whispered, desperately trying to focus. He dashed his hand across his eyes and her heart turned over.

'I do love you,' she said, stroking his harrowed face. 'I think you love me. And I want to be with you. I don't care how long that might be. I want you to be free—'

His mouth descended on hers in a hard and impassioned kiss. He was moaning, muttering words of love and delight, saying how deeply he felt and that he wanted to be with her for the rest of his life.

'You mean everything to me,' he said passionately, holding her shoulders and staring intently into her eyes. 'I can't imagine life without you. With you, it's a miracle. An amazing feeling of serenity and exhilaration. Every part of my heart and mind and soul is filled with love for you. I adore you, Laura. Worship you.'

'Whoopee! I've got a Mum!' yelled Jai from behind them.

'I've got a Dad!' crowed Adam.

She and Cassian smiled ruefully at one another. 'And we've got gooseberries,' she giggled.

'I think,' Cassian whispered, 'we'll get the gooseberries fed and up to bed and have a little party of our own down here.'

'Whoooo*oo*!' the boys chorused.

Laura blushed. And turned to the towel-draped boys, her eyes full of love and amusement.

'Go away, you horrible children!' she laughed.

Jai and Adam looked at each other in resignation. 'Huh. Parents,' Jai pretended to grumble. And they scampered upstairs again, screeching with joyous laughter.

Cassian hugged her. 'Rascals,' he said fondly. Then he caressed her cheek. 'I've never been so happy,' he said roughly. 'Not in the whole of my life.'

'I think you might be,' she purred. 'After chocolate torte for supper. And after that…'

The love in his eyes touched her heart. Wonderingly, she reached up and touched his mouth. Then she lifted her face to his and lost herself in his kisses. Now she was truly, deeply happy. And all her dreams were on their way to coming true.

She sighed and sank deeper into Cassian's arms. Perfect love. Perfect lover. She was, without doubt, the luckiest woman in the world.

'Marry me,' Cassian whispered. 'Be my wife. I want that more than anything. I want us to have children. More gooseberries,' he said with a laugh.

Her face was radiant, her eyes sparkling like a bright blue sea beneath a blinding sun. 'I would love to be your wife,' she said shakily. She giggled. 'And to have your gooseberries!'

Cassian gave a shout of laughter and kissed her passionately.

'About time! Thought he'd never ask,' came Jai's stage whisper from the doorway.

Modern Romance™
...seduction and
passion guaranteed

Tender Romance™
...love affairs that
last a lifetime

Sensual Romance™
...sassy, sexy and
seductive

Blaze
...sultry days and
steamy nights

Medical Romance™
...medical drama on
the pulse

Historical Romance™
...rich, vivid and
passionate

29 new titles every month.

*With all kinds of Romance for
every kind of mood...*

MILLS & BOON®

Makes any time special™

MAT4

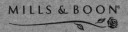

Treat yourself this Mother's Day to the ultimate indulgence

3 brand new romance novels and a box of chocolates

= *only £7.99*

Available from 15th February

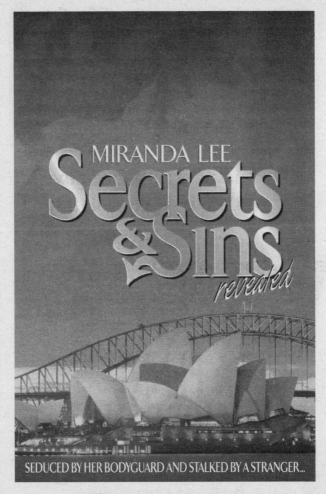

MIRANDA LEE

Secrets & Sins *revealed*

SEDUCED BY HER BODYGUARD AND STALKED BY A STRANGER...

Available from 15th March 2002

*Available at most branches of WH Smith,
Tesco, Martins, Borders, Eason, Sainsbury's
and most good paperback bookshops.*

0402/35/MB34

Starting Over

Another chance at love...
Found where least expected

PENNY JORDAN

Published 15th February

Available at most branches of WH Smith,
Tesco, Martins, Borders, Eason, Sainsbury's
and most good paperback bookshops.

FREE!

2 Books

and a surprise gift!

We would like to take this opportunity to thank you for reading this Mills & Boon® book by offering you the chance to take TWO more specially selected titles from the Modern Romance™ series absolutely FREE! We're also making this offer to introduce you to the benefits of the Reader Service™—

- ★ FREE home delivery
- ★ FREE gifts and competitions
- ★ FREE monthly Newsletter
- ★ Books available before they're in the shops
- ★ Exclusive Reader Service discount

Accepting these FREE books and gift places you under no obligation to buy; you may cancel at any time, even after receiving your free shipment. Simply complete your details below and return the entire page to the address below. *You don't even need a stamp!*

YES! Please send me 2 free Modern Romance books and a surprise gift. I understand that unless you hear from me, I will receive 4 superb new titles every month for just £2.49 each, postage and packing free. I am under no obligation to purchase any books and may cancel my subscription at any time. The free books and gift will be mine to keep in any case.

P2ZEB

Ms/Mrs/Miss/Mr ....Initials ....

BLOCK CAPITALS PLEASE

Surname..

Address...

....

....Postcode ....

Send this whole page to:
UK: The Reader Service, FREEPOST CN81, Croydon, CR9 3WZ
EIRE: The Reader Service, PO Box 4546, Kilcock, County Kildare (stamp required)

On the Run

Stone stood on his knees behind a big boulder and unscrewed the top of his canteen. It was half full, and there was no telling when he might find water again.

He raised the canteen and took a swig. It was silent in the canyon. Stone was so hungry his stomach ached. He regretted not eating raw rabbit that morning, or stealing something from the farmhouse he and McDermott had seen.

He wished he'd listened to the old owlhoot when they were back at the farmhouse. McDermott understood survival, and all Stone knew was a war where the mess tents were never far behind.

He sat beside the boulder and peered at the opening in the mountain. If they came for him, they'd have to come one at a time. He'd get the first three, and after that it'd be his jackknife until the bitter end.

LYNCH LAW

Josh Edwards

CHARTER/DIAMOND BOOKS, NEW YORK

LYNCH LAW

A Charter/Diamond Book/published by arrangement
with the author

PRINTING HISTORY
Charter/Diamond edition/November 1990

ISBN: 1-55773-327-9

PRINTED IN THE UNITED STATES OF AMERICA

10 9 8 7 6 5 4 3 2 1

LYNCH LAW

THE SUN WAS a pan of gold in the clear blue sky over Dumont, Texas. John Stone stood on the main street, looking at a sign that said SHERIFF. People walked past on the planked sidewalk, and Stone was covered with the dust of the trail. He reached for the doorknob and entered a square room of medium size. The sheriff was reading an old newspaper, his feet propped on top of the desk. The jail to his rear was full of prisoners behind steel bars.

Stone walked toward the sheriff's desk, his spurs jangling. He wore two Colts in crisscrossed gunbelts with the holsters low and tied to his legs, and removed an old Confederate cavalry officer's hat.

The sheriff had a white mustache with the ends turned up. "What can I do for you?"

Stone took a small photograph in a silver frame out of his shirt pocket and handed it to the sheriff. It showed a young blond woman in a high-necked dress, gazing at the photographer. One of the prisoners murmured something, and the others laughed, but Stone couldn't make out what was said.

"Ever see her?" Stone asked.

The sheriff lowered his feet from the top of his desk and opened the top drawer, removing a pair of eyeglasses with wire rims. He put on the eyeglasses and examined the photograph again.

"Who is she?"

"Friend of mine."

The sheriff returned the photo. "Never saw her, I don't think."

Stone pushed the photo back into his shirt pocket and buttoned down the flap.

"Got a cigarette?" asked a voice behind him.

Stone turned and saw an unshaven man wearing black pants, a black shirt, and a black hat. He gripped the bars with his hands and reminded Stone of a spider on a web.

"Mind if I give him some tobacco?" Stone asked the sheriff.

"Give him anything except your guns."

Stone walked toward the jail and handed the prisoner his bag of tobacco with some rolling paper.

The prisoner's hair was long and unruly, and he looked wild, as if he'd been living in the elements most of his life. He was in his late twenties like Stone, but shorter and slimmer. He rolled himself a cigarette.

Stone took out the photograph and showed it to him. "Ever see this woman?"

The man in black looked at it. "Can't say I have." He pinched off the ends of the cigarette and put it in his mouth. Stone lit it with a match.

"Much obliged," the prisoner said.

Stone walked back to the sheriff. "What's a good restaurant in this town?"

"Gallagher's, down the street on the left."

"What's that man back there done?"

"That's Tad McDermott. He shot a man."

Stone looked at McDermott, and McDermott looked back at him. *Waiting for the hangman.* Stone turned and walked out of the sheriff's office.

It was late in the afternoon, and two middle-aged matrons passed by. Stone took off his hat and wiped his forehead with the back of his arm. His face was tanned and weatherbeaten, and his eyes were steely blue. His hat was discolored where the old Confederate Army insignia had been torn off.

He returned the hat to his head and tipped it low over his eyes, then headed for the restaurant. He passed a barbershop, a general store, and came to the JACKPOT SALOON.

He'd intended to go to the restaurant, but his throat was awfully dry. He opened the doors and entered the Jackpot Saloon.

It was a large square room, with a painting of naked women in a Turkish harem above the bar. Men sat at tables, fingering cards and drinking whiskey. A few whores sat with them.

Stone stepped to the bar. "Whiskey."

The bartender was young, and placed a glass and a bottle on the bar; Stone filled the glass halfway. Pushing back his hat, he raised the glass to his lips and took a swig.

He'd been on the trail five days, and there was nothing like a good saloon. Stone felt himself unwind as he carried the glass and bottle to a table and sat with his back to the wall. The saloon was redolent with the fragrance of good whiskey, tobacco, and ladies' perfume.

He rolled a cigarette and thought of Tad McDermott in jail, waiting for the hangman. *Wonder who he killed?* Stone lit the cigarette and saw through the haze a figure descending the stairs that led to the rooms on the second floor. She was blond, slim-waisted, and bore a resemblance to Marie. Accompanying her was a cowboy tucking in his shirt.

She kissed the cowboy's cheek, then placed a hand on her waist and surveyed the room like a hawk searching for meat. Her eyes raked over Stone, came back, and settled. Then she opened her black fan and walked toward him.

The closer she came, the more she didn't resemble Marie. This woman's features weren't as refined, she was muscular rather than graceful, and she didn't have that sparkle.

"Mind if I sit down?" she asked with a smile.

Stone arose and pulled back her chair. She motioned to the bartender for a glass. Her face was covered with cosmetics and she looked like a wicked doll.

"Don't reckon I ever seen you here before," she said. "What's yore name?"

"John Stone."

"I'm Mary Ellen. Where you comin' in from?"

"Indian Territory."

"Were you with that wagon train that pulled in this mornin'?"

"Yes."

"Heard that wagon train had quite a fight with injuns."

Stone didn't reply. He took another sip from the glass.

"Where's yore wife?"

"Don't have a wife."

"Want to come upstairs with me?"

"No thank you."

She smiled. "Don't think I'm pretty?"

"You know you are."

"Only two dollars for the screw of yore life."

"I'm engaged to get married." Stone took out the picture of Marie and handed it to her. "Ever run into her?"

"If'n I seen her, I would've remembered her, so I guess I ain't." She returned the picture and looked at Stone's old Confederate cavalry hat. "My brother Bobby Joe was killed as Murfreesboro. Were you at Murfreesboro?"

"No."

"Bobby Joe would've been about yore age. Sure wish the war never happened. What were you before the war?"

"We raised cotton."

"My daddy worked in the post office, and that's what he did in the army too, but Bobby Joe went to the front."

The bartender brought a clean glass for Mary Ellen, and Stone poured whiskey into it. "Do you know who Tad McDermott is?" he asked.

"They're a-gonna hang him Saturday."

"What's he done?"

"Stealin' and killin' for about ten years. Last week he tried to hold up the bank all by his lonesome, but got caught. Folks from miles around will come to the hangin'. You sure you don't want to come upstairs?"

"Sorry."

She slugged down the whiskey and wiped her mouth with the back of her hand. "Got to get back to work. If yore pecker ever gits hard, you know who to see."

She walked away, and Stone remembered the dismal day he'd returned home from the war, and found out his father and mother were dead, his home had been burned to the ground by Sherman's army, and Marie had disappeared. An old friend of his father's said he'd heard Marie went west with a Union officer, but Stone found that hard to believe. Marie had been a true daughter of the South, and she might've gone west, but not with a Union officer.

Stone remembered sitting near the ashes of Marie's home one afternoon, wearing his tattered old uniform, smoking a cheap cigar, and wondering what to do with himself. It didn't take long to conclude that he'd lost everything except his need to see her again.

He'd been looking for her ever since, and had just arrived in Texas on the wagon train. Now he intended to go from town to town showing her picture, hoping someday a person would say he knew where she lived.

He finished his whiskey and walked out of the saloon. On the sidewalk, an old woman in a hoop skirt held a conversation with a small dog on a leash. He turned and walked toward the restaurant, his stomach grumbling. He'd have a meal, take a bath, and have a night of drinking and cards.

He came to Gallagher's Restaurant, and two drunken cowboys, their arms around each other's shoulders, staggered out the door. Stone let them pass, then dusted himself off and walked inside.

It was filled with businessmen, ranchers, cowboys, gamblers, and ladies. Brass coal-oil lamps were affixed to the walls and polished wood frames surrounded the windows. A crude painting of a steer hung from one of the walls.

Stone couldn't see any empty tables and didn't know anybody with whom to sit. He thought he'd better look for a restaurant that wasn't so busy.

"Care to sit down?"

Stone turned and saw a well-dressed couple seated at a table for four against the wall. The man was in his mid-thirties and had a receding hairline, and the woman was early twenties, with black hair and almond eyes. She looked like a panther in a pearl necklace.

"Wouldn't want to intrude," Stone said.

"No intrusion at all. Have a seat."

Stone hung his hat on the peg, and the man introduced himself: "I'm Craig Delane, and this is my wife Cynthia."

"John Stone."

Stone sat at the table, and his heavy guns knocked against

the table legs. The Delanes were drinking coffee, and on the white tablecloth were plates covered with the residue of the pie they'd had for dessert.

"If you're wondering what to order," Delane said, "may I suggest the steak? They also serve a fine whiskey."

His accent was from the northeast, and they were dressed impeccably in conservative upper-class fashion. Stone became aware of his trail-worn clothes and dusty boots. He smelled like a horse.

"You work on one of the ranches around here?" Delane asked.

"Just passing through."

"What brings you to Dumont?"

Stone took out the picture of Marie. "Ever see her?"

Delane looked at the picture, and Cynthia leaned her head close to his. "Let me see too."

"She's very beautiful," said Craig Delane. "Who is she?"

"Friend of mine."

Cynthia asked, "How did you lose her?"

"That's a long story."

The Chinese waiter arrived, wearing a white apron, carrying a glass. He was skinny, with straight black hair. "What you want?"

"A steak with whatever vegetables you've got."

The Chinese waiter scurried away, writing on his notepad, harried and overworked, and his pants were too short, showing white stockings and strange Chinese slippers.

Stone poured some whiskey into the glass. "Where are you folks from?"

"I represent a consortium of investors from New York," Delane explained. "I'm setting up a ranching operation for them."

Cynthia looked at Stone with her velvet eyes. "How did you lose your lady friend?"

"It's kind of personal."

Silence came over the table, and Stone felt Cynthia's eyes boring into him.

Delane lit a cigar. "You look like you've had a hard day," he said to Stone.

"I arrived on that wagon train that came in this morning."

"You sound as if you have an education."

"So do you."

"Where did you go to school?"

"West Point."

"I take it you were a Confederate officer during the war?"

"Yes. Were you in the war?"

"No."

Stone figured Delane bought his way out of the Union Army. *A rich man's war and a poor man's fight.*

"I'm always on the lookout for a good hand," Delane said. "If you're interested, we can put you on the payroll."

"I'd intended to head south."

"If you change your mind, see me at the HC Ranch."

Cynthia looked at Stone and said, "Is that woman in the picture your wife?"

"No."

"How'd she get lost?"

"Dumont County must be quite a change for two New Yorkers. What do you think of the frontier?"

"It gets boring out here," Craig said. "Neither of us hunt, and that's generally the pastime."

"Most people drink a lot," Cynthia added. "And we're not accustomed to having no police. Violence can break out at any moment, and there's nothing you can do."

"We're near the Dunstall River northwest of here," Craig said. "Why don't you come out and have dinner with us one night before you leave? It's so seldom we find someone we can speak with."

"Most people only talk about horses and cows," Cynthia said. "I feel as if I'm in the most remote corner of the world." She looked at Stone. "How long have you been looking for that woman?"

"Since the war."

"That's nearly five years. What'll you do if you don't find her?"

"Cynthia," said Craig, "don't you think that's a rather personal question?"

"Just curious."

On the other side of the restaurant, somebody bellowed, "Where's my goddamned grub!"

Stone saw a heavyset cowboy with a beard sitting at a table

with two other cowboys. The skinny Chinese waiter shuffled toward them.

"Dinner not ready yet!" the waiter said. "Wait little while longer!"

The heavyset man arose and grabbed the waiter by the front of his shirt, picking him off the floor and pinning him against the wall.

"I'm tired of waitin', you slant-eyed son of a bitch! You better git my grub out here, or I'll beat yore ass!"

Stone could see the terror on the waiter's face as he stretched paralyzed against the wall. The heavyset man picked him up and threw him toward the kitchen, and the waiter stumbled, crashing into a table, upsetting a group of diners, but they arose meekly, food all over their clothes. The waiter picked himself up off the floor and ran into the kitchen.

The heavyset man laughed as he strutted back to the table and sat down, reaching for his glass of whiskey. One of the cowboys at the table patted him on the shoulder and murmured, "You showed him who's boss, Wayne."

"Who's that?" Stone asked.

"Wayne Dawson, son of Hank Dawson, who owns the Circle Bar D and most of Dumont County. I've been negotiating with Hank Dawson for the purchase of cattle for my herd."

"He didn't teach his son good manners," Stone said.

Cynthia replied, "He's a pig, and you can't expect a pig to have good manners."

Craig raised his finger to his lips. "Not so loud. We don't want to get on the wrong side of these people."

"I despise him," Cynthia said. "It's disgusting the way everybody bows and scrapes before the Dawsons."

"Keep your voice down, Cynthia."

She raised her cup of coffee, and Stone looked at Wayne Dawson spitting something dark and vile onto the floor. Then he reached for the bottle of whiskey on the table.

"A chink ain't nothin' but an injun turned inside out," Wayne said loud enough so everyone could hear. "A good chink is a dead chink!"

"Maybe we ought to kill one before we go back to the ranch," one of the cowboys said.

The people in the restaurant ignored them and continued to dine quietly. The door to the kitchen opened and the waiter came out, carrying a plate of food. His face was cold and stoical as he placed the plate in front of Wayne Dawson.

Dawson took one look at the food and banged his fist on the table. "That's not what I wanted!"

"You say chicken!" the waiter replied.

"I said roast beef!" Dawson jumped up and grabbed the waiter by the throat, shaking him in the air as though he were a rag doll. The waiter flailed desperately with his legs and arms, and was turning a bright shade of green.

"You son of a bitch!" Dawson roared, drawing back his fist. He held the waiter steady and punched him solidly in the mouth, and the waiter's head was knocked backward. The cowboys at the table laughed as if it were hilarious. Dawson readied his fist again and slammed the waiter in the face, and the waiter went flying against a wall, sliding down and lying in a heap on the floor.

Dawson advanced toward him, an expression of his contempt on his face, and he recited an old ditty he'd heard at his father's knee when he was a boy:

> "Chinky, chinky Chinaman
> eats dead rats.
> They're good for his belly
> and they make him fat!"

Dawson raised his foot to stomp the waiter's head, and something struck the back of his leg. He lost his balance and dropped awkwardly to the floor. The restaurant became still. Wayne looked up and saw John Stone towering above him. Stone looked at him coldly, then turned and walked back to his table.

"You shouldn't've done that," Delane said.

Stone sat and reached for his glass of whiskey. People arose from their tables and headed for the door. Hank got to his feet, looked at his men, and their hands were near their guns.

"I'll take care of this," Wayne said.

He hitched up his gunbelts and walked noisily across the room toward the table where Stone sat with Craig and Cynthia Delane.

"On yore goddamned feet!" Dawson shouted to Stone.

Stone gave him a deadly look. "Get away from me."

"Git up or I'll whip you where you stand!"

Craig took Cynthia's hand and together they moved away from the table. Stone's blue eyes were chips of ice as he looked up at Dawson. Most of the patrons had left the restaurant, and the rest pressed their backs against the walls. Wayne's two cowboy companions arose from their table.

Delane decided he must do something to stop the mayhem. He took a step forward, but one of Dawson's gunfighters turned around, yanking out his six-gun and pointing it at him.

"Hold it right there," said the gunfighter.

Delane stepped back toward the corner. The waiter was out cold, blood on his face, and Stone stared at Wayne Dawson, who looked as though he was going to explode.

Dawson let out a roar and charged, baring his teeth and leaping into the air. Stone waited until the last moment, then dodged out of the way. Dawson crashed into the table and fell to the floor, rolling around and getting to his knees like a big black bear.

Stone stood beside the window, his cavalry hat slanted low over his eyes. Dawson got to his feet and wiped his nose with his finger. Stone saw three armed men in front of him, and felt the old zing of combat in his blood and bones.

Wayne worked the muscles in his jaws and balled up his fists. The cowboys' hands hovered above their guns, and one of them said, "We'll shoot him for you, boss."

"I'll take him out," Wayne said, raising his fists.

He advanced, and Stone leaned to the right, leaned to the left, and uncorked a smashing right jab that caught Dawson on the mouth. Without breaking motion, Stone followed with a crushing left hook to Dawson's ear, and Dawson felt as if a train had run into him. When his mind cleared he was on his knees, and he looked up at Stone standing solidly in front of him, his blue eyes gleaming.

Wayne let out a roar and got to his feet unsteadily. His lips were pulped and bells rang in his ear.

One of the cowboys said, "Just give us the word, Wayne."

"I can handle him," Wayne replied.

He raised his fists and moved toward Stone, while Stone circled to the left. Wayne followed him, then lowered his head and charged. Stone switched direction suddenly and feinted a left jab to Wayne's nose, but when Wayne raised his guard to protect his face, Stone hammered him in the guts three times, then as Wayne lowered his guard, Stone smacked him in the face.

Wayne backpedaled, trying to escape the blows raining upon him. Whenever he tried to cover one part of his body, Stone punched another part. Wayne fell against the wall, dodged into a hard right hook, and all the lights went out.

When he opened his eyes he was lying on the floor, floundering, the room spinning. All he could do was open his mouth and scream: "Kill him!"

Stone and the two cowboys dropped their hands to their holsters and hauled iron. The room echoed with booming shots, and the cowboys were caught before they could thumb back their hammers. Stone triggered his Colts as fast as he could, and the cowboys faltered, peppered with holes. One managed to fire a wild shot at the far wall before he collapsed, while the other cowboy staggered from side to side, trying to hold his gun steady for one last final shot, and Stone fired again. The impact of the bullet sent the gunfighter sprawling backward, and he fell at Cynthia's feet. She opened her mouth to scream, but no sound came out.

Dawson saw his two henchmen sprawled out on the floor. He'd been reaching for his own gun, and suddenly the shootout was over.

"Raise your hands slowly," Stone said.

Wayne looked down the barrel of Stone's gun and saw the flames of hell. He lifted his hands.

The patrons gazed at the two dead men bleeding on the floor. Cynthia's eyes were riveted on Stone's face. She'd never seen anybody killed before, and felt faint.

Craig placed his arm around her shoulders. Stone and Dawson stared at each other, and Stone's gun still was pointed at Dawson's head.

"You'll pay for this," Dawson said.

Stone realized he'd better get out of town immediately. The frontier was notorious for crooked trials and rigged juries. He walked swiftly to the swinging doors, holstered his guns, and stepped onto the sidewalk. A white-haired man in his fifties, wearing a badge and followed by deputies and armed citizens, marched across the street, heading toward him, and all had drawn their guns. Nonchalantly Stone sauntered toward his horse, when the door to the restaurant opened behind him and Wayne, his face bloodied, stumbled outside.

"Arrest him!" Wayne hollered.

The sheriff and his men closed in a tight circle around Stone. "You're under arrest," the sheriff said to Stone. "Hand over yore guns."

"It was self-defense," Stone replied. "They drew on me first."

"Tell it to the judge."

The sheriff pointed his gun at Stone, and Stone wasn't ready to shoot a sheriff and fight a town. A deputy stepped forward and took Stone's guns.

"Head for the jail," the sheriff said.

2

TAD MCDERMOTT GRINNED when he saw the sheriff herd Stone toward the cell.

"Figured you'd be back," McDermott said.

A deputy unbuckled Stone's gunbelts and pulled his knife out of his boot. The sheriff unlocked the cell door.

"Get in," he ordered.

Stone passed through the door, and it was the first time in his life that his freedom had been taken away. The sheriff slammed the door and locked it. Two drunks lay on the floor, and McDermott sat like a sinister specter in the corner. The sheriff and his deputies walked to the desk, speaking in low tones. Stone grabbed the bars and shook them, but they were solidly mounted.

"What'd you do?" McDermott asked.

"Shot two cowboys from the Circle Bar D."

"Not a smart thing."

"That's what I thought when I heard about your bank robbery."

The door of the sheriff's office was thrown open, and Wayne

Dawson entered, stomping toward the cell, his face bruised and mangled.

"You're as good as dead!" he shouted, and spit on Stone's face before he could move out of the way. Wayne Dawson stared hatefully at Stone for a few moments, and Stone wished he could tear the bars apart. Dawson spat on him again, then turned and walked toward the sheriff.

"If he escapes, it'll be yore ass."

"Don't worry, Mr. Dawson. He won't escape."

"He'd damn well better not."

Dawson stormed out of the sheriff's office, and Stone wiped the spit from his face. The sheriff scowled at Stone, who reached for his tobacco. It was sinking into his head that he was in serious difficulty. McDermott looked at the tobacco hungrily. Stone threw it to him.

Both men rolled cigarettes and looked across the cell at each other.

"They'll probably lynch you tonight," said McDermott.

Stone puffed his cigarette and wondered if there was a way to escape. He arose and examined the back window.

"The iron bars are sunk in concrete," McDermott said. "It'd take a cannon to blast you out of this cell."

"Heard you killed a man."

"Killed more than one, but they had the money and I wanted it."

"You killed just for money?"

"Ain't no better reason to kill a man. Why'd you kill them cowboys?"

"We had a disagreement, you might say."

"You must be fast, but nobody's faster'n a rope. It squeezes out yore life and there ain't no place to run. If they're a-gonna lynch you, I reckon they'll probably lynch me while they're at it. Just think—I don't know you, and you don't know me, but we're gonna die side by side tonight."

A windmill spun in the breeze as the sun sank toward the horizon. Craig Delane rode his buckboard toward the main house of the Circle Bar D Ranch, and two of his cowboys accompanied him on horseback.

A crowd of men lounged on the front porch of the main house. Not far away on the lawn, an American flag on a high pole fluttered in the breeze. The main house was painted white, vast and sprawling. Nearby was a corral full of horses.

One of Craig's cowboys tied up the team of horses to the hitching post at the front gate, and Craig climbed down from the buckboard. The men on the front porch stirred, pushing back the brims of their hats. Three stood and hitched up their gunbelts.

Delane walked toward the front porch, followed by his cowboys. A few of Dawson's men swaggered toward him, and one was Jesse Atwell, the ramrod of the Circle Bar D. He was heavyset and in his forties, with pudgy jowls and a button nose. A four-inch scar was on his left cheek, and they said he got it in a saloon in Dodge.

"What can we do fer you today?"

"I'd like to speak with Hank Dawson."

"Search him, boys."

Delane raised his hands, and two cowpokes patted him down. One removed the pistol from Delane's holster and handed it to Atwell.

Atwell said, "I'll hold on to this."

Delane was used to getting frisked at the Circle Bar D. It was part of doing business with Hank Dawson. Atwell jammed the pistol into his belt.

"Have a seat on the porch, while I see if Mr. Dawson's in."

Delane followed Atwell and his men to the porch, dropping onto a caneback chair as Atwell entered the house. Craig sat uneasily among the gunfighters Hank Dawson employed to protect his holdings and advance his interests.

He'd heard rumors that John Stone would be lynched that night, and Cynthia had urged him to visit Hank Dawson and talk him out of it. But he felt intimidated by the gunfighters sitting around him on the porch. One of them laughed, and Craig was certain it was at his expense.

The door opened and Atwell stuck his head out. "Mr. Dawson said to go to his office."

Craig entered the house, and it was a few degrees cooler than outside. The living room had massive furniture strewn on the rug, and the heads of game mounted on the walls. Over the fireplace hung an oil painting of a chubby young woman, Hank Dawson's dead wife. She'd died several years ago.

Delane strolled down a corridor whose walls were decorated with Indian blankets, and entered Hank Dawson's office. Hank sat at a desk covered with documents and envelopes. He was obese, with gray hair and a full gray beard. "What can I do for you, Delane?" he asked in a deep baritone.

"I'm not here on business," Craig said. "I just wanted to tell you this: I was in the restaurant today when your men were killed. I saw the whole thing, and John Stone was sitting at my table before the trouble started. He fought in self-defense, and I think he deserves a fair trial."

Hank Dawson spat into his shiny brass cuspidor, then lifted a box of cigars off the top of his desk.

"No thank you," Delane said.

Dawson took one and lit it. His head disappeared in a cloud of blue smoke. "My son tells a different story. He was having a problem with a waiter, and Stone butted in."

"Your son wasn't having an argument with the waiter. He was beating him up, and the waiter hadn't done anything wrong that I could see. That's when Stone stepped in."

Dawson's small eyes glittered like obsidian. "Nobody pushes my son around, and nobody shoots my men. A man either stands with me or against me. Where do you stand, Mr. Delane?"

"Why not let a judge decide who's right and who's wrong?"

"This ain't New York City. We make our own laws out here. You got to adjust to our ways, Mr. Delane. We ain't gonna adjust to yours."

Delane heard footsteps behind him, and Wayne Dawson walked into the room. "What's *he* doin' here?"

"We're talkin' business," his father said.

"He's a friend of that saddle bum that shot our men and nearly shot me!"

"Leave us alone, son. I'll speak with you later."

"Don't let him talk you into anythin', Pa."

Wayne Dawson shuffled out of the room, leaving Delane alone with Hank Dawson.

"It's been hard raising him," Hank said. "You know how rambunctious young people can be."

"I'd say he's a little more rambunctious than most, Mr. Dawson."

"He's high-spirited, like a fine thoroughbred horse, and

that's always the best kind. 'Course, I couldn't expect you to know much about horses, you bein' from the East and all, Mr. Delane. Now if you don't mind, I've got a lot of work to do.''

Delane walked out of the office, and Jesse Atwell was waiting in the hallway. Delane followed Atwell down the long, winding corridor to the porch, and Atwell gave Stone his gun back.

Delane holstered his gun and descended the steps of the porch. His men waited for him near the hitching post, and one of them untied his team of horses. Delane climbed onto the front seat of the buckboard and glanced back toward the porch.

Wayne Dawson stood at the railing, glowering at him. Delane slapped the reins on the backs of his horses and headed back toward the HC Ranch.

Cynthia sat in the parlor of her ranch and sipped a cup of tea. There was no one to visit, no stores for shopping, no social life, concerts, or plays.

She felt isolated and lonely whenever Craig was away. Outside were snakes, scorpions, dangerous wild animals, and swarms of flying insects. She had nothing in common with the cowboys, who were brutal and insensitive, from what she could see. They avoided her whenever possible, although sometimes she caught them examining her from underneath the brims of their hats. They exuded a raw masculinity that disgusted and attracted her at the same time. Craig seemed almost effeminate compared to them.

She stared out the window at the great rolling plains, and wondered what she was doing here and why she'd ever married Craig Delane.

He was a wonderful man with decent instincts, always considerate of her feelings, but he lacked something. Sometimes she thought he was too nice.

The gunfight at Gallagher's Restaurant had blasted her loose from her moorings. Blood flowed like wine over the floor. She'd looked at Stone standing with a smoking gun in each hand, and hadn't been the same since.

What a strange man he was. He'd killed calmly and coolly, like a smooth well-oiled machine. She'd known the frontier would be wild, but never suspected this. A lynching would take place that night, unless Craig could stop it.

The prairie was endless and the sky immense. She felt small and insignificant, a mere speck on a vast land.

A buckboard and riders surmounted a hill in the distance, Craig returning from the Dawson ranch. Cynthia arose and looked at herself in a mirror. She saw lines around her eyes and thought she was getting old, although she was only twenty-five.

She moved toward the window, pulling back the white lace curtain. Craig and his escort rode toward the hitching rail in front of the house, and Craig climbed down from the buckboard. He issued orders to his men, then brushed the sleeves of his frock coat and walked up the path toward the front door of the house.

Cynthia was in the vestibule when Craig opened the door. Craig was covered with trail dust and looked pale as a ghost.

She kissed him lightly, careful not to get dust on her. "What happened?"

"I couldn't budge him," Craig said. "Two of his men were killed, his son was humiliated, and somebody's got to pay. There's no judge that we can talk to, and Sheriff Perkins is an employee of Hank Dawson."

"I can't believe there's nothing we can do," she replied. "I mean, they're going to *kill* him. Maybe we should go to town—perhaps we can do something there. We can at least talk with John Stone and comfort him during his last hours."

"That'd be awkward. Hank Dawson wouldn't like it, and we're in sensitive negotiations."

She placed her hands on his shoulders. "Please, Craig."

"I'll have the men bring the buckboard back."

"Everybody up!" Sheriff Perkins said, and two of his deputies were behind him, aiming their guns into the cell. "Let's go! Move it!"

Stone, McDermott, and the two drunks got to their feet. Sheriff Perkins inserted a key into the lock in the cell door.

"Get back," said Sheriff Perkins, "and if any of you tries somethin', it'll be the last thing you ever try."

The sheriff opened the cell door, and Stone looked at the outer office, tempted to make a run for it, but they'd shoot him down like a dog.

The sheriff called the names of the two drunks. "You men git out of that cell. You're free."

"What about me?" McDermott asked.

"Don't make me laugh."

The two drunks shuffled out of the cell. The sheriff slammed and locked the door again, and Stone and McDermott were alone. The drunks stood in front of the front desk, and the sheriff gave them their guns back.

"Stay out of trouble," the sheriff said.

The drunks muttered and mumbled as they left the sheriff's office. The sheriff returned to the cell door and looked at Stone and McDermott. "You boys wanna see a preacher?"

McDermott held the bars in his hands. "What do we need to see a preacher for?"

"Some men like to speak to a preacher before they die." The sheriff turned to Stone. "How about you?"

"Yes, I'd like to see a preacher."

The sheriff told a deputy to get the preacher, and the deputy left the office. McDermott sat heavily on the floor of the cell.

"I guess that's it, then," he said. "They're gonna kill us."

Stone didn't say anything. He'd figured the same thing himself.

"I had me some good times and some good women," said McDermott. "If this is the time for me to go, I guess there ain't nothin' I can do."

Stone had faced death many times in the war, but that'd been different, because he'd had a fighting chance, and a man could die with honor. He imagined himself strangling slowly, swinging in the breeze, for nothing.

It was night, and he heard the barking of dogs. He thought of his mother and father, and the old plantation back in South Carolina. He remembered Marie, and the happy times they had.

The door to the sheriff's office opened, and the Chinese waiter from Gallagher's Restaurant approached the desk.

"What the hell do you want?" the sheriff asked gruffly.

"I want talk John Stone."

"You got five minues. Harry, you watch 'em."

Harry, one of the deputies, accompanied the Chinese waiter to the cell.

"My name Hong Fat," the Chinese waiter said. "I very sorry about what happen."

"It's not your fault," Stone replied.

"You are brave man."

Hong Fat and Stone shook hands, and Stone felt a small object in his palm. He grasped the object and closed his fingers around it.

"Good luck," said Hong Fat.

Hong Fat slouched toward the door, and Stone moved deeper into the shadows of the cell. He opened his hand and looked at what Hong Fat had given him. It was a small jackknife with a bone handle. He pulled out the blade, and it was sharp as a razor.

McDermott moved beside him and whispered, "What he give you?"

Stone showed it to him, then dropped it into his boot. He looked out the window again. A cool breeze caressed his face, and a half moon hung in the sky over the mountains in the distance.

The door to the sheriff's office opened and a deputy entered, followed by a man in a black suit.

"Hello, Reverend," the sheriff said. "We got somebody who wants to talk to you."

The sheriff unlocked the prison cell and the reverend stepped inside. He was short, round-shouldered, and bald.

"You got ten minutes," the sheriff said.

"I'm Reverend Skeaping. Which one of you wants to see me?"

"Me," said Stone.

"What can I do for you, my son?"

"My name is John Stone. I'm going to be lynched tonight, and I thought I should speak with a minister of God."

"Do you have a family?"

"No."

"Is there anyone whom you'd like me to notify?"

"No."

"It's not good to be alone. The Bible tells us we must be fruitful and multiply." Reverend Skeaping turned to McDermott. "How about you?"

McDermott sat sullenly on the floor in corner. "I done my

share of multiplyin'," he said, "but they're a-gonna lynch me anyways."

"*Thou shalt not kill.* You've violated the commandment. Love of money is a sin."

"Tell that to Hank Dawson."

Reverend Skeaping looked at Stone. "I suggest you get down on your knees and pray to the Lord our God."

Stone dropped to his knees, and Reverend Skeaping placed his hand on Stone's head. "Dear God," he said, "please have mercy on this man, John Stone. Remember that he's one of your children, as we are all your children. He may've sinned against you, but we are weak vessels. Please help John Stone through the difficult night that lies ahead. Thank you for the blessings you have given us. Amen."

McDermott snorted. "What blessings?"

"Sheriff?" Reverend Skeaping said.

Sheriff Perkins opened the cell door. Reverend Skeaping put on his black hat and left the sheriff's office. Sheriff Perkins stood at the bars and looked at Stone. "Feel better now?" he asked sarcastically.

Stone rolled a cigarette, then threw the bag of tobacco to McDermott. They sat in the darkness and smoked silently. Sheriff Perkins returned to his desk. Stone wondered when they'd come to get him. He wished he'd never set foot in that damned restaurant.

A half hour later, Craig and Cynthia Delane entered the sheriff's office, and they were elegantly dressed as always.

"We'd like to speak to the prisoner," Craig said.

"Right this way, sir." The sheriff led Craig and Cynthia back to the cell. "You're havin' a busy night," the sheriff said to Stone.

Cynthia looked at Stone in the cell, which was small and dirty, and Stone was locked in with a man who appeared to be a hardened criminal.

"I spoke with Hank Dawson," Craig said, "and tried to convince him to let bygones be bygones, but he wasn't receptive."

Stone looked at Cynthia, and her eyes gleamed in the dark. "I wish we could do something," she said.

"Get me a bottle of whiskey."

Sheriff Perkins's voice reverberated across the office. "No whiskey for the prisoners!"

Stone, Craig, and Cynthia stood in silence for a few moments. "I can't believe this is happening," Craig said. "This is still America, a nation of laws."

"Not out here."

Craig turned and walked toward Sheriff Perkins's desk, and Sheriff Perkins looked up from his newspaper.

"I assume you've heard the rumors," Craig said to him.

"I hear rumors all the time. What ones're you talkin' about?"

"The rumors about the lynching. Hank Dawson and his men are going to lynch John Stone tonight. I suggest you deputize some men to guard your prisoner. I volunteer to be one of the deputies."

The sheriff laughed. "You? Mr. Delane, I suggest you take your lady home and forget about bein' a deputy. Why, somebody's liable to take a shot at you, and then what'll you do?"

Craig blushed "If anything happens to this prisoner, I'll report it to the governor."

"Report ennythin' you like, but I recommend you mind your own business. People who go up against Hank Dawson generally don't last long around here."

"I'm not going up against Hank Dawson. I'm going up against you."

"Same difference."

Craig returned to the cell. "They have no concept of the fundamental principles of justice out here. It's really quite shocking."

Stone said ruefully, "If I'd minded my own business, I wouldn't be in jail."

McDermott arose from the floor and took off his black hat. "Ain't nobody gonna introduce me?"

"This is Tad McDermott," Stone said. "If they hang me, they'll probably hang him too."

"You're the bank robber?" Delane asked.

" 'At's me," McDermott said proudly. He looked at Cynthia and grinned. "What's yore name, ma'am?"

"Cynthia."

"You're right purty."

There was a few minutes of awkward silence, then Delane

cleared his throat. "We'd better be moving along. Good luck to you, John Stone. God be with you."

Cynthia reached forward and touched Stone's hand. She wanted to say something, but only platitudes came to mind, and she didn't want to give a man platitudes on his last night on earth.

Craig and Cynthia left the sheriff's office, but Cynthia's perfume lingered behind. Stone and McDermott sat on the floor again.

"Helluva woman," McDermott said. "Wouldn't mind runnin' into her alone on the range some night, but I reckon she'd rather run into you. She was lookin' at you like she wanted to eat you up alive."

Craig and Cynthia stepped out onto the sidewalk as a group of horsemen rode past. Their buckboard was tied to the hitching post, and two of Craig's hands lounged about on the bench in front of the jail.

"I don't feel well," Cynthia said to Craig. "Do we have to go home?"

"Would you like to stay in town tonight?"

"I think it'd be best, if you don't mind, Craig."

They crossed the street arm in arm and headed toward the New Dumont Hotel. Not far away, in front of a saloon, a drunken cowboy fired his pistol into the air.

"Dreadful place," Cynthia said, wrinkling her nose.

"Someday there'll be law here. It might take twenty years, but it'll come."

"A lot of good that'll do John Stone."

They climbed the steps of the New Dumont Hotel and entered the lobby. In one corner, a group of well-dressed businessmen held an earnest conversation, and against the far wall a cowboy slept, his feet propped up on a coffee table.

Craig and Cynthia checked in. The clerk gave them a key and they climbed to the second floor where the best suites were. Craig unlocked the door to theirs and lit a lamp. The suite became bathed in a soft yellow glow.

Cynthia crossed the room and pulled aside the drapes over the window. It faced the street, and she looked toward the jail. "That poor man," she said.

3

STONE SAT ON the floor of the jail, with his back against the wall. The only light came from the lamp on the sheriff's desk, but the sheriff was gone for the night. Harry, one of his deputies, was in charge. He lay on the sofa underneath the rifle racks, fast asleep.

McDermott sat opposite Stone, his unshaven face floating in the darkness.

"It shouldn't be long now," McDermott said.

"They're mainly interested in me," Stone replied. "Maybe you can escape. I'll make a commotion when they open the cell door, to take their attention away from you. Just mingle with the crowd and walk out of here."

Stone took out his bag of tobacco, and there wasn't much left. He rolled himself a skinny cigarette and then threw the bag to McDermott.

"You scared?" McDermott asked.

"I don't know."

"An old owlhoot told me all about hangin' once. He said yore neck snaps right away, and you don't feel nothin'. One minute you're here, and the next minute you're gone."

• • •

The thundering of hoofbeats shattered the silence of the night as a small army of men rode their horses hard in the wan light of the half moon. They were on the wild prairie, heading for the town of Dumont, their horses straining their muscles as they stretched ever forward, the riders giving the horses plenty of rein.

The ground shook with the pounding of hoofbeats, and nocturnal animals ran out of their way. The wind pushed back the brims on the hats of the riders and whipped their clothes. There were over forty of them, grim-faced and heavily armed, all worked for the Circle Bar D. They were on their way to a lynching, and they were mad.

Leading them, riding in tandem, were Hank and Wayne Dawson, father and son, two big men sitting atop big horses. Strings of saliva dripped from their horses' mouths and flew back into the air as the men bounced up and down on their saddles.

An expression of harsh determination was on Hank Dawson's face. Two of his men had been killed and his son had been humiliated. There could be no mercy.

Next to him, Wayne spurred his mighty sorrel and lusted for revenge. A stranger had pointed his guns at him, and he'd never been so afraid. Even women had seen him cringe, a terrible moment. He'd make the stranger wish he was never born.

Behind the two Dawsons rode their private army of gunfighters and cowboys. They were a close-knit brotherhood similar to a military elite, and two of them had been killed by John Stone. They wanted to string Stone up, see the death agony on his face, and watch him twist and turn in the night breeze.

The riders sped through the night, on their mission of hate. No one spoke; all knew what they had to do. In the distance they saw the lights of Dumont twinkling and sparkling in the valley.

Cynthia Delane lay in bed beside her husband, staring at the ceiling. She couldn't sleep, thinking about John Stone sitting in jail, facing the hangman's noose.

The bed was soft and comfortable, and she sank deeply into it. Her hips and shoulders touched her husband, Craig. Neither of them had brought bedclothes to town, so were clad only in their underwear, with a sheet and light blanket to protect them from the cool night air.

Cynthia thought it must be after midnight, and wondered when the lynching would take place. Was it possible that Hank Dawson had had a change of heart?

She'd met Hank Dawson a few times, and he'd disgusted her. He was big and fat, sloppy and unkempt, and his body exuded a sour stench. Yet he was the most powerful man in the region and everybody, including her husband, deferred to him.

Hank Dawson had come to Dumont County ten years ago with a bunch of gunfighters, and gobbled everything up chunk by chunk as if it were a pie. If no one was on the land, he took it for his own. If someone was there, he convinced him to move away. If there was resistance, he overcame it with armed might. Now he was undisputed ruler of thousands of acres, and God pity any sodbuster who happened to wander onto his land.

Cynthia wished she were home, so her maid could prepare a glass of warm milk to help her fall asleep. She was troubled by a headache and an upset stomach, but most of all she was troubled by John Stone. The man made her feel uneasy whenever she thought of him.

I must be crazy, she thought, because she realized she was attracted, in a perverse way, to John Stone. Stone had walked into danger without hesitation to help a stranger, and should be praised, not lynched. She couldn't imagine Craig intervening to help somebody, as Stone had done. Cynthia never had seen such a display of raw courage in her life.

She heard a low rumble in the distance, and at first it sounded like a tornado, but then she realized it was a large number of horses being ridden hard. *Here they are*, she thought. Craig stirred next to her.

"I think they're coming."

He rolled out of bed and walked to the window, and he was lean and ghostlike in the light of the moon. He looked at the street and saw lamps in some of the windows across the street. The sound of the horses became louder, and Cynthia got out of bed, moving toward the window.

The street was deserted, and she heard horse's hooves

pounding the ground. Then the first of the riders turned the corner and came into view. She recognized Hank and Wayne Dawson in front, not by their faces, which were obscured by their hats, but by their corpulence. The rest of the riders followed, grasping the reins of their horses. Hank Dawson pulled out his six-gun and fired a shot in the air. Then his men drew their guns, and a fusillade of shots exploded into the night as the riders passed in front of the New Dumont Hotel.

Cynthia watched the horsemen ride up the street, heading for the jail. Some horsemen yipped and yelled, as though they were herding cattle. Cynthia looked across the street and saw faces in windows. Other citizens were awake too, and everybody knew what was happening.

"Why doesn't somebody do something!" she said.

Craig placed his slender arm around her shoulders. "Hank Dawson will kill anybody who stands in his way."

Stone stood and placed his hands on the bars of the cell. "Here they are."

McDermott raised himself off the floor. The deputy turned up the wick on the lamp, then strapped on his gunbelt.

"Guess this is it, boys," he said.

The sound of horsemen came closer, and it reminded Stone of cavalry. He heard the firing of guns and whoops of cowboys. The horsemen came to a stop in front of the sheriff's office.

Stone turned to McDermott. "Remember what I told you. I'll start something, and you make a run for it."

They heard the sound of boots on the boardwalk outside the sheriff's office. The door was flung open and Hank Dawson walked in, gun in hand. Behind him was Wayne, and then came the cowboys.

"We want your prisoner," Hank Dawson said.

"Can't have him," the deputy replied weakly.

"That's what you think."

Jesse Atwell stepped forward and lifted the gun out of the deputy's hand. A few of the Dawson men chortled.

"Turn around and shut up," Atwell said to the deputy.

Harry turned around and shut up. Wayne Dawson stomped

toward the cell and looked at Stone. "You're dead meat," he said.

Atwell opened the top drawer of the sheriff's desk and took out the ring of keys. Meanwhile, Hank Dawson walked to the cell and looked at Stone. He was curious to see the man who'd shot two of his gunfighters and menaced his son.

Stone stood solidly, his hands on the bars. Hank Dawson looked at his face and saw an aquiline nose and gleaming eyes. Stone's body was muscular and suggested tremendous power. Dawson hated Stone, because Stone made him feel like a fat slob.

"Get him," Dawson said.

Atwell stuck the key into the lock and twisted. Stone stook a step backward and looked at McDermott. The door opened and Atwell entered the cell, followed by a swarm of his cowboys.

Stone leapt forward and punched Atwell in the mouth, and Atwell went sprawling backward. An expression of panic came over Hank Dawson's face, and he turned pale. He opened his mouth to give an order, but no sound came out.

The other gunfighters didn't need orders. Charging forward, they tackled Stone, and he twisted, punched, and kicked. They tried to grab his arms but he broke loose and smashed one cowboy in the stomach, doubling him over with pain. He kicked the next cowboy in the groin, flattened the nose of another cowboy, and slugged a third cowboy on the jaw.

A wild melee broke out in the darkened cell, and it was difficult to see what was going on. A cowboy managed to grab Stone around the waist, but Stone brought his fist down onto the cowboy's head, and the cowboy's arms went slack. Stone kicked him in the face, jumped over him, and landed in front of Hank Dawson.

Horrified, Hank Dawson backed away, and a group of cowboys moved to protect him. Stone punched one of them in the mouth, elbowed another in the throat, but a third cowboy was behind him and brought his gun down hard on top of Stone's head.

Stone saw stars, and his knees gave out. He fell to the floor, but before he could land he was caught by hands that drew him up to his feet again. Stone was dazed, hearing bells and birds. Pinwheels of light flew in front of his eyes.

"We got him," said Atwell, blood dripping out of his nose.

One cowboy held Stone's right arm, and another held Stone's left arm. Stone's consciousness returned and he struggled to break free. A cowboy stepped in front of Stone and punched him in the face. Stone brought up his foot and kicked the cowboy in the gut. The cowboy bellowed like a wounded animal and dropped to his knees in front of Stone.

"Hold his legs!" hollered Hank Dawson.

Two cowboys dived on Stone from either side, clasping their arms around his thighs. Two more cowboys held his waist. Stone worked his right arm loose and swung it at the nearest cowboy, clobbering him on the eye, but two more cowboys twisted the arm behind his back. Another man joined the one who was holding Stone's left arm. Stone couldn't move.

Blood trickled down his forehead, and cowboys from the Circle Bar D crowded around him. Hank Dawson stepped forward.

"You're going to pay for that," he said.

Stone saw the folds of fat around Hank Dawson's neck and looked at Dawson's massive belly. Gravy stains were on Dawson's shirt, and a button had been popped by his considerable girth. Stone raised his gaze and examined Dawson's face. Dawson had tiny pig eyes and a fleshy mouth curled into a sneer.

"Without your men," Stone said, "you wouldn't be anything."

Dawson bared his teeth, raised his fist, and punched Stone in the mouth, but Stone didn't budge.

"My grandmother used to hit me harder than that."

Hank Dawson's knuckles stung as he turned to Wayne. "He's all yours."

Wayne stepped forward, reached into his back pocket, and took out a pair of black leather gloves. Smirking at Stone, he put them on.

"Remember me?" Wayne asked playfully.

"You like to fight people who can't fight back."

"You're gonna be sorry you ever set eyes on me."

Wayne pulled the tight black gloves onto his hands and worked his fingers. "Hold him steady, boys."

Stone tried to break loose, but couldn't move. Wayne's black beard twitched as he stepped forward and raised his right fist. "See this?" he asked, shaking it in the air.

Stone didn't reply.

Wayne continued to shake his right fist, and then brought his left fist around, slamming it into Stone's forehead, and Stone's head snapped backward from the force of the blow. Wayne pounded Stone twice in the stomach, then whacked him in the face again.

Wayne grinned as he worked Stone over, and Stone struggled to stay on his feet, because he didn't want to surrender. Wayne punched Stone again and again. Cuts and bruises appeared on Stone's face, and his lower lip split open, dripping blood. Stone closed his eyes and went limp in the hands of the cowboys and gunfighters who were supporting him.

"He's out cold," Wayne said. "Somebody git a bucket of water."

Stone's head hung down and he was swimming through a sea of darkness. Wayne stood in front of him, sweat trickling through his black beard, breathing heavily. His knuckles hurt, but he felt good. Stone was just like any other man. When you beat on him he shut up.

A cowboy came through the crowd, carrying a bucket of water. He stopped in front of Stone and upended the bucket over his head. The water cascaded down upon Stone, and he opened his eyes. For a split second he didn't know where he was, then felt the pain come on him again. He saw Wayne Dawson rocking back and forth on the balls of his feet, pulling his black gloves on more tightly.

"How're you feeling?" Wayne asked jovially.

Wayne wound up and delivered an uppercut to the point of Stone's jaw. Stone's head snapped back, and Wayne rained blows upon Stone's face. Wayne could feel every hit reverberate through his arms and shoulders, all the way down to his toes. He banged and smashed Stone with wild abandon, and Stone fell unconscious again, but that didn't stop Wayne, who continued to pummel Stone.

"That's enough," said Hank Dawson. "There won't be nothin' to lynch if you keep at him." He turned to the others. "Carry him out and tie him on a horse."

• • •

Cynthia sat on a chair in her hotel room, wearing one of the sheets from the bed as a robe. "They've been in there an awfully long time. I wonder what they're doing?"

Craig stood at the window, wearing the pants from his suit. "It doesn't look good."

"Do you think they'll lynch him in the jail?"

"That's not the way they do it."

"I wish we'd never come to Texas."

Craig saw people emerging from the sheriff's office. "Here they are."

Cynthia moved toward the window like a ghost wrapped in the sheet. She stood beside Craig and peered in the direction of the sheriff's office, where men were mounting horses, and a few fired guns in the air. Cynthia turned to the windows across the street and saw faces looking down the street toward the jail. Everyone wanted to see what was going on, but nobody had the courage to do anything.

The group of riders advanced up the street, heading toward the hotel. Cynthia searched for John Stone, but it was too dark. It reminded Cynthia of a funeral procession. Hank and Wayne Dawson led the pack, and Wayne was smiling as he talked to his father.

"Damn—that felt good!" Wayne said. "Son of a bitch was lookin' for somethin', and I sure gave it to him."

The riders came abreast of the hotel. Cynthia spotted a man slumped on a horse in their midst. "My God—I think I see him!"

They looked at Stone with his head hanging low, his arms bound tightly to his body, hands tied behind his back.

"He's unconscious," Craig said softly.

Cynthia stared at Stone, and it was difficult for her to accept what was happening. She was from New York, where people didn't walk into jails, take prisoners out, and lynch them. In New York, you could always call policemen.

The riders turned the corner and Cynthia stepped back from the window, returning to her chair. They'd find a tree, throw a rope over a branch, and string John Stone up.

"I need a drink," she said.

"It's too late to get anything."

"I wish you'd do something."

"What can I do?"

Cynthia recalled Stone at the table in the restaurant, such a decent man, with a touch of mystery. He was looking for a woman whose picture he carried, and wound up with a noose.

"Craig," she said, sitting in the darkness, "I want to return to New York."

Craig turned around at the window. "I know how you feel, but don't do anything hasty."

"This is a dreadful place. There's no respect for human life. It's the law of the jungle."

"Let's see how we both feel about it in a few days. Maybe I'll leave with you."

"You won't leave with me. You'd never give up your position with the Consortium."

Craig thought for a few moments. "That's true—the Consortium is a once-in-a-lifetime opportunity. If I can turn a profit, I'll be a successful man. Then we can do whatever we want."

"I want to go back to New York."

"It's important for our future that we stay here. I know how you feel about John Stone, and I feel the same way, but we have to be reasonable."

"They're lynching a decent man right now, and I'm supposed to be reasonable? Hank Dawson is a business associate of yours, and I'm supposed to be nice to him next time I see him? I'll spit in his eye!"

"If that's the way you feel, maybe it'd be better if you did leave. A vacation in the East might do you good."

"This won't be a vacation in the East, Craig. If I leave, I won't come back. I can't abide cold-blooded murder, and that's what they're doing to John Stone."

Craig sat limply on the bed. "I don't know what I'll do without you."

"You could come with me."

"I can't leave the ranch."

"You'll have to choose between the ranch and me."

"A woman should stay with her husband, no matter where he happens to be."

"I can't bear this murderous place any longer. You can come with me if you want to, but I'm leaving anyway. My mind is made up. I'm sorry."

• • •

John Stone was aware he was riding a horse. His head was spinning, he ached all over, and his hands were tightly bound behind his back. He raised his head and saw riders surrounding him; ahead was the open range. Nobody said a word. Stone spat blood onto the ground. He felt as if a horse had trampled him.

He knew what was going to happen now. It was a lynching party and he was the man who'd swing in the breeze. He remembered Hong Fat's little knife in his boot, but couldn't reach it. He'd got out of many tight scrapes in his life, but didn't see how he'd get out of this one. It looked as though he was going to die.

He'd never been married, never built a house, never had a son. All he'd done was go to war. He tried not to think about what was going to happen.

Ahead were trees, and the riders veered toward them. Wayne Dawson worked his horse close to Stone. "You still with us?" Wayne asked with a grin. "Guess what's gonna happen now?"

Stone didn't reply, and Wayne punched him hard in the mouth.

"I'm gonna put the rope around your neck with my own two hands. Then I'm gonna watch your face turn blue and your tongue stick out of your mouth. You won't be such a smart feller when you're hangin' by your neck, let me tell you."

Wayne laughed as he maneuvered his horse away from Stone, and the other riders coalesced around Stone. One rider held the reins to Stone's horse. The stand of trees came closer.

Stone's life was coming to an end, and he felt like a block of ice. They entered the stand of trees, and the moon shone down on crooked, gnarled branches, casting weird shadows on the ground. The riders passed among the trees, their horses snorting and jerking their heads around as if they knew something terrible was going to happen. An owl screeched and flew out of a tree, flapping its wings noisily as it fled the scene. A mist arose from the ground, and Stone felt a chill come over him.

The valley of the shadow of death, he thought, and became afraid, but then his old soldierly spirit returned, and he sat straighter in his saddle. *All I can do is go down like a soldier*.

"This looks good enough," said Wayne. "Shorty, gimme the noose."

A man on a horse tossed a length of rope with a noose on the end to Wayne, who circled it in the air a few times and threw it over the branch above Stone's head. The noose hung near Stone's face, and it was rough, with splinters of hemp sticking out like needles. It was going to hurt like hell.

"Yore time has come," Wayne said. "You done fucked with the wrong people, and you don't get no second chance in Dumont County."

He slipped the noose over Stone's head, and Stone saw brigades of Yankees in front of him; he got ready to charge. It was silent as a graveyard in the grove of trees, and then a loud shot rang out!

Stone's horse shuddered at the sound, and Stone saw Wayne sag to the side, blood gushing out of his neck. Wayne's eyes rolled crazily and he leaned back at an impossible angle.

Stone heard the booming voice of Hank Dawson. "What the hell happened there?"

Wayne fell out of the saddle and dropped to the ground heavily. More shots followed in rapid succession, and Stone heard an oncoming rider. He turned around, the noose still around his neck, and saw a tall, lean man on a horse speeding toward him. A ray of moonlight broke through the trees and shone on the rider's face; it was Tad McDermott.

McDermott tore the noose off Stone's head and hollered, "Come on!"

Stone spurred his horse, and the spooked animal leapt forward, broke into a gallop, and plunged through the confused cowboys.

Shots were fired wildly by Dawson's men, and meanwhile McDermott continued to shoot his gun at the riders around him. Stone and McDermott broke away from the hanging party and cut out for the open range. Stone bent low in the saddle, gripping with his legs as much as he could, gritting his teeth, expecting a bullet in the back at any second.

His horse thundered over the prairie, kicking up dirt and

stones. McDermott turned around in the saddle, took aim with his gun, and pulled the trigger.

Click! McDermott stuffed the gun in his belt, looked at Stone, and laughed. "The jail was never made that could hold Tad McDermott!"

Stone, his hands still bound behind him, was having difficulty remaining in the saddle. He bent forward and bit the horse's mane, holding on for dear life as the animal galloped across the prairie, burning the wind.

Back in the woods, Hank Dawson knelt on the ground, looking at the body of his son. His men surrounded him, and everyone was silent. A single sob escaped from Dawson's lips as he saw the black hole in his son's throat. He wanted to drop onto the ground and cry like a baby, and at the same time he wanted to attack his son's killer with an ax.

It had happened so suddenly, and had been so hard to see. A rider attacked, killed his son, turned Stone loose, and got away before anybody knew what had taken place.

Hank Dawson was in a state of shock, heartbroken as he cradled his son in his arms. All he could think of was revenge, and his son's killers couldn't be far away. He could mourn for his son later. First he must catch those killers.

"Ramrod!" he shouted.

"Yes, sir," replied Atwell, standing beside him.

"Have a few of the men carry Wayne back to the ranch and lay him in his bed. The rest of us'll catch those bastards. Anybody see what happened?"

Tom Reece stepped forward. "It was Tad McDermott what done it."

"That's right," said Burkers. "I saw him too."

"He was alone?" Dawson asked.

"As far as I could see."

Dawson felt frustration rip through him. "Why didn't somebody stop him!"

The men shuffled their feet nervously. A few had fired their guns at McDermott, but failed to hit him. The others had been afraid to use their guns, because they might shoot each other in the darkness.

Dawson recalled McDermott in jail with Stone, and realized

he'd gotten away somehow when Wayne was beating on Stone. "Which way did they go?" he asked.

"That way," Atwell replied, pointing to the south.

"Mount up, men!"

Dawson and his men climbed onto their horses, pointed them toward the south, and galloped into the night, leaving Wayne with the three cowboys who were supposed to carry him home, and the empty noose dangling in the breeze.

Stone and McDermott rode toward a gurgling little brook in the middle of a vast basin.

"We can stop here!" McDermott said. He reached over and grabbed the reins of Stone's horse, pulling backward. "You still got that knife the chink gave you?"

"In my right boot."

McDermott pulled the jackknife out of the boot, opened the blade, and cut the ropes that bound Stone. Stone worked his arms to get the circulation going, and McDermott climbed to the ground, leading his horse to the water.

"You saved my life," Stone said. "Thanks."

"I'd still be in jail if it wasn't for you," McDermott replied, "so we're even."

McDermott lay on the ground and lowered his unshaven face into the water. Stone joined him and did the same. He'd thought he'd never drink water again, and it tasted sweet and cool, better than ever. He drank his fill, as the horses slurped next to him.

"Can't stay too long," McDermott said, raising himself up. "Got a lot of ridin' to do."

"Where are we going?"

"Leave it to me. I know every Robbers Roost in these parts."

They climbed onto their horses. Stone turned around in his saddle and scanned the prairie, but could see no sign of Dawson and his men.

"They won't catch us," McDermott said. "I been dodgin' posses all my life, and that one weren't much. When you had that noose around yore neck, what was you thinkin'?"

"I was thinking about the war. Were you in the war, McDermott?"

"Too busy robbin' banks and stagecoaches. Were you scared?"

"I think so."

"Sometimes I think about gittin' hanged. Enough people sure want to toss that old rope around my neck, but they ain't caught me yet. Think I'd rather get shot than hung. How about you?"

"I'd rather die in my sleep when I'm old and gray."

"Men who git in trouble don't git old and gray. Think about that sometime."

They mounted their horses and rode off into the night as stars blazed in the sky above them.

The posse stopped on a large expanse of rock and the men dismounted. Jesse Atwell knelt and looked at the rock. "Can't see anythin'," he said. "Think we lost 'em."

Atwell gazed at Hank Dawson's face, a block of granite in the moonlight. The death of his son was still sinking into him, and he felt a terrible sadness.

Stone and his accomplice had got away for the time being. His men couldn't track them farther at night. He turned to Atwell. "Send somebody back to the ranch for three days' supplies, and get me an injun to track those sons of bitches. I want the supplies and the injun here by sunup."

Dawson sat on the rock and took a small cigar from a silver case. He lit it and puffed until the end was cherry-red, trying to calm down and live with what happened. He'd tear John Stone limb from limb when he got his hands on him, but didn't have him yet. It might turn into a long hunt, but Dawson was resolved to stay on the trail until he caught Stone and McDermott. It might take a week, it might take a month, it might take ten years. Dawson would never give up until the killers of his son were dead.

Atwell approached Dawson. "I sent Mullins back to the ranch. Anything else?"

"Send somebody to look for a water hole."

Atwell walked off to carry out Dawson's latest order, and Dawson puffed his cigar. Stars twinkled in the heavens above and he wanted to go someplace and cry. Climbing to his feet, he walked several paces over the rock, his spurs jangling in the night. He turned his back to his men, stared out at the prairie, and his eyes filled with tears as his body shuddered and a sob arose from his throat. His men heard him and turned their heads away. It was embarrassing to see the boss cry.

Tears dropped from Dawson's eyelashes down his cheeks, and his lips were pinched together. *I'll get them if it's the last thing I do!*

4

It was morning and the sun shone brightly as Craig Delane rode his buckboard down the lane to his ranch house. Cynthia sat beside him, her eyes staring and hollow after a sleepless night, and their three cowboy escorts sat on their horses, talking among themselves about the beating in the jail and the lynching. Craig stopped the buckboard in front of the house and pulled the brake lever.

"I'm going to my room," Cynthia said. "I don't want to be disturbed."

A cowboy dismounted to help Cynthia get out of the buckboard. Cynthia raised her skirt and accepted his hand, climbing to the ground.

Bernice, their middle-aged spinster maid, opened the front door, and Cynthia stepped inside.

"What's wrong, Mrs. Delane?" Bernice asked.

"Draw me a bath," Cynthia ordered, heading for the staircase that led to her bedroom upstairs.

Craig watched the front door close. He jumped to the ground and said to his cowboys, "Take care of the wagon."

One of the cowboys dismounted and tethered his horse to

the rear of the wagon. He climbed into Craig's seat and flicked the reins. The buckboard and cowboys headed toward the barn, leaving Craig alone in front of his ranch house.

Craig had three cups of coffee for breakfast and it was doing something bad to him. The lynching had been disturbing, and now Cynthia was leaving him. She was impossible, but she'd always been impossible. If it wasn't one thing, it was another. Sometimes he thought he didn't measure up to the standards she expected in a husband.

She'd never said she'd leave him before. This was something new, and Craig didn't like it. The frontier was too much for her, and he could understand how she felt. It was too much for him too.

Delane strolled aimlessly into the fields, his hands in the pockets of his suit, and his big pearl-colored hat on his head. He had paperwork to do, but it could wait. The real work would come when the cattle operation was going full blast.

He didn't have any cattle yet, and had been negotiating for them with Hank Dawson. Maybe Cynthia could leave, but he couldn't. His reputation was on the line. If he walked away from the operation now, so early in the game, it might be difficult to get another job. His parents were rich, but they weren't about to support him for the rest of his life.

Delane wandered through the fields. In a few months they'd be swarming with cattle mooing and chomping on grass, but now it was deserted and silent, stretching for as far as he could see. He found a tree stump squared off on top and sat on it.

He took out a long, thin cigar and lit it. If Cynthia left him, he'd be all alone in a strange land, with no friends. It would be tough and he'd get lonely. Cynthia and he'd been together nearly every day since they were married nearly three years ago. It'd be hard to adjust to being alone.

He wished she wouldn't go, because he loved and needed her. He thought she was the most beautiful and exciting woman he'd ever met, but wished he could have more contentment with her.

He didn't know whether she'd leave or not, but had to think about his future. Maybe he could send for books and spend his time reading. It'd be a good time to catch up on world events and the latest advances in knowledge. But books wouldn't compensate for Cynthia. She was so wonderful in every way, except for her moods.

Then he thought of John Stone, and his problems seemed petty in comparison with what had happened to the former cavalry officer. Beaten and hung. What a terrible way to die. *Poor fellow*, Craig thought. *I guess that's what happens to people who don't mind their own business out here*.

Cynthia sat on a chair in her bedroom, staring out the window at the blue sky. Her mind was a blank. She was exhausted and depressed.

There was a knock on the door, and Bernice entered the room, carrying a silver tray with a silver pot of coffee and a cup. She placed the tray on the small circular table beside Cynthia and poured the coffee.

"I'll get your bath now, ma'am."

Cynthia sipped her coffee, and it revived her somewhat. She turned to the mirror, and she was pale, with bags underneath her eyes and lines around her mouth.

She'd known that the frontier was a wild place before she came out here. New York newspapers frequently reported on Indian massacres and other killings west of the Mississippi. But Cynthia never thought it'd touch her. Money always had insulated her from unpleasantness.

Since she'd been in Dumont, she'd heard stories about killings and shootings, but it had been part of the local color. Never did she dream one day she'd be involved.

She thought of John Stone getting lynched, and shuddered, wondering what had become of his body. If it was found, she and Craig ought to give him a decent burial.

Bernice poured hot water into the bathtub in the next room, and Cynthia wanted to soak for a long time. Then she'd go to bed, sleep for the rest of the day, and when she woke up, she'd start packing.

Stone heard a twig snap and awakened with a start. He pulled his six-gun out of his belt and rolled over, aiming at the front of the cave. All became silent. Stone was aware McDermott wasn't in the cave with him.

A figure came into view, dressed in black, carrying a dead rabbit by its hind legs. McDermott stepped inside the cave and looked at Stone. "I didn't think you was up." He held the rabbit in the air. "Look what I got."

"How're we going to cook it."

"We're not gonna cook it. The smoke might attract the posse. We're gonna eat it raw."

"Raw?" asked Stone.

"You'll eat it if you're hungry enough."

Stone's stomach felt like an empty cavern. He jammed his holster into his belt. "Wish I had some tobacco."

"We got more important things to worry about."

"How'd you catch the rabbit?"

"With a length of twine I found in my saddle. It's easy to catch rabbits early in the morning. That's when they're up and around."

McDermott tied the hind feet of the rabbit to a protruding rock in the cave, and let the dead animal hang head down. Then McDermott took out Hong Fat's knife and made incisions around the hind feet of the rabbit. He peeled the fur down until he could grip it with his fingers, then tore the fur quickly off the animal's body.

"He's a fat little bugger," McDermott said. "Feed must be good around here."

Stone looked at the rabbit, and suddenly didn't feel so hungry anymore. McDermott removed the remaining fur from the rabbit, picked off a few spare tufts of hair with his fingers, and untied the rabbit, flinging him down on the floor of the cave. Wiping the knife on his filthy trousers, he cut the rabbit's leg.

"Real tender," McDermott said.

"You're not really going to eat him raw, are you?"

"Ain't I?"

McDermott pulled the rabbit's leg loose from his body and raised it to his mouth, biting off a huge chunk. Stone looked at the maimed rabbit.

"Might be the last food you'll get in a while."

"I'm hungry, but not that hungry."

McDermott ate noisily, picked the bone clean, and tossed it over his shoulder.

"Sure you don't want the other leg?"

"I'm sure."

McDermott cut that one off. "You'll get so hungry in a little while you'll eat the ass out of a skunk." McDermott gnawed on the rabbit's leg. "I think we should hide out here all day and travel at night."

"To where?"

"Eagleton. 'Bout thirty miles south of here. We can get supplies."

"We don't have any money."

McDermott pulled out his gun. "We don't need any money."

"Holdups aren't my game."

"You're on the dodge now, pardner. You'd better realize it before somebody kills you."

Stone craved a cigarette and hot black coffee. His face was swollen and bruised and his body hurt every time he moved. He had a map of the area in his saddlebags, but his saddlebags were in the New Dumont Hotel. He had no idea where he was.

"Is there a sheriff in Eagleton?" Stone asked.

"You ask a sheriff for help, you'll find yourself on the southern end of a rope, only this time I might not be around to save yore ass. Hank Dawson owns everybody and everything in this county. Don't 'spect no help from anybody."

The truth sank into Stone's brain. He was a wanted man and it didn't matter whether or not he was innocent. Hank Dawson owned the law in Dumont County.

"I've never robbed anything before," Stone said.

"Stealin' is a lot easier than bein' a cowboy, in my opinion," McDermott said, his mouth full of raw rabbit meat. "The main thing to remember is most people are afraid of guns. You just point one at them, and they'll give you anything you want."

"Mr. Dawson—the mules are coming."

Hank Dawson lay in a thicket, green grass all around him. Scowling, because he was at his worst when he woke up in the morning, he drew himself to a sitting position.

The sun shone bright and warm. The first thing that entered his mind was an image of his son shot through the throat. The rage and frustration returned. Narrowing his eyes, he looked at the approaching mule train. His men were guiding it into camp. These would be his supplies for the expedition against the men who killed his son.

"Where's the coffee?" Dawson asked.

"Cookie's startin' a fire right now, Mr. Dawson," Atwell said. "It'll just be a few more minutes."

Dawson lit a cigar, and his foreman backed away. Dawson figured the sun had been up at least an hour. Somewhere out there, the killers of his son were also awake, fleeing. Dawson rose to his feet and slapped the dirt off his pants.

Mullins approached across the clearing, accompanied by a flabby Indian in his forties.

"This here's Red Feather," said Mullins. "Supposed to be the best tracker in the territory."

Dawson looked at Red Feather and wasn't impressed. Red Feather looked as if he lain around on his ass too much. Red Feather was stone-faced as he met Dawson's eyes, standing stiffly like a young warrior.

"I want you to find the killer of my son," Dawson said.

"How much?" Red Feather asked.

"Name your price."

"One hundred dollars."

The amount was so outrageous that Dawson was tempted to whack Red Feather in the face. "I could get ten trackers for one hundred dollars."

"Get them."

Dawson didn't have time to hire other trackers. His son's murderers were getting away farther with every passing moment. "I'll give you fifty dollars, and that's generous, damn generous."

"One hundred dollars," said Red Feather.

"Seventy-five."

Red Feather curled his lips in contempt. "You bargain for the killers of your son?"

"All right," Dawson said. "It's a deal. We lost their trail on those rocks over there. See if you can pick it up."

Red Feather turned and walked off in the direction of the rocky plateau. He moved swiftly, with a sense of urgency and purposefulness, carrying his rifle in his right hand. When he reached the designated area, he got down on his hands and knees and brought his eyes close to the rock, searching for the lost trail.

The old grandfather clock in Craig Delane's office struck ten, and Craig paused, his pen in his hand. He was seated at the desk in his office on the ground floor of the HC Ranch, and the clock had been delivered all the way from New York, to provide a touch of home on the frontier.

Every week he had to write a report of his activities, and that's what he was doing. When finished he'd have one of his men take it to town and mail it.

He'd been working on the report about an hour, but it'd been a struggle. There wasn't much to write about, and he had difficulty concentrating. Cynthia was upstairs packing.

There was a knock on his door.

"Come in!"

The door opened, and it was a tall, lanky cowboy with leathery features, Delane's foreman, Everett Lorch.

"What is it?" Delane asked.

"Figgered you might want to hear the latest news, Mr. Delane. That feller John Stone escaped from the lynchin' last night, and Wayne Dawson got killed."

Delane nearly dropped his pen. "How do you know that?"

"I was in town with Curly buyin' supplies, and everybody was talkin' about it. Old Hank Dawson is tryin' to track Stone down."

"How did he get away?"

"The way they was sayin' it in town, some friends of Stone interrupted the lynchin' party just as they dropped the noose around Stone's neck. They shot Wayne Dawson and a few others of Dawson's men, and rode away with Stone."

"If you hear anything else about John Stone, be sure to let me know immediately."

Lorch tipped his hat and got out of Delane's way. Delane left his office and climbed the stairs to the second floor. He stopped at his wife's door and knocked.

"Who is it?" asked Bernice.

"Mr. Delane."

Bernice opened the door. "Mrs. Delane is taking a bath right now, sir."

"Tell her I want to speak with her. It's important."

Bernice walked away, leaving Delane standing in the doorway. Clothing, suitcases, and trunks were piled everywhere. Bernice returned.

"Mrs. Delane will see you now, sir."

Craig walked across the bedroom and into the next room,

where Cynthia sat in a porcelain bathtub, her graceful shoulders visible above the suds, and her hair piled high on her head, tied with a ribbon.

"Good news," Craig said to Cynthia. "John Stone wasn't lynched last night after all. Some men freed him, and Wayne Dawson got shot in the process. Hank Dawson is trying to track Stone down, but evidently hasn't found him yet."

Cynthia had taken Stone's death for granted, and now suddenly he wasn't dead. A smile of relief spread over her face.

"Cynthia," Craig said, "I was hoping you wouldn't leave, now that Stone's still alive. It was my impression that you were going back to New York because you thought he'd been killed."

"It's not just Stone," she said. "It's the lawlessness of this country. I don't like it, and I'll never like it."

"It's not as though we'll have to stay here forever. Just another two or three years. That's not so long."

"I don't think I could last two or three years."

"I wish you'd think it over a little more, Cynthia. You're taking everything much too seriously. This position is a wonderful opportunity for us. I can make my fortune out here."

"I don't like murder."

"People get murdered in New York too. We didn't see it, but it happened. We shouldn't run from life just because it gets a little unpleasant. You used to say you were bored in New York and wanted a change. That's one of the reasons we came out here in the first place."

Cynthia sat naked in the bathtub, soapy warm water eddying around her. She thought of John Stone somewhere on the prairie, running like a hunted animal from Hank Dawson and his men.

"Don't do anything today," Craig said. "Just consider it. Then, if you still want to leave, you can resume packing. That's not such an unreasonable thing to ask, is it?"

"No," she admitted.

"Bernice," Delane said, "put Mrs. Delane's clothing back in her closets. And have the suitcases and trunks sent back to the attic."

"Yes, sir."

Bernice walked out of the small room, leaving them alone. Craig gazed at Cynthia soaking in the bathtub, and she looked delicious. He bent over and kissed her cheek. "You're so beautiful," he murmured.

She felt the touch of his lips, but her mind was far away. She was wondering where John Stone was just then.

"I hope he's all right," she said.

"He's probably on his way to Mexico," Craig replied, touching his lips to her throat.

Hank Dawson sat in the sun, his hat low over his eyes, drinking a cup of coffee. His men were gathered around him, eating breakfast. Dawson wanted to hit the trail and hunt down Stone and McDermott, but Red Feather still hadn't found their trail.

Hank Dawson was a simple man. He worked, cheated, lied, bullied, and killed until he had what he owned now. Everything had been going well, and he'd planned to extract top dollar from Craig Delane for cattle. His long-range plan was to harass Delane's operation and make him sell out in a few years for next to nothing. Then Dawson would wind up with the cattle, land, and Delane's money too.

Now Dawson's son was dead, and Dawson felt as if he was living in a bad dream. It had happened so suddenly, and with such finality. His only boy shot through the throat by Tad McDermott or John Stone.

I should've shot McDermott and Stone in jail while I had the chance, Dawson thought, *and to hell with the lynching*. Dawson wished he could go back to last night, but he couldn't. All he wanted to do was get Stone and McDermott in front of him. He wouldn't be able to rest until he killed them.

Dawson sat facing the rocky flats where Red Feather had disappeared a half hour ago. He was waiting impatiently for the Indian to return. Red Feather may've been the best tracker in the territory, but he hadn't accomplished anything yet. The Indian was old and in poor physical condition.

Dawson drained his cup of coffee, and just then Red Feather's head appeared above a pile of boulders. The Indian walked back to camp, and Dawson hoped he'd picked up Stone's trail.

"More coffee, Mr. Dawson?" asked Cookie, holding the pot in the air.

"Yeah," said Dawson.

Dawson sipped the fresh coffee. It was hot and black, bitter as a killer's heart, just the way Dawson liked it. Dawson felt wide awake and anxious to move out. He was tired of sitting around.

Red Feather approached and squatted down in front of Dawson.

"I found their trail," Red Feather said, and he pointed south. "They went that way."

Dawson looked at Red Feather, measuring the man. Could this physical wreck of an Indian really track somebody? He turned to Atwell. "Tell the men to saddle up."

Atwell got to his feet and shouted orders to the cowboys, who gathered their gear. Dawson didn't have to load his belongings, so he lingered with his cup of coffee. He watched Red Feather climb onto his horse and ride south over the rocks, and realized the Indian sat straighter in his saddle and seemed more vital than when they'd first met. He'd become a young bloodhound again.

Dawson arose, threw his tin mug toward Cookie, and waddled toward his horse. He stuck his foot in the stirrup and laboriously raised himself into the saddle, knowing in another few years he'd need somebody to help.

Dawson and his men drifted south, following the old Indian sitting on his horse like a young warrior.

Stone and McDermott rode across a terrace fringed with silver spruces. "I'm purty sure we lost 'em," McDermott said.

Stone replied, "Dawson won't give up easily. I'm sure he's still out there, trying to find us. He'll do anything to catch us."

"You ever see the old man?" asked McDermott.

"Only for a few minutes."

"Big fat son of a bitch, and when I say fat, I mean fat. The man looks like a whole country walkin' around on two legs. Once I seen him eat in the saloon in Dumont, and I swear the man swallowed an entire pig. It just went on and on, with the yams in honey sauce, the biscuits, and afterward he ate a whole apple pie. Then he burped, farted, and grabbed a waitress's ass."

"What about Wayne's mother?"

"Been dead a long time. Some folks say the old man killed her. Hank Dawson does anything he wants and everybody in Dumont County works for him except two crazy sons of bitches, you and me." McDermott laughed. "I guess we showed old

Hank Dawson he can't fuck with all the people.''

"I admire your confidence, considering we have three bullets between us, no money, and no friends.''

"We'll be okay once we get to Eagleton. We'll get fresh horses and food there, then we'll head for Mexico and find us some friends. Ever screw a Mexican señorita? Like wrasslin' a tiger. And then there's the mescal. Ever try mescal? Smoothest stuff you ever drank, and it makes you see things like colored lights dancin' in the air, and places you ain't never seen, and that never was.''

Stone didn't want to go to Mexico, but had to hide from Hank Dawson until things cooled down. Then he could return to Texas and resume his hunt for Marie.

"There's this little general store in Eagleton," McDermott said. "We'll waltz in with our guns in our hands and take what we need for the trip south. I know you don't want to do it, but you got to. A man can't worry about other people's feelin's when he's on the dodge. It's their feelin's against yore life, and which you think is more important?''

Hank Dawson sat heavily on his horse, outside the cave. His men surrounded him, looking inside the murky darkness from which Red Feather was emerging.

"This is where they sleep last night," Red Feather said.

"Where are they now?"

"I not know yet."

"Well find out, goddammit. What the hell d'ya think I'm payin' you for?"

Red Feather looked up at Dawson and frowned. Then he turned around and gazed at the ground. He dropped to his knees, examining tracks, then arose again and walked into the bushes. Dawson reached for his canteen and took a swig. The sun was hot and he was impatient. Stone and McDermott were getting away.

He sat in the shade and wished he had something to eat, but they had to conserve their food. He felt that he was getting weak from lack of nourishment, and took off his hat, wiping his forehead with the back of his hairy arm. Stone and McDermott had been here, gloating over killing Wayne. Dawson felt a cold, bitter anger. He wanted to pound them to death with clubs.

Red Feather returned, huffing and puffing. Sweat poured off his body and soaked his shirt. "I found their tracks," he said to Dawson. "They still head south. My guess is they go to Eagleton. I know shortcut through mountains. If we leave mules and chuck wagon behind, we can beat them, maybe. I say maybe. I not promise anything. The decision is up to you, Mr. Dawson."

Dawson lit a cigar and thought Red Feather made sense. Stone and McDermott needed supplies, and Eagleton was the next town south on the way to Mexico. He turned to Atwell.

"Leave Standfield and a few other men with the mules and chuck wagon. Tell them to follow us to Eagleton."

Atwell rode off to carry out the orders. Dawson looked at Red Feather, who'd mounted his Appaloosa. Red Feather wore a knife on one side of his belt, a holster on the other side, and a rifle in a scabbard attached to his saddle.

"You'd better be right about this," Dawson said.

"I not know whether I right," Red Feather replied, "but I know I find the men who killed your son. They not get away. I swear it."

Red Feather kicked his heels at the belly of his Appaloosa, and the horse stepped away from the cave. Dawson followed him, and the rest of his men gathered behind in a column of twos. The main body of riders headed south, leaving the mules and chuck wagon trailing behind.

Craig and Cynthia Delane, and a few of their men, were riding on the open prairie. Cynthia wore a white cotton shirt and blue jeans that'd shrunk considerably since she'd bought them in town.

"Take a good look at this land," Craig said to Cynthia, "because it won't be this way for long. In another month or two, cattle will be spread out for as far as the eye can see. We'll get rich out here, if we can just hold on."

Cynthia looked around at the vast rolling plains and the purple mountains in the distance. It certainly was beautiful, she couldn't deny that. The sun shone brightly and she wore a wide-brimmed cowboy hat to shield her eyes. She always felt expansive and almost spiritual when she was on the prairie. Raising her eyes, she looked at the blue sky.   •

"Remember the plans we made in New York?" Craig said to her. "They can all still come true, Cynthia. I wish you wouldn't leave me now. I can't do this without you."

"I don't know what to think anymore, Craig. Last night was very disturbing."

"We can't let it stop us, because we're stronger than anything, or at least we should be."

Cynthia thought of the evenings they'd spent at their apartment on Fifth Avenue, reading books about the West, making plans and dreaming dreams. They were going to build a great future for themselves, and still could do it.

She had to admit that she loved the land. She'd never imagined that geography could be so enthralling. New York was dirty and crowded, and the soot in the air made you cough, but here the air was sweet and pure, fragrant with green grass growing in the sun.

"Injustice is everywhere," Craig said. "But this is virgin land. Lawlessness will decrease as it's settled, and we're building a first-class, large-scale cattle operation. In ten years we'll wield enormous power, and we'll have friends in Washington. Then we can fight Hank Dawson and everything he represents from a position of strength."

Cynthia felt her resolve weakening. Maybe she shouldn't panic and run from a decent marriage and promising opportunity, just because of an unpleasant incident in a restaurant.

"I suppose I'm rather confused," she said.

He placed his hand on her shoulder. "Take your time. Think it through. Whatever you decide, I'll understand, but it'll be hell here without you."

The plains spread out all around her, and a hawk floated lazily in the sky. The vast space filled her with a strange euphoria. She turned to look at Craig, wearing his business suit as he bounced up and down on his saddle. He looked out of place on the prairie, but he was determined to make it his land, and she couldn't help admiring him.

"I'll give you my answer tonight," she said. "Just let me think it over a little while longer."

"Take as long as you like," he replied. "There's no rush."

Some treated their wives like servants, but not Craig. She

was his equal partner in life, helped him with the business. They were good friends and good companions.

She began to wonder how she could ever seriously consider leaving him.

5

THE FARMHOUSE WAS a small squat structure made of logs taken from the woods nearby. A woman hung wash on the line in the backyard, and a few dozen cattle grazed in the adjacent field. Smoke curled into the air from the stone chimney on the roof.

Stone and McDermott lay on their stomachs on top of a hill on the southern side of the farmhouse. They smelled baking bread, and Stone's mouth watered.

"I don't see no men about," McDermott said, his eyes scanning the barn and fields surrounding the farmhouse. "Think she's alone?"

"She looks alone."

"Her menfolk prob'ly went to town, or maybe they're out ridin' the range."

"They can't be too far away," Stone said. "They wouldn't leave her alone."

"They're far enough for us to go down there and take what she's got."

"What are you talking about?"

"Them horses for openers, and we can git some grub. She's

prob'ly got a rifle too, and ammunition. She might even have money. I been through this before, and I know how to pull it off."

McDermott made a motion to return to his horse. Stone grabbed his sleeve.

"Wait a minute."

McDermott looked at Stone's hand on his sleeve, then looked Stone in the eye. McDermott's beard had grown longer and he was starting to resemble a wolf in black clothing. "What's the matter?"

"I can't rob that woman."

"Why the hell not?"

How could Stone argue morality with a man who had none? "I'm not a thief."

"I'll need you to cover my back. We got to have fresh horses, food, guns, and ammunition. The meanest man in West Texas is after us with a posse. We got to take care of ourselves, or we'll wind up buzzard food." McDermott looked him in the eye. "Are you gonna help me or aren't you?"

Stone shook his head. "Can't do it."

McDermott stared at him. "What kind of goddamned fool are you anyways?" he asked. "Do you want to live or do you want to die?"

"We can take what we need at Eagleton."

"A miracle you got this far in life. Maybe it's time we split up."

"Whatever you say. I don't want to get in your way, and I don't want you to get in mine. Thanks for saving my life." Stone held out his hand. "It's been good to know you."

"I should've left you swingin' from that noose." McDermott looked at the farmhouse longingly. "We can't split up now. Two guns is better than one."

"It's up to you," Stone said.

"Let's get out of here."

They crawled back to their horses, picketed at the bottom of the hill, and climbed into the saddles. They headed south, while down in the valley, the woman continued hanging wet clothes on the line.

Red Feather led Hank Dawson and his men through a narrow defile in the mountains. The trail twisted to the left and right and then curved back on itself, and in some spots there were only inches between the men's elbows and rock walls.

Dawson sat on his horse and watched Red Feather pass out of sight around a bend in the trail. Dawson had never known about the defile, although he'd been in this part of the country approximately ten years ago, checking on a herd on a nearby range. The damned Commanches knew the country better than any white man.

Dawson glanced at the sun, directly overhead. He was tired and hungry, accustomed to sitting in his office, and his muscles were slack on his bones underneath the thick layers of fat.

He knew he shouldn't be away from the ranch for long. His management skills were required on a round-the-clock basis, because so many important decisions had to be made. The hunt for Stone and McDermott was becoming a major expedition. Dawson figured he would've caught them by now.

He thought of his son, lying on his bed back at the ranch. It was a hot day and the body wouldn't keep long. Dawson decided if he didn't catch Stone and McDermott today, he'd return to the ranch with some of his men, and let the others keep after them. He'd hire more men and order them to comb the countryside. Sooner or later Stone and McDermott'd have to show their faces someplace, and then they'd get it.

Up ahead, Red Feather stopped his horse and raised his hand. Dawson, his big belly hanging over his belt, continued to ride until he reached Red Feather's side.

"What're you stoppin' for, injun?" Dawson asked.

Red Feather pointed straight ahead. Dawson looked in the direction of his finger and saw a little town a few miles away in the valley, basking in the sun.

"Eagleton," Red Feather said.

The farmhouse receded into the distance behind them. Stone and McDermott rode along silently, and Stone could see McDermott was mad. The outlaw's eyes were half closed and his jaw set in a grim line. He looked like a naughty little boy whose mother had just told him to keep his cotton-picking hands out of the cookie jar, and Stone let loose a peal of laughter.

McDermott was startled and turned toward him. "What the hell's the matter with you?"

"You're mad because I wouldn't let you shoot that poor housewife."

"I wouldn't've shot her unless she got ornery."

"How could you shoot a woman? What's wrong with you?"

"Once I was in a whorehouse in Dodge, and a whore took a shot at me. Her gun jammed, otherwise I wouldn't be here right now. I didn't have my clothes on at the time, otherwise I would've plugged her dead game."

"Why'd she want to shoot you?"

"I tried to git out without payin'."

"Have you ever in your life had a job?"

"What the hell do I want a job for? I want to be free."

"You're not free. You live like a hunted coyote."

"Better'n a job, and more fun too. 'Course you have to be ready to use that thing in yore holster. Some men wears 'em for decoration, but not Tad McDermott."

They came to the top of a hill. McDermott raised his arm and pointed. "Looka there."

Stone saw trees and bushes straight ahead, a water hole. They rode toward the trees, and their horses moved more eagerly, because they'd smelled the water. Stone was thirsty too, and still ached from the beating he'd taken in jail.

They drew their guns and rode among the trees, glancing about, looking for Indians. The horses walked faster, and Stone thumbed back the hammer of his pistol. The horses came to the water hole and lowered their heads into it. Stone and McDermott climbed down from their saddles, took their canteens, and dipped them into the water. They filled the canteens and raised them to their mouths, leaning back their heads, drinking deeply.

McDermott wiped his lips with the back of his hand. "Let's rest here for a little bit," he said. "Then we'll **head into** Eagleton and rob the general store."

McDermott stretched out on the ground and fell asleep as if lying on a sofa in his living room, and Stone realized McDermott was at home when he was on the dodge. It was his natural way of life and the bare ground was his furniture.

Stone looked at the bushes and trees. Once, when he was scout on the wagon train, he'd been ambushed by Indians at a water hole like this. They'd shot arrows at him, and one went through his leg.

He'd survived the Commanches, and wondered if he'd survive Hank Dawson. He knew Dawson was out there someplace, looking for him. Dawson was a rich and powerful man, and would spare no expense.

It was wide-open country, and there were lots of places where a man could hide. Everything would be all right once they got more weapons and ammunition in Eagleton.

A half hour later McDermott opened his eyes. "How're you doin'?" he asked, scratching his ribs. "You might as well git some shut-eye now, and I'll look out fer you."

"That's all right," Stone replied. "I'm not that tired. Let's go to Eagleton and get the dirty work over with."

"Can't wait, huh? I know the feelin'. There's nothin' like the power a man feels when he points his gun at a man's nose and says, 'Hand over everythin' you got.'"

Stone and McDermott climbed onto their horses and rode out of the little oasis, heading toward Eagleton.

It was just a main street with buildings on both sides. In the center was a general store and saloon combined. Across the street was the stable, and the whorehouse a few doors down.

A woman sweeping her front porch looked up as the men on horseback approached, and she recognized Hank Dawson immediately because he was the fattest man in Dumont County and owned Eagleton.

Dawson pulled back the reins of his horse, and his horse stopped in the middle of the street. His men brought their mounts to a halt all around him.

"Atwell—post two men at one end of this street, and two men at the other end. Tell 'em to keep their eyes open fer Stone and McDermott. Then git another man with good eyesight and tell 'em to git on the highest roof in town, to see anybody comin'. The rest of us'll git somethin' to eat."

Dawson spurred his horse, and the animal clomped down the street. The woman on the porch stared at Hank Dawson and wondered what he was doing in town. Dawson stopped his horse in front of the saloon, climbed down from the saddle, and stepped onto the boardwalk, which creaked underneath his weight. He scuffed toward the doors of the saloon and pushed them open.

He entered a dark room that smelled of coffee. A bar ten

feet long was straight ahead, with tables in front. Pants and shirts hung from the rafters nearby. On the floor were burlap bags full of beans, coffee, and rice.

Nobody was in sight. "Who the hell's in charge here?" Dawson bellowed.

A bony little mouse of a man came running into the saloon from a corridor. "Mr. Dawson!" he expostulated. "I'm so glad to see you! What can I do for you?"

"Whiskey for me and my men."

"Yes, sir! Coming right up, sir!"

Dawson and his men sat heavily on the chairs that surrounded the tables, but nobody dared sit at the same table as Dawson. Nobody sat at the same table with Red Feather, either. The proprietor placed bottles and glasses on each table. When he came to Red Feather's table, he paused.

"Should I serve likker to the injun?" he asked Dawson.

"No," replied Dawson.

Red Feather's face didn't change its expression, but his heart boiled with anger. He wanted to walk out of the saloon and ride away, but he was being paid to find the killer of Dawson's son, and couldn't walk away from Hank Dawson.

Dawson poured whiskey into his glass and guzzled it down. The ride had been long, and he was tired. Stone and McDermott wouldn't suspect anything, he didn't think. They'd just ride into town and get shot down in cold blood.

Stone and McDermott might not come to Eagleton, he knew. They could be headed to some other town, but Dawson didn't think so. He'd learned to trust the hunches of Indians, although he didn't trust Indians themselves. He thought they were murdering, thieving sons of bitches.

The proprietor walked up to Dawson's table and bowed slightly. "Anything else, Mr. Dawson?"

"You got fresh meat?"

"I've got steers out in back."

"Steaks for me and my men."

"Yes, sir."

The proprietor walked away. Dawson scratched his thick gray beard and took out a cigar, scraping a match on top of the table and lighting the end of the cigar with it. He took off his hat and hung it from the back of the chair next to him. His

men murmured to each other. They were afraid to talk loud
for fear of disturbing him.

Dawson thought of his son. It hurt, but whenever he stopped
to relax, that's where his mind drifted. Dawson felt dead himself. It wasn't fair, what happened to Wayne. Dawson wanted
to kill Stone and McDermott slowly, and watch them suffer.

"I'm offerin' a hundred dollars bonus to the man who brings
me Stone and McDermott alive!" he said.

That was over three months' pay. The cowboys sipped their
whiskey and thought about saloons with roulette wheels and
beautiful girls who'd do anything you want for five dollars.

At the table by himself, Red Feather watched the men drinking whiskey, and an insatiable thirst for firewater increased in
his throat. He wanted some desperately, but all he could do
was sit still and stare at a Commanche Indian blanket hanging
on the wall.

He wondered how the proprietor came by the Indian blanket.
Had a Commanche traded it for whiskey? Or had the Commanche been killed and the blanket taken from him.

Red Feather hated the white man and hated himself for doing
the white man's odd jobs, but he was lazy; he liked to hang
around towns and drink whiskey. He didn't want to hunt or go
to war unless he was being paid. Turning his head slightly, he
looked out the corner of his eye at Hank Dawson.

Dawson was a great chief of white men, but he was so much
different from a Commanche chief, who earned his position
by virtue of his skill at hunting and war. Dawson seemed to
have no skills whatever. All he had was money. Red Feather
had learned that money was everything in the new world the
white man was making, and he was anxious to get more money
for himself, so maybe he could buy some land and hire cowboys
to work for him.

Dawson would pay him a hundred dollars for tracking down
Stone and McDermott, and an additional hundred dollars bonus
if he captured them alive. That was enough to get started in
the ranching business.

I will catch them, Red Feather said to himself. *They are
mine.*

A wagon trail wound its way over the plains like a tan ribbon,
and at its end was Eagleton. Stone and McDermott rode on the

trail, looking at the town shimmering in the distance, a few miles away.

"I been to this town before," McDermott said, "and believe me, there won't be nothin' goin' on today. All we gotta do is walk into the general store and take what we want. You just leave ev'rythin' to me. I'll put my gun on the man, and you take rifles, ammunition, money, supplies, ennythin' you kin lay your hands on. There's burlap bags behind the bar—just fill 'em up. Grab a couple bottles of whiskey while you're at it. We'll have us a little party on the prairie tonight. This is a town that don't even have a sheriff. Bein' a crook is easy, sometimes. You might even git to like it."

Tom Reece was perched on the highest roof in Eagleton, looking north toward Dumont. His hat was low over his eyes to keep the sun from blinding him, and his eyes swept the prairie from side to side and back again, searching for riders. Then he turned around and searched the terrain on the southern side of the town, in case the riders decided to come in the back way.

He turned to the north again and looked at the rolling grassy plains. He had a headache, but needed to spot Stone and McDermott before they got close to town.

Reece took off his tan, wide-brimmed hat, wiped his balding head with his hand, and put the hat back on again. He loosened the bandanna around his neck and unbuttoned a few buttons on his shirt. It was hot as hell on the roof and rivulets of perspiration dripped down his face and plastered his clothing to his body. He wished Atwell would've picked somebody else for the lookout job.

Then he saw something. At first he thought his eyes were playing tricks on him, because the heat made everything shimmer in the distance, but then he perceived two men riding on the wagon trail that led to town. Reece knew what Stone looked like; he'd been in the jail the night Wayne Dawson had beat him up, but couldn't recognize him in the distance. He didn't recognize the other man either. Reece wondered whether to wait until they came closer, or report to Dawson immediately. He decided not to take any chances, and tell Dawson somebody was coming.

It wasn't easy to get down from the roof, because it was steeply slanted and one wrong move could send him tumbling to the ground. Slowly, gingerly, he crept over the clapboard shingles to the edge, then turned and looked at the two riders again. They were closer now, and he could see that one of them was dressed all in black, Tad McDermott the outlaw. The other was tall and broad-shouldered, and had to be John Stone.

Reece looked down at the ground, approximately a ten-foot drop. Taking a deep breath, he jumped off the roof and fell to the dirt, rolled over, and got to his feet, running toward the saloon.

Hank Dawson sat in the saloon, eating a massive steak with fried potatoes and a bowl of beans. A drop of gravy stained his shirt but he couldn't see it, and even if he did, he wouldn't have cared. All that mattered was the quantity and quality of the food, and the former was more important than the latter.

Dawson's mind was totally concentrated on chewing and swallowing. There was a terrible emptiness in him that he always was seeking to fill. It had driven him all his life.

He wasn't thinking about his dead son while he was eating. He wasn't even thinking about Stone and the ambush he hoped to spring. He was just concentrating on masticating food and gulping it down like any other big dull animal.

Reece burst into the saloon. "I just saw 'em! They're on their way into town!"

Dawson stood and wiped his mouth with the back of his hand. "The sons of bitches are here! Take your positions! You know what to do!"

Stone and McDermott rode closer to Eagleton over the winding road rutted with tracks left by wagon wheels.

"I don't see anybody around," Stone said.

"Like I told you, it's practically a ghost town most of the time."

"Seems there should be somebody up and about."

"The less people the better."

The road inclined toward Eagleton, constructed on a basin in the middle of the plains. Mountains were in the distance on all sides of the town. Stone's mind often functioned militarily: it was something that happened automatically, not out of conscious effort. In his cavalryman's eyes, he viewed the town as a military objective, and wondered how to capture it. He often found himself planning military strategies, although the war had ended years ago.

First he'd shell the town with artillery placed on the heights surrounding the town, then send in a troop of cavalry on a feint from the south. That would turn the enemy, while he'd send his main force against the northern end of town.

Stone blinked his eyes. The artillery batteries and troops of cavalry disappeared. Eagleton lay silently in the sun. Stone could see the main street, and a spotted dog was walking down its middle, but there were no people around.

"I don't like this," Stone said. "It's too quiet."

"You worry too much," McDermott replied. "I tell you— it's going to be a picnic."

Hank Dawson and his men crouched behind windows and doorways, holding their rifles and pistols ready, waiting for Stone and McDermott to come abreast of them. Their orders were to open fire on Dawson's command, but they were to aim for arms and legs, wound their quarries but not kill them. Dawson wanted to reserve that great pleasure for himself.

Hammers on pistols were thumbed back. Rifles were cocked and ready to fire. Each man wanted to capture Stone and McDermott, for the hundred-dollar reward. They looked at each other and grinned. At last they were going to capture the men who'd murdered Wayne Dawson and made fools out of them for nearly two days.

Atwell was on the east side of the street with half the men. Dawson was on the west side with the rest of them. They hoped to catch Stone and McDermott in a murderous cross fire.

They heard the faint sound of hoofbeats approaching from the northern end of town. The hoofbeats came closer, and the men tensed, peering out the windows, tightening their fingers around their triggers.

Stone and McDermott advanced steadily into the town.

"I still don't like it," Stone said. "At least there should be a drunk or a housewife or *somebody* on the street."

"It ain't that kind of town," McDermott replied.

"Something's telling me to get the hell out of here."

"The general store is halfway down the street on the left side. We'll just ride up to it real easylike, hitch our horses to the rail, and go inside. I'll draw on the shopkeeper as soon as he comes out, and you grab everything we need. Got it?"

"What if there's shooting?"

"Shoot back, and don't be so serious, for Christ's sake. You look like you're goin' to a damn funeral. All you got to do is pay attention to what I say." McDermott laughed. "I'll make an owlhoot out of you yet."

The sound of hoofbeats came closer. Sweat dripped down Hank Dawson's face and seeped into his beard. He was on his knees beside a window that faced the street, and his men were all around him. They outnumbered Stone and McDermott and should be able to shoot them down without any great difficulty, but gunplay always was unpredictable and dangerous. Stone or McDermott might get off a few shots and kill somebody. Anything could happen.

Dawson moved the curtain aside and peered down the street. He saw John Stone and Tad McDermott approaching, and clenched his jaw. The revenge he thirsted for would soon be his. He gripped his gun more tightly. "Git ready now," he said softly. "Here they come."

The inhabitants of Eagleton had been told by Hank Dawson's men to stay indoors and out of sight. They hid under beds, in closets and pantries, and behind furniture, and some took advantage of the opportunity to take a nap.

Louisa Perez was one of those taking a nap. She lay on her bed with her four-year-old son Tino, her arms wrapped around him, dozing softly. The windows and side door were open to let in fresh air, and curtains fluttered in the breeze. The town was silent, and Louisa fell more deeply into slumber. She was tired because she'd been scrubbing floors all morning.

Young Tino opened his eyes and lay still for a few moments, watching a fly buzz in lazy circles over his head. He was a chubby little boy with a round face and straight black hair worn long like his father's, who worked at the stable.

Tino was well rested and didn't feel like lying in bed anymore. He wanted to get up and play, but didn't want to wake his mother because he knew she was tired. She'd give him a smack across the top of his head if he woke her up.

Gently and smoothly he crawled out of her arms. She moaned and rolled over, turning her back to him. Tino's teddy bear lay on the floor. Tino slid down from the bed and picked it up.

He hugged the teddy bear, bright light came to him from the door, and he moved toward it like a moth to flame. He pushed it open and stood in the alleyway between two houses. To his left was the street. He liked to watch the horsies, so he turned in that direction to see if any were around. Clutching his teddy bear closer to him, he shuffled barefooted toward the street.

Stone and McDermott rode down the main street of the town, and Stone still didn't like the way it looked. He pulled the six-gun out of its holster.

McDermott noticed him. "What the hell you think you're doin'?"

"I feel safer with it in my hand."

"You tryin' to tell ev'rybody you're an outlaw? Put it away!"

"Something's wrong here."

"You'll scare everybody before we git to the store, you damn fool!"

Stone thought McDermott might be right. He had to settle down and behave normally, so he pushed the gun into its holster.

"It'll be easy," McDermott said. "We're almost there."

Stone looked at the deserted sidewalks and still thought something was wrong.

The sound of the hoofbeats came closer. Dawson could see Stone and McDermott more clearly now, and the corners of his fat lips turned up in a grim smile.

"Here they are, boys," Dawson murmured. "They're walkin' right into our laps. Get ready now." Dawson licked his lower lip as Stone and McDermott came abreast of him. "Fire!"

His men raised their guns and poked them out the windows, then saw something that stopped them cold.

A little Mexican boy shuffled onto the sidewalk directly in their line of fire, and the men's trigger fingers froze.

Dawson hesitated too. He was a rotten son of a bitch, but he didn't want to shoot a kid.

Stone and McDermott saw guns and rifles on both sides of them. They ducked and slammed their spurs into the withers of their horses. The horses sprang forward and Stone pulled out his gun. The two horses kicked clods of dirt into the air as they plunged down the main street of Eagleton.

Dawson saw his quarry getting away. "Stop them!" he shouted. "Bring them down!"

His men jumped out the windows and charged out the doors, firing down the street at the two riders.

"Don't let them get away!"

Dawson ran out the door and saw Stone and McDermott approaching the far side of town at a fast gallop. His men let out a barrage of fire, but the riders were fast-moving targets getting smaller every moment.

Bullets flew all around Stone and McDermott, slamming into the ground, whizzing past their ears. They were out of town now, on the open range, heading for the mountains in the distance.

"I told you that town wasn't right!" Stone hollered.

McDermott flashed his desperado smile. "They'll never get Tad McDermott!"

The smile vanished from McDermott's face, and a red flower appeared on the back of his shirt. He closed his eyes and tilted to the side. Stone watched in horror as McDermott fell off his horse and hit the ground.

Stone pulled back on his reins, and the animal dug in his heels. He jumped out of the saddle and ran to McDermott, lying on his back on the ground. McDermott opened his eyes.

"Get goin'," he croaked. "I'm a goner."

"You're coming with me."

McDermott raised his gun and pointed it at Stone's head. "I said git goin', and I ain't kiddin'."

Stone looked toward Eagleton. Riders were coming fast, firing guns, and dirt exploded into the air near Stone and McDermott. Stone knew he had to move.

"You was right about the town," McDermott whispered, his lips ringed with blood. "Guess I ain't as sharp as I used to be. It was nice meetin' you, pardner. If you're ever somewheres with a purty gal, give her one fer me."

McDermott coughed, and blood burbled out of his mouth. A bullet whacked into the dirt ten feet from Stone. He looked at the oncoming riders and knew it was time to get going.

Stone ran and jumped onto his horse, digging in his spurs. His horse snorted and charged forward. Stone turned around in his saddle and saw the posse spreading out over the prairie and galloping toward him, firing their guns.

Stone faced forward and looked at the mountains in the distance. The windstream washed his face and bent the brim of his hat. *If I can just get into those mountains, I might have a chance*. He had to push his horse even if he rode it to death.

The horse's hooves pounded on the ground, and Stone thought of McDermott lying on the ground, bleeding to death, the owlhoot's luck run out. Something had told Stone to stay out of Eagleton, but he'd gone along with McDermott because he thought McDermott knew what he was doing. *Should've trusted myself*.

A bullet cracked over Stone's head, and another ricocheted off a rock about ten feet away. Stone hunkered down in his saddle and clenched his teeth as his horse raced wildly toward the mountains.

6

THE GALLOPING HORSEMEN approached the prostrate body of McDermott lying on the green prairie grass.

"Atwell!" Dawson shouted. "Take the men after Stone and bring him back to me!"

"Let's go, men!" Atwell hollered.

Atwell maneuvered his horse in front of the posse, and they rode hard after the lone rider approximately a thousand yards ahead of them. Dawson pulled back on his reins and slowed down, allowing his men to pass him by. He angled the head of his horse toward McDermott's body, and it walked in that direction, snorting from the exertion of carrying an extremely heavy man.

The horse approached McDermott, and Dawson looked down at him. McDermott opened his eyes to half mast and saw Dawson towering above him, the sun above his right shoulder. McDermott tried to raise his gun, but didn't have the strength. His life was ebbing away and he could barely think.

Dawson raised one stout leg over his saddle and stepped down from the stirrup onto the ground. He pulled out his six-gun and walked to where McDermott was lying.

McDermott watched him come closer. His consciousness was leaving him, but he recognized who it was. "Well looka who's here," he said with a rasp. "The fattest man in the world."

"You killed my son," Dawson said, pointing his gun at McDermott's head.

"If I had the chance," McDermott wheezed, "I'd kill you too."

"You don't have the chance."

McDermott knew what was coming, and closed his eyes as his body was wracked by a paroxysm of coughing. Dawson waited until he was finished, then brought the barrel of his gun to within an inch of McDermott's head. Dawson thought of his son and pulled the trigger.

The gun fired, and Dawson looked at the mess he'd made. Holstering his gun, he walked back to his horse, feeling a sense of accomplishment. "One down, one to go," he said.

He climbed onto his horse and followed the assembly of riders galloping over the prairie in the distance.

Stone noticed his horse slowing down, and the mountains were still far away. "C'mon, old boy," he said to the horse. "Don't give up now."

A fuzzy, unwholesome sound came out of the horse's nostrils every time he breathed; his body was coated with sweat and his eyes were bloodshot.

"Just a little bit farther," Stone coaxed.

Stone turned and saw the posse gaining on him. He wished he had old Troop C of the First South Carolina Cavalry with him. Then he'd turn around and charge the bastards.

A bullet whizzed by his left shoulder, and another struck a few feet from his horse's hooves. Stone crouched lower in the saddle and uttered a prayer.

He thought of the farmhouse he'd seen earlier in the day with McDermott. Good horses had been in the corral, but he didn't want to steal one. Now he realized a good horse might spell the difference between living and dying. He wished he'd stolen one of those horses in that corral. McDermott had been right.

He flashed on McDermott, lying on his back in the grass. He probably was dead by now. "Poor son of a bitch," Stone muttered. "I hope there's a good whorehouse wherever you are."

Stone only had three cartridges, and that was another good reason they should've raided the farmhouse. He couldn't make much of a stand with only three bullets. *McDermott must be laughing, wherever he is right now.*

He noticed his horse straining more. "Just a little farther, boy," he said. "Don't stop now."

"He's slowin' up!" Atwell shouted. "We got the son of a bitch."

The thunder of the posse's hooves echoed all around him, and the men could see they were drawing closer to Stone; each wanted to be the one who put a bullet in his hide.

Red Feather was on the right flank of the posse, and he wanted that extra hundred dollars. In order to get it, he'd have to fire the first clear shot at Stone, and there was only one way to do that. He'd have to bring him down before he got into the mountains, and he didn't have much farther to go.

Red Feather saw a low hill to his right. He pulled his horse's head to the side and angled it toward the hill, separating himself from the rest of the posse. Atwell saw him out of the corner of his eye. *Where's that crazy injun goin'.*

The posse continued its headlong charge toward Stone, and Red Feather's horse galloped up the side of the hill. The horse charged onto the top and Red Feather pulled on the reins. He yanked his rifle out of its boot and jumped to the ground. Dropping onto his stomach, he raised the butt of the rifle to his shoulder and lined the sights up on Stone.

It wouldn't be an easy shot because Stone was three hundred yards away and moving at an angle to Red Feather, but Red Feather had been a crack shot in his youth and still thought he had a good eye.

Red Feather took a deep breath and held it. He clenched his teeth, led Stone slightly, and squeezed the trigger. Stone was low in his saddle, moving his body in tandem with the motions of his horse. The trigger moved the final fraction of an inch and the rifle fired. It kicked into Red Feather's shoulder, and Red Feather saw Stone's horse go down.

• • •

Stone thought the horse's fighting heart had finally given out, and the next thing he knew he was hurtling toward the ground. He raised his arms to protect his head, crashed into the sod, and flipped in the air. He landed on his back and rolled over quickly to avoid landing underneath the horse. Bruised and aching, he climbed to his feet. His horse was trembling, its eyes wide with horror. Blood oozed out of a hole in its ribs. Stone wanted to put the animal out of its misery, but couldn't waste the ammunition.

He looked up and saw the posse bearing down upon him. The only thing to do was run like an animal. A bullet kicked up dirt a few feet away. Stone pulled the canteen off the pommel of the saddle and slung it over his shoulder, running toward the mountains. A bullet whistled past his left shoulder, and Stone dodged to the right. His long muscular legs propelled him forward as he summoned up his last remaining reserves of strength.

A bullet struck the ground near his feet as he was running around the base of a hill. The mountains were a hundred yards away, and he dug his boots into the ground, gasping for air. He could hear the hoofbeats of horses in the posse behind him and knew he didn't have much time. He had to find shelter quickly, or else he was a dead man.

His heart chugging in his chest, his mouth dry as paper, he saw a pile of boulders at the foot of the cliffs. It was as good a place as any to make a stand.

He couldn't see the posse now. The hill was between him and them, which meant they couldn't see him either. He ran the final yards flat out, gulping air, and dived behind the rocks.

The moment he landed he drew his gun and made sure it was ready to fire. Then he reached for his canteen, unscrewed the lid, and took a swig, wondering if it were the last drink he'd ever swallow. The posse wasn't in sight yet, and he had a few more minutes to relax before the final grand surge of his life.

He sat against the rock cliff and everything was still around him, but in the distance he could hear oncoming riders. At least he'd be able to die fighting like a man, instead of swinging from a noose.

A jackrabbit scurried out from beneath a bush and ran toward the stone wall of the mountain. It looked as if it were going to collide headfirst with the wall, but somehow kept going, disappearing out of sight into the wall.

Stone wrinkled his brow and sat straighter. The rabbit had run through the cliff! Stone crouched low and moved toward the spot where the rabbit had gone. The rock was darker than the rest of the wall, but as Stone drew closer, he noticed it was an optical illusion. The rock wasn't really darker. There was an opening in the mountain!

It wasn't a big opening, and in fact was barely big enough for a man Stone's size to squeeze through, but it offered the possibility of escape. Stone wondered where it led.

He turned back toward the posse, and it still was out of sight behind the hill. He squeezed himself into the opening, the rough rock walls scraping against his shirt and jeans. He saw that it turned to the right, and continued to push himself along, hoping he'd find a safe place to hide.

The passageway widened after the right turn, and then he saw a left turn. It narrowed again, and he squeezed through, bruising his ribs.

Then he stopped, dazzled by what he saw before him: a wide canyon basking in the sunlight. Boulders were strewn all around, and there was a sea of grass. It was a lost place, a freak of geological nature.

He wriggled through the last few feet of stone passageway and wondered if he were the first man ever to set foot in the hidden canyon.

The posse galloped past Stone's horse, still in its death throes on the ground. No one stopped to put the horse out of its misery, because all the riders wanted John Stone. They galloped up the top of the hill, looked ahead at the mountains, and Stone was gone. Atwell raised his hand and the riders pulled their horses to a stop. The horses danced and shifted in their excitement as the men held tightly to their reins.

"He must be hidin' someplace!" Atwell shouted. "Spread out and look fer him!"

Red Feather climbed onto his horse. He was still on the hill where he'd shot Stone's horse, and had seen Stone run away. From his vantage point, he'd been able to follow Stone's path of retreat, and knew approximately where Stone had sought shelter.

Red Feather rode his horse down the side of the hill. He was confident he could find Stone, especially since Stone was now on foot. Red Feather's main worry was that one of the white riders might find him first.

Red Feather didn't want to be obvious. If he rode directly to the spot where he'd last seen Stone, the other riders would notice and try to get there first. They knew he was the expert tracker, and would try to anticipate his moves.

Red Feather decided to take his time. Stone was dismounted and couldn't go far, so there was no hurry. He saw the other posse members riding back and forth at the foot of the mountains, and Red Feather smiled, because the fools were only obscuring Stone's tracks.

He heard hoofbeats behind him, and it was Hank Dawson.

"Where the hell is John Stone?"

Red Feather pointed toward the mountains.

"He got away?"

"I find him for you, Mr. Dawson."

"What the hell happened?"

"I shoot his horse."

Dawson spurred his horse and rode toward the mountains, and Red Feather followed more slowly. He came to Stone's horse groaning and trembling on the ground, lying in a pool of blood. Red Feather dismounted, yanked out his long knife, and cut the horse's throat.

Red Feather saw where Stone had fallen, gotten up, and walked to the horse. Then Stone's tracks headed for the mountains. Red Feather saw spots on the ground where bullets had landed. *I not shoot straight as I used to*, Red Feather thought, *but I kill John Stone anyway*.

The men from the posse had dismounted and were searching among the rocks at the base of the mountains. Their rifles and pistols were in their hands and they were ready to shoot Stone when they found him. Atwell puffed a cigarette and watched the search. Stone had to be around here someplace, but where the hell was he?

Atwell heard hoofbeats behind him and turned around in the

saddle. He saw Dawson galloping toward him, and Atwell didn't look forward to speaking with him.

Dawson stopped beside Atwell and looked toward the mountains. "Where the hell is he?"

"Somewheres in there."

"You stupid son of a bitch!" Dawson spurred toward the base of the mountains. "He's around here someplace, men!" he shouted. "If you don't find him—you're all fired!"

Stone stood on his knees behind a big boulder and unscrewed the top of his canteen. It was half full, and there was no telling when he might find water again.

He raised the canteen and took a swig. It was silent in the canyon. Stone was so hungry his stomach ached. He regretted not eating raw rabbit that morning, or stealing something from the farmhouse he and McDermott had seen.

He thought of McDermott dying in the grass, and wished he'd listened to the old owlhoot when they were back at the farmhouse. McDermott understood survival, and all Stone knew was a war.

He sat beside the boulder and peered at the opening in the mountain. If they came for him, they'd have to come one at a time. He'd get the first three, and after that it'd be his jackknife until the bitter end.

Dawson was becoming increasingly frustrated. Stone could not've vanished into thin air. Where the hell was he?

Not far away, Mullins and Reece approached the rocks near the passageway and saw tracks, but thought they might've been made by other men in Dawson's posse. They walked over Stone's tracks and looked behind the rocks, but he wasn't there. They searched about and saw the passageway, but the shadow made it appear a solid wall of rock. Mullins and Reece walked away, holding their guns before them cautiously, ready to fill Stone full of holes.

Meanwhile, Red Feather rode toward Dawson. He was dreaming about the good time he was going to buy with the reward money. He'd lay in bed with a young woman and do all the things old men dream of.

"Where the hell have you been?" Dawson demanded as Red Feather pulled alongside him.

"Where you want me to be?"

"I want you to find that son of a bitch!"

"I find him, you not worry, Mr. Dawson." Red Feather pointed toward the base of the mountains. "Your men are fools. I was raised in this country, and know these mountains well. I find your man."

"That hundred-dollar reward is yours if you bring him to me dead or alive, and I already owe you a hundred dollars for the tracking job, but if you bring him alive, I'll give you an *additional* hundred dollars."

Red Feather pondered that vast amount of money for a few moments. "We are talking about three hundred dollars altogether, yes?"

"Yes," said Dawson, perceiving the greed in Red Feather's eyes.

Red Feather saw himself as a rancher, raising cattle, having a young wife. "I have him for you tonight," he said.

Red Feather rode to the area where he'd seen Stone disappear. He pulled his rifle out of its scabbard, jacked the lever, and dismounted. Looking at the ground, he saw the marks of horse's hooves and men's feet. If Stone had left tracks, surely they were obliterated by now. But he had to be someplace close, hiding, maybe even looking at Red Feather just then.

Red Feather felt a chill go up his back. Narrowing his eyes, he scanned the cliffs and ledges in front of him for the telltale silhouette of a man. Stone wouldn't dare shoot, because that would give away his position, but he'd shoot if he realized he'd been discovered. Red Feather would have to be careful.

He stepped forward and searched among the bushes at the foot of the mountains, holding his rifle ready to fire. He peered behind rocks and gazed into depressions in the ground. He came to a tree and looked up at its branches, but no one was there. Systematically he scoured the area where Stone had gone.

Finally he came to the pile of rocks where Stone had first taken refuge. He saw the many tracks of boots on the ground and cursed underneath his breath. His work would be easier if he were alone.

He searched behind the rocks and realized it would be a good place for a man to make his last stand. He would've chosen this spot himself, if he were the fugitive. He crouched behind the rocks and saw many tracks of boots. Dawson's men had been here, but had Stone been here too? Red Feather looked at the passageway, but the shadow was darker and the opening more difficult to see than before.

He realized there was something familiar about this spot. Searching his memory, he recalled playing in this area as a child, and there was something special about it, but he couldn't remember what. His mind drifted back over the decades, and doors that had been closed for years opened. Finally it came to him. There was a hidden canyon on the other side of the mountain, and it was possible to reach it through openings in the rock wall.

Red Feather arose and walked toward the side of the mountain. As he drew closer, it seemed impenetrable. He reached out to touch it, and his hand went right through. At first he thought he had a powerful medicine, but then realized with a jolt that this was one of the openings into the hidden canyon.

He smiled and poked his rifle into the opening. Through the dark mists of memory, an incident came back to him. He'd played in this very spot as a child, and with his friends had passed through the opening to the hidden canyon.

Stone could've gone through here. Red Feather realized he'd picked up his trail. He looked back at the white men, and didn't want them to know what he'd found, because they'd come over and make a racket. You had to creep up on your quarry. The white men all were busy, running around in the dark like chickens with their heads cut off. Nobody was paying any attention to Red Feather.

Slowly, with no abrupt motion that might attract attention, Red Feather sank into the rocks. He saw a scrape mark and some crumbled dust on the bottom of the opening. The mark was fresh.

I found him, Red Feather said to himself. He crept forward and found another scrape mark and more crumbled dust. It was about the distance of a full stride from the other mark. Raising himself up, he looked at the sides of the passageway. There were white spots where ends of rocks recently had been knocked away by somebody pushing his body past them.

Red Feather was convinced that Stone had come this way, and there was no longer any need to study tracks. He sucked in his belly and moved through the passageway, aiming his rifle straight ahead in front of him.

• • •

"What happened to the injun?" Dawson said.

Atwell pointed toward his left. "I thought I saw him over there."

"No," Dawson replied, pointing toward his right. "I thought he was there."

"I don't think so, Mr. Dawson."

Dawson shrugged. "Well, there's nothin' to worry about. He knows his way around these parts. He seemed awful sure he could find Stone."

"They say injuns can find anything they want," Atwell said. "They're the best trackers in the world."

Red Feather came to the end of the passageway, crouched low, and pointed his rifle straight ahead. If Stone was out there, he might have his gun trained on the opening of the passageway. If Red Feather were a young man, he'd move swiftly to a position of safety behind boulders, but he wasn't a young man.

He could go back and get the others, but then he'd have to share the reward money. No, he'd better press on by himself. He still had the old Commanche cunning.

He looked down, and the grass was pressed in the shape of a boot. He filled his lungs with air and jumped out of the passageway, running toward the nearest big boulder, expecting a bullet to smash into him at any moment, but seconds later found himself huffing and puffing behind a huge boulder.

He saw white dots in front of his eyes, and his chest ached. It was the most he'd exerted himself in months. He told himself he ought to return to his people and get back into shape, but they didn't have any whiskey, and the old chiefs always were telling him what to do. He didn't want to go back to his people. He wanted to live like a white man.

Stone evidently had come this way. Looked like he kept going, and was on the far side of the canyon by now. Otherwise he would've shot Red Feather dead, because Red Feather knew how slow he'd been.

Red Feather poked his head out from behind the boulder. The canyon was silent and still. He bent down to study Stone's tracks. The tracks weren't hard to decipher. Stone hadn't even tried to cover them up.

Red Feather stepped forward, following Stone's tracks. He

knew Stone didn't have much ammunition. It was possible Red Feather would find him passed out somewhere in the canyon.

Red Feather approached a boulder eight feet tall and shaped like a giant potato. He walked past it, following the tracks. His once-acute hearing had been dulled after years in the white man's towns, and he didn't hear the footfall behind him, or the rustle of clothing. Suddenly, out of nowhere, an arm clamped around his chest and something sharp entered his throat.

Red Feather gasped, and everything went black before his eyes as Stone slit his throat from ear to ear. The Indian fell to a heap on the ground, and Stone glanced back to the passageway, to see if anyone else was coming. Below him lay great treasure. Red Feather had a knife, rifle, pistol, and plenty of ammunition.

He stripped the bandoliers of ammunition from Red Feather's shoulders and dropped them over his own shoulders. He picked up the pistol, knife, and rifle. The rifle wasn't new, and no soldier would ever permit his rifle to become so dirty, but otherwise it seemed to be in good condition.

Stone turned and ran deeper into the canyon, as Red Feather lay behind him, bleeding in the late-afternoon sun.

"Where'd that injun go?" Dawson asked Atwell. "He's been gone for a long time. Maybe you'd better send some men to look for him."

"I'm sure he's all right," Atwell replied. "He's one smart injun."

Atwell rode forward to pass the orders to the men, and Dawson took out a cigar. Stone should've been found by now, but was nowhere in sight, and now the injun had disappeared.

Dawson looked toward the horizon, and the day was coming to an end. It they didn't get Stone before dark, they probably wouldn't catch him at all. Stone had killed his son and made a fool out of him at every turn.

Meanwhile, Atwell gathered his men around him.

"Anybody seen that injun?" he asked.

Tom Reece pointed toward the mountains. "I seen him a little while ago over there."

Atwell drew his pistol and fired three shots in the air, making the horses skitterish. He waited a few minutes, then fired three more shots. Red Feather didn't fire back.

"Spread out and look for him," Atwell said.

Stone heard the first three shots, and then three additional shots followed by a long silence. Evidently they were signaling one another on the other side of the mountain.

He continued to make his way around the base of the mountain, looking for a passageway out. The air became cooler and he heard the gurgling of water. Rushing forward, clawing branches away from his eyes, he came to a stream not more than a foot wide.

"Thank God," he said, dropping to his knees beside it. He lowered his lips, kissed the water, and drank.

The sun touched the horizon. Burkers and Finch, two of Dawson's men, approached the rocks, their rifles in their hands.

Both were tired of searching for Stone and the Indian. After a few hours, every rock looked alike, and they were hungry. The chuck wagon hadn't caught up to them yet.

They looked at the passageway, but didn't see it. The shadows were too long now, the day becoming too dusky. Then they passed on. They wanted to return to their bunkhouse, have a meal, and go to bed. To hell with Stone. They were getting tired of the chase.

Dawson sat on the ground and realized Stone had gotten away. Meanwhile, his son needed burying. He looked at the rock cliffs, knowing Stone was waiting for him to leave. But he wasn't going to leave. His men would stay here until hell froze over or John Stone came out of hiding.

Dawson shouted, "Atwell!"

Jesse Atwell, at the base of the mountain, heard his boss's voice. He wheeled his horse around and galloped toward him, climbing down from the saddle before the horse had come to a full stop.

"Stone's around here someplace," Dawson said. "He'll have to come out sooner or later, so leave half your men here to wait for him, and the rest of us'll go back to the ranch. And make sure you tell the men who stay that my offer still stands. It's a hundred dollars to the one who kills him, but two hundred dollars if he's brought back alive."

7

IT WAS DARK when Hank Dawson and his men brought their horses to a halt in front of Dawson's ranch house. Dawson walked toward the front door, where a lamp burned behind the window. He didn't bother with his horse; he just let it stand there snorting. A cowboy grabbed the reins and led the horse to the stable.

The veranda shook as Dawson walked across it and opened the front door. The hallway was dim, and Dawson hung his hat on the peg. One of his gunfighters sat in a chair near the stairs.

Dawson climbed the stairs, and the planks of wood creaked underneath his weight. A carpeted corridor was at the top of the stairs, and Dawson walked down it, toward his son's bedroom.

He came to the door of the bedroom and paused, to prepare himself for the shock he knew would come. Wayne was on his bed, his promising young life finished.

Dawson opened the door, and a sickly sweet odor struck his nostrils. A dark form lay on top of the bed. His boy was dead, and nothing could bring him back.

Dawson swerved away from the bed and opened the windows, to get the stink out. He'd have to bury Wayne first thing in the morning, because of the heat. He lit a lamp on a dresser and carried it to the bed, forcing himself to look at the corpse of his son.

It was gray and stiff as a board. The cheeks had sunk in and the lips were blue. Wayne had been full of life just a short time ago. He loved to ride horses and go hunting, and now was a rotting corpse.

Hank Dawson placed the lamp on the night table, and sat on a chair near the bed. The bedroom was large, with stuffed heads of an antelope, bear, and mountain sheep on the walls. At the far end of the room was the rocking horse that Wayne had played on as a child.

Wayne loved horses all his life. He owned twenty fine horses personally. Hank would buy his son anything he wanted. Hank knew he spoiled Wayne, but why not?

Hank Dawson had been poor as a child. His father owned a little dirt farm in Illinois, and there was never enough of anything. All Hank Dawson had was a skinny mongrel dog. They were so poor they couldn't afford to feed the dog, so it had to survive on its wits, killing squirrels and rats. Once the dog tried to kill a skunk, and came home stinking. Everyone thought that was funny, but the dog almost died.

Dawson's mind returned to the bad smell in the room. He'd always thought Wayne would come to his funeral, and instead he was going to Wayne's.

Wayne was the only person Hank Dawson ever loved. He hadn't liked the boy's mother much; she nagged too much, but he took care of her when Wayne was four years old. Rat poison in her dinner, followed by a fast funeral in the backyard.

The boy hadn't missed her; he'd always loved his daddy best. Hank bought him whatever he wanted: horses, guns, women, and whiskey. Let the kid have a good time, because life was short and there was no hereafter except in the minds of stupid idiots.

Wayne had been a terror as a child. He hollared at the maids and cowboys, and all the Dawson employees had been ordered to do whatever young Wayne said, ever since he was five years old. It was funny, seeing grown people jumping at the whims of a five-year-old. They actually were afraid of him.

Everybody had been afraid of Wayne Dawson, and Hank had liked that. It meant no one would ever harm the boy, and the boy loved to fight. He was big and strong and whipped everybody. People stayed out of his way, and he took several gunmen wherever he went. Yesterday, at the restaurant, had been a fluke. He'd only been with two men because it was a busy day at the ranch and most of the hands were working.

The boy had been a good worker. Could hold his own with the strongest cowboys, but didn't like work much, preferring hunting, drinking, gambling, and whoring.

Hank Dawson had thought he'd live forever through his son, his son's son, and so on into the future. He'd been thinking lately of who should marry Wayne. Most of the families in the area would be happy to wed their daughters to the son of Hank Dawson. The boy could have his pick.

Dawson had been about to sound out his son about these matters, so that together they could pick the lucky girl. It would've been a good night of drinking and laughing. Wayne had looked up to his father the way a puppy looks up to his master. The future had appeared so bright. Nothing could go wrong, or so it had seemed.

Now all those dreams were shattered in one night with one bullet, and it was the fault of John Stone. If John Stone hadn't ridden into town that day, Wayne would still be alive.

Hank thought of John Stone as he'd seen him in the jail house the previous night. The man had a presence that Hank hadn't liked the moment he'd set eyes on him. He'd watched as Stone had fought off his men, and it had been an impressive display of fighting ability. Hank Dawson didn't like people who were extraordinary, because they made the most trouble.

Dawson knew Stone was out there in the night, and sooner or later his men would find him. He'd blanket the country with riders, put them in all the towns, and wait for Stone to show his face. Stone didn't even have a horse. He couldn't get far, and sooner or later he'd be caught. Dawson would string him up by the heels and beat him to death.

A breeze blew through the bedroom, rustling the hem of the bedspread underneath Wayne Dawson's corpse. The light flickered in the lamp, casting weird shadows on the wall. Hank Dawson had a stomachache and his head hurt. His rear end felt sore from so many hours in the saddle.

He had many things to do, but somehow couldn't raise himself from the chair. All he could do was sit and gaze at the corpse of his son, and think about all that could have been if it hadn't been for that goddamned John Stone.

At the Delane Ranch, Craig and Cynthia were seated at opposite ends of their long dinner table. It was covered with a white tablecloth and a candelabra that held six glowing candles. Craig and Cynthia wore evening clothes, and raised their glasses of champagne.

"To the Consortium!" Craig said.

They were too far away to touch glasses, so they smiled and lifted the glasses to their lips, tasting the fine old French champagne that Craig had imported all the way from New York for special occasions, and tonight was a special occasion. He and Cynthia had reaffirmed their love and Cynthia agreed to stay on the ranch for at least another year.

Craig lowered his glass and gazed at Cynthia, whose face glowed in the light of candles. Her eyes were catlike and her high cheekbones gave her face a dramatic cast. Craig thought she was absolutely stunning.

The door opened and Bernice appeared, carrying a silver tray on which was a silver tureen filled with chicken consommé. She served the consommé to Craig and Cynthia, then backed out of the dining room.

Cynthia tasted the consommé, and no one in New York City, even in the finest restaurant, would taste any better. Bernice was an excellent cook, and the staff grew plump chickens. It was nice to live luxuriously on the frontier.

Cynthia decided to stay with Craig because the more she thought about it, the more she realized she no longer missed the gay social whirl of the city. A person could feel on the crest of a new wave on the frontier. They were creating a great new land.

But something nagged her. She was unable to push John Stone out of her mind. Where was he?

She recalled seeing John Stone pull out his guns and open fire in the restaurant. What kind of man could do such a thing? Cynthia still was amazed by how calmly and confidently Stone had stepped into danger, and why? To help a person he didn't even know? Cynthia wished she could talk with Stone and find out what made him tick. He'd come all this way to find a woman, how strange.

Craig finished his bowl of consommé and looked up at Cynthia, whose fingers were poised on her spoon, a faraway expression on her face.

"What are you thinking about?" he asked.

She smiled and gazed down the table at him. "How happy we're going to be together."

Jesse Atwell sat on his heels beside the campfire and jabbed a long, thin branch into the red-hot coals. The end of the branch burst into flame, and Atwell drew it back to the cigarette between his lips. He inhaled and filled his lungs with the rich, tasty smoke.

He took a few steps back from the fire and looked ahead at the mountains. The injun still hadn't come back, and it was clear to everybody that John Stone must have killed him.

Atwell reasoned there must be a hidden cave or other hiding spot someplace that his men had missed. He'd ordered them to search for such a spot, and that's what they were doing. Atwell sat with Shorty by the fire, and Shorty whittled a piece of wood.

The prairie was vast and the night dark. It wouldn't be hard for Stone to escape now, but he wouldn't get far on foot. The man had no food, unless he could live off the land like an injun. Atwell expected Dawson to hire more injuns in the morning. Then Stone might be found.

Atwell and the others would have to be cautious. Stone was fighting for his life and was dangerous as a rattlesnake.

Times had been easy for Atwell and his men before John Stone arrived. No one ever dared defy the men from the Circle Bar D, and they'd ridden roughshod across the land. Then Wayne had to get into a fight with John Stone.

Atwell wasn't bereft by the death of Wayne Dawson, because Wayne had humiliated Atwell on many occasions. None of the men had liked Wayne much, but stayed for the good money and easy work.

Atwell wondered what would happen to the Circle Bar D now that Wayne was gone. There'd be a lot less damned foolishness probably. They'd get more of the real work done, without Wayne interfering, and Hank Dawson would get richer than he was already.

"Somebody's comin'," said Shorty, whittling his stick.

Atwell heard the sound of hoofbeats, and a form materialized out of the night. It was Jack Mullins on horseback; he came to a stop in front of Atwell.

"Cain't find 'im," Mullins said.

"Keep lookin'," Atwell replied.

"The men're gittin' tired. We din't have hardly no sleep last night. How's about some of us hittin' the hay for a spell?"

"Maybe later," Atwell said, "but in the meanwhile, git back and keep lookin'."

"Oh, shit, come on, Atwell. Don't be a hard ass."

"I said git back there and keep lookin'. Don't forget that reward money. Maybe you'll be the lucky cowpoke who'll wind up with it."

Mullins took off his hat. "If we ain't caught him now, we ain't gonna catch him. There's no tellin' where he might be right now."

"He's around here someplace. The man ain't got wings. The boss'll git hot under the collar if we don't find him."

"Let the boss pick up his big ass and find 'im, if he thinks it's so easy."

"Nobody said it's easy. Git goin'."

Mullins wheeled his horse and rode toward the base of the mountains. Shorty chortled at he whittled his stick of wood.

"What're you laughin' at?" Atwell asked.

"Funny how everything's changed," Shorty said. "Nobody would've dared talk like that when Wayne was alive, because he was always with us. But he ain't around no more, and we can speak our peace."

"No you can't," Atwell said, "because I'm still here, and I won't tolerate anybody criticizin' the boss."

Shorty chortled again. "Come off it, Atwell. Ain't nobody around here afraid of you."

Atwell puffed his cigarette. He wasn't the fastest gun in the outfit and everybody knew it. But he was still the ramrod, and wanted to keep his job.

"You wanna git fired, Shorty?"

"Who's gonna fire me?"

"Me, and Dawson will back me. He always has."

"You fire me, and I'll kill you, old man."

Atwell was older than most of the men at the Circle Bar D, but he was only thirty-eight, and that wasn't so old.

"Anytime you're ready to kill me, make your play," Atwell said. "I'll be a-waitin' for you."

"Don't worry about it, old man. I will."

Stone dropped to one knee. He'd been searching the canyon and hadn't found any caves, valleys, tunnels, or other ways out. His stomach was empty and numb, and he felt a lightness in his head. He thought he could go without food several days, as long as he had water, but after that he'd collapse. He had to resolve his food problem.

He couldn't get over the mountains; they were too steep and high. The only alternative was go out the same way he came in, and face Dawson's cowboys.

He was sure they were out there. Dawson wasn't the kind of man who'd walk away from a feud, and Stone realized that's what he was in, a feud. Dawson wanted to kill him and everything he stood for, and he had to fight back if he wanted to stay alive.

It was dark and gloomy in the shadow of the canyon, but Stone had learned in the war that the night could be your best friend. High up on the mountains, wind whistled through the few trees. Stone crouched and peered ahead across the floor of the canyon, ready to dive to the ground at the sight of danger. He wished Tad McDermott were still alive. Together they'd have a better chance, covering each other, four hands were better than two.

Stone felt somehow he'd let McDermott down. He should've talked him out of going into Eagleton. He'd known there was danger. He could smell it.

Stone saw movement ahead, and dropped to his stomach behind a bush. He raised his rifle to his shoulder and sighted down the barrel. Nothing happened. Stone waited several minutes, ready to fire his rifle, but there was no more movement. Maybe it was a bird, or a small animal.

He rose to his feet again and continued to move across the floor of the canyon, holding his rifle tightly, ready to fire.

* * *

Tom Reece and Billy Finch searched the base of the mountains on the other side of the canyon. They were dismounted, carrying rifles, poking in bushes, and peering around boulders.

"I'm gittin' sick of this shit," said Reece. "Let's have us a smoke."

"We're supposed to be lookin' fer John Stone."

"To hell with John Stone."

"I want that two hundred dollars."

"He could be ten feet away right now, and we wouldn't see him. You can't find somebody at night."

Finch looked around fearfully under the brim of his big hat. "Let's have that smoke," he said. "These boulders look like a good place."

They sat behind the boulders and leaned their rifles behind them. Reaching into their pockets, they took out bags of tobacco.

"I'm gittin' plumb tired," Reece said. "I want to roll up in my blanket and get some shut-eye."

"Atwell might find us."

"So what if he did? I ain't afraid of that son of a bitch."

Reece's paper tore as he was rolling the cigarette. He threw the torn piece over his shoulder and reached for another. Meanwhile, opposite him, Finch watched the paper fly through the air. He expected it to bounce off the wall, but somehow it kept going, seemingly *through the wall*.

"What the hell was that?" Finch asked.

"What the hell was what?"

Finch arose and walked toward the wall. He raised his hand and it went right through.

"Well I'll be damned."

"What's the matter?" asked Reece, turning around.

"There's a cave here."

Reece stood and walked toward the opening. They looked inside and saw pitch-blackness.

"Are you thinkin' what I'm thinkin'?" Reece asked. "Maybe this is where Stone went. Let's go back and tell the others."

"What the hell for? You wanna share the two hundred dollars with them? Let's get Stone for ourselves."

"He killed the injun."

"We're white men, and we can handle him. Are you afraid?"

"Hell no, but I don't feel like goin' up against him with just you."

"I thought you said you wasn't afraid."

"Let's get the others in on this. John Stone ain't nobody to fuck with. He killed a lot of people tonight."

Finch turned around and cupped his hands around his mouth. He was about to yell when Reece clamped his hand over his mouth.

"Wait a minute!" Reece said. "What if this cave is only three feet deep? You might call everybody over here for nothin', and make fools of us. Let's at least check it out a little bit on our own."

Finch could see the sense in that. "Okay."

Reece entered the narrow passageway, pointing his rifle straight ahead. He took a step, and then another step. The passageway inclined to the right. Reece pawed ahead with his rifle, and it didn't touch anything.

"The cave keeps going," Reece said.

"I think I'd better go back and tell the others."

Reece looked into the darkness. John Stone could be straight ahead, his gun cocked, and Reece wouldn't be able to see him. "I'll wait for you right here," Reece said.

Finch turned around and called out. "We found a cave!"

There was a pause for a few seconds, and then he heard Atwell's voice echoing through the night. "Light a fire so's we can see where you are."

Finch gathered some twigs and set fire to them with a match. It wasn't much of a fire, but it could be seen in the darkness. Soon the sound of horse's hooves came to Reece and Finch. Standfield and Burkers galloped up, and a few moments later Atwell arrived, followed by the rest of his men.

The men climbed down from their horses and pulled their rifles out of the boots.

"What the hell you got here?" Atwell said, stepping forward.

"This cave," said Finch, pointing to it.

Atwell didn't see any cave. He dismounted and walked toward the spot Finch indicated, reaching out tentatively with his foot, and it vanished in the darkness. Now he saw it, but didn't want to be the first one in. Stone might be waiting in there, rifle in hand. The only thing to do was get down on his belly and crawl. He was ramrod and had to lead the way.

"Shorty," he said, "stay with the horses. The rest of you follow me."

He crawled into the passageway, expecting to run into a wall, but the passageway inclined to the right and it turned over onto itself like a big snake. Atwell heard his men behind him, grunting and scraping over the floor of the passageway. He expected a bullet to blast into his head at any moment. Finally he saw a shaft of moonlight and realized he'd passed through the base of the mountains.

"There's a canyon in here," he said. "Stay ready. Stone might be just ahead."

Atwell moved forward cautiously and came to the edge of the passageway. His men crowded behind him.

Reece pointed straight ahead. "There's somethin' lyin' out there."

Atwell saw a shadow in the shape of a man lying next to bush. "Follow me," he said.

He crept toward the shadow, and his men followed cautiously. The canyon was dark and silent as they moved deeper into its stillness. Atwell drew close to the shadow. "It's the injun."

Red Feather lay on his back, his arms spread out and his throat cut from ear to ear. He'd been stripped of weapons and ammunition, and now Atwell knew what happened to Stone.

He pointed to the tracks on the ground with the barrel of his rifle. "Spread out and go after him. Watch yore step—you can see what he's done to the injun."

Atwell stepped forward, following the tracks that led into the canyon. His men came behind him, examining rocks and bushes around them. The moonlight glinted on the barrels of their guns as they advanced deeper into the canyon.

Stone, behind a nearby boulder, watched them disappear, following his old trail. If they stayed on it, they'd roam the canyon for hours. A coyote howled on a distant ridge, and Stone waited, to make sure they were far away.

Finally he came out of his hiding place and stepped toward the passageway, listening for sounds of someone coming the other way, then moved through it silently, alert for danger, and upon reaching the end peered into the rolling hills.

He saw the boulders where he'd hidden, and a hundred yards beyond them were horses crowded together and saddled. Nearby a man sat cross-legged on the ground, his rifle lying across his knees. The man's head was inclined forward and it looked as though he was asleep.

Stone pulled the Indian's knife out of the sheath in his boot, and held it blade up in his fist. Then he got down on his belly and crawled toward the guard.

The guard raised his head, and Stone stopped. It appeared as though the guard heard something. The guard looked in Stone's direction.

"Who's there?"

Stone lay still on the ground. The guard arose and walked toward him, leaning forward, holding his rifle. Stone could drill him through the eyes with his rifle, but the sound would give him away.

The guard stopped ten feet from Stone, stood rooted to the same spot for a few seconds, then turned and walked toward where he'd been sitting. He dropped to his haunches and stared aimlessly into the night.

Stone had to creep up on the guard, but the night was still and sound carried far. He crawled forward, and the guard's head snapped around. The guard rose to his feet, and Stone gripped his knife tightly in his hand. The guard appeared to be looking directly at him.

"What the hell's goin' on?" the guard said.

The guard advanced cautiously, and Stone lay on the ground in front of him, moonlight dappling his body and making it look like a pile of rocks.

Suddenly Stone sprang to his feet and lunged forward.

"Hey!" shouted the guard, raising his rifle.

Stone slammed the rifle down and jabbed the knife into the guard's jugular. A sigh passed between the guard's lips, then his knees became jelly and he fell to the ground at Stone's feet. Stone wiped the blade of the knife on the guard's trousers, dropped the blade into his boot, and ran toward the horses.

They were picketed a short distance away, and Stone appraised them quickly, settling on the biggest one. He untied the others and slapped their haunches, shooing them away.

Stone tightened the cinch on the big horse, then untied the reins and climbed into the saddle. He prodded the horse with his spurs, and the animal moved off into the dark, billowing night, leaving behind the dead guard with his eyes wide open, staring sightlessly at the moon.

8

HANK DAWSON SNORED loudly as he sat on the chair in his son's bedroom. The lamp flickered, casting dancing shadows, and the heads of dead animals mounted on the walls seemed to be winking.

Dawson hadn't eaten, changed his clothes, or taken a bath since he'd come in from the trail. He'd just sat with the body of his son and gradually dropped off to sleep.

The sound of his snoring reverberated through the house as he dreamed of Wayne as a little boy. Hank bought Wayne a puppy, and Wayne pulled the puppy's tail and ears. The puppy died about a month after Hank bought it, and little Wayne cried when a cowboy buried it in the backyard. Hank dreamed about how he'd held Wayne in his arms and comforted him. He told him he'd buy another puppy to replace the dead one, but little Wayne played rough and killed that one too.

Hank Dawson awoke with a start, and the first thing he saw was the form of his son lying on the bed. Rigor mortis had set in and Wayne was stiff as a board. Hank Dawson took out his pocket watch, and it was midnight. Why had there been no word about John Stone?

Dawson arose and approached the bed, looking at his son. It still was hard for him to believe Wayne was dead.

He walked toward the door, and one of his men dozed on a chair in the corridor. Dawson kicked a leg of the chair, and the man went sprawling toward the carpet, reaching for his gun as he went down. At the last moment he recognized his boss standing above him. He smiled sheepishly and returned his gun to its holster.

"Guess I must've dropped off."

"You better be careful I don't drop you off'n a cliff. Any word from Atwell?"

"I ain't heard nothin', Mr. Dawson."

"Go out and see what he's doin'. Then report back to me."

Dawson descended the stairs and headed for his office. In the moonlight near the window he poured himself a glass of whiskey, drank it down, then filled another glass, carrying it upstairs to Wayne's room.

The stench hit him when he opened the door, and he realized it had become much stronger during the past few hours. He hadn't noticed, because he'd been in the room all that time, but now it was horribly apparent. He couldn't go back.

He continued down the corridor to his own room, furnished with a big brass bed, rustic chairs, a dresser, and a desk. As in his son's room, the heads of dead animals were mounted on the walls.

He placed the glass of whiskey on his night table and sat on the bed, pulling off his boots. Then he lay back on the bedspread and closed his eyes.

He'd find Stone even if he and his men had to search every square foot of Texas.

Cynthia sipped the remaining champagne in her glass. She sat on one of the upholstered chairs in her living room, and Craig lay on the sofa opposite her, his feet propped up on a pillow. He picked one of the cookies off the plate on the coffee table beside him, and dropped it into his mouth.

"I think I'm going to bed," Cynthia said.

Craig arose from the sofa and took her hand, kissing her cheek. They walked toward the stairs as Bernice cleared away the empty bottle, glasses, and plate of cookies.

Craig and Cynthia made their way down the corridor to her

bedroom. The cool breeze ruffled the chiffon drapes that covered the windows as Craig lit the lamp on the dresser. The room carried the fragrance of Cynthia's French perfume.

The centerpiece of the room was a huge canopied bed that had cost a small fortune to ship from New York. Its bedposts were ornately carved and the fabric of the canopy was pure white satin.

"Unbutton me, would you, Craig?"

Craig opened the back of her dress, revealing her smooth white skin blemished only by one mole on the nape of her neck. Craig bent over and touched his lips to the mole. She closed her eyes and felt the tip of his tongue, thinking of John Stone.

It was strange how he kept intruding himself into her mind. It was as though he were the third person in the room. Somehow she couldn't stop thinking about him.

Craig peeled the dress off her shoulders, kissing and urging her toward the bed, and together they sank onto the mattress, rolling over, embracing.

Ahead was a gully with a stream running into it. Stone pulled back on the reins and the horse stopped in front of the flowing water. Stone climbed down from the saddle and let the horse drink. He pulled the saddlebags off the horse and sat on the ground, to see what they contained.

Opening the flap, he reached inside and found three biscuits. He groped around more and pulled out a handful of jerked beef. Hungrily he stuffed the food into his mouth, barely chewing it. In the other saddlebag he found an unopened bag of tobacco, some cigarette papers, and a box of matches. He was tempted to have a smoke, but a light would carry far at night. He decided to forgo the pleasure till morning.

He continued searching the saddlebags and found a clean pair of socks and a shirt too small for him, and a folded sheet of thick paper. He unfolded the paper and held it up to the moonlight. It was a map of the area.

Stone studied it while his horse slurped water and flicked a fly off his haunch with his tail. Stone located Eagleton and found the approximate location of the mountains where he'd tried to hide. From the mountains he determined his approximate current position. The big question was where to go from here.

McDermott's plan had been to go to Mexico, and Stone thought that was still a good idea. He looked up at the sky, saw the Big Dipper, and found the North Star. If he slept by day and traveled by night, he ought to reach Mexico in a week.

Stone learned long ago in the war that you must never do what your enemy expects. He looked at the map again and thought maybe he should head north, or west, or even east. Somehow he had to trick Dawson and his Indian trackers.

The best alternative would be to find a safe place to hide for a week or two until the trouble blew over. Dawson couldn't have his men searching constantly. Sooner or later he'd have to get on with the business of operating his ranch.

If only there were a cave someplace, or if he had friends someplace. Then he realized he did have friends in the area: the Delanes. Hadn't Delane said his HC Ranch was west of Dumont?

Stone held the map up to the moonlight and looked for Dumont, a mere dot on the map, and then heard hoofbeats in the distance.

He reached for his rifle and got down. He and his horse were in the gully and couldn't be seen unless the riders came directly into it with him. Stuffing the map into his shirt, he climbed toward the top of the gully and looked onto the prairie.

He saw the shadowy indistinct shapes of two riders in the distance, heading toward the mountains, and he figured they must be Dawson's men, because who else would be riding hard that time of night?

Stone hoped his horse wouldn't make any noise. He took off his hat and held his head low so his silhouette couldn't be seen in the moonlight. The riders seemed to be unaware of his presence and continued to head toward the mountains. A few minutes passed and the night swallowed them up. Stone couldn't hear their hoofbeats anymore.

He dropped to the bottom of the gully and took out the map again, holding it in the moonlight. Dawson's men would scour the countryside for him, and he needed a hiding place.

He found Dumont on the map and looked to its west: a chain of mountains and another dot. Beside the dot was written: *HC Ranch*.

Stone kneeled at the stream and took a drink of water. He still felt sore from the beating, but at least was alive.

He threw the saddlebags over the hindquarters of the horse and climbed into the saddle. Pulling the reins to the side, he headed for the HC Ranch.

The riders who'd passed Stone were Clint Standfield and Al Burkers, two of Dawson's men. They rode their horses hard because they knew Dawson was anxious for the latest news.

They approached the base of the mountains where Stone had disappeared, and saw horses scattered about. Standfield and Burkers looked at each other in surprise. Horses normally were picketed together. How come these horses were loose?

"Atwell!" Standfield hollered. "Where the hell are you?"

There was no answer, and Standfield scowled. He pulled back the reins of his horse, and so did Burkers. Their horses slowed to a stop.

"Where the hell is everybody?" asked Burkers, who wore a thick black mustache.

"Damned if I know," said Standfield, a blond. "It don't look good to me." He took out his pistol and fired a few shots in the air. "That ought to bring 'em, if they're still around."

Burkers drew his pistol and fired two shots, then paused and fired two shots more. The sound of the shots echoed back and forth among the mountains.

"What the hell's that?" Atwell asked, raising his head.

"It's shots," replied Finch, standing behind him.

"I know it's shots, you damned fool, but who the hell's firin' 'em?"

"Sounds like it's comin' from outside the canyon."

Atwell looked in the direction of the shots. He and his men still were in the canyon, following the trail left by Stone.

"Sounds like trouble," he said. "Let's go."

They ran across the canyon floor, heading for the passageway that led to the outside. The shots hadn't sounded like a gunfight, but as if somebody was giving a signal.

Atwell worried Dawson would fire him if Stone got away, because it wasn't easy to get a good foreman job. He might have to become a cowboy on some lesser spread someplace, and that'd be hard to take after the soft life he'd enjoyed as Dawson's ramrod.

They came to the passageway, and Atwell moved through it swiftly, but instead of seeing his horses picketed nearby, there was nothing.

"Shorty!" he said. "Where the hell are you?"

There was no answer. Atwell looked off into the prairie and saw the dark forms of horses. Suddenly shots were fired. Atwell dropped to one knee.

"That you, Atwell?" called the voice of Clint Standfield.

"It's me all right."

"Fire your gun so's I kin see where you are."

Atwell pulled out his pistol and fired a shot into the air. Two horses galloped toward him from the prairie straight ahead.

"Look—it's Shorty!" said Finch.

Atwell looked in the direction Finch was pointing and saw a figure lying on the ground. Atwell walked toward the figure and gazed down. It was Shorty all right, his throat slit open and his tongue sticking out.

Two riders approached out of the night, reined their horses, and looked at Shorty.

"What the hell happened to him?" Standfield asked.

"Somebody carved him up, looks like."

Atwell took off his hat and scratched his head. Dawson would be furious. He looked up at Standfield. "What the hell're you doin' out here?"

"Dawson sent us to see if you caught Stone yet, but I guess you ain't. I'd better go back and tell him."

"I'll tell him myself. You and Burkers round up the horses."

Standfield and Burkers rode off to collect the horses, and Atwell rolled a cigarette. *Looks like I'm out of a job*, he thought. *I wonder if they're doin' any hirin' over at the HC.*

Cynthia Delane lay in bed and stared at the ceiling. Craig had returned to his bed an hour ago, leaving her alone, and somehow Cynthia couldn't fall asleep. Maybe it was the coffee she'd drunk with dinner, or maybe it was her troubled mind. She wore a white diaphanous nightgown and was covered with a light sheet. Her windows were open and a cool breeze floated through the room, causing the curtains to billow in the air.

She wondered if she'd done the right thing by agreeing to

stay with Craig in Texas, because she realized she felt no great passion for him and never had. She liked him as a friend or brother, but not a husband.

She'd thought passion was silly when she'd married Craig, and her love for Craig was spiritual. They shared many similar interests, and their union had brought together two fine old New York families, but now Cynthia craved something more.

Craig was too gentle, too nice, too much of a gentleman. They had good communication, but not so good that she could tell him what she wanted. Besides, she didn't want to tell a man what to do. She wanted a man who knew what to do.

John Stone seemed like a man who knew what to do. He walked through the world as if he owned it. Cynthia closed her eyes and thought how wonderful it'd be to have a man like John Stone sweep her up in his arms and carry her away.

The snoring of Hank Dawson reverberated throughout the big ranch house. He was in a deep sleep without dreams when he felt someone shaking his shoulder. He opened his eyes and saw a dark form above him.

"I got bad news," Atwell said. "Stone got away."

Dawson sat up in bed as the clock downstairs struck three. He still was wearing his clothes, and the odor of death clung to them. "How'd he get away?"

Atwell explained how Stone had killed the injun and Shorty, and stolen a horse. "I guess I should've left more men guardin' the horses, but I wanted to have as many with me as I could, in case we had a shootout with Stone in the canyon."

"He outsmarted you."

"Reckon he did."

Atwell thought for sure he was going to be fired as Dawson rolled out of bed and lit a lamp. Then he used the flame from the lamp to light a cigar. His pants were drooping low on his hips so he thumbed his suspenders back onto his shoulders. He paced the floor back and forth a few times, then stopped and turned to Atwell.

"First of all," he said, "get the undertaker and preacher out here first thing in the morning. Next, hire a bunch of injuns to track down John Stone. I figger Stone's headed for Mexico, so make sure you got all the main trails covered. Then send a few men to each town around here, in case Stone shows up

lookin' for supplies or a fresh horse. You say he's got one of
our horses?''

"That's right, sir."

"It's got my brand on it. Make sure everybody knows they're
supposed to be lookin' for a stranger on a Circle Bar D horse.
And I'm uppin' the reward. From now on it's five hundred
dollars to the man who gets Stone dead or alive, and dead is
as good as alive as long as I got the son of a bitch. If you
don't have enough men, hire as many as you need, but get me
John Stone.''

Atwell walked out of the room, and in the corridor smelled
the odor of Wayne's putrefying body permeating the house,
getting into every nook and cranny.

At least he hadn't been fired. Dawson needed his old ramrod.
Atwell put on his hat as he descended the stairs to the ground
floor. He crossed to the front door and made his way to the
bunkhouse, his spurs jingling in the stillness of the night.

He opened the door and heard snoring and wheezing from
the men who hadn't been out yet.

"Everybody up!" he hollered, stamping his foot on the floor.
"We got work to do!"

The men groaned as they rolled around and opened their
eyes, trying to see in the dim light.

"What's goin' on?" one of them asked sleepily.

"On yore feet, you bunch of bastards! Mr. Dawson is offerin' five hundred dollars to the man who gits John Stone dead
or alive!''

John Stone saw the buildings of the HC Ranch sprawled out
ahead of him in the night. He pulled back the reins of his horse,
and the animal snorted and danced around on the grass.

He knew Delane would have at least one guard posted to
watch for Indians. He also assumed some if not all of Delane's
men were working part-time for Hank Dawson, reporting Delane's activities, because Dawson would want to keep an eye
on the man who headed the Consortium. Stone would have to
get into the house and talk with Delane without Delane's hired
hands knowing about it.

He couldn't take the horse with him because it carried the
Circle Bar D brand. Stone guided the horse toward a cotton-
wood tree, dismounted, pulled off the saddle, and stashed it

under the tree. Then he slipped off the bridle and reins. The horse was naked, looking at Stone curiously. Stone patted the horse's mane. "Go far away from here," he said. "Don't give me away to the Dawson gang."

Stone whipped the horse in the ass with the reins, and the horse leapt away in surprise. It broke into a gallop and ran off into the night.

Stone listened to the sound of its receding hoofbeats, and then the only sound was the chirping of crickets. He threw the saddlebags over his shoulder and carried the rifle in his right hand, setting off for the ranch nestled in the valley below him.

The Circle Bar D Ranch was the scene of frantic activity. Some men galloped toward the border, hoping to catch Stone on the way down, and others rode toward the towns in the area, in case Stone showed up in one of them. Every man wanted that big five-hundred-dollar reward.

Dawson watched the men ride away while smoking a cigar next to the bedroom window. His lamp was lit, bathing the room in a soft glow. The putrescent odor of his son's corpse filled the house.

He saw Atwell ride out of the barn, followed by four men. Atwell passed in front of the ranch house and waved at Dawson, but Dawson didn't bother to wave back. Atwell was on his way to Dumont to fetch the undertaker and preacher, to hire Indian trackers and more men.

Dawson had been tempted to fire Atwell, but controlled his temper because he didn't have anybody better. But he'd replace him first chance he got. He needed somebody smarter. In Dawson's opinion, most cowboys were drunken fools. They worked like slaves for their miserable wages, then spent it all on whiskey and whores, incapable of thinking beyond next weekend.

Stone was only one man, and he couldn't hope to elude the small army that Dawson was sending out to catch him. "You'll never get away from me," Dawson muttered. "I'll catch you no matter how long it takes, and how much it costs."

Pausing in the shadow of a tree, Stone looked at the HC ranch house and knew he couldn't simply walk up to the front door and knock. Somehow he'd have to get into the house without awakening the guards.

He saw open windows on the second floor. A large tree beside the house had branches that extended to the roof of the house. Stone heard a sound and froze in the shadow of a pile of wood. The door to the bunkhouse opened and a cowboy staggered out, half asleep, on his way to the privy. Stone held his rifle ready and watched the cowboy enter the privy and close the door. Soon thereafter the door to the privy opened again and the cowboy reappeared, making his way back to the bunkhouse.

The cowboy entered the bunkhouse and Stone waited a few minutes until everything settled down again, then crouched low and ran toward the tree that grew beside the ranch house. Slinging the rifle over his shoulder, he jumped up and grabbed a branch, swung his legs back and forth, and hoisted himself onto it.

The grounds surrounding the ranch house were still quiet. The guard probably was asleep. Stone waited a few moments, then climbed to the roof, stepped onto it, and made his way to the nearest open window.

He came to the opening and saw a large bed with a white canopy. From the distance, he couldn't discern whether one or two people were in the bed. He swung one of his long legs over the sill and entered the bedroom, then unslung his rifle, holding it ready to fire.

The sweet fragrance of ladies' perfume arose to his nostrils, and he heard a feminine sigh. He could see only one person in the bed now, and it was Cynthia Delane, rolling over onto her back, sweeping the thin sheet off her.

Stone stood still; he didn't want to frighten her. Cynthia finished her movement and lay supine. Stone waited a few seconds, then approached her slowly, his finger tight against the trigger, in case a cowboy with a gun in his hand burst through the door.

Cynthia had thrown the sheet off her, and her nightgown raised high above her knees. A strap of her nightgown had fallen off her shoulder, and nearly all her right breast was exposed. Stone stopped beside the bed and looked at her. She was nearly naked and he hadn't been with a woman for a long time. Her dark hair was tousled on the pillow and her mouth was half open.

She was another man's wife, and he was pledged to another

woman himself, but he couldn't help gazing at her with lust in his heart. The fragrance of her body rose to his nostrils and made him dizzy.

His life was in danger and he needed these people to help him. He had to calm down and awaken Cynthia without alarming her.

Meanwhile, in the depths of her sleep, Cynthia felt something was wrong. She didn't know what it was—only a vague uneasiness—but it prodded her to consciousness. She opened her eyes and saw a big man standing over her.

At first she couldn't believe he was there. Then she realized she wasn't dreaming, and a man indeed was in her bedroom leering at her! She opened her mouth to scream.

Stone clamped his hand over her mouth. She tasted his salty fingers and could feel the tremendous strength of his body.

"It's me, John Stone," he said. "Please calm down."

She recognized his voice, and he removed his hand from her mouth.

"I need someplace to hide," he said. "Will you help me?"

Cynthia saw his face in the moonlight filtering through the window. "Of course we'll help you," and then realized she was half naked in bed. She pulled down the hem of her gown and raised the silken strap to her shoulder, arose from the bed, and put on her robe. "We were worried about you. Let me get Craig."

"Some of your people might be working for Dawson. Don't tell anybody I'm here."

She left the room, and Stone sat on a chair beside the bed, thinking of Cynthia lying resplendent in bed. There'd been a moment where he'd almost grabbed her.

Cynthia returned to the bedroom with Craig, who wore a blue and white striped robe, and his eyes were heavy-lidded from just being awakened.

"My God—this is a surprise!"

"I don't want to put you to any trouble," Stone said, "but I had no place else to go."

Delane patted him on the shoulder. "You came to the right place. We'll take care of you. Last thing we heard, you were going to be lynched. We saw you pass by the New Dumont Hotel, surrounded by Dawson and his men. How'd you get out of it?"

Stone gave them a quick rundown of what happened. "I didn't know where to go, because the countryside is full of Dawson's men. You're the only people I know in this area."

"Your worries are over," Craig said. "You can stay in our guest room. I'll get Bernice, our maid, to fix it up for you."

"Can you trust her?"

"Of course we can trust her. What makes you think we can't?"

"I wouldn't be surprised if some of the people who work for you are also working for Dawson. He controls everything and everybody in this area. You and he are in negotiations, aren't you?"

"I don't think he'd spy on me."

"I wouldn't put anything past him. He's ruthless and a little crazy, especially now that his son is dead. You mustn't let any of your people know I'm hiding here."

"We can trust Bernice," Cynthia said. "We brought her with us from New York, and she doesn't know anybody around here. She's worked for my family for years."

Cynthia left the room, and Craig looked at Stone.

"Are you hungry?"

"I could use a drink."

Cynthia returned to the room with Bernice, who wore a nightcap with her robe.

"This is John Stone," Cynthia said to Bernice. "He'll be staying with us for a while, but nobody must know he's here. Please make up the guest room for him."

"Before you do that," Craig said, "bring us some whiskey and my box of cigars."

Bernice left the room, and Craig lit the lamp on the dresser while Cynthia sat on the bed.

"Mind if I roll a cigarette?" Stone asked.

"Not at all, but would you prefer a cigar?"

"I'd rather have a cigarette."

Stone took the tobacco pouch from the saddlebags and rolled a cigarette as Cynthia gazed at his broad shoulders. Stone radiated raw masculine vitality, and she could feel it across the room. Craig was a scarecrow compared to him. What had she been thinking about when she married Craig?

She'd been a girl, and had a girl's needs. Now she was a woman, and had a woman's needs.

Stone raised his head and looked directly into her eyes, and it was like two streams of fire meeting in outer space.

9

THE CASKET WAS white pine, unpainted, with the lid nailed shut, and the odor of Wayne Dawson's rotting corpse seeped through. Ladies in long dresses held their handkerchiefs to their noses.

Hank Dawson stood beside the casket, his hat in his hands, his head lowered as Reverend Skeaping delivered the funeral oration. A few feet from the casket was the deep hole into which the casket would be placed, and the onlookers thought the sooner Wayne was buried, the better, because the stench was getting worse in the hot sun.

"Dear Lord," said Reverend Skeaping, his white chin whiskers quivering with emotion, "please gather unto yourself the soul and spirit of our dearly departed Wayne Dawson. He was a good man, kind to all who knew him, a friend to those who needed friends, and he has been taken from us cruelly, in the very prime of youth. Remember all the kind things he did in his young life, and forgive him the unkind things, because deep down he was a decent boy."

Reverend Skeaping's voice droned on, and the assembly stood solemnly, knowing he was lying about Wayne Dawson, because Wayne had been a hellion with a vicious streak a mile wide. Everyone present except Hank Dawson was glad Wayne was dead.

"Ashes to ashes and dust to dust," the Reverend Skeaping said. "The Lord giveth and the Lord taketh away. The righteous shall live at the right hand of the Lord forever and ever. Amen."

Reverend Skeaping winked at Thomas O'Neil, the undertaker, and O'Neil cleared his throat. The six cowboys from the Circle Bar D lowered the casket into the grave.

The casket came to rest at the bottom of the grave, and the cowboys grabbed shovels, tossing dirt onto it. Hank Dawson stepped forward and looked into the grave, tears rolling down his cheeks. Wayne was gone and there was no bringing him back. Hank let out a sob and closed his eyes, as clods of earth filled the hole in the ground.

Bernice stood over the hot stove, frying bacon and eggs. She wore an apron and her funny little maid's hat from New York City.

Cynthia entered the kitchen, eating an apple. "Bernice, I want to talk with you."

Bernice flipped over the strips of bacon so they could cook on both sides. "What is it, ma'am?"

"I know Mr. Delane spoke with you about this last night, but I want to make sure you understand that you mustn't say a word about Mr. Stone to anybody, do you understand?"

"I understand, ma'am."

"Just make believe Mr. Stone isn't here, because you wouldn't want anything to happen to him, would you?"

"No, ma'am."

"After you cook his breakfast, I want you to wash his clothes, but don't hang them outside on the line. Hang them someplace upstairs in the attic, where none of the hired hands can see them."

"Yes, ma'am."

Bernice shoveled the eggs and bacon on plates, while Cynthia cut thick slices of bread and laid them on another plate. Bernice arranged the plates and a pot of coffee on a tray, and prepared to pick it up.

"I'll take it," Cynthia said.

Cynthia lifted the tray and headed for the stairs. She passed Craig coming from the other direction.

"I've got to go to town," Craig said. "I should be back later this morning."

They touched lips lightly. Craig wore a gray New York business suit with cowboy boots and a cowboy hat. He looked like a dude.

"Will you be back in time for lunch?" she asked.

"I think so."

Cynthia carried the tray up the stairs and down the hall, kicking the door of the guest room with her foot. She heard the rush of water, and a few moments later the door was opened by John Stone, wrapped in a large towel.

"Oh, you were still taking your bath," Cynthia said. "I didn't mean to disturb you."

"That's all right. I was finished."

"I brought your breakfast."

She entered the room and placed the tray on the table. John Stone was nearly naked, a towel wrapped around his waist. He had dark blond hair on his chest, arms, and legs.

"Did you sleep well?" she asked.

"Yes, thank you."

"Is there anything I can get you?"

"I wish I had some clothes."

"I could lend you some of my husband's clothes, but I don't think they'd fit. I told Bernice to wash your clothes, and she'll hang them in the attic where no one can see. Sit down—your breakfast is getting cold."

Stone sat on a chair, placed the tray on his lap, and proceeded to dine. Cynthia looked at his big shoulders, the expanse of his chest, and he had bruises everywhere. He wolfed down the food, and she knew she had no legitimate reason to stay in the room, but somehow couldn't leave.

"Have a seat," he said.

She dropped to a chair opposite him and felt ill at ease, because she was attracted to him, and she was a married woman.

He could see her discomfort as he poured a cup of coffee. He was nervous too, and tried not to think about how she'd looked in bed last night.

"Has Craig gone to town yet?" he asked.

"Yes," she replied. "You and I are alone. Well, not really alone. Bernice will be here, and of course our hands will be in the vicinity."

He drank a half cup of coffee, then rolled a cigarette and lit it. She looked at his round biceps, his prominent pectoral muscles, the sinews of his forearms.

"I think I'd better be going," she said, getting to her feet. "If you need anything, just walk down the hall and knock on my door."

She walked out of the room, and Stone blew smoke out of the corner of his mouth. She was beautiful, and Craig was away from the ranch. All he had to do was . . . but she was a married woman, and he was practically a married man.

Marie's picture was on the dresser, and Stone picked it up. He gazed at it and tried to think about Marie, so he wouldn't think about Cynthia.

Cynthia sat in the chair beside her window, a frown on her face. *I practically threw myself at him.*

She thought of John Stone half naked, sitting before her in the chair and casually drinking coffee. He'd looked like a beautiful lion, instead of a man.

She'd never known much about men before marrying Craig, but she was learning. Sometimes she had desires that frightened her. She stood and paced the floor, balling and unballing her fists. He was just down the hall, and all she had to do was go down there, knock on his door, and take off her dress. She knew he wouldn't resist her. She'd seen the lust in his eyes and knew what men were like. They were animals.

She wished Craig would return soon, and realized she shouldn't have let him go to town without her. *What am I going to do now?*

Eugene Tregaskis, president of the Dumont Bank, looked up as Craig Delane entered his establishment. Tregaskis, an overweight man with a bald head, put on his best banker's smile and stepped around the cage, holding out his hand.

"Good morning, Mr. Delane," he said. "My wife and I missed you at the funeral this morning."

"What funeral was that?"

"Wayne Dawson's funeral."

"Didn't know anything about it."

"It was first thing this morning. Guess Hank Dawson didn't have time to notify you. A lot of people didn't get notified. There was a rush to get the funeral over with. The climate, you know. What can we do for you today?"

Craig handed him checks and drafts, and Tregaskis invited him back to his office. Delane sat on a chair while Tregaskis transacted the business, and Delane thought of Cynthia and Stone back at the HC Ranch. He felt uneasy about them being together on the second floor of the house, but knew he was being ridiculous. Cynthia was a responsible person, and he could trust her.

Tregaskis handed Craig the receipts. "By the way, I don't know if you've heard it yet or not, but Dawson is offering five hundred dollars for John Stone, dead or alive."

"What about the law?"

"You're not in New York now, Mr. Delane. We don't have much law here."

Delane walked out of the bank, dismayed that everybody accepted the domination of Hank Dawson as long as he let them make money.

He crossed the street and entered the general store, where Stephen Connor, proprietor, stood behind the counter, and five men sat around a table playing cards.

"I want to buy a pair of pants, a shirt, and a pair of stockings," Delane said.

"For yerself?"

"One of my men."

Connor led Craig to the section where shirts and pants were folded on shelves. Craig selected a red shirt and tan jeans in large sizes for John Stone. Then he picked a pair of black socks out of a barrel. He paid for the garments and walked out of the store, heading for the buckboard.

He noticed a crowd of armed men spilling out of the saloon and onto the sidewalk. From their midst came two cowboys, one tall and one short, walking into the middle of the street. They didn't look at each other, and their faces were stern as they paced off, turned around, and faced each other, their hands above their guns and legs spread apart.

"Git out of the street!" somebody shouted at Craig.

Craig stepped toward the sidewalk, his eyes fastened on the

two men. He'd heard about duels in the main streets of towns, and thought them more myth than reality, but it looked as if that weren't so.

They went for their guns at the same moment, raised them up, and fired. The street echoed with gunshots, and smoke filled the air. The tall man staggered from side to side, tried to hold his gun steady for another shot, and was shot again by the short man. The impact of the bullet sent him reeling backward, and the holes in his body let out spirals of blood as he fell to the ground.

The short man pushed his gun back into his holster and walked toward the saloon. The bystanders followed, and some patted him on the back. A dead man lay in the middle of the street, as normal morning business traffic resumed.

Craig couldn't take his eyes off the body. A hand fell on his shoulder, and it was one of his cowboys.

"You all right, Mr. Delane?"

"What was that all about?"

"Probably a whore. That's what they usually fight over, or maybe somebody got caught cheatin' at cards."

A cowboy rode past the corpse, glanced at it, and kept going. Nobody was disturbed that a dead man was lying in the middle of the street. Craig walked toward his buckboard, trying to understand what he'd just seen. It was unthinkable, but it happened. *A human life doesn't mean anything out here.*

Craig's men waited for him beside the buckboard, and he climbed into the seat. They unhitched the horses from the rail and accompanied him out of town, heading back to the HC Ranch. Craig looked back and saw the body lying in the same place as a stagecoach rolled past, and the passengers poked their heads out the window, gawking at it.

In the kitchen of the HC Ranch, Bernice stood at the counter sifting flour for bread that she intended to bake. In front of her was a window, and through it she saw Everett Lorch, ramrod of the HC, advancing toward the main house. Bernice rinsed the flour from her hands and smoothed the front of her uniform. The door to the kitchen opened and Lorch stepped inside.

They looked meaningfully at each other. Bernice motioned with her head to the pantry. She walked into the pantry and Lorch followed her, closing the door behind them.

They were alone with cans of fruit and bags of beans. Lorch leaned her against the wall and wrapped his arms around her waist, hugging her toward him, kissing her lips. The old spinster sighed as the weatherbeaten cowboy pressed his stubbled cheek against hers.

"Rory told me you wanted to see me," he whispered into her ear.

"You'll never guess who's upstairs," she replied.

"I imagine Mrs. Rich Bitch is up there."

"And somebody else too." She looked about conspiratorially. "John Stone."

He pulled back from her. "Here? How'd he git in?"

"He climbed through one of the upstairs windows last night."

"Hank Dawson is offerin' a big reward for him," Lorch said.

"That's why I'm telling you. We can split it, but don't tell anybody I told you."

Everett Lorch patted her rear end, then walked out of the pantry. He left the house and made his way to the barn, where he saw Curly, one of his hands, pitching hay.

"Curly," Lorch said, "put yore shirt on. I want you to take a message to Hank Dawson."

Curly dropped the pitchfork and reached for his shirt, hanging on a peg nearby. Lorch took out his notepad and wrote on a sheet of paper.

JOHN STONE HIDING AT THE HC.

Lorch folded the paper and handed it to Curly, who unfolded it and read it. His jaw dropped open and he looked up at Lorch.

"Don't say a word," Lorch said. "Just do what I told you. Make sure you give it to Hank Dawson himself, understand?"

Curly winked, turned around, and walked out of the barn, heading toward the corral. Lorch rolled a cigarette and raised his eyes to the second floor of the main house. John Stone was up there someplace, thinking he was safe. *Boy, is he in for a surprise.*

John Stone lay on the bed in the guest room, trying to read a two-week-old issue of an El Paso newspaper, but wasn't able to concentrate. He kept thinking about the beauteous Cynthia Delane down the hall.

He was tempted to knock on her door but forced himself to read about the election they were holding in El Paso. He'd never be able to live with himself if he made love to Cynthia Delane.

He sat up in bed and wished he had clothes to wear. Walking toward the window, he stood to the side and looked outside. A horse and rider were in the distance, heading toward the open range.

He sat on the chair near the window and tried to think of Marie, but he hadn't seen Marie for years, whereas Cynthia Delane was a few feet away down the hall. He tried to plan what he'd do when he left the HC Ranch, but his thoughts kept returning to Cynthia Delane. He recalled how she'd looked last night as she'd lain in bed with her nightgown above her knees and her breasts nearly exposed. *I've got to calm down.*

Cynthia Delane chewed her thumbnail and sat on the edge of her bed. She'd changed to jeans, a shirt, and cowboy boots because she thought she ought to get out of the house and take a ride.

She couldn't stay with him any longer. It was driving her mad, and the worst part was she knew she was capable of being unfaithful to her husband. It would be easy, and no one would know. She knew he desired her as much as she desired him. *Things like this happen to other people.*

She'd heard gossip about women being unfaithful to their husbands, and had always looked down on them, thinking they were tramps and sluts. Now she realized it had little to do with nobility of character, and everything to do with a wild passion that made no sense but urged you onward into the most exquisite hell.

I've got to get out of here. She put on her cowboy hat and left her room, walking down the hallway. She passed John Stone's door and forced herself to keep walking down the stairs and out the front door.

She saw her husband riding his buckboard toward the ranch house, accompanied by three of his cowboys. He waved, jumped down from the buckboard, and walked toward her, carrying his briefcase and the clothes he'd bought for John Stone.

"How's our guest?"

"Seems to be all right."

"Have you looked in on him?"

"Earlier."

He looked into her eyes for the lie, but they were clear and green as always. "Where were you going?"

"For a ride."

"Maybe I'll join you later."

He kissed her cheek, entered the house, left his briefcase in his office, and climbed the stairs to the second floor, knocking on Stone's door.

Stone thought it was Cynthia, and was afraid to open the door. The knock came again, and he arose from the bed, expecting Cynthia, but instead saw Craig standing in the corridor and holding the clothes he'd bought.

Craig entered the room and dropped the clothes on the bed. "Hope they fit."

"Any news in town?"

"Hank Dawson is offering five hundred dollars for you, dead or alive. Wayne was buried this morning. Hank Dawson's gunmen are everywhere."

"They'll probably come out here before long."

"I don't think so," Craig said. "They'll never suspect me."

Curly sat on his saddle and crouched low as his horse galloped through a grassy swale. The windstream pushed back the brim of his hat and made his shirt flutter against his chest as he crossed a coulee and descended into a wide basin.

He couldn't wait to reach the Circle Bar D, because he thought he was entitled to a piece of the five-hundred-dollar reward for reporting the presence of John Stone at the HC Ranch.

His job at the HC Ranch was the strangest he'd ever had. Whoever heard of a ranch without cows, but that's what the HC was. Mostly he and the others pretended to work in the absence of much real work to do. They reported Craig Delane's activities to Hank Dawson, and Lorch even went into the office and read private company papers. It was the easiest job he ever had.

His previous employment had been at the Circle Bar D, and he'd gone hunting and whoring with Wayne, but never had much to do with old Hank Dawson. Curly couldn't wait to see the expression on Hank Dawson's face when he told him that John Stone was hiding at the HC Ranch.

Curly wondered what Hank Dawson would do to the Delanes for hiding John Stone. He might even burn down the HC Ranch and shoot Craig Delane.

Ahead was a conglomeration of boulders ten feet high. The trail Curly was on led through the middle of them. He sped toward the boulders, wondering how much of the reward he could get.

He saw something flash above him, looked up, and saw an Indian diving toward him from the top of a boulder, and the Indian had a long knife in his hand. Curly let go of his reins and reached for his six-gun. The Indian landed on top of him, plunging the knife into his chest.

Curly screamed as he fell off his horse, and the Indian fell with him, holding onto his shirt with one hand and stabbing him repeatedly with the other.

Curly lay still on the ground, bleeding from holes in his chest. Other Indians came out from behind the boulders where they'd been lurking in ambush. One was mounted, and he rode after Curly's horse. The others stripped Curly of his weapons, clothes, and boots. Within a minute, Curly was naked on the ground. The Indian who'd killed him grabbed his hair with one hand and scalped him.

The Indians gathered Curly's belongings. One put on Curly's plaid shirt, covered with blood, and searched through the pockets. In one pocket was a bag of tobacco and some cigarette papers. The other pocket contained a folded sheet of paper.

The Indian unfolded the sheet of paper and looked at the writing on it, but couldn't read English. Shrugging, he tossed the piece of paper over his shoulder, and the breeze whisked it away.

The Indians carried their booty to their horses and mounted up. Singing a victory song, they rode off to their encampment in the hills.

It was midafternoon, and Hank Dawson sat in his office, drinking a cup of coffee. He had nearly a hundred men searching for John Stone, plus a dozen Indian trackers, and his spies were everywhere, but no one had been able to find him.

Hank Dawson couldn't work, because he was obsessed with John Stone. Where was he hiding? How had he managed to get away?

Dawson lit a cigar. His mouth tasted bitter and he had a cramp in his stomach. The house still carried the noxious odor of Wayne's corpse although the maids had scrubbed Wayne's room and laundered the bedclothes. Dawson believed he'd lose respect if he didn't kill John Stone. You don't let somebody shoot your son.

Dawson drummed his fingers on his desk. He'd like to torture John Stone, kill him slowly, maybe even burn him at the stake. Dawson spat into his cuspidor and wiped his mouth with the back of his hand. "Where the hell is the son of a bitch?"

In the office of the HC Ranch, Craig and Cynthia could hear Stone pacing back and forth above them. Stone's footsteps made the ceiling creak as he went from one side of his room to the other. Craig raised his head and looked at the ceiling, then returned to his accounting.

Cynthia was trying to concentrate on the letter she was writing to her mother, but all she could think about was John Stone. She was telling her mother that everything was all right at the HC Ranch, when in fact everything wasn't all right. They were hiding a wanted man upstairs, and Cynthia was in love or lust with him, she didn't know which.

"You look distraught," Craig said, "if you don't mind me saying so."

"I am distraught. Aren't you distraught?"

"Of course." He reached over and placed his hand on her shoulder. "This'll all be over in a few days."

"I hope we can last that long."

Everett Lorch sat on a bale of hay in the barn and lit a cigarette. He'd sent Curly Soames to the Circle Bar D early in the morning, and now it was nearly suppertime and Curly hadn't returned. Throughout the entire day he'd expected Hank Dawson to show up with his men. *What the hell happened?*

He knew Hank Dawson wanted to get his hands on Stone,

so Lorch had to assume Dawson hadn't received the message he'd written, but why? Where was Curly?

Lorch listened to the men hammering nails into the privy. It was only a two-hour ride to the Circle Bar D. Lorch didn't know what had gone wrong, but had to do something.

He took out his notepad and wrote:

JOHN STONE IS HIDING OUT AT THE HC RANCH
ON THE SECOND FLOOR IN THE GUEST ROOM

He tore the sheet of paper out of the pad and folded it. Then he walked out of the barn, approaching Carruthers and Hannah, repairing the privy.

"Put yore shirts on and saddle up yore horses," Lorch said, handing Carruthers the note. "I want you to deliver this, in person, to Hank Dawson."

Carruthers took the note, opened it up, and looked at it, but he couldn't read. He and Hannah put on their shirts.

"Hurry up!" Lorch told them.

Carruthers and Hannah strapped on their gunbelts and dropped their hats on their heads. They walked toward the corral to get their horses.

Lorch figured Dawson should get the message around nightfall, and then the fun would start.

10

THE SUN WAS a giant orange ball sitting on the tree line to the west of the HC Ranch, sending streaks of violet and gold through the sky. Craig Delane glanced at it through a window as he climbed the stairs to the second-floor corridor of his ranch house. He walked down the corridor and knocked on the door of the guest room.

"Come in."

Delane entered the room and saw Stone stood near the bed; he'd been pacing when Delane knocked.

"Sounds like you're restless up here," Delane said. "Guess it's no fun being confined to a room this size all day."

"I'm leaving as soon as it gets dark," Stone told him. "Think I'd be safer on the open range. Sleep during the day and ride by night, and in a few days I'll be far away. I'll have to ask you to lend me a horse and some supplies. I'll send you a check as soon as I get settled."

"Don't worry about that," Craig replied. "Are you sure this is the right thing to do?"

"I don't want to get surrounded in this house."

Craig looked out the window. "It'll be dark in about another hour. I'll take care of everything."

Craig descended the stairs and saw Cynthia in the living room, reading a magazine.

"John has decided to leave as soon as it gets dark," Craig said. "Bring him his supper, while I have the men saddle a horse."

Carruthers and Hannah galloped underneath the carved wooden sign that said CIRCLE BAR D. It was night as they made their way to the main ranch house, lamps burning in the windows. Tethering their horses to the hitching rail, they walked toward the front porch.

Jesse Atwell sat in the darkness, smoking a cigarette, and arose as they approached.

"What're you fellers doin' here?" Atwell asked.

"Got a message for Mr. Dawson, from Lorch," Carruthers said. "Lorch told me to give it to Mr. Dawson in person. He said it's important."

"Follow me."

Atwell led them into the house and through the corridors to Hank Dawson's office, opened the door, and saw Dawson seated on the big armchair in front of his desk, a cigar perched between his sausage fingers. Dawson's face was haggard; his eyes had dark, wrinkled pouches underneath them.

"What is it?" Dawson growled.

"These men have a message for you from Everett Lorch at the HC."

Dawson looked at Carruthers and Hannah, his eyebrows knitted together. Carruthers stepped forward and handed the piece of paper to Dawson, who unfolded it and read the words scrawled by Everett Lorch. Dawson's eyes widened and he sat straighter in his chair as he read the note again. A faint smile appeared on his face as he turned to Atwell.

"Saddle up as many men as you can," he said, "and make sure they're fully armed."

Cynthia carried the tray into John Stone's room. "Supper."

He took the tray and sat on the chair beside the window. Before him was a slab of roast beef, mashed potatoes, sliced carrots, and a pot of coffee.

She sat on the chair opposite him. "Craig said you're leaving us."

"Time to move on."

She watched him eat, and something told her he wasn't going to make it.

"You don't think you'll be safer here?"

"I'll be hard to find on the prairie."

He placed a forkful of mashed potato into his mouth. She wanted to rush over and take him in her arms. The door opened and Craig walked in.

"My foreman is saddling my best horse," he said. "I've named him Thor, and he's got tremendous speed and endurance. I don't think you'll be disappointed in him."

"I don't want to take your best horse," Stone said.

"I can always get another. It's the least I can do."

"Wish I could pay . . ."

"It's been our pleasure, isn't that right, Cynthia?"

In the barn, by the light of a lamp, Everett Lorch threw a saddle onto Thor, the fine black stallion that Craig Delane had bought from one of the local horse breeders. He pulled the straps down and tightened the cinch.

Then he took a step backward and sat on a barrel, wondering what to do next. He knew why Craig Delane told him to saddle the horse. John Stone was going to make a run for it.

Lorch wasn't a great gunfighter, but knew how to shoot straight. He wondered if he should kill John Stone as he was trying to leave. Just drill him in the back and bring him down, then collect five hundred dollars.

Lorch debated the pros and cons with himself. It'd be dangerous, because if he missed, Stone would surely kill him as he'd killed so many others.

There was one other option. Four other cowboys were in the bunkhouse, having supper. Maybe he could let them in on the secret. Together they could rush Stone and kill him, and split the five-hundred-dollar reward. That'd give each of them one hundred dollars.

There was a hitch. Stone was fast. He'd killed many cowboys since arriving in Dumont County. Lorch was torn between fear of Stone and greed for money.

He heard footsteps approaching.

"Lorch!" called Craig Delane. "Do you have Thor ready?"

"He's right here!"

"Bring him outside!"

Lorch didn't have time to rustle up the boys in the bunkhouse. If he was going to stop Stone, he'd have to do it alone. Grabbing the bridle of the horse, he led him toward the door and saw in the darkness three figures approaching across the yard.

Lorch walked out of the barn, and Thor clip-clopped beside him, jerking his head up and down. Delane was on the left, his wife was in the middle, and John Stone was on the right, carrying a rifle in his hand and saddlebags over his shoulder, huge in the moonlight. Five hundred dollars was a lot of money, but Lorch decided that his life was worth more.

Delane grasped Thor's bridle. "You can go to the bunkhouse now, Mr. Lorch," he said.

Stone stepped in front of Lorch. "Do you know who I am?"

"I think so," Lorch replied, and felt a shiver up his spine.

"Keep your mouth shut."

"Right," Lorch said. "Yessir."

Lorch walked toward the bunkhouse. He didn't want to go up against John Stone.

Stone, Craig, and Cynthia stood with Thor in front of the barn. The moonlight cast long shadows all around them.

"I appreciate all you've done for me," Stone said to Craig and Cynthia. "Don't know how I would've made it without you."

"Good luck to you," said Craig, holding out his hand.

Stone shook it, then turned to Cynthia. She moved forward and hugged him. "Be careful."

He gave her a squeeze, and never wanted to let go. They released each other, took a step back, and gazed into each other's eyes one last time. There was a lump in Stone's throat as he climbed on top of Thor. He wheeled him around and rode away from the barn, heading for the open prairie.

Craig and Cynthia stood side by side and held hands, watching him disappear into the night.

Twenty minutes later, Craig and Cynthia heard a rumble in the distance. At first they thought it might be thunder, but it became a continuous roar, the sound of horses galloping across the plains.

Craig and Cynthia lowered their forks, looked at each other, and rushed to the window of the dining room.

Forty riders rounded the bend next to the barn and charged toward the front of the house. They pulled back on their reins, bringing their horses to a halt in a huge cloud of dust, then dismounted, yanked their rifles out of their scabbards, and surrounded the main house.

Hank Dawson, followed by several of his men, walked toward the front door.

"Go to your room," Craig said to Cynthia. "I'll take care of this."

"I want to be with you."

Craig saw the determination in her eyes. There was a loud knock on the door.

Bernice entered the living room. "Should I get it?"

"No," said Craig. "I'll go."

Craig decided not to arm himself and give them an excuse to shoot him. There was another louder knock. He pulled down the points of his vest and walked toward the front door, Cynthia following him.

They heard Hank Dawson's booming voice: "Open up this damned door or I'll break it down!"

Craig grasped the knob of the door and pulled it open. He saw Hank Dawson in front of him, a rifle in his hand, and a crowd of men behind Dawson.

"We want him," Dawson said. "Git out of the way."

Dawson nodded to his men and they rushed the door, pushing Craig and Cynthia to the side. Dawson's men invaded the house, heading for the staircase, grim-faced and hard-looking, climbing the stairs to the second floor.

Craig stepped in front of Dawson. "Where I come from, people don't enter other people's homes without an invitation."

Dawson pointed his rifle at Craig's belly. "I ought to kill you."

Craig looked down the long barrel of the gun, and Cynthia blanched.

"You knew John Stone killed my son," Dawson said evenly. "Why did you hide him?"

"He was our friend," Craig replied.

There was a commotion upstairs, and Dawson heard slamming and banging as his men tipped over beds and knocked dressers onto their sides. They opened closet doors, threw clothing out, and peered up fireplaces.

"Let me through!" said a voice behind him.

Dawson turned and saw Everett Lorch making his way through the crowd of Circle Bar D cowboys on the front porch. Lorch was followed by the other cowboys who were ostensibly employed by Craig Delane, but who really took their orders from Dawson.

Lorch came to a stop in front of Dawson. "Stone left about a half hour ago!" Lorch pointed north. "He went thataway!"

"Why did you let him get away?"

"He had the drop on me."

Dawson stepped into Craig's living room and cupped his hands around his mouth. "You men git down here! He's got away!"

The men rumbled down the stairs. Dawson turned to Craig and Cynthia. "I'll take care of you after I get Stone."

Dawson stomped across the porch, as his men followed, carrying their rifles and guns. They all climbed onto their horses.

"Let's git him!" Dawson bellowed.

Dawson shoved his spurs into his horse, and the animal bounded away. Dawson's men followed, heading north after John Stone. Craig and Cynthia watched them go, and their hoofbeats receded into the night.

Craig and Cynthia turned around, and Bernice stood at the end of the vestibule, light from a lamp aureoling behind her.

"It was you who told them, wasn't it?" Cynthia asked.

Bernice said nothing. She looked down at the floor.

"You're fired," Cynthia said. "I'll expect you to leave in the morning."

The stars in the Milky Way blazed like fire, and Stone had the whole night ahead of him. Thor moved steadily beneath him, and Stone could sense the great power of the animal. A coyote howled in a cave nearby, and Stone rocked back and forth in the saddle, holding the reins in his right hand. He'd take his chances on the open plains any day.

His thoughts drifted back to Cynthia Delane, and he was glad he'd never tried anything. He'd escaped a powerful temptation, and in a corner of his mind wished he'd given in, because she'd been so lovely.

He heard something, and his ears perked up. It was a low roar somewhere behind him, barely perceptible. He pulled Thor to a halt, and the animal snorted, twisting his head from side to side because he wanted to keep going.

"Be still," Stone said.

Thor understood, raising his massive head and twitching his ears. Stone turned around in his saddle. The roar became louder, and Stone heard it more distinctly. He'd heard that sound before, and his heart sank, because he knew what it was: a large number of horses galloping, like a squadron of cavalry, in the night.

Stone sat in his saddle and wished it was the wind in the trees, or an approaching storm, but he was an old cavalry soldier and knew horses when he heard them. They were behind him, headed his way. He didn't know how they'd found him, and there was only one thing to do.

He touched his spurs to Thor's withers, and Thor lunged forward, stretching out his long, powerful legs, plunging them into the ground. Stone crouched low in the saddle as the horse galloped across the plains.

A few miles behind him, men rode hard through a forest of trees opulent with leaves, the hooves of their horses pounding into the ground and tearing it apart. The moon shone down and the wind threatened to rip their hats off.

Hank Dawson rode in front, peering ahead for any trace of John Stone. Twelve Indian trackers rode a hundred yards in advance of the main body of men, yipping and yelling, adding to the excitement of the chase. They shook their rifles in the air, and each hoped to kill John Stone for the five-hundred-dollar reward.

Hank Dawson rode a big muscular horse who strained his neck forward with every leap he took. Dawson flew through the air, wind whistling in his beard. "Faster!" he shouted. "Don't let him get away!"

Thor broke his stride, faltered, and Stone was nearly thrown out of the saddle. Thor slowed down and began to limp.

Stone pulled back on the reins, bringing the horse to a halt.

He climbed down from the saddle and checked the horse's legs, as the hoofbeats behind him became louder, and then saw the loose shoe.

Stone turned around and brought the horse's hoof between his knees. He pulled out his pistol, held the barrel in his hand, and used the grip as a hammer, banging in the nails, his strokes rang sharply into the night. Stone checked the horseshoe again, and it was tight. Holstering his gun, he jumped into the saddle, and Thor already was running away.

A shot rang out, and a bullet whizzed over Stone's head. He turned around and could make out the heads of riders appearing over the rim of a hill. If he could see them, they could see him. He cursed the loose horseshoe as he hunkered down in the saddle.

Thor galloped over the prairie, and Stone heard the yelling of Indians behind him.

"Faster," he murmured into his horse's ear as he crouched lower in the saddle. "We've got to get away!"

The men in the posse fired, and he recalled what had happened the last time they'd chased him. They'd shot his horse out from underneath him, and if he didn't have that mountain range nearby, they would've run him down and killed him.

He unfolded the map of the territory in his mind, and it occurred to him that the town of Dumont was only a few miles away. Dawson and his men would catch up with him eventually, and he'd have to make a stand someplace. The town of Dumont would be as good a place as any. He could hide, play hit-and-run in the alleys, take many of Dawson's men with him before they got him.

He estimated the location of Dumont and pointed Thor in that direction. A bullet cracked over his head, and he dropped lower in the saddle. Then he remembered Hong Fat, the Chinese waiter in Gallagher's Restaurant where the whole mess began. Maybe he could find Hong Fat, and Hong Fat could hide him.

A bullet kicked into the ground about ten feet away and another whistled past his ear as he worked his body smoothly with the motions of Thor. Together they streaked across the plains toward Dumont.

● ● ●

Hank Dawson saw his Indian scouts veering off to the right, and realized that Stone had changed the direction of his run. Dawson and his men followed the Indians and galloped off in the new direction, their legs flapping against the ribs of their horses.

Dawson wondered why Stone had changed course. The darkness and intensity of the chase had disoriented him. Jesse Atwell, his ramrod, was riding at his side, and Dawson turned to him.

"What's up ahead?" Dawson called out.

"Dumont!" Atwell replied.

Dawson's face creased a smile as he realized where he was. He raised his immensity a few inches higher in his saddle and yelled, "He's a-headin' toward Dumont, boys! We got him where we want him now!"

11

THE LIGHTS OF Dumont glittered in the night, and John Stone rode toward it, hoping he could find shelter. Thor ran steadily, gobbling up miles in his pounding hooves, and gradually was pulling away from Dawson and his men.

But Stone knew he couldn't elude them forever. Thor would tire before long, and Dawson held all the high cards. Dawson could buy fresh horses easily, whereas Stone couldn't. Dawson had an army of spies working for him, and Stone was alone.

He rode down the incline to the town and approached the Chinatown district. Thor continued to run swiftly, stretching out his legs, straining his neck. Stone saw the town draw closer, made out the shapes of buildings. He headed toward the back alleys where the sheds and privies were, figuring he had a five- to ten-minute lead.

Reaching a tree in a backyard, he pulled back Thor's reins, and the horse dug in his hooves and came to a stop. Stone jumped down from the saddle and pulled his rifle out of its boot. Thor snorted and blew air out of his rubbery lips. He turned his head around and showed Stone his long white teeth.

Stone patted his gleaming black mane. "Thanks for the ride, old boy."

The horse's large eyes were fixed on Stone as Stone ran toward the back of a building. Stone saw lights in the windows and figured somebody had to be there. He came to the back door and pounded on it with his fist. People jabbered in Chinese on the other side of the door. Dawson and his men weren't in sight yet, but they should be showing up soon. Stone pounded on the door again.

The door was opened by a middle-aged Chinese woman with the build of a mosquito.

"What you want!" she said.

Stone didn't have time for an explanation. He leapt past her into the room and closed the door behind him.

He found himself in a Chinese restaurant. Chinese people sat around tables and ate strange-looking food with chopsticks. All of them stared at him.

The woman moved in front of him. "What you want!" she demanded. "This not white man part of town. White man go other part of town!" She pointed to indicate the direction she wanted Stone to go.

"I want to see Hong Fat," Stone said. "It's important."

"Hong Fat not here."

"Can you get him for me?"

"Hong Fat not here."

Stone realized the Chinese people weren't going to help him, and Dawson would show up at any moment. He moved toward the window and peered outside. It looked as though he'd make his last stand here.

He heard a chair scrape on the floor. A tall, middle-aged Chinese man dressed in white man's clothes walked toward him.

"What you want Hong Fat for?" he asked.

"I need help."

"Why should Hong Fat help you?"

"I did him a favor once."

The Chinese man turned around and said something in his language to another man sitting at a nearby table. The man said something in reply, and the first Chinese man looked at Stone again.

"Are you John Stone?" he asked.

Stone was surprised the man knew his name. "That's right."

"I know who you are," he said with a smile. "We will help you. What is wrong?"

"Hank Dawson and his men are after me, and they'll be here in a few minutes. They want to kill me."

"I am Jimmy Wing. Come with me, please."

Jimmy Wing walked toward an open doorway, and Stone followed him, wondering if Jimmy Wing was going to betray him for five hundred dollars. Jimmy Wing said something in Chinese to the people in the restaurant, and they resumed eating. Jimmy Wing and Stone entered the kitchen, where two cooks flipped food in strange spherical frying pans, fat spattering into the air. The cooks looked up at Stone for an instant and then returned to their work. Jimmy Wing spoke to them in Chinese, then led Stone to another door, opened it, and beckoned for Stone to follow.

The door led to an alleyway. Stone and Jimmy Wing crossed it and came to another building. They approached a door and Jimmy Wing knocked. A window opened in the door and two eyes looked out. Jimmy Wing said something in Chinese. The door was opened.

Stone followed Jimmy Wing into a long, dark corridor that exuded a peculiar fragrance. They came to a dark smoky room where Chinese and a few white men lay on the floor next to tall-necked opium pipes. The air was filled with sweet smoke so strong it made Stone cough. An old man with a long pigtail shuffled up to Jimmy Wing and started to say something, but Jimmy Wing waved him away.

They came to a door on the far side of the room, passed through, walked down another corridor, and came to an office.

"In here," Jimmy Wing said.

Stone entered the office and Jimmy Wing closed the door behind him. The office was furnished with a desk, a few chairs, and a sofa against the far wall beneath a shelf that held a black shellacked wooden statue of the Buddha.

Jimmy Wing moved the chairs out of the way in front of the desk, and underneath the chairs was a thick maroon rug. He peeled the rug away, revealing a trapdoor. He opened the trapdoor, and Stone looked down at a flight of stairs that led to a basement.

"Down there," Jimmy Wing said.

Stone hesitated. It looked like a dungeon.

Jimmy Wing smiled. "You are the man who saved Hong Fat from Wayne Dawson, when Wayne Dawson was beating him up. You help one of us, so now we help you."

Stone descended the steps into the cellar, and the trapdoor closed over him. It was dark, and he heard the rug and chairs moved into place over his head. He made out the shape of a cot against the far wall, and sat down upon it, laying his rifle over his knees.

He still wasn't sure Jimmy Wing wouldn't betray him, and there was no way out of the cellar except through the trapdoor. He saw a candle on a little table near the head of the cot, and lit it. The walls were red brick and the floor hard-packed dirt. Some crates were on the other side of the room. The air smelled damp and musty.

Stone reached into his shirt pocket and took out his bag of tobacco. He was safe for the time being, but wondered how long it would last.

The Indians were dismounted, holding the reins of their horses and looking at the ground. Occasionally a few of them would get down on their hands and knees and examine hoofprints. They were approaching the Chinatown section of Dumont, and behind them were Hank Dawson and his men on horseback.

Chinese people looked fearfully out the windows of buildings at the horde of men moving toward them. The Indians found the spot where Stone had left his horse, and followed his trail to the back of the restaurant.

"He go in here," one of the Indians said to Hank Dawson.

Dawson climbed down from his horse and yanked out his Colt. His men followed his example, preparing their rifles and guns for shooting. They looked at the windows of the building where the restaurant was, and saw Chinese people staring back at them. Dawson turned to Atwell, and Atwell walked up to the door and opened it. Atwell aimed his gun straight ahead and stepped into the restaurant, followed by Dawson and his men.

The small restaurant quickly became crowded with gunmen. Dawson swaggered to a table where a Chinese family was trying to eat, and kicked the table over onto them. Dishes and bowls crashed to the floor and the Chinese people stood, lo mein and chunks of fried beef clinging to their clothes.

"Where is he?" Dawson demanded.

A little Chinese woman wrung her hands as she shuffled meekly toward Dawson. "Where is who?" she asked in a trembling voice.

"John Stone!"

"I not know him!"

"A big white man! He was just here!"

"I not know him."

"Liar!"

The woman cringed in front of Dawson, and he wanted to pistol whip her, but turned to Atwell instead. "Search the place! He's around here somewhere."

Atwell relayed the orders to his men. Some went upstairs, others bullied their way into the kitchen. Dawson sat at a table and lit a cigar. He tried to put himself in Stone's shoes and figure out what he'd do.

He realized that Stone wouldn't dare go to the white man's part of town, because he wouldn't last a minute there. Anybody who owned a gun would try to shoot him for the five-hundred-dollar reward. So he'd come to the Chinese section, where he thought he'd be safe, but whatever gave him that idea? Dawson would track him down if he had to tear Chinatown apart board by board.

His men returned from the kitchen and upstairs.

"He ain't here," Atwell told Dawson.

"If he ain't here, he's in one of these other buildings. Spread the men out and tell them to search through Chinatown. Rip the goddamn place to pieces if you have to, and tell the chinks I'm offerin' five hundred dollars to the one who'll tell me where John Stone is hidin'."

Dawson's men stormed out of the restaurant and into the surrounding buildings, breaking down doors. They barged in on Chinese people sleeping in their beds, searched through kitchens, closets, cellars, and attics. The men showed no courtesy or gentleness. They shot through walls, in hopes of finding secret hiding places. People who protested were punched in their mouths, and if the cowboys saw something they fancied, a watch, piece of gold jewelry, or an ivory knickknack, they put it into their pockets.

Dawson accompanied Atwell and one of the groups of men, but Dawson didn't do much actual searching. He mostly sat and puffed his cigar while his men terrorized Chinese people and tore their homes apart.

The marauding army smashed through Chinatown, destroying anything that impeded their progress, beating up those who dared protest, throwing pots and pans, upending trunks full of clothes, pushing children out of their way, breaking open casks of soy sauce, tearing down wallboards, abusing women and humiliating their husbands.

Hank Dawson and Jesse Atwell, plus eight of Dawson's gunfighters, kicked in the door of the whorehouse. Semiclad young Chinese women screamed and ran in all directions as their customers struggled to put on their clothes, wondering what all the commotion was about.

The madam, an old Chinese woman in a purple silk dress with a high collar and a slit up the side, advanced toward Hank Dawson.

"What you do?" she demanded. "Why me?"

Dawson pushed her out of the way, and the old woman went sprawling to the floor. Dawson's men shot holes in furniture, looked in closets, and stampeded up the stairs to the second floor, where they searched rooms, looked under beds, poked their rifles behind the drapes.

Dawson's men worked themselves into a frenzy. They knew John Stone was somewhere in the vicinity and all they could do was vent their fury against the people they ran up against. They slammed their rifle butts into the faces of Chinese men and ripped the dresses off the prostitutes.

On the first floor of the whorehouse, Dawson bent over the madam and grabbed the front of her dress in his big hairy fist. She lay on the floor beneath him, her eyes wide open with terror.

"Where is he?" Dawson replied.

"Where is who?"

"John Stone!"

"I not know him!"

"Liar!"

Dawson backhanded her across the mouth, and the old

woman shrieked like a wounded animal. Dawson couldn't bear the sound, and backhanded her again.

The woman whimpered and held her hands to her bleeding mouth. Jesse Atwell and several men clomped down the stairs.

"He ain't here," Atwell said wearily.

Dawson chomped his cigar. "Let's move on."

They left the whorehouse and barged through the front door of the next building. A sweet, smoky fragrance assailed their nostrils as they marched down the corridor, opening doors, searching rooms. The rooms were tiny and crowded with cots on which Chinese men slept. Dawson's gunfighters tipped the beds over and kicked the Chinese men, who covered their heads with their hands to protect themselves from the blows.

At the end of the corridor they came to a locked door. Dawson stepped forward and banged the handle of his pistol on it.

"Open this goddamned thing up!" he said.

The little window in the door slid open and two slanted eyes looked out. The little window slid closed, but no one opened the door. Dawson stepped back and Atwell aimed his rifle at the doorknob, firing three shots. The doorknob shattered and sparked, and the corridor filled with gunsmoke. Atwell threw his shoulder against the door, and it burst open. A Chinese man stood a few feet down the hall, a pistol in his hand. He hesitated a moment, and that was all Atwell needed. Atwell fired two quick shots, and the Chinese man staggered, his knees knocking together. The Chinese man dropped his pistol, sagged against the wall, and dropped to the floor.

Dawson and his men trampled the dying man as they made their way down a smoke-filled corridor. They came to the opium den and saw men lying on the floor in a stupor next to their pipes.

Dawson wrinkled his nose at the smell of the opium, and felt disgust for the men lying on the floor. He kicked one of them in the ass.

"You filthy son of a bitch!" Dawson snarled, but the man on the floor didn't move a muscle; he was in a deep trance.

The little old man with the beanie and pigtail shuffled toward Dawson and bowed. "How I can help you, sir?" he asked in a quavering voice.

"Where's John Stone?"

"I not know him."

"I'll give you five hundred dollars if you tell me where he is."

"I not know him."

Dawson hit the old Chinese man on the temple with the barrel of his gun, and he collapsed at Dawson's feet.

Dawson sat on a heavy wooden chair, lit another cigar as he listened to his men demolishing the building. In the distance he heard the screaming of women. It seemed as though John Stone should've turned up by now.

It was clear to him that the Chinese were hiding Stone. He didn't know why, and then a wild idea entered Dawson's brain: *Maybe he should set fire to Chinatown!* That would flush John Stone out of his hiding place, but then Dawson realized that a fire would be difficult to control, and it might burn down the rest of Dumont also.

Dawson didn't want to burn down Dumont because he owned most of the real estate and it represented a great deal of wealth. It would be like burning money, and Dawson loved money.

Dawson wracked his brain and tried to figure out what to do. All he could think of was continuing the search for John Stone, who had to be someplace in Chinatown. Dawson clamped his nicotine-stained teeth down on his cigar.

Atwell walked up to Dawson. "We found Jimmy Wing," he said.

Dawson had sold property to Jimmy Wing, and knew him fairly well. Jimmy Wing was the wealthiest Chinese man in Dumont, and a leader of the Chinese community.

Dawson followed Atwell into the corridor, and a new thought entered his mind. He'd negotiated with Jimmy Wing in the past, and maybe he could negotiate with him now. Jimmy Wing had always been a reasonable man, and knew everything that happened in Chinatown. Perhaps they could cut a deal.

Dawson walked into Jimmy Wing's office, and Jimmy Wing sat calmly behind his desk, his hands folded before him. He wore a white shirt, and his straight black hair was cut short, without a pigtail. Several of Dawson's men were in the office, pointing their guns at Jimmy Wing. A closet door was open and clothing lay on the floor. Papers, pencils, books, and ledgers were also scattered about.

Dawson approached Jimmy Wing's desk and stood on the rug in front of it. "Guess you're surprised to see me here this time of night."

Jimmy nodded. Three shots erupted outside in the street. There was loud maniacal laughter, and then the scream of a woman.

Dawson grinned. "My boys are havin' themselves a little fun."

Jimmy Wing's face was like rock.

"I guess you don't like what's goin' on," Dawson said.

Jimmy Wing didn't reply.

Dawson sat on a chair in front of the desk and leaned forward. "You tell me where John Stone is, and I'll call my men off. We'll leave Chinatown, and your friends and neighbors won't be bothered anymore. But if you don't tell me where John Stone is, we'll get rougher."

"Who's John Stone?"

"Don't git me mad, Jimmy."

"I don't know who he is."

Dawson blew a cloud of cigar smoke at Jimmy Wing. "My men are givin' your people a bad time out there, and you can stop it if you just tell me where the son of a bitch is."

"I don't know what you're talking about."

Dawson wondered why Jimmy Wing wasn't cooperating. Maybe there were too many people in the room. Maybe he didn't want to say anything in front of so many witnesses.

Dawson turned to Atwell. "You stay here with me, and pick two other men. The rest of you get the hell out of here."

Atwell selected Al Burkers and Billy Finch to remain in the room, and the others filed out the door. Dawson held out his silver cigar case to Jimmy Wing. "Want one?"

Jimmy Wing shook his head.

Dawson looked at Jimmy Wing and tried to measure him. Jimmy Wing had come to town penniless about fifteen years ago and got a job in a laundry. He'd saved his money, invested in opium, made deals, and now was rich. Dawson realized he'd been using the wrong approach with Jimmy Wing, who was essentially a businessman. When dealing with a businessman, you had to talk money.

"You tell me where John Stone is, and I'll give you five hundred dollars, cash on the barrelhead."

"I told you I don't know who he is."

"Six hundred."

Jimmy Wing said nothing.

"Seven hundred. A thousand."

"I can't help you."

"I always thought you were a smart chink, but guess I was wrong." Dawson pulled out his gun, aiming it at Jimmy Wing's head, cocking the hammer with his thumb, and it made a loud *click*. "John Stone killed my son, and if you don't tell me where he is, I'll kill you."

Jimmy Wing's face showed emotion for the first time, as he looked at the gun in Dawson's hand, but then his countenance returned to its usual placid cast.

"You're just another slant-eyed chink son of a bitch as far as I'm concerned," Dawson continued, "and you got three seconds to make up yore mind. Tell me where's John Stone, or I'll put one right between yore goddamned eyes." Dawson aimed his gun at Jimmy Wing's head and said, "One!"

Underneath Dawson's feet, below the trapdoor, John Stone stood on the stairs looking up. He knew Dawson was directly above him, heard the hammer being cocked and Dawson's voice counting. Stone raised his arms and placed his hands against the trapdoor.

"Two!"

Dawson aimed down the barrel of his gun and saw a man who wasn't flinching. Jimmy Wing looked coldly at him, his face immobile, ready to die, and Dawson thought: *He must be telling the truth, because nobody dies for somebody else.* Jimmy Wing was no fool, and maybe the Indian trackers were wrong. John Stone probably was in Dumont, but not Chinatown. Somebody would betray him sooner or later, if a large enough reward was posted. There was no need to shoot Jimmy Wing; perhaps they could transact more business in the future.

Dawson eased forward the hammer of the gun. "This is yore lucky day," he said to Jimmy Wing. "I'm not gonna kill you."

Dawson plopped the gun into its holster and turned to Atwell. "I want fifty men in Dumont at all times, watchin' the town—and I don't mean gettin' drunk and screwin' whores—I mean *on duty*, lookin' for John Stone actively, day and night—you set up the roster personally. Then have posters printed and nailed up all over town. As of right now, I'm offering *five thousand dollars* for John Stone, dead or alive!''

In the cellar, Stone heard footsteps heading toward the door above him, and one chorus of boots sounded like an elephant: Dawson himself. Stone thought of raising his gun and shooting Dawson through the floorboards, but there was no guarantee of success, and it would draw the attention of Dawson's army.

The last footsteps left the office, and it became silent above him. Stone descended the ladder to the basement floor, and lay on the cot. It had been a close call. He'd been ready to push through the trapdoor and open fire, but Dawson backed off at the last moment.

Stone didn't know why Dawson backed off. Blood never stopped him before. There must be a reason, but Stone had more important knots to untangle. He was trapped in a cellar in Dumont, and a small army was searching for him. He looked at the hard-packed dirt walls of the cellar, and it was nearly as bad as the Dumont jail. How long could he last down here, and how long before somebody turned him in for the five-thousand-dollar reward?

He heard the scraping of chairs above him, and the rug being pulled across the floor. The trapdoor opened, and Jimmy Wing descended the stairs.

''They leaving Chinatown,'' he said. ''You're safe.''

''Why didn't you tell him where I was?''

''Mr. Dawson hates to give up money,'' Jimmy Wing replied, ''and I make money for him. That is why he did not kill me.''

''What if you'd figured wrong?''

''I understand my opponent, and understanding is half the battle. Also, Hong Fat is the cousin of our priest, Mew Fong; so you see, when you helped Hong Fat, you were helping an important member of this community, and we are all beholden to you. I'm sure Mew Fong'll come to pay his respects soon.''

They heard the sound of footsteps in the room above them, and legs appeared on the stairs. Three Chinese men descended to the cellar and chattered to Jimmy Wing in Chinese. Jimmy Wing replied, then turned to Stone.

''Hank Dawson is leaving for his ranch,'' he said, ''but many of his men are staying behind.''

''Five thousand dollars is a lot of money.''

"There will be no takers in Chinatown. You do not understand how revered Mew Fong is."

It was dark on the main floor of the HC Ranch, and Craig looked through the living-room window at the night, his rifle in his hands.

Before him lay the barn and outbuildings. His cowboys were gone and, before departing, took all the horses in the corral. If the Commanches found out the HC Ranch was unprotected, they'd steal everything he had, scalp him, and God only knew what they'd do to Cynthia.

She held a rifle and looked out the window at the opposite side of the room, and was wearing tight jeans and a buckskin jacket, plus high-topped boots. Her view was of the open range, and the moonlight made the bushes and trees appear like an army of Commanches.

Cynthia was frightened, but had managed to hold herself under control so far. A few times she'd wanted to scream, but grit her teeth and swallowed the fear back down. If the Commanches came, she'd fight as long as she could.

Craig said, "Why don't you lie down and get some sleep? I'll watch for a while."

"I can't sleep," she said. "Maybe you should lie down."

"I can't sleep either, but the Commanches probably don't know we're alone yet. We'll leave for town first thing in the morning."

"Maybe our hands didn't leave horses, in which case we're trapped out here, and it's only a matter of time before the Commanches get us."

"I didn't see anybody turn loose the horses in the barn. We'll get out of here, don't worry. The Consortium won't let us down."

It fell silent in the living room as they both stared out their windows, looking for Commanches. Craig wondered what the Consortium would do when they found out he'd botched the job, because that's the way they'd see it. They'd probably fire him and send a replacement. Craig would become a failure in the first important endeavor of his life.

Cynthia said, "I wonder if they've caught John Stone."

"I think you'd better stop worrying about him and start worrying about us. At least he's got a horse and knows how to fight. I don't know a damn thing, and neither do you."

Craig was certain he saw something move in front of the corral. He aimed his rifle at it and fired. Cynthia jumped involuntarily as the house reverberated with the blast. Craig looked into the yard and wondered if he'd killed a Commanche, or if his eyes were playing tricks on him.

"Is somebody there?" Cynthia asked, her heart pounding.

"Don't know. Hard to see."

"I need a drink."

"This isn't a time to be drinking alcoholic beverages. We need to keep our wits about us. There may be Commanches out there."

"Perhaps we should invite them in for a drink and make friends with them, as it were. I'll give them some beads, and you can give them a horse, if we have any horses left."

She arose, went to the cupboard, and poured some whiskey into a glass.

"I'll have one too," he said in a low voice.

She poured a glass for him, placed it in his hands, and returned to her post at the window. She'd feel safe with John Stone, whereas poor Craig was probably as frightened and useless as she. She looked at him crouching beneath the windowsill and laughed.

"What's so funny?" he asked.

"I think the tension is unhinging my mind."

"Try to hang on until morning, Cynthia. It's not too far away. Then we'll leave this place forever."

"What if we don't have horses?"

"We'll cross that bridge when we come to it."

"You know, Craig—we just might die out here."

"We can walk to town tomorrow, if we don't have horses."

"What if we run into Commanches?"

"We can't let fear control us. We must be optimistic and keep striving."

Cynthia sipped some whiskey, and it settled her down. She knew Craig was right; they couldn't simply surrender.

"In hindsight," Craig said, "I guess we should've been more careful who we associated with, but John Stone seemed like such a gentleman. I had no idea he'd shoot people."

Cynthia saw something move in the darkness and fired two

wild shots out the window. Craig ran across the room and joined her, looking at the moonlit plains.

"What was it?"

"I thought it was an Indian!"

She pointed with the barrel of the rifle, but he saw only the dim outlines of hills and foliage.

"We're firing at shadows," he said. "We'd better calm down."

He returned to his window and wanted to light a cigar, but was afraid a Commanche might see it.

"If we ever survive this," he said, "it'll be a helluva story to tell back in New York."

"You have doubts we'll survive, Craig?"

"I guess we have to realize anything can happen out here. This isn't Fifth Avenue."

He wasn't reassuring. She sat in the darkness near the window and sipped her whiskey, trying to stay calm.

Stone lay on his cot in the cellar, the lantern on, and he was smoking a cigarette. It felt like a dungeon, damp and musty, with nothing to do and no place to go. He felt restless and trapped, and sometimes it seemed as if the earthen walls were closing in on him.

He thought he'd made a mistake by coming to Chinatown, and should've taken his chances on the open range. He'd learned the principles of leading trackers astray from Tad McDermott, one of the best in the game. If they caught him, at least he'd die like a cavalryman instead of a rat in a hole in the ground.

He couldn't lie still any longer, got up, and paced the floor back and forth like a caged animal, leaving trails of cigarette smoke behind him. Dawson had fifty men in town; how could he get out? Stone felt desperate, as if he might spend years in this hole. He'd look like one of those lizards who live in caves and never see the light of day. There was a possibility he'd lose his mind.

He heard furniture being moved above him, and then the trapdoor opened. He faced the stairs and saw a slim figure in a pale blue silk dress descending. It was a young woman with long, straight black hair to her shoulders, and she was carrying a tray with dishes and bowls.

"I am Mai Wing, daughter of Jimmy Wing, and I have brought you something to eat. You are hungry?"

"I was about to start chewing on my boots."

He sat at the table and she placed the tray in front of him. He knew what rice was, but the rest was unfamiliar.

"It is only chicken and vegetables," she said. "I think you will like it better than your boots."

Stone placed food in his mouth, and it tasted new and exotic, making him want more. He ate heartily and looked at Mai Wing, who sat pertly on her chair, and he figured she was seventeen. Her dress was high-necked and she had a simple friendly manner, not seductive and not the least bit nervous about being alone with a man.

Stone realized a little Chinese world existed in Dumont alongside the rootin' tootin' American frontier town. When Stone had arrived in Dumont, he'd had no idea it was just a few hundred feet away, opium dens and Chinese whorehouses, tea parlors and beautiful young girls with the most extraordinary eyes.

"Do you ever go out?" he said.

"Not very often. It is dangerous."

"What do you do with your life?"

"I take care of my father, and I study with Mew Fong."

"What do you study?"

"The Buddha."

"Don't know much about that."

"If we pray to the Buddha, our lives will become pure."

He looked at her and realized that's what she was: pure and innocent, a child in the body of a young woman.

"Tell me about Mew Fong."

"He is a very wise priest trained at a great monastery in China. Everybody places great weight on what he says."

"What does he say?"

"Depends on what you ask him."

"You must know your neighbors well. Do you think there's anyone who might betray me for the five-thousand-dollar reward?"

"If someone took it, he would be banished from the community, and no one wants that."

"With five thousand dollars, he could go to another community."

"I think you will be safe. No one would want to make Mew Fong mad at him, because Mew Fong has great powers."

Stone finished eating and pushed back his chair, lighting a cigarette as Mai Wing loaded the dishes on the tray.

"I will see you tomorrow," she said.

She walked toward the stairs and climbed them, and the trapdoor was closed. Stone sat alone again, thinking there must be at least one person in Chinatown who'd betray him for five thousand dollars. He looked at the walls and low ceiling. There was only one way out, and if Dawson set fire to the building, Stone would roast to death.

He'd have to live cooped up in the cellar, in constant fear someone would betray him, and it wouldn't be easy. He wondered how much he could take before going stark raving mad.

Hank Dawson sat before a table cluttered with plates of food in the Presidential Suite of the New Dumont Hotel. He'd decided to spend the night in town and go home in the morning.

A maid had given him a bath, and he wore clean clothes. He sliced into a huge slab of venison, which was tender as newly fallen snow, and placed the meat in his mouth, chewing contentedly while cutting a potato in half. Before him were dumplings in gravy, slices of cheese, an assortment of vegetables, a loaf of bread, a plate of beans, and a rhubarb pie.

He ate steadily and systematically, stuffing his great stomach and making it sag low over his belt. He'd been troubled about losing John Stone, but now felt better as great gobs of food were passing down his throat and into his gut. He'd spend a peaceful night in Dumont, and tomorrow would ride to the HC Ranch, settling his account with the Delanes. They, more than anyone else, were responsible for Stone still being on the loose. Dawson didn't know what he wanted to do with them, but whatever it was, it'd be exquisitely horrible, because he couldn't let them off easy after what they'd done.

Meanwhile, outside in Dumont, his men were prowling the streets and back alleys, looking for John Stone. Stone would have to show himself sooner or later, and Dawson was willing to wait him out.

Someone was hiding him, and Dawson wondered who it was. Probably some well-intentioned idiot who went to church every Sunday and believed the foolishness about The Good Samaritan.

That might work for a few days, but then the reality of five thousand dollars would sink it. The average cowboy would have to work fourteen years to earn that much money. It was a tremendous stake and a person could literally live on it for the rest of his life by investing in cattle or some other business.

Sooner or later somebody would step forward, Dawson thought, his mouth full of food. *Nobody could resist five thousand dollars for long.*

12

IN THE MORNING the trapdoor opened and Hong Fat climbed down the stairs, followed by a gnome in a black robe lined with white silk.

"This is Mew Fong," Hong Fat said.

Mew Fong's head was shaven, he wore glasses, and had a friendly smile. "Thank you for helping my cousin, Hong Fat," Mew Fong said with a bow. "One wins merit when one stands up for the good and the right." Mew Fong held out the tray. "Your breakfast."

Stone lifted the lid off the plate and saw bacon and eggs with biscuits and coffee. Sitting at the table, he wolfed it down.

Mew Fong and Hong Fat sat silently and watched him. The coffee was especially delicious, and Stone felt new life surging into him. He'd slept well, and there'd been no trouble all night. He was beginning to feel safe in the cellar.

They waited until he finished the last morsel and was rolling his after-breakfast cigarette. Then Mew Fong said, "We will make everything here as comfortable for you as possible. I will visit every day, and so will Mai Wing. You will have the best food, and someone is collecting things for you to read. One day you will leave this place."

"Dawson'll never give up."

"Everyone gives up sooner or later. Even you, one day, will give up."

"Dawson might live another twenty years. I don't want to spend that long in this cellar."

"Charging ahead in a time of danger only hurries the catastrophe. You must be patient."

They were interrupted by the sound of feet running on the ceiling overhead, and then somebody shouted a warning in Chinese. Hong Fat and Mew Fong arose from their chairs.

"Dawson's men are coming!" Hong Fat said. "We must go!"

Hong Fat and Mew Fong scurried toward the ladder and climbed to Jimmy Wing's office. The trapdoor closed, and Stone sat at the table, pouring another cup of coffee. Heavy footsteps approached the room above, and Stone figured they were the boots of Dawson's men.

"What the hell's goin' on in here!" demanded Finch, followed by four gunmen.

"A business meeting," replied Jimmy Wing.

"Search the closet, boys."

Stone heard footsteps move toward the closet, and something fell to the floor. In his imagination, he saw them throwing dynamite into the cellar.

"Nothin' in the closet," Burkers said.

"We'll shoot anybody who's hiding John Stone," Finch said, "but you tell us where he is, and it's five thousand dollars in yore pocket."

Stone heard the cowboys leave the office, and there were several minutes of silence. Then the trapdoor opened again and Mew Fong came down the stairs.

"A brief unpleasantness," Mew Fong said, "but nothing dangerous. You are very tense—I can see it in your body. You must relax and let your Buddha mind speak to you."

Mew Fong took a small statue of the Buddha out of his robe and held it in the palm of his hand. The Buddha's diamond eyes glittered and gleamed in the light of the lamp, and Stone felt sleepy.

"Lie down," Mew Fong said gently.

Stone felt himself arising and stumbling toward the bed. He sat on the edge of it, didn't have the energy to pull off his boots, and stretched out, closing his eyes.

Mew Fong sat on the chair beside the bed, held the statue up, and said, "Time is precious, but truth is more precious than time."

It was morning at the HC Ranch, and Cynthia was trying to light the stove. She stuffed in the newspaper and wood, lit it, and it smoked pitifully for several seconds, then went out. She was dusted lightly with ashes from head to foot and getting angrier every moment.

Bernice had lit the fire every morning, and Cynthia cursed herself for not watching and learning how it was done, but she'd never dreamed a day would come when she'd have to light a fire.

Muttering, she pushed the remaining newspaper into the firebox, but her hand hit a hot surface. She shouted, pulled back suddenly, and slammed her hand unintentionally against the stove door. A small cut had opened on the back of her hand, and she covered it with her handkerchief as she looked out the window at Craig walking toward the barn.

I hope they left us horses, he thought as he advanced toward the big proscenium door. If there were no horses, he and Cynthia were doomed. He felt a choking sensation in his throat as he approached the door and looked inside. *Please God,* he thought, and then in the dimness saw the two horses that pulled the buckboard. They were looking at him, and he supposed they wanted to be fed.

He had no idea what to feed them, but vaguely recalled seeing cowboys use pitchforks to toss hay before the horses. Two pitchforks were leaning against the bin filled with hay, and he picked one up, stuck it into the hay, and threw a stack in front of the horses, who lowered their heads and chomped on it.

Nearby was the harness, but Craig didn't know how to hitch the buckboard to the horses. He realized how dependent he'd been on his cowboys, and how dangerous it was to be ignorant of basic knowledge that people needed to survive. *I'll figure it out somehow,* he said to himself, and then heard the sound of horses in the backyard. His heart soared with joy, because help had arrived at last!

He ran out of the barn, the pitchfork in his hand, and was dismayed to see Hank Dawson leading thirty of his men toward the main house. Craig realized he'd left his rifle in the barn, a stupid move. Dawson pulled his horse to a halt and looked coldly at Craig standing at the edge of the yard.

Meanwhile, Cynthia came onto the porch. She recalled Dawson saying he'd take care of them later, and now was back, true to his word. Turning, she ran back into the house, made her way to the kitchen, and picked up her rifle, carrying it to a window and poking it outside.

A gun fired, and splinters of wood flew into her face. Coughing and sputtering, she dropped to the floor.

"Keep that rifle out of sight," Dawson hollered, "or I'll shoot yore stupid husband!"

Cynthia raised her head and saw a cowboy with a smoking gun in his hand, aiming in her direction. She held up her hands where he could see them. Dawson turned to Craig.

"Been thinkin' about you, Delane," he said. "Intended to kill you, but that'd be too easy, so instead I'm a-gonna *destroy* you." He turned to Atwell. "Burn everything to the ground."

Atwell shouted orders to his men, and Cynthia and Craig watched in horror as cowboys dismounted and walked toward the house, barn, and outbuildings. Cynthia followed the cowboys into the kitchen and one of them picked up a lamp and hurled it at the wall, splattering glass and coal oil in all directions. Then he threw a match onto the puddle of coal oil on the floor. Cynthia moved to stamp out the match, but a cowboy grabbed her arms.

"Try it and I'll break yore neck," he snarled.

The oil caught fire, and flames crept across the floor and up the wall. Another cowboy threw a lamp against the wall in the living room. Cynthia heard more cowboys climbing the stairs, and then heard another lamp shatter.

She tried to break out of the cowboy's hands, and he laughed, hugging her tightly against him and biting her neck. She screamed, kicked him in the shins, and he squeezed her so hard she thought she'd faint from the pain.

"I like a filly who fights me," the cowboy said. "I got a mind to show you who's boss."

Atwell walked into the house. "What the hell's goin' on here."

"Bitch is actin' up," the cowboy said.

The cowboy released his grip, and Cynthia looked at the sheet of flames on the kitchen wall. She could feel the heat on her cheeks, and it was spreading toward the living room, sending out clouds of acrid smoke.

The cowboys hopped down the stairs and entered the kitchen. "Set three fires up there," one said.

"Back to yore horses," Atwell replied.

The cowboys filed out the front door, leaving Cynthia staring in disbelief at her kitchen going up in flames. She didn't know what to save first and was thoroughly confused. It was difficult for her to believe it was happening.

The kitchen became hotter, and she realized there was gold upstairs in Craig's office. Somehow she had to get it, because they'd need gold if they ever made it to Dumont. She ran to the pitcher of water next to the basin, poured it over herself, picked up the poker, and ran toward the stairs.

The living room billowed with flames, and she saw her furniture going up in smoke. Coughing, holding her hand over her mouth, she ran up the stairs and down the corridor, bursting into Craig's office.

Craig's desk was on fire and so was the painting of the Hudson River hanging above it. She opened the desk drawer with the poker and pulled out the ring of keys, then opened the closet door and bent in front of the safe.

Coughing and choking, she tried to work the lock, but could barely see through her smarting eyes. The heat was on her back and something told her the house would become her funeral pyre, but then the key turned and the door opened.

She saw the gold coins, certificates, and other important papers. *How can I carry it all?* Then she remembered Craig's briefcase next to the desk, turned to it, and saw that it was enveloped in flames. Her mind raced—she knew she didn't have much time—and remembered the pillowcase on her bed in the next room.

She ran down the smoke-filled corridor, entered her bedroom, and saw her magnificent bed on fire. The smoke was so thick it nearly overcame her, and she backed out of the room, coughing, and made her way to Craig's room.

It too was burning, but the bed hadn't caught fire yet. She pulled the pillowcase away, ran toward Craig's office, and heard Craig call her from downstairs.

"I'm up here!" she hollered.

"Get out of there!"

She made her way to the office, kneeled in front of the safe, and scooped everything into the pillowcase. Craig climbed the stairs and rushed into the room.

"Are you crazy?" he said, grabbing her arm.

"We've got to get the money!"

"The money?" he said, and then the realization struck him. He got on his knees beside her and helped gather it up.

The office filled with smoke, and they coughed from deep in their lungs. Cynthia spat something, worked frantically, and finally the safe was empty. Turning, they saw a wall of thick black smoke in front of them. He took his hand in hers, charged the door, missed by a few feet, and his head crashed into the wall.

He fell to the floor in a daze, and she helped him up.

"Hurry!" she said. "We don't have much time!"

He got to his feet and lunged at the door again, this time finding the opening. There was less smoke in the hall, but downstairs at the bottom the stairs were boiling flames.

"We'll never make it," she said.

"Out the window of your bedroom!"

He grabbed her hand and pulled her down the corridor, opening the door to her bedroom, and there was a path to the open window. Craig threw the pillowcase out, then helped Cynthia onto the roof, as wisps of smoke arose from the shingles.

He followed her down the slope to the same tree Stone had climbed, and then onto the branch. The barn and other buildings were ablaze, but the two horses were hitched to the rail in front of the house. Craig had managed to get them out, plus saddles, blankets, and bridles, before joining Cynthia in the main house.

They climbed down the tree to the ground, and Craig ran back to the wall, picking up the pillowcase full of wealth. "We've got to get out of here before the Commanches see the smoke!" he said. "Come on!"

They ran across the yard to the horses, and the two saddles

strewn on the ground nearby. Craig and Cynthia hastily saddled their mounts as the blaze swallowed the house and barn, and timbers crashed through the flames, sending out showers of sparks. They climbed into the saddles and rode away from the inferno, their clothes soiled and scorched, heading toward Dumont.

Dawson rode onto the front yard of the Circle Bar D Ranch and laboriously raised his leg, dropping down out of the saddle. He turned and looked to the west, seeing a long trail of black smoke rising into the sky. He smiled thinly and made his way toward the backyard as cowboys escorted his horse to the barn.

He was thinking about the Delanes and how terrified they'd been when he set their spread on fire. Shooting would be too good for them. He preferred long, slow suffering for his enemies.

Dawson approached Wayne's grave and squatted crosslegged on the ground, his belly nearly touching the grass.

"We're makin' progress, Wayne," he said. "I put out a five-thousand-dollar reward for John Stone, and somebody'll step forward anytime now. Then, when I git the son of a bitch, I'll tie him to a tree and shoot little pieces off him, till he dies."

Stone opened his eyes and saw total blackness, as if his eyes still were closed. He reached into his pocket, took out a match, and lit the lamp next to the bed.

He had no watch and didn't know whether he'd slept an hour or ten hours. It had been a deep sleep, and he'd dreamed of Marie.

Somehow the walls didn't seem so confining. It was cool in the cellar, and the sun wasn't burning his eyes out. There were no snakes and scorpions to contend with. Could be much worse.

He remembered the dream of Marie, about the first time they'd made love. It had been in her bedroom late at night when they'd been sixteen. He'd snuck into her house and crawled into her bed, as she'd previously left all the appropriate windows and doors open. They spent the whole night together, and it had been glorious.

The dream brought it all back, second by second it seemed, from the moment he approached her family's home with special treats for the dogs, all of whom he'd befriended during the preceding years for just such an eventuality.

When she'd opened her door, he'd seen her face in the moonlight, and she'd been half terrified by what they'd done, but they locked the door, got into bed, and that's how it began.

Stone took the picture out of his pocket and held it up in the light of the lamp. A terrible longing arose in his heart. During the war, one of the men in his troop wore a tattoo on his arm that said:

ONE LIFE
ONE LOVE

Stone thought that's the way it was for Marie and him. Occasionally he felt attracted to other women, but his main pull was toward Marie.

He heard the trapdoor open and pulled out his gun. Jimmy Wing, carrying a burlap bag, stepped down the stairs and walked toward him. "Newspapers," Jimmy Wing said, holding out the bag, "but I have something more important." He reached inside and pulled out a sawed-off, double-barreled shotgun, another Colt, and boxes of cartridges.

"Nobody loves the Buddha more than I," Jimmy Wing said, "but sometimes it's best to have a shotgun."

Stone accepted the shotgun and cracked it open. A man couldn't ask for a better weapon in close quarters.

"At least you will have the satisfaction of knowing you will take some of your enemies with you," Jimmy Wing said. "I know what you need the most."

Jimmy Wing threw a strange oriental salute and walked back to the stairs, climbing them, closing the trapdoor, leaving Stone with the shotgun. He thumbed in two loads, closed it, and then filled his guns with cartridges.

They might trap him like a rat, but that didn't mean he had to die like one. Now he'd be able to do some damage, before they got him. His eyes fell on the burlap bag, and he reached inside, pulling out an old *Houston Gazette*. The headline said:

TRANSCONTINENTAL RAILROAD
OPENS NEXT MONTH

Craig and Cynthia rode side by side on the trail that led to Dumont, and behind them smoke trailed into the sky from the smoldering embers of the HC Ranch.

They were bruised, burnt, dirty, and smudged, and their clothing was in tatters, but their main worry was Commanches. They searched the hills and gullies around them for Commanches, and knew they wouldn't have a prayer if they saw some.

They'd debated earlier about whether to use the trail or travel over open country, and decided on the trail because it was faster and they wouldn't get lost, but it also would be the most likely place to run into Commanches.

The sun beat down, and their hats had been lost in the fire. Perspiration plastered their clothing to their bodies, and they hadn't brought water. It hadn't occurred to them when they left the ranch.

Their mouths and throats were parched, they had headaches, and they recalled all the stories they'd heard about Indians scalping white people, torturing them, raping women, castrating men, and so on. They'd always been sympathetic to the problems of Indians, but now wished somebody had exterminated them long ago.

"I think we're about halfway," Craig said, scanning the trail ahead, where boulders were piled high, a perfect spot to ambush somebody. He drew his gun and held it ready in his hand.

"What's wrong?" she asked.

"Just a precaution."

She drew her gun too, and wondered if she'd have the courage to shoot a man. They approached the boulders, craning their necks to see if anybody was hiding behind them, and passed without incident. On the other side, Cynthia holstered her gun, but Craig held on to his.

She looked at him with the gun in his hand, his shirt torn, his hair tousled on his head, and he looked almost masculine, but he was as frightened as she, maybe more frightened, pretending a bravado he didn't feel.

He'll always be my friend, she thought, *but if I ever get out of this alive, I'm leaving him.*

Stone read old newspapers all morning, and found out that the Central Pacific and Union Pacific railroads were scheduled to meet soon somewhere in Utah, and for the first time people and goods could travel from coast to coast via the rails.

Congress passed the Fifteenth Amendment last February, giving former slaves the right to vote. During the Christmas season, President Johnson had issued an amnesty to remaining Confederate soldiers not included in his previous two amnesties. Ulysses S. Grant was inaugurated President of the United States in January.

The conqueror of the South now governed the nation, while John Stone lived in a cellar.

Stone often wondered how a drunken failure like Ulysses S. Grant could rise to leadership of the Union Army, defeat the Confederacy, and now become President. It was almost incomprehensible.

Stone refought the war for an hour, then Mai Ling brought lunch, a meat and vegetable stew over rice.

She sat opposite him as he ate, and he was so big, while she so small. "I am curious," she said. "Most Americans do not like Chinese, yet you helped Hong Fat when he was in trouble. Why?"

"Damned if I know," Stone said.

"Mew Fong says nothing is chance, and everything we do has a deep meaning."

"What does Mew Fong say my deep meaning is?"

"He says you are a Buddha who's come to this world to help people."

Stone tried not to smile, because he didn't want to offend her. "The main person I'm trying to help is myself."

"What about Hong Fat?"

"If I'd known what was coming, I would've eaten my meal and kept my mouth shut. I respect Mew Fong's wisdom, but if you knew what kind of thoughts I had sometimes, you'd know I'm not a Buddha."

"What kind of thoughts do you have?"

He looked into her eyes and smiled, and her face turned red.

"You are no Buddha," she announced. "This time Mew Fong is wrong."

Craig and Cynthia rode over the crest of a hill and saw Dumont lying on the plain before them. They looked at each other and shouted, "We're here!"

Since early morning they'd lived in terror of Indians, but now were safe at last. There was a hotel, bank, restaurant, and stagecoach leaving for the East at the beginning of every month.

Craig took out his handkerchief and wiped his brow. His face was pink from the sun, whereas Cynthia had been turning a deep bronze, like an Indian.

"There were moments, Cynthia, when I didn't think we'd make it," he said.

"All I want to do is eat," she said, "and then I want to take a bath for at least an hour."

"I'll order a bottle of champagne," he told her. "We'll have a celebration, and be back in New York before you know it."

They came to the edge of town and rode onto the main street, looking like two derelicts from the open prairie. Approaching the general store, they saw Stephen Connor on the front porch, and Delane waved to him.

Connor turned the other way and walked back into his store.

"Maybe he didn't see me," Craig said.

"He was looking right at you."

They came to Gallagher's Restaurant, rode to the hitching post, and dismounted. Cynthia was sore and starving as she threw her horse's reins over the rail and stepped onto the sidewalk.

Mrs. Minnie Grayson, whom she knew from the church, was approaching with her nephew Frankie. Cynthia was about to say hello, but Mrs. Grayson turned away, pulled Frankie toward her, and walked by. An icy fear gripped Cynthia's heart as the truth dawned on her. When Hank Dawson said he'd *destroy* them, he'd meant something more than merely burning the HC Ranch.

Craig joined her on the sidewalk. "I've given thousands of dollars' worth of business to Steve Connor since we've been here, and now he pretends I don't exist."

"They may not serve us in there."

He took her hand and led her to the door of the restaurant where they'd eaten whenever they'd come to town, two or three times every week since they'd first arrived in Dumont. They entered the restaurant, and instead of hearty greetings from their acquaintances and neighbors, there was silence; everyone looked away from them.

They sat at a table in the middle of the restaurant, and could feel hostility in the air. The waiter—a tall, lanky, toothless old ex-cowboy—ignored them.

"May we have menus?" Craig asked loudly.

The ex-cowboy sauntered toward the table and drawled, "We don't serve yore kind in here."

"Why not?"

"Orders from the boss."

"Where is he?" Craig said. "I demand to talk with him!"

"If'n you don't leave, I'm a-gonna call for the sheriff."

Craig's sunburnt complexion turned a deep shade of maroon, and his lips thinned. Cynthia could see he was enraged, where she was in mild shock. She'd never been denied service in a restaurant in her life.

The waiter walked away, and the restaurant fell silent except for forks and knives scraping against china. Craig and Cynthia looked into each other's eyes as the full weight of their predicament sank into them. Hank Dawson owned the town, and they wouldn't be able to buy anything. They might as well be in the middle of the desert.

They arose from the table and walked out of the restaurant, passing people whose homes they'd visited, and who'd visited their home, but who ignored them. Craig lit a cigar with shaky hands, and Cynthia needed a strong cup of coffee.

"Think the hotel'll take us?" she asked.

"They'd better."

They walked side by side toward the New Dumont Hotel, crossing the street, pausing in the middle for a bullwhacker with a wagon load of huge crates, then proceeding to the other side.

Craig thought he was having a nightmare, and would awaken soon in his bedroom, with the morning breeze filtering through the drapes, and the fragrance of bacon and eggs frying in the kitchen downstairs. He was hungry, thirsty, and afraid of being killed. His saddlebag was full of money, but he couldn't buy a meal in a restaurant.

They came to the front of the hotel, a two-story building in the middle of a block, with a veranda in front, and a few ladies sat at tables, sipping tea. Cynthia knew all of them, but they pretended she wasn't there, chattering like parrots as she and Craig crossed to the door.

They entered the lobby, and a few tough-looking cowboys

sat on chairs, smoking cigarettes. Craig had seen them at the Circle Bar D Ranch and knew they worked for Hank Dawson.

"It's the dude," one of them said derisively, and the other laughed.

Craig walked to the front desk, where the clerk was reading a newspaper, and Cynthia followed, feeling as if her legs were ready to give out.

"A room for the night," Craig said to the clerk.

"All filled up," the clerk replied, not looking up from his newspaper.

"You're a liar," Craig replied. "This hotel has never been filled up in its history."

"I told you the way it is, mister. If you don't like it, you know what you can do."

Craig leaned over the counter. "Let me tell you something. This may be Dumont County, but it's still the United States of America, and there are laws here. This is a public hotel and you're required to rent rooms to the public. I'd like to speak with the manager, if you don't mind."

"He's not in."

"We'll see about that."

Craig moved toward the opening that led behind the counter when he heard a voice to his rear.

"That'll be far enough, Mr. Delane."

Delane turned around and saw the three cowboys standing and aiming their guns at him.

"He givin' you any trouble?" the cowboy asked the room clerk.

"Just get him out of here."

The cowboys walked toward Craig and Cynthia, their guns pointed at them, and Cynthia was surprised to realize she wasn't afraid.

"Get going," said one of the cowboys.

Craig and Cynthia walked to the door, stepping onto the veranda. The ladies sipping tea continued to ignore them. Cynthia and Craig stared at the sun baking the dirt and muck that comprised the street.

"There's only one thing to do," Craig said, puffing his cigar nervously. "We'll have to sleep on the prairie close to town and live off the land until the next stagecoach leaves. There's game out there, and who knows what else we might find."

"You've never shot game in your life, and what about rattlesnakes and scorpions?"

"I don't see where we have any choice." Then his eyes fell on the BANK OF DUMONT on the other side of the street, and he thought of Eugene Tregaskis, the president, with whom he'd transacted so much business in the past.

"Come with me," he said to Cynthia, taking her hand.

He led her across the street and onto the sidewalk, passing the barbershop and a lawyer's office, and then entered the bank. Two people stood in line in front of the teller, and Mr. Tregaskis was behind the cage with another customer.

"Eugene," Craig said, "could I have a word with you?"

"If you have any business to transact," Eugene Tregaskis said coolly, "take it up with the teller."

Tregaskis led his customer to his private office and closed the door. It was the first time the banking system ever failed Craig, but he brought himself under control, turned, and walked out the door.

Cynthia joined him on the sidewalk, and a couple whom they knew walked by and paid no attention to them. Cynthia sat heavily on the bench outside the bank and wondered if they were going to starve to death in Dumont.

Craig sat beside her, puffing the butt of his cigar and trying to think. He realized now that he'd had no concept of how much power Hank Dawson had. He'd always believed there was a solution for every problem, but there appeared to be no solution to this one. Where would they sleep, what would they eat, and who would let them drink from their well?

"What about Reverend Skeaping?" Cynthia asked. "He's another of Dawson's toadies, but he's an ordained minister, and I don't think he'd refuse us sanctuary until the stagecoach comes. We've always contributed generously to his church."

They arose and walked down the street toward the white church steeple in the distance, as a crowd erupted out the door of the saloon halfway down the block.

"My God!" said Cynthia.

It was Everett Lorch and Bernice with several other cowboys who'd worked at the HC Ranch, and they all looked drunk. Bernice was dressed like a lady, in a high-necked white dress, but her hair was mussed and her eyes half closed.

"It's Mrs. Rich Bitch and her sissy husband!" Bernice cackled.

"We'd better cross the street," Craig said.

They walked to the end of the hitching rail and stepped onto the street, noticing with dismay that Lorch, Bernice, and the cowboys were doing the same.

"Maybe we can go another way," Craig said.

"I'm not running from my maid," Cynthia replied, raising her chin a fraction of an inch and walking imperiously toward the other side of the street.

Craig caught up with her and side by side they tromped through the muck as the coalition formed in front of them. One of the cowboys laughed, and Bernice sneered.

"Mrs. Rich Bitch don't look so rich today," she said.

Cynthia kept walking, and Bernice got in front of her, spreading her legs and placing her hands on her hips.

"Mrs. Rich Bitch can't take a shit unless somebody holds the pot for her."

Bernice blocked Cynthia's way, but Cynthia wasn't about to stop or walk around her; she set her jaw and kept going. Bernice balled up her fists, and an expression of contempt came over her face. She thought Cynthia would retreat or swerve out of the way, but Cynthia kept coming, determination in her eyes, and Bernice had been drinking with Lorch since leaving the HC Ranch. Bernice didn't budge, and Cynthia walked right into her.

Bernice shrieked angrily, clawed at Cynthia's face, and Cynthia punched Bernice in the nose. Blood trickled out, Bernice licked it off her upper lip and grabbed two handfuls of Cynthia's hair, pulling down with all her might, and Cynthia saw the ground coming up fast toward her face. At the last moment she dived toward Bernice's legs, tackled her, and brought her down.

They rolled around in the middle of the street, scratching, biting, trying to gouge out each other's eyes, but Cynthia was twenty-five and sober, whereas Bernice was forty and half drunk. Cynthia was no weakling, not puny, and she was mad.

Cynthia saw an opening, hauled off, and slammed Bernice in the nose. This time the bone and cartilage cracked, and Bernice hollered in pain. Cynthia rolled Bernice onto her back and socked her again, as Bernice tried to scratch Cynthia's face with her fingernails.

"We'd better stop it," Lorch said.

Cowboys surrounded the two women and pulled them away from each other, holding their arms. Bernice's face was bloody and hair awry, while Cynthia was scratched and dirty, with a torn shirt. Cynthia struggled to break loose from the cowboys who held her arms, while Bernice kicked at Cynthia long distance, showing her muddied petticoats.

Lorch laughed, his thumbs in his gunbelt. "Ladies sure do put on a show once they git started." He stepped in front of Craig. "How're you doin' today, Boss Man? You ain't so high and mighty anymore. Where you think you're goin'?"

"Out of my way," Craig mumbled.

Lorch was blocking his path, and Craig knew he'd have to collide with him, as Cynthia had done with Bernice. Craig couldn't turn the other way after what Cynthia had done. He'd have to fight Lorch, a rough cowboy who'd been brawling in saloons since he could belly up to the bar.

Lorch raised his fists, and Craig bent himself into a fighter's crouch. Lorch uncorked a sharp uppercut to the point of Craig's chin, straightening Craig up, and then Lorch hit him with a left hook to the body and a straight right to the head, sending Craig reeling to the ground.

Craig's mouth was filled with blood and he thought he had a broken rib. The street spun around him, and everybody laughed.

"You used to talk to me like I was shit," Lorch said, standing with his legs spread in the middle of the street, "and now you're the one lyin' in the shit."

Craig looked down at his hands and saw they were indeed resting on a fresh pile of horse manure. The stench rose to his nostrils and cleared his head. He arose from the ground, wiped his hands on his pants, and spit a piece of dirt out of his mouth.

Lorch poised his hand above his gun. "I see you're armed today, Mr. Delane. You know how to use that thing in yore holster?"

Craig flashed on the gunfight he'd seen on this very street a few days ago, and wasn't going to be the one lying at the curb when the stagecoach came by.

"I don't know how to use it as well as you," Craig said to

Lorch, "so I'm not going to duel with you. However, I want you to understand this: if my skill were equal to yours, I wouldn't hesitate."

Lorch laughed. "Mr. Fancy Pants and Mrs. Rich Bitch. Wonder if Mr. Fancy Pants knows what Mrs. Rich Bitch was doin' in John Stone's room while Mr. Fancy Pants was in town?"

Craig glanced at Cynthia and felt a terrible stab of pain.

"It's not true, Craig," she said.

Lorch, Bernice, and the cowboys roared with laughter. Craig took Cynthia's hand, and together they walked through the crowd. When cowboys wouldn't move out of their way, they swerved to avoid them. One cowboy held out his foot, tripping Craig, and Craig let go of Cynthia's hand as he fell to the ground. The cowboys laughed louder, and one of them kicked Craig in the rear end. That was the last straw for Craig, and he jumped to his feet, reaching for his gun.

"No!" screamed Cynthia.

A shot was fired, and the gun flew out of Craig's hand. A red ribbon rolled down Craig's palm, and Craig saw Lorch standing with his gun in his hand and a smirk on his face.

"It's real easy to die," Lorch said.

Craig's hand was a world of pain, and blood dripped to the ground. Cynthia tore the bottom off her shirt and wrapped it around the wound, as Craig stared white-faced at her.

"You bunch of cowards!" she said through clenched teeth. "You push around a man who doesn't know anything about guns, and who isn't as strong as you, but you haven't done so well when you're more evenly matched!"

She took Craig's hand, and he walked woodenly, the pain radiating up his arm. Cowboys stepped out of their way as Cynthia and Craig moved toward the white steeple jutting above the roofs of Dumont.

Stone finished reading the last newspaper and lay it on the table in front of him. Incredible events were taking place all over the world, and he was confined to a small dank place underneath the ground like a mole. He looked at the walls, and they seemed closer than before. He was a man of action, accustomed to riding long distances, and felt penned in. His lungs craved fresh air, instead of the musty atmosphere in the basement. He wanted to stretch out his legs and run, or go to a saloon where they had dancing girls. He could think of a million things to do, but couldn't do anything in the cellar.

Frustrated and claustrophobic, a mad thought entered his mind. Maybe he should take the shotgun and fight his way out of Dumont, jump on the first horse he saw, and ride away. He wanted a fighting chance, instead of a slow, lingering death from bad air and inadequate exercise in the cellar.

He stood, picked up the shotgun, and cracked it open. Dawson's men probably were lulled into stupefaction by the lack of activity, and might not even realize anything until he was riding out of town. They'd chase him and the outcome would depend on who had the best horse.

Then the rational part of his mind took hold. It'd be better to break out at night, when lack of visibility would favor him. One of the Chinese could leave a horse outside. Stone would be riding hard across open range before Dawson's men knew what happened.

He placed the shotgun on the table and sat on his chair, rolling a cigarette. He'd talk over the escape plan with Jimmy Wing next time he came down the stairs.

He looked at the four walls in the tiny cellar. *I've got to get out of here.*

Cynthia and Craig approached the rectory in back of the church, and it was white like the church, with curtains drawn back from the windows.

"Skeaping is as corrupt as the rest of them," Craig said bitterly. "I don't think we can expect much from him."

"He's a man of God—he'll have to help us," Cynthia replied, raising her hand and knocking on the door. There was no answer, and she knocked again. "Maybe he's not in."

Craig was angry and kicked the door hard. "Maybe he's hiding underneath one of his pews!"

A few moments later the door opened, and Mrs. Bunberry, the gray-haired housekeeper, appeared.

"We'd like to see Reverend Skeaping," Cynthia said.

"I'm sorry, but he's not in."

Craig waved his bandaged hand in the air erratically. "I know he's in there!" he shouted. "You can't fool me!" He pushed Mrs. Bunberry out of the way and invaded the house. "Skeaping—where the hell are you?"

There was no answer, and Cynthia realized that Craig had become deranged. This definitely wasn't the man she'd married, who observed even the tiniest points of decorum at all times, but it sounded as though he was knocking things over in Reverend Skeaping's dining room.

Cynthia climbed the stairs and entered the room, seeing her husband standing near the fireplace, wielding the poker like a saber. "Skeaping—you hypocrite!" Craig hollered. "Come out of your rat hole!"

Reverend Skeaping, minus frock coat and tie, appeared in the doorway behind the stove. "Figured you'd be here before long," he said wearily. "Mrs. Bunberry, would you please bring the lemonade."

"Lemonade, hell!" Craig said. "We're damn near *starved* to death!" He reached into his saddlebags and pulled out a handful of coins, throwing them onto the table. "If you need a contribution to this miserable excuse for a church that you've got, take it!"

"Dear me," Reverend Skeaping said. "This is so awkward." He turned to Mrs. Bunberry. "Please prepare food for our guests, after you fetch the lemonade." Then he sat at the table and leaned back in his chair, crossing his legs. "Don't worry," he said to Craig and Cynthia, "I don't believe they'll harm you here. Have a seat."

Craig and Cynthia sat at the table, and Reverend Skeaping frowned. "Your problem, Mr. Delane, is you've made the mistake of thinking we're more or less like New Yorkers. You've never realized we have our own codes and traditions, and our own ways of doing things."

"Like lynching, shooting, and stealing!" Craig replied. "I can understand the others, because they're ordinary people trying to get by, but you're supposed to be the conscience of this town, and you're the worst bootlicker of all!"

Reverend Skeaping shrugged. "It's true that I defer to Dawson, but so did you. Believe it or not, most of the people in this town need what little of God's spirit that I'm able to give them. You won't find many men willing to take this pulpit, and the town could end up with a preacher far more corrupt than I."

Mrs. Bunberry appeared, placing a large pitcher of lemonade on the table, with three tall glasses.

"Would you please bring my pipe," Reverend Skeaping said to Mrs. Bunberry.

She retreated from the room, and Reverend Skeaping watched Cynthia and Craig slurp lemonade thirstily. He was amazed at how disheveled they were, like a couple of derelicts instead of the fashionable and intelligent easterners with whom he'd enjoyed so many interesting conversations.

"What happened to your hand?" Reverend Skeaping asked.

"Lorch, my former foreman, shot a bullet through it."

"Lorch is a gunfighter. You're lucky you're still alive."

Mrs. Bunberry returned to the table, carrying a corncob pipe and a pigskin tobacco pouch.

"Would you please call Dr. Merriwether, Mrs. Bunberry."

She headed for the door, and Reverend Skeaping tamped tobacco into the black bowl of his corncob. Cynthia and Craig were on their second glasses of lemonade, drinking like fiends.

"Let me explain something to the both of you," Reverend Skeaping said. "Dawson does whatever he pleases here, and he takes an extremely harsh view of events. You don't step on such a man's toes, and you definitely don't help his enemies. John Stone is a drifter, and should've drifted right on through, but instead he put his nose where it didn't belong, and that's spelled trouble for him and everybody else ever since."

Cynthia asked, "Do you know where he is now?"

"They say he's hiding in Chinatown. I would say his future doesn't appear promising at this point."

"Do you have anything to eat?" Craig asked plaintively.

"We have biscuits you can chomp on until Mrs. Bunberry does her cooking."

Reverend Skeaping lit his pipe, and his head disappeared in a cloud of blue smoke. Then he arose through the smoke and walked toward the kitchen, leaving behind the fragrance of his tobacco.

"We're safe," Craig said. "All we have to do is wait for the next stagecoach."

Cynthia agreed absentmindedly, thinking about John Stone. He was somewhere in town, possibly close by, and she wished she could see him again. Reverend Skeaping returned with a plate heaped high with biscuits, and a bowl of butter, placing both on the table.

Cynthia and Craig dived on the biscuits and butter like ravenous animals, and Reverend Skeaping puffed his pipe contentedly, feeling at peace with the world.

Five hundred yards away, in the depths of Chinatown, John Stone explained his escape plan to Jimmy Wing, who listened attentively and then said, "I think you should wait a few days."

"I can't wait a few days. I'd rather make a run for it."

"It will take at least a day to make all the preparations, and today is almost finished, so you will have to leave tomorrow night at the earliest. Is all right?"

"Is fine, but there's just one problem—I can't afford to pay for the horse and saddle, but maybe you can collect from Craig Delane. He's a friend of mine and should be good for the money."

"Mr. Delane and his beautiful wife have had many misfortunes since they saw you last," Jimmy Wing explained. "Dawson's cowboys burned his ranch to the ground."

Stone was stunned by this information. "I should never've gotten them involved," he said. "It's my fault."

"Everybody is responsible for what he does," said Jimmy Wing. "The Delanes will probably leave Dumont with their lives, at least. We cannot be so sure about you."

13

It was ten o'clock at night, and Cynthia had just awakened. She was lying next to Craig on the bed in the guest room of the rectory, and had been sleeping since four o'clock in the afternoon.

Craig mumbled something in his sleep. The doctor had cleaned and bandaged his wound, but he had a fever. She touched her hand to his forehead, and it was hot, covered with perspiration.

She felt desolate and abandoned, and knew a great ordeal lay ahead. Somehow she and Craig would have to get out of town, and there was no telling what Dawson might do.

She didn't think she could depend on Craig. He'd been acting as if his mind had cracked. She realized now that a woman should marry a man who wouldn't break under pressure.

It wasn't because she was weak herself and needed somebody to take care of her. She could take care of herself, but she wanted a man who could take care of himself too.

Craig was a hothouse flower. Until now, everything had been easy for him. He'd come out west to prove himself, and failed the test. She'd help him any way she could, but their married life was over.

She remembered the feeling she'd had when she'd been with John Stone in the guest room of the HC Ranch, and had an irresistible urge to hug him, but managed to fight it down.

Men were no mystery to her, and she'd seen the mad gleam of lust in his eyes. He wanted her too, but wouldn't make advances to the wife of a friend.

What if she's weren't a wife anymore? There'd be nothing to stop them. Love was a rare and magic thing, and no one could make it happen. Years could pass, and she might never have that feeling again. It was possible she'd become an old maid and die alone. She'd had a great-aunt like that.

She wished there was some way she could see John Stone, so she could tell him she wasn't married anymore. Then he could stop his search for a dream woman, and have a real woman who'd hold him tightly and love him with every ounce of her being.

Her heart beat faster, and she smiled. She was getting carried away. Stone and she'd never discussed philosophy, religion, politics, child-rearing, or any of the important subjects. She didn't even know his interests, or even if he had interests.

But she already had somebody who shared her interests, and it wasn't enough. She wondered if somehow she could reach John Stone. It would be dangerous to go to him in Chinatown, but something told her she ought to try, because she might never meet another John Stone in her life.

She rolled out of bed, wearing a white cotton nightgown Mrs. Bunberry had lent her. Folded on the chair were clean jeans and a shirt, and she put them on, tying a red bandanna around her throat. She looked at herself in the mirror and combed her hair, then put on a wide-brimmed cowboy hat with a braided horsehair band.

Craig stirred on the bed, and she froze in the shadow, looking at him, his thin legs illuminated by a shaft of moonlight. He rolled over and was still again, and she opened the door, passing into the corridor. She made her way to the dining room, un-latched the door, and was greeted by a chorus of crickets as she stepped into the backyard.

A half moon floated in the sky, outlining a silvery mountain range on the horizon. She walked around the house, passed through the alley, and came to the street. Removing her hat, she eased her head out from behind the building and looked toward the saloon district, and could hear faint strains of piano music. Chinatown was to her left in the darkness at the edge of town. She pulled her hat low over her eyes and stepped onto the sidewalk, imitating the slow, rolling gait of a man as she headed toward the shadows of Chinatown.

Hank Dawson sat in the moonlight next to his son's grave, drinking a jug of whiskey. He hadn't put up a headstone, and only a mound of brown earth covered the spot where Wayne lay buried in the ground.

Dawson had bought the best casket available, but it was wood and the rats probably had chewed through it by now. He imagined them tearing Wayne's flesh apart with their tiny teeth, and worms crawling into Wayne's ears.

A tidal wave of sorrow struck him in the heart. Life was miserable now that Wayne was gone. His vast wealth, his land, and his cattle didn't mean so much to him anymore.

Wayne had been a good boy, all a father could ask for. He liked all the things men liked, and enjoyed life, whereas Hank Dawson mainly liked to eat, and had been eating more than ever since coming home.

Beside him, wrapped in a napkin, was the roasted leg of a turkey. He unwrapped the napkin and took a huge bite, working his jaws, mashing the meat into paste. Hank had been happy when Wayne was alive, because Wayne would tell him the things he did, and it was as if Hank had done them himself.

Now everything had turned grim, and the turkey tasted like dust in his mouth. It wasn't fair the way the boy had been taken away from him, and burning the HC Ranch had given him no great satisfaction. He needed his pound of flesh, and it could only come from John Stone.

John Stone was in Dumont, but where? He might stay hidden for weeks or months, and Dawson knew that the vigilance of his men would slacken after a while. Perhaps Stone might slip out of town on a dark night, and then Dawson would never be able to track him down.

Dawson sipped whiskey and felt himself getting angry. It wasn't often that his goals were thwarted. Sometimes he thought Wayne was looking down at him reproachfully for not avenging his death.

Wayne had been killed, but no one had paid. Maybe it was time to start spilling blood. There was nothing like death to bring people to their senses.

He knew his men would end up in the saloons and whorehouses of Dumont no matter what his orders were, and decided to move his headquarters to town and supervise the hunt personally. If he was serious about avenging Wayne's death, he'd get up off his fat ass and throw some terror into the hearts of the good citizens of Dumont.

He drained the jug of whiskey and rose unsteadily to his feet. Staggering from side to side, he got his bearings and stumbled toward the bunkhouse, where a light shone in the window. As he drew closer, he heard one of his cowboys playing a guitar and singing a song about the señoritas of Laredo.

Dawson threw open the door of the bunkhouse and saw a group of men gathered around the table playing cards, while others snored in their bunks. The guitarist at the window stopped playing at the sight of Dawson.

"Where's Atwell?" Dawson asked.

"In his bunk."

The cowboy pointed, and Dawson ambled back to where Atwell slept beneath his blanket, a faint smile on his face. Dawson shook Atwell's shoulder roughly.

In a sudden movement, Atwell pulled his gun from underneath his pillow and pointed it at Dawson's nose, then recognized who he was.

Dawson stank of whiskey and stale sweat, and his beard carried bits of turkey. "Round up every man on the spread," Dawson ordered gutturally. "We're going to tear up Dumont, until we find John Stone."

Cynthia walked along the darkened sidewalk, passing a drunk sleeping in the gutter, then came to a long row of buildings locked and shuttered for the night.

At their end was Chinatown, deserted, with nothing to indicate a strange race from a far-off land lived here. Cynthia knew it was extremely dangerous to wander around Dumont at night, but was driven by a deep need.

She thought of knocking on the first door, and awakening the people inside, but realized that might cause a commotion, and she didn't want to attract attention to herself. Maybe there'd be somebody awake at the rear of the buildings.

She turned into the first alley, making her way toward the shaft of moonlight shining through the tree at the end. Halfway through the alley she noticed a figure sprawled on the ground. Stopping, she realized it was a midget Chinaman with a pigtail, wearing a black beanie, sleeping soundly.

Suddenly the Chinaman became aware of her presence and woke up, his eyes bulging at the sight of her. He screamed, jumped to his feet, and ran on stubby little legs toward the backyard, his pigtail dancing in the moonlight.

Cynthia followed him toward the privies and sheds in the backyard. All buildings were darkened, and she pinched her lips together, wondering what to do next, when she became aware of a dim orange light in a window not far away.

She made her way to it, passing a wagon, a chicken coop, and a stack of firewood. The light shone through the window of a room on the ground floor of a small building. She approached the door and knocked.

The door opened and a tall, slope-shouldered Chinese man stood before her. "What you want?" he demanded.

"Could you take me to John Stone? It's very important that I see him."

The door slammed in her face. Turning, she saw another light glowing behind a small window. It hadn't been on before, and she moved toward it, wondering what to say.

She knocked on the door, and footsteps came to her from the other side. The door was opened by a small man wearing glasses and a black robe.

"I must see John Stone," she said. "It's very important."

He stared at her for a few moments, then bowed and said, "Come in."

She entered his room. Incense burned in a pot beside a mat on the floor, and in the corner was a two-foot black statue of the Buddha seated in meditation.

"What is your name?" the Chinese man asked.

"Cynthia Delane."

"I am Mew Fong. Please follow me."

He opened a door and plunged into a long, dark hallway, and she followed, her heart beating wildly.

John Stone sat at the table in the cellar and studied a map to determine where he would go next. He'd rejected south to Mexico because he thought Marie would more likely be in the United States. There was no point going east, because that was where he'd started from. The choice was between north and west, but he'd just come from the north on the wagon train, so he'd go west to New Mexico and Arizona.

Tomorrow night he'd be on his way. The horse would be saddled behind the building, and he'd sneak out at two or three in the morning, making his run for the Pecos.

His lungs felt clogged and weak, from breathing the musty air of the cellar. He longed for the clear air of the prairie, the sunlight, and the vast seas of buffalo grass.

He heard a sound above his head and reached for the shotgun. Blowing out the lamp, stepping back into the corner, he pointed the shotgun at the stairs.

The trapdoor opened, and he saw a pair of men's cowboy boots and a pair of pants. The figure stepped lower, and Cynthia Delane emerged, illuminated by light from the office above.

"John Stone?" she asked, peering into the darkness.

He was astonished to see her and came out of the corner, holding the shotgun. The trapdoor closed above them, and an expression of tense expectation was on her face.

"How did you find me?"

"A Chinese man brought me here."

"Where's Craig?"

"He was shot in the hand by Everett Lorch."

"You took a big chance coming here."

"I had to talk with you." She looked into his eyes and moved closer. "I'm leaving Craig," she said, and waited for him to take the hint.

"What happened?"

"I don't love him."

"Maybe you'll change your mind, once you return to New York."

"My mind is made up."

She was a few feet away, and they were alone, with a bed in the corner. He reached for his bag of tobacco, thinking it over, and she realized with dismay that if he had to think it over, he wasn't feeling what she was feeling. A few awkward moments passed.

"I think I'd better be going," she said, trying to regain her composure.

"There's no hurry. Have a seat."

Confused, she sat at the table opposite him. Their eyes met and he looked away.

"What are your plans?" she asked.

"I'm making a run first chance I get."

"Dawson's men are all over town. You'll have your hands full."

"That's the way it's always been."

"It won't be easy for us to leave either. Dawson's angry because we helped you. Craig and I didn't realize what we've been up against out here. We've really been rather naive, but then I suppose I've been naive all my life. I never should've married Craig."

"You seem to get along well."

"There's more to life than just getting along well."

They sat in silence for a few moments, afraid to make a move.

"Well," she said, "I wanted to find something out, and I did. Guess I'll be on my way. It's been nice knowing you, John Stone. Maybe someday, in some other place, we'll meet again, who knows."

She arose and walked unsteadily toward the stairs, and he didn't know whether to run after her or remain still. She stopped at the foot of the stairs and looked at him quizzically for a moment, then climbed the steps and knocked on the trapdoor.

He watched her pass from sight, and the trapdoor closed again. Lighting his cigarette, he sat at the table and stared into space.

Cynthia walked home, trying to keep from crying. She'd offered herself to him, and now felt ugly and unwanted. The woman he wanted most was in his pocket, and Cynthia was second-best, thrown away, and now what kind of life could she expect?

She had to leave Craig; there was no doubt about that. She didn't love him and had to be true to herself, but it'd be no fun as an old maid. Her future was uncertain, and she couldn't even be sure she'd get out of town alive.

She passed along the darkened sidewalk when suddenly a shadow moved in a doorway beside her, a hand shot out and grabbed her arm so tightly it hurt.

She screamed and found herself looking into the leathery face of Everett Lorch. "Where d'ya think you're goin'?" he asked with a sneer.

Craig felt someone shaking his shoulder and opened his eyes. The face of Reverend Skeaping floated above him in the darkness. "Hank Dawson and his men just rode into town. Thought you might want to know."

Craig turned to Cynthia, and she wasn't there. "Where's my wife?"

"Don't know."

He called her name, but there was no answer. Worried, he got out of bed and pulled on his boots, then followed Reverend Skeaping through the rectory and into the church, passing the silent pews to the windows in front.

Craig looked out a window and saw horsemen in front of the New Dumont Hotel. One of them dismounted, and he was round as a barrel. Hank Dawson shuffled toward the steps of the hotel, and then his men climbed down from their saddles. An enormous crowd was in the street, over a hundred armed men.

"Looks like trouble," Reverend Skeaping said. "You'd better hide in the root cellar."

Craig returned to his room and strapped on his gun. Then he sat on the bed and tried to think of what had happened to Cynthia. Where had she gone?

He couldn't hide in the root cellar while Cynthia was roaming around in the night. Arising from the bed, he put on his hat and walked toward the door.

Dawson entered the lobby of the New Dumont Hotel and saw his gunfighters and cowboys lounging about on sofas and chairs. When they spotted his monstrous figure, they sat straighter and tried to appear alert although it was two o'clock in the morning. Lorch walked toward him, hat in hand.

"I caught the Delane woman comin' from Chinatown," he

said. "We think she was talkin' to John Stone."

Dawson followed Lorch down the hall, remembering his Indian scouts tracking Stone to that Chinese restaurant. They entered an office, and Cynthia sat in the corner. Other cowboys were in the office guarding her, and a bottle of whiskey sat on the desk.

Dawson walked toward Cynthia and looked into her eyes. "Where is he?"

Cynthia didn't reply, repelled by the odor coming from his mouth, the hair sprouting out of his nose and ears, and his unbelievable massive grossness.

He raised his hand to slap her face, and she sat stoically, looking him in the eyes. Dawson lowered his hand.

"You're sure she was coming from Chinatown?" Dawson asked Lorch.

"Saw her myself."

He looked at her. "What were you doing in Chinatown this time of night?"

"Taking a walk."

One of the cowboys chortled, and Dawson turned down the corners of his mouth. He doubted she knew Chinese people well enough to visit, so she must've gone to see John Stone, which meant Jimmy Wing had outbluffed him the other night.

A cowboy sat behind the desk, but got out of the chair when he saw Dawson move toward him. Dawson dropped heavily into the chair, lit a cigar, and stared at Cynthia.

He'd heard about Cynthia spending time alone with Stone at the HC Ranch. If Stone were in Chinatown, Jimmy Wing would know where he was. The problem was Jimmy Wing wouldn't talk, and neither would Cynthia. He could slap the shit out of her, and she'd remain silent. Some people could handle pain.

But could they handle somebody else's pain? Dawson recalled meeting Jimmy Wing's pretty young daughter, and Jimmy Wing had been so proud of her. Dawson wondered if Jimmy Wing would be so cavalier with his daughter's life.

Dawson thought of Wayne lying cold beneath the earth, eaten by rats, bugs, and worms. The time had come to avenge his death.

"Somebody stay with Mrs. Delane," he said. "The rest of you come with me."

He arose and moved toward the door, followed by his men, heading toward Chinatown.

Jimmy Wing descended the stairs, followed by Hong Fat and a few other Chinese men. Stone still sat at the table, wondering if he'd been a fool when he'd let Cynthia Delane get away.

"Big trouble," Jimmy Wing said. "Dawson and his men are headed this way. You be extra quiet and turn out your light."

They climbed the stairs, and Stone opened the box of shotgun loads, stuffing them into his pockets. Then he checked his guns, tipped the table onto its side, and crouched behind it, laying the shotgun beside him.

Dawson and his men hit Chinatown like a tornado, shooting locks off doors, busting through windows. Women screamed, babies cried, and men stood by stolidly as Dawson's cowboys invaded their homes and wrecked everything in sight.

One contingent, led by Dawson, made their way to Jimmy Wing's building. Lorch shot the lock off the door and men spilled into the corridors, as Dawson followed, heading for Jimmy Wing's office.

The door to the office was closed. Dawson nodded, and Atwell turned the doorknob. The door opened and revealed Jimmy Wing sitting behind his desk, with Mew Fong and Hong Fat sitting in front of him on the rug. Dawson raised his gun and fired point-blank at Hong Fat. The explosion shook the room, and Hong Fat's eyes rolled up into his head as blood poured from the hole in his chest.

Dawson turned and aimed his gun at Jimmy Wing. "We got the Delane woman, and we know she was here. Where's John Stone?"

Jimmy Wing looked at Dawson coldly and didn't reply.

"You goddamn chink!" Dawson was so mad he wanted to kill Jimmy Wing, but that would accomplish nothing. "I'll make you talk," he said through clenched teeth.

There was a commotion in the corridor, and Mai Wing screamed. Dawson smiled as he saw the consternation on Jimmy Wing's face. Mai Wing entered the room, wearing a pale green silk robe, her straight black hair hanging loosely to her shoulders, and behind her was a group of Dawson's gunmen.

Dawson pointed his gun at her. "Against that wall."

Mai Wing, trying to be calm, stood where he told her, looking down the barrel of his six-gun.

Dawson turned to Jimmy Wing. "Here's yore choice. Tell me where John Stone is, or she dies."

Jimmy Wing's face lost its composure. "Please," he said. "Not my daughter. She is so young. Kill me instead."

"You'd love to die for somebody you don't know, you crazy chink, but you don't want yore daughter to die, eh? Well that's what she's gonna do if you don't start talkin'. One."

Dawson aimed his gun at Mai Wing and sighted down the barrel, and a sob arose from her throat. Dawson heard a sound from the cellar, paid no attention, and said, "It's my son for yore daughter, you goddamned chink! Two!"

Suddenly the floor exploded as John Stone threw open the trapdoor with all the strength in his body. The chair with Hong Fat tumbled through the air, landing on Dawson and knocking him off his feet. John Stone erupted out of the cellar, the shotgun in his hands, while Atwell, Lorch, and the other cowboys dropped their hands toward their holsters.

Stone pulled both triggers, the office was rocked by a tremendous roar, and tiny pellets of steel chopped holes through the cowboys. Stone dropped the shotgun, yanked both his Colts, and fired another barrage, then pivoted and aimed his smoking pistols at Dawson, who was on his knees, swinging his gun toward Stone.

"Drop it!" Stone shouted.

Dawson looked at Stone, and his heart filled with black hatred. Here was the man responsible for the death of his son! But Stone had the drop on him. Dawson grimaced as he dropped his pistol to the floor.

Suddenly the sound of rushing footsteps came to them, and another group of Dawson's men rushed into the office. Stone turned toward them and triggered his guns, spewing forth a hail of bullets that threw them backward. Stone kept firing as they clutched their wounds and dropped through the swirling gunsmoke to the floor.

Dawson saw his chance and made one last desperate move. He reached for his gun with trembling sausagelike fingers.

"Watch out!" cried Jimmy Wing.

Stone wheeled and fired both guns at Dawson. One bullet drilled through Dawson's fat gut, another pierced his chest. Dawson jerked violently and shot a bullet over Stone's head, then dropped the gun, groaned, and closed his eyes, collapsing onto the floor.

Stone dived behind Jimmy Wing's desk and thumbed cartridges into the shotgun, then reloaded his Colts. The room was silent and full of gunsmoke, and Hank Dawson lay gasping on the floor, blood burbling out of his mouth.

"What the hell's goin' on!" shouted a voice in the corridor.

"Stone's in there!" replied another voice. "Rush him."

Stone heard footsteps stampeding toward the door. Men appeared, their guns drawn, and they saw Dawson lying on the floor directly in front of them, covered with blood. They froze in horror at the sight of their leader, and Stone raised himself, pulling both triggers of the shotgun.

It sounded as if a cannon had fired, and the cowboys were blown to bits. They toppled to the floor and Stone heard a flurry of footsteps fleeing down the corridor.

Stone reloaded the shotgun and handed it to Jimmy Wing as Mai Wing ran across the room and jumped behind the desk next to Mew Fong on the end. Stone considered their situation as he loaded both guns. The room had no windows and only one door. Dawson's men could rush him, but they'd have to come through one at a time, and he'd be able to pick them off. Stone looked at Dawson, and the old cattle baron wasn't gasping anymore. He lay still on the floor, his big belly like a mountain.

Jimmy Wing raised his head cautiously and looked at Dawson. "He is dead?"

"Looks that way."

"Then his men have nothing to fight for anymore."

Stone realized that was true, because when Dawson died, so did the five-thousand-dollar reward. He raised his head higher and shouted toward the hallway: "Hank Dawson is dead! There's no more five-thousand-dollar reward! You might kill me, but I'll get a lot of you first, and you'll die for nothing because Dawson can't pay you anymore!"

Stone paused to let his words sink in, and recalled Chancellorsville when the word came down that Stonewall Jackson had been shot. The men went into a state of shock and lost their will to fight for several days. Stone hoped the same malaise would strike Dawson's men, because Dawson was their commanding officer, and they were used to following his orders.

It was silent in the corridor. He was sure the word was rippling among them. Atwell and Lorch, their other two leaders, were dead too, and the cowboys were unsure of what they were risking their lives for. Stone thought the time had come for him to take a calculated risk. He holstered his guns and moved toward Dawson, picking his limp body off the floor and cradling him in his arms. Dawson's head hung backward, his arms and legs were splayed, and he was covered with blood. He was heavy as a small horse but Stone was strong, carrying him steadily toward the door and passing through into the dark hallway.

He saw men in the shadows, guns in their hands.

"Take a good look at him!" Stone shouted. "He's a dead old man!"

Stone kept walking, and it was silent in the hallway. The men gazed solemnly at their fallen leader, the undisputed ruler of Dumont County, who'd dominated every facet of their lives, and who'd provided their daily sustenance. They felt lost without him, and in awe of the man who'd taken his life and could actually *carry* him.

They moved out of Stone's way. Their king was dead, covered with gore, and so was their ramrod. They wilted, letting Stone pass.

The word traveled back that Stone was coming with Dawson in his arms, and a crowd gathered in the street in front of the building. Some of the people carried torches, and little children were among them, their eyes wide open and staring. Everyone's world was turned upside-down and they didn't know what to do.

Stone passed through the doorway and stepped onto the sidewalk, blood dripping from Dawson's head onto the wooden planks. Stone heard the people in the crowd suck wind. Some of the men took off their hats and placed them over their breasts. It was as silent as the inside of a tomb. Stone walked into the middle of the street, and men got out of his way. He stopped and let Dawson's body go.

Dawson fell to the ground, and the people in the crowd

stepped back. Dawson's head was covered with blood, and it was coagulating in his beard. His shirt was soaked with blood, and he was a horror.

The light from torches flickered on Stone's face, and he was ready to draw and fire. Someone in the crowd coughed. People crowded around, but nobody dared come too close.

Stone turned and walked away. He didn't know exactly where to go, but had to get out of there. The people made way, gazing at him with reverence.

Stone walked calmly, but was ready to fight if anybody tried something. He passed cowpunchers, gunfighters, Chinese men and women, and even a few Chinese children.

He came to the edge of the crowd, where Cynthia stood with Craig and Reverend Skeaping. Stone touched his finger to the brim of his hat and strolled away.

Rows of buildings were on both sides of him, and the road ahead led to the open prairie. A horse whinnied to his right, and it sounded familiar. Stone saw a group of horses hitched to a rail, and one was big and black, turning his head around, looking at him.

Stone walked toward the horse and realized it was Thor, wearing a saddle from the Circle Bar D Ranch. Stone patted his side, tightened the cinch, and untethered him from the rail. Then he placed his foot in the stirrup and raised himself up from the ground, settling into the saddle.

He looked down the street at the vast crowd of people illuminated by torches in the middle of the dark night, then turned Thor's head toward the prairie and touched his spurs to the animal's flanks.

The people watched silently as the tall man on the big black horse rode out of town.

WESTERNS!

at least a savings of $3.00 each month below the publishers price. Second, there is never any shipping, handling or other hidden charges—Free home delivery. What's more there is no minimum number of books you must buy, you may return any selection for full credit and you can cancel your subscription at any time. A TRUE VALUE!

Mail the coupon below

To start your subscription and receive 2 FREE WESTERNS, fill out the coupon below and mail it today. We'll send your first shipment which includes 2 FREE BOOKS as soon as we receive it.

Mail To: 557-73327
True Value Home Subscription Services, Inc.
P.O. Box 5235
120 Brighton Road
Clifton, New Jersey 07015-5235

YES! I want to start receiving the very best Westerns being published today. Send me my first shipment of 6 Westerns for me to preview FREE for 10 days. If I decide to keep them, I'll pay for just 4 of the books at the low subscriber price of $2.45 each; a total of $9.80 (a $17.70 value). Then each month I'll receive the 6 newest and best Westerns to preview Free for 10 days. If I'm not satisfied I may return them within 10 days and owe nothing. Otherwise I'll be billed at the special low subscriber rate of $2.45 each; a total of $14.70 (at least a $17.70 value) and save $3.00 off the publishers price. There are never any shipping, handling or other hidden charges. I understand I am under no obligation to purchase any number of books and I can cancel my subscription at any time, no questions asked. In any case the 2 FREE books are mine to keep.

Name _____

_____ Apt. # _____

_____ State _____ Zip _____

_____

_____

(if under 18 parent or guardian must sign)
Terms and prices subject to change.
...bject to acceptance by True Value Home Subscription Services, Inc.

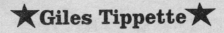